## MOONSTRUCK

They were standing on the deck looking up at the luminous full moon.

"You see that?" Micah said, pointing to the celestial body. "Tell me, doctor, what effect does the moon have on us?" As he looked down into her upturned face, he inquired in a husky voice, "Is the gravitational attraction limited to the ocean?"

"No it's not," Gaea replied, looking away. "Rivers and lakes are also affected."

"And humans?" Micah asked as he bent his head. "Because I believe I'm moonstruck, doctor." He said this so close to her ear that his clean, warm breath on her neck sent shivers of delight coursing down the length of her body.

He pulled her close to his chest. Gaea exhaled slowly as Micah placed his finger beneath her chin and tilted it upward. He gently followed the curve of her jaw with his forefinger. Gaea's heart thudded in her chest.

"Micah, I don't know anything about you," she said, her voice barely a whisper.

His mouth was a fraction of an inch away from hers. "I'm thirty-five. I'm single, unattached. Healthy. I brush and floss after every meal and I think you're beautiful."

Micah leaned in and their lips met.

He pulled her firmly into his embrace and Gaea's arms wrapped themselves around his strong neck. Their mouths hungrily devoured any semblance of unfamiliarity. She knew the taste, the feel of him. Sweet, utterly male. He knew firsthand her softness and her quiet strength. And they wanted more knowledge of each other.

# BOOK YOUR PLACE ON OUR WEBSITE AND MAKE THE ARABESQUE ROMANCE CONNECTION!

We've created a customized website just for our very special Arabesque readers, where you can get the inside scoop on everything that's going on with Arabesque romance novels.

When you come online, you'll have the exciting opportunity to:

- View covers of upcoming books
- Read sample chapters
- Learn about our future publishing schedule (listed by publication month *and author*)
- Find out when your favorite authors will be visiting a city near you
- Search for and order backlist books from our online catalog
- Check out author bios and background information
- Send e-mail to your favorite authors
- Meet the Kensington staff online
- Join us in weekly chats with authors, readers and other guests
- Get writing guidelines
- AND MUCH MORE!

**Visit our website at**
**http://www.arabesquebooks.com**

# OUT OF THE BLUE

## *Janice Sims*

Pinnacle Books
Kensington Publishing Corp.
http://www.arabesquebooks.com

PINNACLE BOOKS are published by

Kensington Publishing Corp.
850 Third Avenue
New York, NY 10022

Pinnacle, the P logo and Arabesque, the Arabesque logo are Reg. U.S. Pat. & TM Off.

First Printing: December, 1998
10 9 8 7 6 5 4 3 2 1

Printed in the United States of America

This book is dedicated to my grandparents-in-law, J.Z. and Emma Sims, because they know the value of family. That's what this story is about: the importance of knowing where you come from. It's the only way you'll know where you're going.

A special thanks also to my husband, Curtis, for telling me to "get to work." Our daughter, Rachel, just for being so sweet. And my mom, Lillie Jean Hammond, for her continued encouragement. You guys keep me going.

There are many golden
words which could express
the beauty of . . .

Your eyes, your smile, the
dimples in your cheeks that
make you look so innocent.

But no word ever spoken could
fully capture the way I feel when
your indefinable spirit couples with
mine, and produces . . . love

That all-powerful sense of
completeness which imbues its
giver with the need to believe in
the impossible and its receiver . . .

with the desire to relent.

—*The Book of Counted Joys*

# Prologue

"Gaea!"

Beneath the surface of the waters of the lagoon, the voice of Gaea Maxwell's mother, Lara, barely penetrated the buffer the blue-green water provided. Looking upward through her face mask, Gaea observed the tiny bubbles rising from the snorkel.

That would give her mother some indication as to where she was in the expanse of the placid waters. She'd have to go up for air in a minute or so anyway; but for now, she wanted to continue watching the school of bright orange, black-striped butterfly fish she'd chanced upon a while longer.

It was the summer of 1980 and she was a girl of twelve with golden brown skin, made darker by Florida's relentless sunshine. She was on a private beach in Key West, owned by the Langstons, the wealthy family that employed both of Gaea's parents. The Langstons were childless and ever since Gaea's birth, to their estate manager and personal secretary, they'd tried to spoil her as if she was one of their own children.

What Gaea loved more than anything was the sea, therefore she could be found here, in the lagoon, every day, swimming with the myriad sea creatures that populated these shallow waters, until the time her mother grew impatient and informed her that she'd stayed in the water long enough. There were other things a young lady should be concentrating on, such as piano lessons. Gaea tended to indulge her mother's fantasy of one day seeing her sole offspring become a concert pianist. It was the dream her mother had had for herself but hadn't been able to realize because of financial constraints. Lara had gone to work shortly after high school because her mother had been ill with cancer and the responsibility of caring for her younger siblings had fallen on her shoulders. Her mother succumbed when Lara was twenty-one and, at that point, Lara resigned herself to a life of caring for her siblings.

Four years later, both siblings were in college due, mainly, to their older sister's constant encouragement, and badgering in their opinions, to always do well in school.

The first year they were gone, Lara at twenty-five, felt like a mother in the throes of empty-nest syndrome. Then one night, she was out for a drive to clear the cobwebs, when she decided to skinny-dip on a secluded beach. As she was coming out of the water, she heard a deep, male voice say, "If you're a sea nymph, you're free to go. But if you're human, I'll have to detain you because this is private property and you're trespassing."

"I'm all too human," Lara had replied, turning to look up at the tall, brown-skinned man a few feet away.

Now, she watched as their daughter, half-fish that she was, swam in the very lagoon.

Around Gaea, the school of butterfly fish scattered, not in a hurried manner as they would if a predator were near, but slowly, as though they were making room for some larger creature they had no fear of. Moving her head first to the left, then to the right, Gaea wondered what it was they had sensed nearby.

Then she was roughly nudged from behind, right in the middle of her back. She spun around but saw nothing. Out of air, she surfaced, removing the snorkel and mask. Her heart beating rapidly, she scanned the area closest to her. There, swimming less than five feet away from her was a sleek, six-foot long, gray with a white underbelly, bottlenose dolphin. It raised its body half out of the water in a graceful backward dance, seemingly gesturing to Gaea to follow. Then it emitted a series of high-pitched squeaks. To Gaea, the shape of its beaklike snout made it appear to be smiling at her. She giggled and swam closer.

"Gaea, stay away from that animal," Lara Maxwell cried from the beach. "Gaea, do you hear me?"

Gaea paused mid-stroke. She'd momentarily forgotten her mother's presence. Her slender brown arms and legs flailed in the clear water in order to stay afloat.

The dolphin swam farther out to sea, still squeaking and waving at her with its streamlined body. Gaea fought the urge to follow it. She'd never been this close to an intelligent sea mammal, one that was cognizant of her *and* desired interaction.

She was intrigued. What would happen if she swam after it? Would it lead her out to the deep part of the ocean and when she tired, her arms and legs growing leaden with fatigue, would it allow her to drown, or would it save her, as dolphins were reputed to have done in the tall tales her father loved to recount from his seafaring days? She longed to find out.

However, there was the very real threat of her mother, already hitching up her flowery summer dress to wade into the water in order to retrieve her recalcitrant daughter, she had to consider.

Her mother was not averse to grounding her for a month for disobedience. That meant no exploring. Gaea figured she'd shrivel up and die if she wasn't permitted to dive into the ocean for an entire month. Therefore, she reluctantly turned and swam back to shore.

# PART ONE

# One

"We have whale sign!"

In the middle of the Pacific Ocean, near Sakhalin, Russia, aboard the research vessel, *Cassiopeia,* Dr. Gaea Maxwell stood next to research assistant, Jason Conrad. At thirty she was trim, petite, brown-skinned, with warm, intelligent brown eyes. They studied the aqua-tinted screen of the monitor. Sure enough, sonar detected several distinct shapes. Blue whales.

"They're not far away," Captain Matthew Canady observed. He smiled at Gaea. He thought the excitement of the moment made her open, attractive, golden-brown face glow from within.

"Not far at all," Gaea replied. She was one of four scientists aboard for this data-gathering voyage and it was her turn to oversee the control room. She'd simply been in the right place at the right time.

She reached over and pressed the save key on the computer. They had to make certain the coordinates, time of sighting, depth and other data were properly recorded. After two weeks at sea, this was the first blue whale (Balaenoptera musculus) sign; although, they had come upon various other rorquals, including the gray whale and the humpback. They had even been afforded the opportunity to study a right whale: the bowhead. The blue whale had been more difficult to locate, because, earlier in the century, it had been unmercifully hunted nearly to extinction by whalers of South Georgia, Russia.

According to Gaea's research, in the summer of 1930, more

than 29,000 of the giants were butchered. It wasn't until 1965 that blue whales were given universal protection from being hunted. Today, they were beginning to increase their numbers, miraculous in itself, because baleen whales produce young one at a time, perhaps once every two years, at a gestation length of 10 to 13 months.

At that rate, it took time to replenish the populations.

Unexpectedly, there appeared another, larger, shape on the screen.

"Another research vessel?" Gaea asked of Jason. Her eyes narrowed. "I wasn't informed that we'd have company on this trip."

"Neither was I," Jason assured her, frowning.

On the screen, the shape signifying the other vessel moved in on the whales.

"Interlopers," Gaea said more to herself than anyone else in the control room.

Captain Canady, sitting at the helm of the *Cassiopeia,* tried to raise the unknown vessel via ship-to-ship radio.

"This is Captain Matthew Canady of the research vessel *Cassiopeia* of the Reed Oceanographic Institution. Please identify yourself."

The response was swift. "Good day, Captain Canady. This is Captain William Devere of the *Trickster.* We are presently on a photographic expedition in search of the blue whale. We have just sighted several specimens and are now in pursuit."

"Negative, *Trickster,*" was Captain Canady's calm riposte. "The *Cassiopeia* has been tracking said specimens for two weeks now and we have the logs to prove it. What say you?"

There was a pregnant pause and then a different male voice came on the line. It was American, commanding and to the point. "This is Thaddeus Powers, owner of the *Trickster.* I have a great deal of respect for oceanographic institutions, Captain Canady. However, as a lover of the sea and the creatures in it, I am not about to give up the opportunity of a lifetime. Those are blue whales out there for God's sake! We will get our photographs and then, you and your scientists may study the specimens at your leisure."

Standing next to Matthew, Gaea blew air between her full lips and calmly reached for the handset. "May I, Captain?"

Matthew gave her the handset, then sat back on his chair because he knew what was coming next.

He watched as her sable-colored, almond-shaped eyes narrowed ever so slightly.

"Mr. Powers, Dr. Gaea Maxwell here . . ."

There was dead air for a few seconds.

"Dr. Maxwell, I'm honored." Thaddeus Powers's deep voice sounded genuinely impressed. "Your article on the Amazon dolphin, Inia Geoffrensis, in the *Journal of Marine Science,* was riveting. I'd been contemplating a trip down the Amazon to observe the only pink dolphin known to man. Reading your article was the next best thing to being there."

"Thank you, Mr. Powers. Your reputation precedes you as well," Gaea said pleasantly.

Indeed, Thaddeus Powers was known in marine science circles as a generous contributor to various institutions. He was an avid yachtsman and sailed the world photographing sea creatures in their natural habitats.

"I realize spotting a blue whale isn't an everyday occurrence and you are loath to relinquish your position; however, allow me to remind you that the *Cassiopeia* has permission from the Russian government to be in Sakhalin. Furthermore, according to code 1012 of the International Waters Laws: oceanographic institutions, whose goal is, first and foremost, scientific discovery and enlightenment, should always, when challenged by a private citizen, have the right to collect data before said private citizen."

She paused and took a deep breath, preparing to launch into a diatribe about each person's duty, as a citizen of the world, not to stand in the way of scientific advancements.

"Well," Thaddeus Powers cut in, laughter evident in his voice, "I was unaware of this code, Dr. Maxwell. Please do go ahead with your data gathering. If there is anything I can do to help, feel free to call upon me. The *Trickster* will drop anchor and await your instructions."

Gaea breathed a sigh of relief before pressing the talk button on the handset and speaking into it.

"I knew you'd see reason, Mr. Powers. In appreciation of your cooperation, I'd be happy to supply you with professional-quality photographs in a matter of days."

"That's very kind of you, doctor. Thank you. Well then, I'll let you get to work. Over and out."

Gaea was grinning as she passed the handset back to Matthew.

"Thaddeus Powers," Jason said, shaking his curly maned head. "I wonder what he'll do when he finds out there's no such code?"

Laughing, Gaea bent to study the screen. "I don't care what he does, as long as *we* get first crack at those babies. Imagine if his photographers went after the whales and frightened them off. We only have another week out here, we haven't a moment to lose."

She affectionately grasped Jason's shoulder. "Alert everyone."

"They're all probably still sleeping," Jason reminded her. It was, after all, only 5:35 A.M, Russian time. Dr. Christopher Binder, Dr. David Brennan, Dr. June Ellison and Don Shear, the other research assistant, were all snug in their bunks.

"They'd never forgive us if we didn't awaken them," Gaea told him from experience. None of the scientists on this voyage, including herself, had ever seen a living blue whale. Only photographs and the infrequent carcass that washed ashore in some remote part of the world.

"Alerting the troops," Jason joked as he pressed the general alarm button. The cacophony that ensued made them all place their hands over their ears. Fortunately, however, he only had to leave it on for a few seconds.

Five minutes after the sound had subsided, Dr. Christopher

Binder, chief scientist on the expedition, burst into the control room. His brown eyes, behind thick, horn-rimmed glasses, looked from Captain Canady to Jason and finally settled on Gaea.

"What the hell is going on, doctor?"

Gaea kept her eyes focused on his face, because the doctor had forgotten his pants in his haste to get there. He stood before them in a white T-shirt, jockey shorts with red hearts printed all over them and bare feet, one rubbing the other in an attempt to warm itself while standing on the cold, gray steel floor of the control room.

"We have whale sign," she said simply.

Dr. Binder hurried forward, his gaze on the screen. He grinned broadly, revealing crooked but white teeth in his sun-tanned, bespectacled face. "So we have." He turned to Gaea, taking both her hands in his. "Congratulations, Gaea." Looking over at Jason, he added, "You, too, Jason."

"It just happened to be our watch," Gaea said modestly. But, she was beaming nonetheless.

Christopher gave Matthew, with whom he'd been on at least ten previous expeditions, a high five. "Way to go, Matt."

From the entrance came the sound of a man clearing his throat.

"What is the meaning of this gross interruption of my beauty sleep?" Dr. David Brennan asked as he entered. He rubbed his eyes to emphasize his point.

"And you certainly need it," June Ellison, the fourth scientist aboard the *Cassiopeia,* spoke up from behind him. She playfully shoved the much larger David aside and walked over to the others gathered around the monitor.

"I assume we finally have a blue-whale sign after more than two weeks on this godforsaken tub. No offense, Matthew . . ." June said.

"None taken," Matt said congenially. She was the only one of them who suffered from seasickness, so he understood her viewpoint.

"Well," Christopher began, looking around at the others. "Since we're all here, I suppose the next course of action should be to decide who goes out in the raft to make first contact."

"Don's not here," Jason informed him, looking out for his fellow research assistant.

"Don could probably sleep through the Apocalypse," David joked. "I'll go rouse him."

The remaining scientists continued to observe the various monitors on the control board in the cramped room. The *Cassiopeia* was large by R/V standards. It was a two-hundred footer. And, like all rooms aboard, every square inch of space in the control room was being utilized. In addition to the navigation equipment such as radar and a radio navigation system, the means by which the captain piloted the ship, there were also sonar and imaging equipment that helped the scientists to see underwater without having to actually dive beneath the surface.

Gaea smiled warmly at her companions. They were a motley crew. As serious academicians, they were not given to paying much attention to their physical appearance. A minimum of fuss was the general rule when one spent sixteen-hour days either in the laboratory, the classroom or the sea.

Therefore, for practicality's sake, the women sported short haircuts and the men, those who still had fur on top, followed suit. Clothing was function-oriented. Depending on the climate, it was usually denim shirts, khaki slacks and rubber-soled boots. The decks of ships were slippery.

In Sakhalin, in the middle of spring, the temperature hovered around the thirties and forties, so they all wore thermal underwear when they went outside. The ship's inside temperature was comfortably set at sixty-five degrees.

"I'd love to go," June said regrettably, referring to Christopher's proposal that they choose those who would be venturing out in the raft on their initial data-gathering trip. "But I'm afraid my stomach would never allow it."

"You can stay behind and man the monitors along with Jason," Christopher said sympathetically.

He ran a hand over his white, tightly curled hair and glanced at Gaea. Her deep brown eyes held such a luminous glow of excitement that he was able to discern what her reply would be to his query without actually asking.

"You'll go, of course, Gaea."

"Thank you," Gaea said, nodding. Emotion prevented her from saying more.

"Dave?" Christopher inquired, looking at David Brennan who'd just rejoined them, with Don Shear in tow. Dave scratched his bushy, dark beard. His straight hair was receding, however, he felt he was compensating for the loss with his beard. It was his one bow to vanity. "I'm there," he said cheerfully.

As the best diver aboard, Don Shear wasn't given a choice in the matter.

"We'll need you, Don," Christopher told him.

"I'm looking forward to it," Don said, grateful to be indispensable.

"Then it's settled," Christopher announced. "Shall we have some breakfast and then get the gear together?"

"Wonderful," June piped in with her usual droll sense of humor. "That should give you ample time to locate your pants."

"I *knew* I felt a draft," Christopher replied, looking down at his knobby knees. To which everyone burst into good-natured laughter.


With the temperature outside at twenty-nine degrees fahrenheit, the water temperature was below freezing and as the humans in the large, black rubber raft, making their way toward the behemoths of the sea, did not have blubber protecting them from the cold, they were outfitted with thermal underwear and down parkas. In the case of Gaea and Don Shear, who'd been elected to go into the ocean to take undersea photographs: thermal diving suits, flippers, masks and computerized oxygen tanks, which continually monitored the amount of nitrogen in their bloodstream.

The raft was paddle-propelled so as not to frighten the whales off. In the spring of the year, young females, who were larger than their male counterparts, were returning to the deep after giving birth.

The group the *Cassiopeia* had encountered, as far as they could tell, boasted no less than six calves. A fact which the scientists considered a minor miracle.

Gaea breathed deeply as she held on to the side of the raft. There was a gentle wind blowing, however, there wasn't a cloud in the sky. She loved the sea. Their patience had been rewarded with a beautiful day. The sky above them was a clear, crystalline blue and the sun felt warm on her face even though the temperature was chilly. The waters were remarkably calm and of a slightly pink color that she knew was caused by the abundance of krill, the tiny shrimplike crustaceans the whales fed on, in them. This area of the North Pacific was rich in nutrients the whales required in order to nurture their offspring.

The mothers, a few of whom were more than sixty feet long and eighty tons—the size of two city buses end-to-end—scooped up thousands of the krill in their mouths, then sifted them through baleen plates whose fence-like design allowed the water to drain through, after which the whale swallowed the remaining krill.

Unlike toothed whales, such as the killer whale or the sperm whale, baleen whales did not have teeth, per se. They were not overly aggressive. Their sheer size precluded the need to guard against predators—man being their one true enemy.

"My God," Dave said, binoculars up to his eyes as he got a close-up view of the specimens. "Just *look* at them."

It was impossible for Gaea to keep her eyes off the mammals. The awesome churning power of the creatures was like watching huge locomotives operating at full speed, except the ocean was the tracks and the air and water the whales expelled through their blowholes was the steam.

*The largest animals ever on earth,* Gaea thought reverently. *And I'm only a hundred feet away from them.*

The ever-increasing waves, created by the whales' swimming, rocked the rubber raft. The passengers were knocked off balance more than once as they went about their separate tasks.

Gaea picked up her Minolta and started taking photographs of the whales. As far as they could make out, there were thirteen. Seven adults and six calves. Of course there could have been a few stragglers that sonar hadn't detected yet.

As the Minolta clicked away, the others in the raft adeptly readied the instruments of their trade. Christopher recorded the proceedings on a video camera, providing commentary as he did so. Gaea could tell by the vibrancy of his voice how excited he was. Don Shear rechecked the gauges on the diving gear. Any experienced diver knew his life depended on accurately operating equipment. Dave made certain the underwater camera, encased in an eighteen-inch long cylinder to make it watertight, was ready to go. Gaea, who would be diving alongside Don Shear, was going to be taking the photos.

After exhausting one roll of film, Gaea quickly removed it, placed it in its container and stored it in the waterproof camera bag, then reloaded. Her brown eyes briefly focused on the *Trickster*, which was anchored several hundred feet aft of the *Cassiopeia*. She could make out the tiny forms of three persons on deck watching their progress. She was curious to know what Thaddeus Powers's next move would be. She knew his presence here wasn't coincidental, nor accidental. He had an agenda, he simply wasn't ready to put it on the table yet.

After growing up around the Langstons in Key West, she was familiar with the manner in which wealthy people operated. Powers would not have been so easily talked out of photographing the whales if he didn't have something more important in mind. She'd read his bio in *Time* magazine. What was it, about a year ago, that his company, Poseidon Industries, had valiantly fought off a takeover bid from a British conglomerate? She recalled how she'd wished she could meet a man like that. It appeared as if her wish was about to come true.

Turning her attention back to the whales, Gaea finished off another roll of film. Dave lowered the remote camera into the ocean. On board the *Cassiopeia*, June and Jason would be able to observe the divers via this camera. It was a safety precaution. These waters were populated by sharks. Although the predators usually stayed well clear of blue whales, one could never predict how they would react to human trespassers on their territory.

"We have a go," June spoke into the microphone. In the rubber raft, Christopher read her clearly.

"Positive sound test," he informed his companions. "Good luck, guys."

Gaea and Don lowered their face masks and adjusted the mouthpieces attached to the oxygen tanks on their backs. Their eyes met in silent consensus. They'd made many dives together, so they knew each other's signals well. They resembled seals in black wet suits with bright yellow stripes down the sides.

Don gestured to Gaea to go ahead of him with a curt nod of his blond head. Gaea quickly checked the mesh bag hanging around her waist, which held the underwater camera, an attachable strobe light, a serrated knife and a high-intensity beam. She moved to the edge of the raft and tipped backward, which was enough to propel her into the water.

Once in the ocean, she allowed herself to drop perhaps seven feet, then peered upward and watched as Don mirrored her actions. Visibility was excellent at this depth, but the deeper she went, the presence of sunlight would diminish accordingly, making the artificial light of the beam a necessity.

Now with Don at her side, she removed the camera from the mesh bag and shot several pictures of a mother whale thirty yards away. A twelve-legged sea spider, bright orange, each of its legs at least sixteen inches long, floated past. Since it was usually a bottom-dweller, Gaea, at first, assumed it was dead. Then it moved its legs and she realized it was just hitching a ride on the ocean's currents. Probably moving to an area with richer food sources.

Gaea sometimes thought of the ocean as one huge smorgasbord. It was a case of who's eating whom. The strong and the clever survived, while the rest became dinner. It was the way of nature.

Don grasped her arm, motioning for her to snap the photo of a baby whale approaching them on the left. As she turned, the mother's sixty-foot long body blocked out the sunlight. She and Don dropped down a few more feet and waited, hoping the mother would move farther away, thereby allowing the light through. However, the mother continued to hover, protectively shielding her offspring from the interlopers.

Then, Don swam alongside Gaea and pointed upward. They were then about thirty feet below the surface, the same depth as the whales. Looking in the direction Don had indicated, Gaea realized that another stray calf was swimming toward them. As quickly as the water pressure allowed, she snapped several photos of the light-colored calf. The older whales were mottled bluish-gray, however, as newborns, they were a uniform light-gray color.

Gaea busily clicked away, her legs kicking so as not to sink deeper into the ocean's depths. Suddenly, everything went dark again. The effect was like experiencing an eclipse of the sun. The mother of the inquisitive calf was coming to claim her child.

For an instant, Gaea froze as the whale came within ten feet of her. She knew that if she was hit by its tail, even lightly, she could be in for a world of hurt. She had to remind herself to breathe normally as the mother whale turned, catching the calf in her draft. Much lighter than its mother, the calf was swept with the current, back in the direction of the other whales.

Able to see once more, and breathing a lot easier, Gaea snapped off the entire roll of film as the two mammals rejoined their family.

Don appeared at her side and pointed upward toward the raft. It was time to resurface.

As they came up, they removed their face masks and mouthpieces and foolishly grinned at each other. They laughed nervously, relief flooding their features. "That was fantastic," Gaea said excitedly. "I've never been so frightened in my life!"

"I did feel a bit like Jonah must have," Don concurred, shaking his head in disbelief. "That was a warning. Now we know not to get too close to the calves."

# TWO

Micah Cavanaugh felt a twinge of impatience as he stood with his godfather on the deck of the *Trickster*. Thaddeus smiled faintly, a pair of binoculars held at his eyes.

"They've come back up," he informed Micah. "I'd like to know what they found so amusing. You should see her face. It's radiant." He paused to look at Micah. Micah showed no interest whatsoever in viewing the marine biologist through the binoculars. He didn't dare encourage Thaddeus in his incessant matchmaking. But then, Thaddeus needed no encouragement.

"You can ask her at dinner," Micah said dryly. He turned his back to the railing and yawned. He could be in New York working on the Perryman deal at this moment instead of floating in the North Pacific, indulging his godfather in his latest cause du jour.

James Daly, Thaddeus' assistant, was more willing to go along with his employer's enthusiasm. "I'd love to get a look at Dr. Maxwell," he said, reaching for the binoculars.

Thaddeus handed them over with a smile, winking at James.

"She's quite pretty," James said, providing commentary. "Wait, they're helping her into the raft. She looks so young for one with such extensive experience in the field. That must mean she's quite brilliant, a maverick perhaps."

"Or it could mean," Micah spoke up, "that she devotes all her time to science because she lacks people skills."

"That's a little like the pot calling the kettle black, isn't it?"

Thaddeus asked innocently enough. "You're the worst worka-holic I've ever known. You can't even appreciate your surround-ings—the here and the now—because you're thinking about work. Take a chill pill, son."

"Where'd you pick up that expression," Micah asked with a laugh, "from Angelica?"

Angelica was Thaddeus' sixteen-year-old granddaughter, by his only child, Connor. Connor was happily married to Isobel, whom Thaddeus introduced him to seventeen years ago at a Christmas party at their Long Island estate.

"Where else?" Thaddeus remarked with a note of pride in his voice. He adored Angelica in spite of the fact that she was the proverbial wild child, or perhaps, because of it. She re-minded him of himself at that age: possessing a boundless cu-riosity and a seemingly endless reserve of energy. She drove her parents to distraction.

"How tall would you say she is?" James said, still appraising the comely marine biologist.

"It's hard to tell from this distance," Thaddeus replied. "How-ever, I'd guess five-five, maybe five-six."

Sighing, Micah turned and almost violently wrenched the binoculars out of James's hands.

James chuckled as he let go of the binoculars.

"All you had to do was ask."

"Don't think I don't know what you old foxes are up to," Micah grumbled as he adjusted the lenses. "How tall is she? What difference does it make how tall she is? You're here to offer her a position at Benson College, not to take down her vital statistics."

He could see the four people in the raft clearly now. Both Dr. Maxwell and the other diver were on board removing their headgear and the remaining two men were paddling toward the *Cassiopeia*.

Unfortunately, Gaea's back was to him. All he could see of her was a shapely form and a mop of short black hair, which was the blue-black hue of a raven's wing. He didn't know why he'd thought of a raven. Maybe it was because they were out there, in the elements, surrounded by nature.

He mentally willed her to turn so that he could get a good look at her. That thumbnail black-and-white photo of her in Thaddeus' marine science journal couldn't have possibly done her justice. She'd appeared too young in it for one thing. All of nineteen. A square-chinned face with a cleft in the center of that chin. High cheekbones. Large, widely spaced eyes above a small, but not too small, well-shaped nose. An interesting face, if not picture-book perfect. But then he wasn't attracted to the sculpted faces seen on the covers of fashion magazines. He liked faces with character.

"Come on, one quick glance," he intoned.

Beside him, Thaddeus was smiling with satisfaction. Dr. Maxwell intrigued Micah. He was certain of it.

Across the water, Gaea was removing her flippers while trying to maintain her balance in the swaying boat.

"You should've heard June," Christopher was saying. "She says it's the most amazing footage she's ever seen of a diver interacting with a whale."

"I wouldn't call that interacting," Gaea said with a short laugh. "We were just trying to get out of the way."

Dave laughed as he halted his paddling for a moment to help her with the other flipper.

"Thanks," Gaea told him softly. He resumed his paddling as she reclined and looked up at the clear, blue sky. It was then that she recalled the three people on the deck of the *Trickster* and wondered if they were still there. She turned and squinted in the direction of the *Trickster*. They were.

"We've been under scrutiny ever since we got here," Dave said.

"Would you hand me those binoculars?" Gaea asked, pointing to a pair of high-powered lenses in their case on the raft's floor.

Grunting, Dave reached down, removed the lenses from the case and handed them over.

Gaea brought the binoculars up and focused, first, on the *Cassiopeia*. Then she turned at the waist and looked straight into the face of the man standing on the deck of the *Trickster*, watching them.

She grinned impishly, revealing straight white teeth in her sunkissed face. She relished the almost palpable jolt the fact that he was now the object of her voyeuristic interest seemed to give him. His thick brows shot up in surprise as he lowered his binoculars. He recovered quickly though and gave her a smug smile, after which he raised his binoculars again. Gaea lowered hers, giving him an unobstructed view of her face. *Now,* she thought, *let's see what's behind yours.*

She brought the binoculars back up and was rewarded with a clear look at him. He was of African descent. Medium brown skin. Natural black hair shorn close to his well-shaped head. A square-chinned face. An altogether handsome face. The kind women liked to gaze upon and make impossible wishes in their secret heart of hearts. Almond-shaped eyes of an almost Asian cast. A long nose above a wide, full-lipped mouth. There was something disturbing about that mouth, especially the manner in which it was smiling at her right now. It was as if he was taunting her with the childish refrain: Nah, nah, nah, nah, nah, nah. I made you look!

A trifle annoyed by the thought, she lowered her binoculars and purposely turned her back to him. Let him ruminate on that!

On board the *Trickster*, Micah chuckled.

"What happened?" Thaddeus wanted to know. His tanned features were awash with curiosity. Micah could tell his godfather was thoroughly enjoying this game.

"She let me know, in no uncertain terms, that my attentions are not welcome. And, in essence, told me to bug off," Micah replied, handing Thaddeus the binoculars.

"And you're laughing about it?" Thaddeus cried, amazed. His godson was not accustomed to females snubbing him. On the contrary, Micah was used to fending off overly aggressive women who found him irresistible.

"Secretly, you're rejoicing," Micah accused Thaddeus, a smile curving his full lips. "You got me out here on the pretense that you wanted my opinion on the character of Dr. Maxwell. So, shall we go issue the invitation to our dance? I'm sure the doctor's curiosity must be piqued by now."

"All right," Thaddeus willingly conceded. "I had more than one objective when I asked you along. But, please, don't be too judgmental of Dr. Maxwell because of my bungling."

The three of them began walking toward the stairs that led to the helm. James lagged behind.

"I do still want her for the position at Benson, even if you find her totally unacceptable as a potential mate. Do I make myself clear?"

Micah nodded in the affirmative. "You do. Now, allow me to say this and then I'm done on the subject: You had good luck with your matching up of Connor and Isobel. I know that encouraged you to try your hand at finding me the perfect woman. But I'd rather have that inestimable honor myself, Thad. You take your responsibilities as my godfather seriously and I appreciate most of your efforts, however, I'm thirty-five, reasonably intelligent and attractive and I don't need your help in the romance department."

Giving his godson a sidelong glance, Thaddeus sighed. "All right. Henceforth, I'm staying out of your love life. But don't bite off your nose to spite your face, son. If you find Dr. Maxwell interesting, for God's sake, act on it. Don't let your stubbornness cause you to lose out on a good thing."

Micah made no reply as they ascended the stairs leading to the helm. He then held the door of the room open for the two older men.

"I'm sorry to disappoint you, Thad," he said in low tones. "But a woman who spends most of her time swimming with fish holds no allure for me. I like my women more hot-blooded."

* * *

In the shower in her cabin, Gaea vigorously scrubbed her scalp, then rinsed. Stepping from the tiny stainless-steel cubicle, she located her rubber-soled slippers and began toweling dry.

Five-minute showers. It sounded paltry, however after five years of sailing on various R/Vs, she had it down to a science. The key was to reserve the bulk of your water allotment for rinsing off. While washing, cut the water off and, then, when your body's all lathered up, rinse off. Of course when she returned to Key West, and the luxury of a tub, she wallowed in the water like a pig in mud. To her, a long bath was the epitome of indulgence.

The intercom on the wall buzzed. There was an incoming message for her.

She walked over and pressed the talk button. "Yes?"

"Gaea, Mr. Powers is on the radio for you," Jason's voice said. "Should I tell him you'll call him back?"

"I'm on my way up," she said. "Tell him I'll return his call in ten minutes. Thanks, Jason."

"All right," Jason responded and severed the connection.

Standing before the lone mirror in the cabin, Gaea combed her damp hair away from her face. It would dry naturally in about an hour or so. After that, she smoothed a light moisturizer over her face and neck. She didn't use makeup aboard ship. The wind, the sun and the ocean, itself, wreaked havoc on her skin and she didn't need the added oil and clogging agents that makeup provided. It was one of the lessons she'd learned while at sea.

Her face and neck done, she smoothed the lotion over the rest of her five feet, six inch body, including the soles of her feet. It had the piquant aroma of papaya. She felt a bit exotic rubbing it on her skin. This done, she quickly put on a matching pair of silken bronze-colored bikini underwear and lacy bra. Her outerwear might be utilitarian, but her unmentionables were frilly and feminine. Her little secret.

June came in just as Gaea was preparing to leave their shared cabin.

"I was in the control room when Thaddeus Powers radioed over to talk to you," she said without preamble. "See if you can wangle an invitation to lunch, or whatever. I'd brave the rolling waves to get a look at him." She paused to run a hand through her short, brown locks. "Though God knows what *I* must look like after two weeks at sea."

"I'll see what I can do," Gaea promised, although she didn't know how she would broach the subject with Thaddeus Powers. She turned to smile at June as she reached for the doorknob. "And you look just fine."

Dr. June Ellison was forty-five, with thick, brown hair and dark blue eyes. She was an attractive divorcée who rarely took the time to date. Gaea thought it was wonderful that June was taking an interest in Thaddeus Powers who was, according to that *Time* magazine article she'd read, a widower in his late fifties. She'd try her best to get June aboard the *Trickster* so that she could meet the intriguing philanthropist.

"Never fear, my dear," Gaea joked. "Dr. Maxwell is here to save the day!"

"My heroine," June replied with an infectious grin.

"You just put on your best pair of khakis and get ready to bedazzle Mr. Thaddeus Powers," Gaea admonished.

"It's a done deal?" June said, laughing.

"As sure as the sea is salty," Gaea responded confidently. And with that she walked briskly down the hallway toward the control room. Suddenly, she felt buoyant, having something other than work to concentrate on.

Her parents occupied her thoughts, of course. It was difficult being away from them for weeks, sometimes months, at a time. She missed her mother's warm hugs and home cooking. And she missed her father's deep, baritone relating to her, for the umpteenth time, his various Naval adventures. She was certain hearing those stories as she was growing up influenced her choice of careers. That, and the fact that she grew up with the

Gulf of Mexico in her backyard. It never occurred to her that marine biology was a field few other African-Americans would venture into. But now, sometimes, she found herself hoping to see someone who looked like her looking back at her. That was why, seeing that man on the deck of the *Trickster* was such a pleasant surprise. In the last three weeks, she hadn't seen another dark face.

"Dr. Maxwell," Thaddeus Powers said a few minutes later, "Mr. Conrad tells me that you all haven't celebrated Hump Day yet."

Hump Day was what oceanographers referred to the point at which they reached the middle of their sojourn at sea. Since they were "over the hump," they threw a party to celebrate. It also provided some much-needed stress release in the form of recreation.

"That's true," Gaea said lightly.

"My godson, my assistant and I would be thrilled if you and your associates would join us on the *Trickster* to celebrate the momentous occasion. My chef does a mean roasted chicken with orange sauce and there are spirits for those who partake."

"Excuse me while I run that by our chief scientist," Gaea said into the mouthpiece.

Christopher sat a few feet away with headphones on, listening to the sound of the whales as recorded by hydrophones, which were attached to the bow of the *Cassiopeia*.

Gaea went and tapped him on the shoulder. He looked up at her with an inquisitive expression in his large brown eyes, made even larger-looking by the thick spectacles he wore. "What is it, my dear?"

Gaea told him what Thaddeus Powers had proposed.

"Roasted chicken? When do we put on the feed bag?" was Christopher's response.

Gaea laughed and returned to the radio.

"We'd love to," she said into the handset. "What time would you like us to be there?"

"How does seven sound?"

"Perfect," Gaea said. "It'll have to be informal. We didn't pack our black-tie apparel."

"Neither did we," Thaddeus said, laughing at the notion. "I'm looking forward to meeting you all, Doctor."

"Same here," Gaea assured him. "Over and out."

# Three

"Heaven's here on earth . . ." Tracy Chapman's voice sang sweetly and clearly through the earphones attached to Gaea's Walkman. She was in the ship's darkroom developing the shots she'd taken of the whales only a few hours ago.

The music put her in a rhythm that made the time in the darkroom pass quickly. So far, she had twelve eight-by-tens drying on the line above her workplace. She was surprised by the clarity of some of the shots; she'd been afraid that because of lack of light, they might not turn out well. However, the use of a 20mm lens and a strobe light had brought out the true colors of the subjects.

Her favorite shot was the last one she'd taken: that of the cow and her calf returning to the fold. It gave her a feeling of cohesiveness, a sense of motherly love, that made her miss her own mother that much more.

After hanging twelve more prints, Gaea decided to call it a day. She'd already selected six photographs that she was going to present to Thaddeus Powers tonight at the Hump Day party.

As she left the darkroom, with the finished photographs in a file folder, she allowed herself to wonder about the handsome man behind the binoculars aboard the *Trickster*. Could he be the godson Powers had mentioned earlier? She'd find out soon enough, because as she noted, with a quick glance at her watch, it was already six-fifteen.

She smiled as one of the crew, Armand Trudeau, passed her

in the hallway. He worked exclusively on the ship's engines. She'd met him a couple of times when both of them happened to be getting a bite to eat in the galley. There was no ship's cook, therefore it was every man (or woman) for himself. Meals consisted of microwaved frozen dinners. The fresh fruits and vegetables had been exhausted the first ten days of the voyage, but there were plenty of canned fruits and vegetables in the larder.

"Hi, Armand," she greeted him gaily.

Armand paused to smile at her. He was thirty, five-ten, superbly conditioned. Armand was French, although, he'd told her, he'd recently applied for American citizenship because he loved America.

He had the swarthy complexion of his Basque ancestors. And his short, dark wavy hair was almost black.

It was his eyes that Gaea liked best about his good-looking face. They were slightly downward sloping, deep brown and thickly fringed. Totally sexy.

She had to check herself now as he looked at her and said: "Dr. Maxwell, you are especially lovely tonight."

She blushed. If she'd been a redhead with fair skin, her face would've been as red as a beet. Thankfully, she was brown-skinned, so her cheeks only reddened a minuscule amount.

"What, in these old things?" she joked. She was wearing a purple cable-knit, pullover sweater with her customary khakis and a pair of brown leather, rubber-soled boots.

"How're the engines?" she asked, changing the subject.

"They'll get us back to port," Armand assured her with a gentle smile. "Listen, Doctor, the fellas and I are going to get a game going tonight at around ten, we could use a fourth. Would you join us?"

It wouldn't have been the first time Gaea had played cards with the crew on a voyage. She regretted telling him no. However, she had no idea what time she and the other scientists would be returning from the party on the *Trickster* tonight, so she had to decline.

"Sorry, Armand, but I have other plans. Maybe another time?"

"Of course," Armand replied, attempting to keep the disappointment out of his voice.

He swallowed and his Adam's apple moved in his throat. Gaea didn't know why, but she found the movement utterly masculine.

"Bon soir, Doctor," Armand said softly, backing away from her.

"See you, Armand," Gaea managed.

She turned and hurried to her cabin. Lord, what was wrong with her? Sure, Armand was attractive but her reaction had been almost like that of a schoolgirl in the midst of her first crush. Had it been that long since a man had flirted with her?

She'd given Xavier his ring back five months ago. Five months since she'd learned he'd been unfaithful to her with one of his students. What had really burned her up was when she'd confronted him, he'd asked her to overlook his "slight slip" because the girl had meant nothing to him. What Xavier had failed to understand was to Gaea, marriage meant a lifetime commitment to one person. If he couldn't embrace fidelity before jumping the broom, then he most definitely wasn't going to change his ways simply because of a legal document. Breaking up with Xavier Cross, the head of the biology department at Reed Oceanographic Institution, had been the hardest thing she'd ever done. Number one: he was the only man she'd ever been in love with. Number two: her parents loved him. And number three: all their friends thought they were the perfect couple.

For a long while, she'd felt like a failure. But, not anymore. Xavier had been the one to break their bond. If she could be faithful to him, then he could be faithful to her. She didn't believe in the double standard whereby men get to cheat and women are supposed to understand and forgive them. She needed, no, she deserved a man who could be true to her, alone, for always.

She smiled to herself as she reached for the doorknob to her cabin. So she'd gotten a little hot under the collar when Armand had flirted with her. She was a scientist, not a dead woman.


Gaea was grateful Matthew's report on the mild weather forecasted for tonight had proven accurate. There was a very light breeze, and the full moon gave off just enough light so that they could see where they were going without high-intensity beams. Silence surrounded them. All they could hear, as they steered the raft toward the *Trickster*, was the gentle lapping of the sea against the raft and the steady slap of the oars hitting the water as Don and Jason rowed.

She sat next to June with her right arm about the older woman's shoulders. June was tightly grasping her left hand in hers, denoting that her vertigo had returned. Gaea squeezed June's hand reassuringly.

"We're almost there," she said softly. "And from the looks of that beauty, it's so steady, you won't even know you're at sea."

"One can only hope," June said with a forced smile.

Gaea had to admire her colleague's fortitude. Many marine biologists who suffered from seasickness never went to sea, choosing instead to remain ashore, working in laboratories, analyzing data someone else had collected.

A few minutes later, they were being helped aboard the *Trickster* by two hefty crewmen. Gaea's first impression of the boat was its stately charm. The yacht was easily a hundred and fifty feet. Smaller than the *Cassiopeia,* but what it lacked in size it made up for in luxuriousness. And, as Gaea stood on the deck, she realized it was steady. She turned to smile at June, who gave her a thumbs-up sign.

"Welcome, welcome!"

A silver-haired gentleman stepped forward and grasped Gaea by the shoulders, turning her around to face him.

He was perhaps five-eleven, trim, with a jutting jaw and

broad forehead. He grinned, revealing even white teeth. For a moment, Gaea thought he was going to hug her. Then, he released her and pumped her right hand instead.

"Thaddeus Powers, at your service."

She laughed. The warmth emanating from this man was overwhelming. She liked him at once.

"Mr. Powers, Gaea Maxwell. It's so good to finally meet you."

She motioned for her companions to come forward. "May I present: Dr. June Ellison, Dr. Christopher Binder, doctoral candidate, Jason Conrad, Dr. David Brennan, and doctoral candidate, Don Shear."

Thaddeus shook all the proffered hands, ending with June, whose hand he held on to a little longer than necessary. This was duly noted by June and fully appreciated.

"Welcome to the *Trickster*, ladies and gentlemen. I'd like you all to meet my godson, Micah Cavanaugh."

Micah shook hands with everyone, welcoming them aboard. When he got to Gaea, he said, for her ears only: "That wasn't very nice, turning your back on me like that."

"When you apologize for spying on us, I'll apologize for snubbing you," Gaea returned in an equally low voice.

She smiled at him, then turned to their host. "I have those photographs I promised you," she told him.

"Wonderful!" Thaddeus exclaimed, beaming. "Shall we go down to the lounge? We can have a few drinks and listen to music while Auguste prepares our meal."

The lounge was a large sunken room, richly furnished in modern leather pieces. It was both elegant and warm. The colors were in muted tones and the floor was thickly carpeted, which made their progress across the room completely silent.

Thaddeus directed Gaea to an overstuffed sofa as the rest of the party ordered drinks at the bar.

Sitting across from Thaddeus, Gaea removed the file folder from her bag and handed him the photographs.

She watched as he perused them. His face crinkled in a grin.

"Beautiful." He looked up at her. "You're a talented photographer."

"How did you know I took them?"

"All right," Thaddeus admitted, "you got me. Micah, James, my personal assistant, and I, watched with great interest as you went into the ocean this morning. I saw you taking photos before your dive, so I assumed you'd also be taking the underwater photographs. Am I correct?"

"Yes, you are," Gaea said, appreciating his honesty.

She sat back on the sofa and crossed her legs, getting comfortable. Thaddeus sat back also, his eyes on her face.

"Would you mind if I asked you a personal question?" she inquired suddenly.

"Go right ahead," Thaddeus said, looking intrigued by her interest.

"Why all this?" she said, gesturing to their elegant setting. "And I don't mean the yacht and all the trappings. I mean your years of dedication to gathering data about the ocean. Why do you do it?"

"May I tell you a little story, Dr. Maxwell?"

"I'm all ears, and, please, call me Gaea."

"Gaea. I suppose you realize you're named after the Greek earth goddess? That's ironic isn't it, for someone who spends her time studying the sea?"

"I guess so," Gaea said, smiling. "It was my grandmother's name. She died before I was born."

"Well, I like it," Thaddeus complimented her. He cleared his throat. Then he launched into his story: "My family's from Cape Cod. We have a long history of seafaring. Generations and generations. One of my ancestors, Gavin Powers, was a member of the Royal Society of London back in 1872. . . ."

"That was the year the HMS *Challenger* began a more than three-year expedition," Gaea said excitedly.

To many in the field, the HMS *Challenger*, sent by the British government in 1872 to collect specimens from all over the earth, was the beginning of oceanography.

"We're getting ahead of ourselves," Thaddeus warned gently. "However, you're correct. Gavin Powers was aboard the *Challenger*. All my life, I'd heard about him. I have actually seen some of the original specimens, kept at a British museum. When I was a boy, I practically lived in the ocean. It was my fondest desire to become a marine biologist. But, my father had other plans for me. I fought him all through college, but in my senior year, he had a stroke, making it impossible for him to run his aeronautics business."

He paused to catch his breath and something in his demeanor made Gaea feel the depth of his sadness at having to give up a long-held dream.

"I had no choice but to take over for my ill father," Thaddeus continued. "That, or allow everything he'd worked for to go down the drain. You see, we weren't to-the-manor-born. Oh no, the family, or the American branch, at least, were working people. So, to pursue my dreams, in detriment to my father's legacy, would've been selfish. I learned, and I did well. By the time my father passed away, four years after I'd taken over, the business had grown tenfold. I was good at the bottom line. Ruthless, if the truth is to be told . . ."

"But your heart still belonged to the sea," Gaea said softly.

"Yes," Thaddeus said. He reached for her hand and she placed it in his. "Then you understand the reason why I'm out here."

"It's the same reason *I'm* here," Gaea told him. "It's in your blood."

"Spoken like a true mariner," Thaddeus replied, smiling at her.

He sat up, still holding her hand. "You know, Gaea. I'm on the board of a small school in Long Island, called Benson College. It's predominately black. Now, I don't say that to impress you with my philanthropic works, it's simply a fact. I have great faith in this college. It has a top-notch teaching staff, the administrators are excellent. Everything is first rate. Except the science department; more specifically, the biology department."

"June told me you don't drink alcohol." Micah interrupted them as he sat down beside Gaea. "I hope you like ginger ale."

"Yes, thank you," Gaea said, accepting the tall glass. Micah's dark brown eyes boldly looked into hers. *He's trying to size me up*, she thought. She looked right back at him. She had to admit that he was more intimidating in the flesh than he had been during their encounter through binoculars. For one thing, he was a good six inches taller than she was, and powerfully built. He must work out prodigiously. One couldn't help noticing the muscles straining against his casual attire of navy Dockers and a white Polo shirt. He was wearing navy deck shoes, which she knew had to be a size twelve. What was he, six-one, six-two?

"Sorry to cut in on your conversation," Micah said, not sounding convincing. "But I know Thad. He'll keep you to himself all evening, and I wanted to apologize for my snooping earlier."

His lips weren't smiling, but there was laughter evident in his eyes, which Gaea found challenging. What was his intent? Was it simply his way, to be fun-loving and somewhat of a jokester? The comment he'd whispered in her ear. Did he make it because he truly felt she'd rebuffed him? Or was it to engage her in an innocent flirtation? Or both?

"Your godfather has already explained about that," Gaea told him. She smiled at Thaddeus.

Thaddeus released her hand and got to his feet. "I think I'll get myself a drink. We'll talk about Benson later, my dear."

Gaea didn't notice his parting wink in Micah's direction.

"I can see you're already taken with Thad," Micah said after Thaddeus's departure. "But he's much too old for you. What are you, twenty-five?"

Laughing, Gaea said, "You and Thaddeus are working as a tag team, aren't you? He sweetens me up and then you come in and finish the job."

She sat up straighter on the sofa and looked him squarely in the eyes.

"I'm flattered. Now, if you'll be so kind as to tell me what's going on here, I'd be forever in your debt."

"Forever?" Micah said, looking as though he was contemplating the concept. He closed his almond-shaped eyes for a moment. "What is that heavenly scent you're wearing?"

"Papaya," Gaea replied, straight-faced.

"You smell good enough to eat," Micah murmured, and, once again, his dark eyes held an amused glint.

"I really don't know what to make of you, Micah Cavanaugh," Gaea said through her laughter. "Are you coming on to me? Because if you are, you have to be less subtle. I'm a scientist, and I deal in measurable quantities."

Standing, Micah took her by the hand. "Come with me, doctor."

Gaea rose. Micah's large hand firmly grasped hers as he led her through a nearby exit. She glanced back at the others, wondering if anyone had noticed Micah sneaking off with one of the guests, but they were all engrossed in conversation.

"Don't worry," Micah told her, amused by her hesitancy. "I promise you'll see them again."

Gaea just stared at him.

Soon, they were standing on the deck, looking up at the luminous full moon.

"You see that?" Micah said, pointing at the celestial body. "Tell me, doctor, what effect does the moon have on us?"

"Well," Gaea began, wishing he'd let go of her hand, "for one thing, the moon is presently in its perigee, that's the point where it's closest to the Earth. And the closer it is to the Earth, the stronger its gravitational pull will be. Therefore, we're experiencing high tides."

"So you're saying the moon's gravitational pull is having a cumulative effect on the Earth's waters?" Micah said, looking down into her upturned face.

"That's right," Gaea said, pleased he'd understood. "The effect will increase and then, gradually lessen and, of course, the cycle will begin all over again."

"Is the gravitational attraction limited to the ocean?" Micah inquired, his voice husky.

"No, it's not," Gaea replied, looking away. "Rivers and lakes are also affected."

"And humans?" Micah asked as he bent his head. "Because I believe I'm moonstruck, doctor." He said this so close to her ear that she felt his clean, warm breath on her neck, which sent shivers of delight coursing down the length of her body.

He turned and pulled her close to his chest. Gaea heard a sharp inhalation. It was hers. She exhaled slowly as Micah placed a finger beneath her chin and tilted it upward. He then purposefully bent his head to meet her mouth in a kiss.

"So that's where you got to," Thaddeus' deep voice said loudly from behind them. "We're all waiting on you. Dinner's served."

Micah sighed regrettably.

They parted as Thaddeus joined them at the railing. "Watching the moon, huh? I bet Gaea could tell us some fascinating facts about the moon's effects on the ocean."

"She was just about to enlighten me when you showed up," Micah said.

Gaea walked ahead of the two men, glad to put some distance between Micah Cavanaugh and herself. Maybe it was the moon. How else could she explain the fact that she was about to kiss a man she'd known less than thirty minutes? Moonstruck?

"You looked as if you were making time with our lovely doctor," Thaddeus accused Micah in barely a whisper.

"I find myself strangely drawn to her," Micah admitted.

"Mmm hmm," Thaddeus replied sagely. "She isn't the type of woman whose affections can be trifled with."

"Remember your promise to stay out of my love life, Thad," Micah reminded him in nonthreatening tones.

"Oh, I mean to keep that promise," Thaddeus assured him. "I just don't want to see you get your heart trampled on, that's all."

# Four

As Thaddeus Powers had promised, the food was delicious. His personal chef, Auguste, came out momentarily to greet the guests and wish them "bon appetit," then left them to a feast of roasted chicken with orange sauce, fresh asparagus, new potatoes, tossed greens and flan for dessert. The scientists felt like visiting royalty; it was rare that anyone made a fuss over them.

Gaea was pleased to see June in a lively conversation with Thad, her seasickness all but forgotten. Micah, sitting next to her on the right, asked Christopher, who was sitting beside him, about the purpose of their expedition.

Christopher was in an effusive mood and Gaea knew from experience that his reply would be long-winded.

He began by explaining that the blue whale had been on the endangered species list for decades and that to find that their populations were expanding was very satisfying.

"In a way," he said, "it's like the ocean has been granted a reprieve by Mother Nature. Man tends to believe that the ocean, due to its vastness, cannot die, be destroyed. They are mistaken. Pollution, overfishing, the dumping of nuclear waste, all these factors are killing the ocean. What we do is observe and record our findings. Occasionally, we are invited to Senate Hearings and relate what we've learned to government officials, who, we hope, will enact laws to protect the environment. It doesn't always work that way, however."

"You're telling me!" Gaea said, turning toward Micah in her

chair. "For years, marine biologists have been warning our leaders about the effects of global warming and the government has yet to take adequate precautions."

"No," Christopher spoke up, placing his spoon on the dessert plate. "They're too busy sending probes to Mars. Every year, thirteen billion dollars is spent on space exploration and a measly five hundred million on ocean science. Now I ask you, when the ocean dies, where will the world get water to drink, air to breathe, food to eat? Are the billions of people on this planet going to rocket into space and build condominiums on Mars? No, we'll all be dead. When the ocean dies, we'll all die too."

"No more wine for you," Gaea joked as she reached for Christopher's wineglass.

Christopher placed his hand over hers. "I'm fine," he said, smiling. "I always get a little morose when I think of the injustice, the ignorance of our so-called leaders."

"At any rate," Jason said from his end of the table, "suffice it to say that we are the guardians of the sea, and sometimes the job rankles a bit."

"Like when you're trying to squeeze a livable budget out of the bigwigs," Don said as an example.

"But don't misunderstand us," Gaea was quick to add. "We love our work. We simply wish certain folks wouldn't make it so difficult for us to do it."

"Well," Micah intoned, raising his glass for a toast, "I think what you do is fascinating. Here's to more funding."

After the well wishes had circled the entire table, Thaddeus rose, reaching for June's hand. "I don't know about the rest of you, but I enjoy a stroll after dinner. Would you join me, Dr. Ellison?"

"I'd love to," June said at once, placing her hand in his. The color rose in her cheeks.

Gaea watched them as they departed, hoping that Thaddeus' interest in June was genuine. June hadn't been treated well by her ex-husband. It would be nice if . . .

"It would seem that our host has abandoned us," Christopher said jokingly, interrupting Gaea's train of thought.

"Not to worry," Micah said. "The *Trickster* boasts myriad facilities, which are sure to appeal to all of you. There's a theater. Anyone interested in a film? Thad has classics as well as the latest releases. There's also a game room, a pool and a sauna, a well-stocked library . . ."

"A good book sounds wonderful after that splendid meal," Christopher spoke up. "Just point me in the direction of the library."

"Take the exit and turn left. Up one flight of stairs. It's the first door on the left," Micah instructed.

Christopher got to his feet and bid them all farewell with a reminder to come and collect him when they'd agreed upon a time of departure. He was apt to lose track of time when his nose was in a good book.

"What sort of games do you have in the game room?" Jason asked.

"Chess, other board games. And, I confess to being a video-game junkie, so we have the latest games on disc too."

The remaining three men, Jason, David and Don, nearly tripped over one another in their haste to get to the game room.

"Men and their toys," Gaea said dryly, looking up into Micah's eyes. "Are you sure you don't want to join them?"

"I'm exactly where I want to be," he assured her, that amused glint, as evident as ever, in his dark brown eyes.

With his elbow on the table, and his chin resting in the palm of his right hand, he simply watched her, uninterrupted, for a few seconds.

"When Thad invited us over, he mentioned an assistant. What happened to him?"

"Oh, James," Micah said offhandedly. "He had another bout of seasickness, so I'm afraid he's confined to his cabin, poor guy."

"You're an old hand at sailing?"

"Ever since I was a toddler," Micah replied, smiling. "My dad has always loved the sea. He's a Navy man . . ."

"So's my dad," Gaea told him, wondering if he was aware a dimple appeared in his left cheek when he grinned.

"But my mother's the proverbial landlubber," Micah said with a laugh. "She stands on the dock dressed in black, waving a handkerchief as though she's already a widow when we leave port. She's terrified of the water."

"My mom's just the opposite," Gaea said softly. "She can handle a sailboat as well as Dad can and takes a dip in the ocean every morning. She says it keeps her young."

"Then being a mariner is undoubtedly in your genes," Micah told her seriously. "Your parents' genes did some other remarkable things to your form as well." His eyes rested on her mouth.

He reached out to gently follow the curve of her jaw with his forefinger. Gaea's heart thudded in her chest and her stomach muscles constricted painfully. She tried to breathe normally, but his proximity was playing havoc with her nervous system.

"Micah, I don't know anything about you," she said, her voice barely a whisper. Micah leaned in. His mouth was a fraction of an inch away from hers. The smell of her satiny skin intoxicated him.

"I'm thirty-five. I'm single, unattached. Healthy. I brush and floss after every meal and I think you're beautiful."

"Flossing is very important in an oral-hygiene regimen." Gaea couldn't believe those words had escaped her lips. He'd turned her brain to mush when he'd said he thought she was beautiful. After breaking up with Xavier, she'd vowed she'd never allow a man to reduce her to putty again. And here she was experiencing meltdown under the tender efforts of a perfect stranger.

"Oh God," she breathed, and their lips met.

Micah pulled her firmly into his embrace and Gaea's arms wrapped themselves around his strong neck. She sighed. He moaned. Their mouths hungrily devoured any semblance of unfamiliarity. By the time they parted, eyes locked, they were no longer strangers. She knew the taste, the feel of him. Sweet, utterly male. He knew, firsthand, her softness and her quiet strength. And they wanted more knowledge of each other.

"I never do this," Gaea disavowed, suddenly stricken with a sense of having sinned greatly.

"You don't like kissing?"

"We haven't even been on a date yet."

"Tomorrow, I'll row my boat over to the *Cassiopeia* and formally ask you to dinner. How's that?"

"You know what I mean!" Gaea accused lightly.

Micah nodded. He liked the way her eyes danced when she was slightly peeved.

"But then you and I aren't normal people who met under normal circumstances. You caught me spying on you in the middle of the North Pacific. That was our beginning. I can't imagine anything more . . . normal!"

"Well here's something that's equally askew: All of my colleagues believe I'm engaged."

"You're engaged?" he asked incredulously.

He slowly released her, and they sat up straight in their chairs, regarding each other with clearer eyes.

"No, I'm no longer engaged. However, up until five months ago, I was supposed to marry Xavier Cross. Dr. Xavier Cross. He heads my department at Reed. Anyway, I broke it off, for personal reasons. I left it up to him to make the announcements to our colleagues. For some reason, he hasn't yet seen fit to do so. Therefore, it would appear unseemly for me to be openly flirting with you."

"Are you asking me to sneak around with you?" That glint was back.

Gaea smiled slowly.

"I'm saying I like you. For certain, I should set my colleagues straight about my circumstances, but that would lead to questions and even though I don't owe Xavier any loyalty, his reputation, or his standing in the community, serves as a beacon to the impressionable students at Reed. They look up to him and they are the ones I don't want to disappoint."

"I understand," Micah told her. He leaned in and breathed her essence. Then he looked into her eyes. "I like you, too, and I'd jump through any hoops to be with you. So a few clandestine meetings aren't going to cool my ardor."

Gaea's sable-colored eyes were taking in every centimeter of his square-chinned face. She wondered if there was something to recent scientific reports that most people were attracted to symmetry in the face of a mate. If so, a lot of women must have been drawn to Micah Cavanaugh because his face held all the sought-after lines and planes. Wonderfully constructed, from his large, dark eyes, to his wide, mobile mouth. Yes, he was good to look at. But, what went on behind those hooded eyes of his? She was accustomed to getting to know the man behind the face long before anything physical transpired between them. Was she on the rebound? Could that explain the longing she felt for this man? If so, then she'd better put the brakes on this dalliance right now.

"So there you two are, off alone again. Micah, you've got to stop monopolizing the doctor. I'd like the chance to get to know her too, you know."

Micah reluctantly turned his head to look at his godfather standing in the doorway.

"I thought you and Dr. Ellison were taking a stroll."

"The lady has a thing for Donkey Kong, what can I say? I left her in the game room with the others."

Thad walked into the room, his gray eyes going first to Micah's face, then to Gaea's. *They're blushing,* he thought. *I must have interrupted something interesting.*

"We can have that talk later," Thad offered, turning to leave the dining room.

"No!" Gaea cried, coming to her feet. "Let's talk now. We have to rise at the crack of dawn tomorrow morning, so we'll be leaving shortly. Please. You were telling me about Benson College earlier, I'd like to hear more."

"Well," Micah said, rising, "I think I'll join the others."

He frowned at Thad as he passed his godfather on the way out. Thad merely smiled back.

"We'll be more comfortable in the lounge," Thad said as he approached Gaea. He placed his hand beneath her elbow as they exited. "I hope my godson has kept you entertained this evening."

"He's been very kind," Gaea said.

"I think he likes you," Thad commented. "I'm glad. Micah is a workaholic. I had to practically threaten him with bodily harm in order to get him to take this trip with us."

They went up a flight of stairs and soon were standing at the door to the lounge. Thad held the door open for Gaea to precede him.

"He rarely takes any time for himself," Thad continued. "It's usually work and A Step Up."

"A Step Up?" Gaea asked, seeking elucidation.

"It's the name of the program Micah founded five years ago. It helps inner-city high-school kids prepare for college. And, it also awards scholarships."

"Oh, then he's not just an attorney," Gaea said, then thought that, perhaps, her comment had sounded judgmental. "I'm sorry. I have nothing against attorneys, honest."

"Then you'd be among the few people who don't," Thad replied, laughing softly. "Some lawyers have earned bad reputations, I know. But, Micah is a good attorney. And he's a good man."

"You don't have to convince me," Gaea said, feeling contrite.

"I know," Thad told her, looking down into her upturned face. He smiled at her. "You should see your face, my dear. You'd make a poor poker player. Your embarrassment is flooding your features."

"It's just that I didn't mean anything by that comment. I li . . ." Gaea stammered.

"You're fond of my godson," Thad finished for her. "I won't cause you any further discomfort."

He led her over to the sofa they'd sat on earlier in the evening. After they'd sat down, he turned to her.

"Gaea, what I'm about to put before you should be thought out at length. Don't give me a hasty reply. Take all the time you need."

He paused, leaving Gaea extremely curious as to what he was going to say next.

"As I've already told you, Benson College is a fine institution. Its only weak point happens to be its science department, more specifically, the biology department. What I'm proposing is that you come to work for us as a consultant of sorts. Help me set up one of the best biology departments in the Northeast. I really want you to stay on as a professor, but I know that the work you love best takes you all over the world, so I can't imagine you'd want a position that would require you to spend most of your time in one location."

He paused and grasped her hand in his. "Perhaps Reed would be good enough to grant you a sabbatical. Then, when you've completed your work with us, you could go back to your research at Reed."

Gaea was intrigued. The opportunity to be at the ground level of a new, innovative program which could inspire more minority students to choose marine biology as a career excited her. The fact was, however, that Xavier would never grant her the six months away from her research that Thad's request would require. If the plans for their present expedition hadn't been finalized two years in advance, he wouldn't have allowed her to come to Russia. Ever since their breakup, he'd been refusing to cooperate with her in any way. His behavior was tantamount to blackmail. Until she agreed to take him back, he was going to make her life as difficult as possible.

"I'm very interested," Gaea told Thad now. "But like you've suggested, I should give it some thought. How much longer do you plan to stay here?"

"A couple more days?" Thad replied, looking hopeful.

"I need more time than that to make a decision," Gaea told him.

"Good enough," Thad said with forced enthusiasm. He was disappointed that she hadn't jumped at the opportunity. Perhaps her responsibilites at Reed were quite pressing and she wasn't at liberty to accept his offer.

"Of course we can work around your schedule," he added cajolingly. "You may want to finish up something you're working on back at Reed and then join us at Benson. Whatever suits you best. But we would be so pleased if you'd say yes. I'm certain you would be an inspiration to the students; show them that there are no limits, no glass ceilings to their hopes and dreams."

Gaea was touched by his sincerity.

"I'd love to be able to tell you I'll do it, Thad. But I can't. As a matter of fact, there are things I need to settle at Reed before I can begin to think of going elsewhere."

She was loath to reveal to him that her decision hinged on a disgruntled ex-fiancé. That would make her seem out of control of her own life, which wasn't the case. She loved her work at Reed, she just didn't enjoy being under Xavier Cross's tyrannical thumb. If he kept up his stalking campaign, she might just shock him, and everyone else, by quitting Reed altogther. She had good credentials, she could get on anywhere. Here was a man, sitting right beside her, who was in need of her expertise.

"Give me a couple of weeks," she said decisively. "I promise you, I'll be able to work something out."

"Wonderful!" Thad exclaimed, getting to his feet and pulling her up with him.

He hugged her enthusiastically. "I feel like you're part of the family already."

The sound of a man clearing his throat startled the both of them.

"I assume the talk went well?" Micah said as he stepped into the room.

"Gaea will let us know in a fortnight," Thad informed his

godson. He released Gaea and kissed her on the cheek. "I'm going to challenge Dr. June to a game of Donkey Kong while you two get better acquainted. Excuse me."

"Of course," Gaea said with a grin.

"How about another look at that moon?" Micah suggested when they were alone.

"What if we stay here and talk instead?" Gaea countered. She sat on the couch, hoping he'd follow her cue. The last thing she needed was to come under the influence of the moon, the night and Micah Cavanaugh, yet again. No, she'd stay inside, under the stark light of fluorescent bulbs, where the setting was less conducive to romantic notions. She hoped.

Micah sat down across from her and regarded her with a sardonic smile on his lips.

"Am I missing something? I thought we were getting on quite well."

"Thad told me that you founded a college preparatory program. It sounds interesting, I'd like to hear more about it."

His dark eyes narrowed. "It's an after-school and weekend tutoring program. We go into the schools and choose minority students who are having academic problems, but show a willingness to work hard and truly want to succeed in life. They start in the ninth grade and continue through high school. Most of our students get into good colleges and graduate with honors."

"How did you come up with an idea like that? I think it's a wonderful endeavor. Taking kids under your wing before they are too far gone academically, and turning their lives around."

"There are other college preparatory programs out there," Micah said modestly. "Upward Bound, for example. But sometimes, the other programs don't reach inner-city kids. Some of those kids have a lot of latent talent. Smarts just waiting for someone to tap into."

He smiled at her. "I was one of those kids."

"But I assumed that, since Thaddeus Powers is your godfather, you were born with a silver spoon in your mouth. You said your dad took you sailing when you were a toddler."

"He did, but it was on the East River in a borrowed boat. My dad and Thad met while they were in the Navy, during the Korean War. Pops was brought up in Harlem. Thad, in Cape Cod. They were like night and day, literally. But they liked each other from their first meeting. After the war, Thad entered college and Pops went to work for a shoe factory. When Thad took over the family business, he insisted that my father join him. But Dad has never been one to follow anyone else's lead. He went to night school and became a teacher. He felt black kids needed better role models in the neighborhood."

Micah leaned back on the couch, moved a bit closer to Gaea and lazily draped an arm about her shoulders. "Eventually, he became principal at George Washington Carver High School in Harlem. He's retired now. He and Mom live on Long Island, not far from Thad. They play golf twice a week and Mom is busy trying to fix Thad up with all her lady friends so they can have a foursome for bridge. She misses Thad's late wife, Katherine. They were good friends."

"So you're just doing for your students what your parents did for you: instilling good work ethics."

"Exactly," Micah said, looking down into her large, almond-shaped eyes. "Did you know that when you smile, your eyes sparkle?"

"It's funny, but I grew up on the fringe of great wealth too," Gaea said quietly, carefully skating around his "sparkling eyes" observation. "My father was the estate manager for Cyril and Gwendolyn Langston. Then, after he married Mom, she became the personal secretary to Gwen. I grew up in a mansion in Key West, right next to the Gulf of Mexico. The Langstons tried to spoil me with extravagant gifts, but my parents would have none of that. They made sure I knew where I came from, and what was expected of me. I was not to rely on things being handed to me. I had to work for what I received in life."

"Didn't it make you resentful of the Langstons? Your living in their home, and yet you weren't one of them?" Micah asked.

Gaea laughed shortly. "No, I felt sorry for them. They had every material possession, yet, they weren't as happy as my parents and I were. Later, I realized it was because Mrs. Langston, Gwen, wanted children. But Mr. Langston was sterile. He wouldn't adopt, which made Gwen even more unhappy. So when I came along, she poured her affection out on me. Once, she and Mom got into a shouting match about who my mother was. I was ten at the time. I thought the Langstons were going to fire my parents, or my parents were going to quit. There was no question as to where my loyalty lay: with my parents. But I'd grown fond of Gwen. She'd always been kind and loving to me and I felt her loneliness because I was an only child."

"What happened?"

"The household was as quiet as a tomb for days. Mom and Gwen weren't talking, and they used to chatter away for hours on end. Then one afternoon, Mom was in the kitchen getting a cup of coffee and Gwen came into the kitchen for something or other, which was unusual because it was a household joke that Gwen couldn't find the kitchen even if her life depended on it," Gaea related through laughter.

"Anyway, they took one look at each other and both of them dissolved into fits of tears. They apologized. Gwen promised to stop offering advice on how to raise me. And Mom made the concession that Gwen could take me shopping on Christmas. That was the one time of the year when she could spoil me to her heart's content."

"So that settled it?" Micah said, the dimple in his left cheek putting in an appearance.

"Mmm hmm," Gaea replied.

"And you've made out like a bandit every Christmas since."

"Oh yeah, big time."

Her head was on his shoulder, but she couldn't recall putting it there. Their bodies had automatically drawn closer as they sat together on the sofa. It had taken her two years to feel that comfortable with Xavier.

She'd been in awe of Xavier's accomplishments. At thirty, he was already a full-fledged professor. Ten years her senior, he was an icon in his field. He exuded confidence and charm and on campus, he was held in such high esteem that students built their schedules around his classes. His lectures were always packed. And because he was such a handsome, commanding, larger-than-life figure, women threw themselves at him. Gaea was more than taken aback when he strolled into her laboratory one afternoon and asked her to have dinner with him that evening. She wished she'd had the gift of foresight, because little did she know, underneath his suave, debonair exterior beat the heart of a philandering schemer.

Now, as Micah drew her into his arms, she didn't resist, as she had thought she should. She *wanted* to believe in fidelity. She wanted to believe that there was at least one man on the face of the earth who could be sincere, and hide not a single nasty quirk beneath his armor.

"You never did finish telling me about the moon and the apogee and the perigee," he said softly into her ear.

Gaea turned in his arms to look into his face. "I never mentioned the apogee, only the perigee. You know more about the moon than you're letting on."

"I paid attention in science class," Micah told her. He took advantage of an upturned face and planted a kiss on her mouth. A tiny buss which left her wanting more. "Make me your student, Gaea Maxwell. Give me the benefit of your years of experience. Mold me, shape me into the model pupil."

"What exactly are you talking about, marine science or something else?" she asked, her deep brown eyes regarding him with a mixture of humor and suspicion.

"I'm feeling emotions I haven't felt in a long time," Micah said softly. "There's something about you, Gaea, that makes me want to learn everything there is to know about you. Your work, your hopes and desires. Everything."

"You're different," Gaea told him quietly. Her suspicion had been tempered by desire. "A brother who says he wants to know everything about me. That's novel. Xavier was content with my presence. He didn't want to know what I was thinking. Just that I was there to complement him."

"He sounds selfish to me," Micah stated.

"It wasn't all his fault. I was dazzled by his brilliance. I was an acolyte at his feet. I would've followed him anywhere. Something's wrong when a woman closes her eyes to a man's true personality. She's living in a dream world."

"So what was it that awakened you?"

"I'm afraid I'll shock you if I tell you. We've just met, Micah. And even though we're attracted to each other, a wrong word, a bad impression could kill what's happening between us."

"The fact that we don't know each other well makes it easier for you to bare your soul, Gaea. I won't judge you. I'm not someone you have to face every day of your life. You may decide to go back to Key West and never see me again. So what we have is the here and now. Don't hold back."

Sighing, Gaea rose and turned her back to him. Micah went to her and grasped her about the shoulders, forcing her to face him.

"I'll go first," he said softly. "I'll tell you something I've never told anyone else: I was engaged to a beautiful, talented woman about a year ago. She left me for a man who had better prospects. Money has never been a priority with me. Sure, I make a good living. I don't want for anything. I make certain my parents don't suffer financially. But that wasn't enough for her. She wanted more. That broke my heart." He laughed. "A big dude like me, getting torn to shreds by a woman who knew her own mind. I can't fault her for that, can I?"

"You have a right to be angry," Gaea said emphatically. "You thought she loved you, when it was your money she was after all along."

"But your pain is different from my pain," she continued, looking him in the eyes. "You're due your anger. I, on the other hand, feel a sense of guilt about what happened between me and Xavier."

Micah gently caressed her silken cheek. "Why?"

"I didn't give him what he needed," Gaea replied. "I'm a virgin." She waited to witness the usual surprise that was sure to register on his features. He appeared mildly intrigued, but far from nonplussed.

"Even when we became engaged, I firmly held on to my beliefs. I thought that I was saving some great prize to offer him on our wedding night."

"But he knew, didn't he?" Micah inquired, concern mirrored in his dark eyes.

"Of course. I told him when we first broached the subject of going to bed together. I explained that because of my religious background, and my upbringing, I'd chosen to wait until marriage. Actually, until I started seeing Xavier, my work kept me so busy, I never dated anyone for any significant length of time. So maintaining my celibacy was no great burden. Plus, I've always believed I had to be in love with a man before I could trust him enough to make love to him. You understand?"

"My God," Micah breathed, "you're a throwback to another era."

Seeing the hurt expression in Gaea's beautiful eyes, he hugged her to his chest. "I didn't mean it that way." He held her tightly. "I think it's marvelous that you can stand by your convictions in this day and age." He looked down into her up-turned face and smiled slowly. "I suppose you did shock me a little. It's just that you're so vital. Your face, your form. You must have had lots of offers?"

"I'm thirty and I haven't lived in a convent all my life, so yes, I have," Gaea said angrily. She tried to wiggle out of his embrace. He held her securely.

"Now don't get upset with me, Gaea," Micah cajoled, still smiling. "It's not every day that I meet a woman who's made it to her thirtieth birthday without having slept with anyone."

"Let go of me!" Gaea warned through clenched teeth.

"Why, so you can kick me in the shins and stalk out of here without finishing our conversation? Those boots you're wearing look wicked. Besides, I like holding you."

"You were right," Gaea threatened. "I will go back to Key West and never speak to you again. You laughed at me, after you'd promised you wouldn't judge me."

"Let me school you on the male psyche," Micah said, ignoring her protests. "Xavier was probably delighted that you were saving yourself for him. It's the ultimate high for a man. However, the pristine ideals he desired for you were impossible for him to live up to. Am I right?"

Gaea relaxed in his embrace.

"He cheated on you and you blamed yourself. The mind games some men inflict on unsuspecting women! It's monstrous. Before Xavier, you were untouched in more ways than one. Now you know how duplicitous the male animal can be. Learn from it, Gaea."

Enfolded in his embrace, Gaea felt emotionally wrung out. He released her and took a step backward, standing with his muscular arms akimbo.

"Go ahead, give me a good swift kick. I deserve it," he entreated her.

Gaea's expression held no discernible emotion. She didn't know what to make of him. She simply spun on her heels and walked out of the room.

Micah stood rooted to the spot, silently cursing himself for his honesty. Instinctively, though, he knew he'd done the right thing. He'd never met a woman as complex, intriguing, and mercurial as Gaea Maxwell. He wasn't ready to throw in the towel just yet.

# Five

When research is supported mainly by government grants, you feel compelled to give the big guys their money's worth. Or that's what Gaea was thinking as they paddled out toward the pod of whales early the next morning.

For much of the night, Captain Canady had trailed the whales at a speed of five knots. This morning, the mother whales were feeding on the abundant krill and allowing their offspring to suckle.

The day was sunny and bright, however Matthew had warned the scientists that the weather service was predicting a storm, coming in from the east in the afternoon. So their time in the water would be cut short.

To Gaea, Christopher Binder appeared a bit green behind the gills. There was a reason why spirits were usually taboo aboard research vessels.

"Basically, what I want you and Don to do today is get as many shots of the calves as possible," Christopher was instructing Gaea.

He reached out and grasped the sides of the raft, hoping to steady his roiling stomach. "Oh God," he said, his voice thick. He leaned over the side and retched.

Gaea handed him a bottle of spring water when he could hold his head up again.

He took a swig, rinsed and spit into the ocean.

"Better?" Gaea inquired, concerned.

"I should have taken your advice last night," Christopher said through a wry smile. "But, yes, I do feel better. Thank you."

Dave and Don busied themselves with the underwater microphone and the oxygen tanks, respectively. Their added attention might have made their leader feel even more self-conscious than he already felt.

Outfitted in black thermal wet suits and flippers, Don helped Gaea on with her oxygen tank and she returned the favor. Then they adjusted their mouthpieces and goggles.

"Have a good one!" Dave called after them as they went into the water.

To Christopher he said, "I didn't want to mention this in front of a lady, but you look like . . ."

"Save the euphemisms," Christopher interrupted as he bent over the side, gagging.

"It must have been the expensive wine," Dave said, shaking his head in sympathy. "We're more used to the rotgut variety."

Christopher would've laughed if he didn't feel so miserable.


Over a leisurely breakfast, Thad tried, unsuccessfully, to pry the details of what went on between Gaea and Micah the previous evening.

Micah wore an enigmatic smile and ate with abandon. The sea air always gave him a ravenous appetite.

"She didn't even glance at you when they boarded that infernal raft to head back to the *Cassiopeia*," Thad prompted him. "I have a right to know if you've messed up my chance to get her for the project."

That brought a sigh from Micah's lips. He looked down at his godfather through hooded eyes. "I don't think the lady operates like that. She's a professional. Nothing I could do or say would deter her if she's interested in your proposal."

His reply appeased Thad somewhat, however it still didn't answer his questions.

Thad threw his linen napkin onto the tabletop and rose. "I've got some work to do, if you gentlemen will excuse me."

He nearly stomped off the deck, he was so peeved.

James chuckled.

"I wish I had been at the party last night."

"I see you're feeling better," Micah said dryly, glancing at the prodigious amount of food on James's plate.

"Wonderful," James affirmed. There was some color in his cheeks this morning. Of Irish descent, he had brown eyes and thick, nearly black hair with gray streaks. He wore it combed away from his rather round face. At forty-five, he'd been Thaddeus Powers's righthand man for nearly twenty years. Widowed since his wife, Mary, died seven years ago, he was the father of two adult children: a son, James, Jr. and a daughter, Kathleen. He enjoyed working for Thad. His job took him all over the world and he got the opportunity to meet many fascinating people. Besides that, he liked Thad as a person. Something not many employees could say about their employers, he'd wager.

"He only wants what's best for you," he said of Thad now. "As of late, you've been reminding him of himself too often. The way he looks at it, he's had his Katharine. The great love of his life. And you? You are pushing forty and you've experienced no great love. He worries about you."

"I won't be forty for five years," Micah said with a laugh. He drank the last of his coffee and gazed out at the expanse of blue ocean seen from the starboard deck where they were having breakfast.

"Thad has to learn that he can't manipulate other people's lives. He's been chairman of the board far too long. Always in control. Besides, I'm my father's son."

Placing his cup down, he got to his feet. "I'm stubborn, just like my old man. But, I'll give Thad this much: I'm glad he convinced me to come on this trip. Otherwise, I might never have met Dr. Maxwell."

"Charming, is she?" James inquired, his bushy eyebrows arched in anticipation.

"Very," Micah said simply as he walked away from their umbrella-topped table.

On account of the distance she and Don had to maintain in order to get full-body shots of the whales, Gaea didn't think they'd call attention to themselves like they did yesterday. She wasn't desirous of another confrontation with a one-hundred ton mother whale.

She snapped shot after shot as Don hovered nearby, serving as her eyes and ears. The sea was alive with creatures great and small. A school of grunts, their dark, striped bodies glistening in the sunlight streaming downward, glided past her line of sight.

They appeared to be heading toward the whales but, seemingly as a last-minute decision, altered their course and turned in the opposite direction. They weren't in danger of becoming prey for the blue whales. Gaea guessed the grunts were acting on instinct. Any object in their path bigger than they were was automatically suspect. A good rule to live by in their eat-or-be-eaten environment.

Don tapped her on the right shoulder denoting that she should look to the left.

She did, and, there, coming toward them, was a bottlenose dolphin. *What's he doing this far out to sea?* Gaea wondered. Bottlenose dolphins were inshore feeders, and being highly social creatures, usually traveled in groups.

Perhaps he was hunting the grunts. Of course, he could be curious about the humans in his watery world. Dolphins were notoriously inquisitive.

Gaea snapped off several photographs of their visitor. He floated to within six feet of her and made a graceful arch, spinning in circles in the water.

Gaea smiled. He reminded her of the time when she was twelve and a dolphin of the same family beckoned to her to follow him out to the open sea. She remembered the distinct markings on that dolphin of almost twenty years ago. He had a white spot the size of a half dollar on his melon, that rounded mass of blubber located on his head in proximity to the beak. That wasn't a common feature to bottlenose dolphins, she was to learn years later.

She was able to zoom in on the melon of their curious visitor now. He had the identical marking. Impossible. The dolphin in her past was seen in the Gulf of Mexico in Key West, Florida. That was thousands of miles away. It couldn't be the same specimen. She was aware that dolphins were thought to live into their thirties, but this was simply too coincidental. Could there be a subspecies of bottlenose dolphin as yet undiscovered? That would be exciting. But in all the years of research other scientists had put in, wouldn't at least one other person have recorded the sighting of this new species?

The dolphin ceased its acrobatics and went to the surface for air. Gaea felt as though she could use some fresh air too and pointed upward. Don nodded his consensus and they began kicking upward, gliding almost as effortlessly as the dolphin had until they broke the surface.

Gaea removed her mouthpiece and breathed in the sea air. She inwardly chided herself for her ludicrous thoughts. The same dolphin? Impossible. Maybe her twelve-year-old powers of observation left a lot to be desired. She was only a child, after all.

Off to their left, the dolphin was up on its tail, putting on a show for his human audience.

"What a big flirt," Don commented.

They swam slowly toward the raft, taking their time.

"What's he doing out here?" Dave wondered aloud as he helped Gaea aboard.

"It's not uncommon for a dolphin to haunt certain areas," Christopher offered by way of explanation. "An old friend of mine, former chief scientist for the National Oceanic and Atmospheric Administration, once told me about a dolphin who followed her for days when she was on a photographic expedition in the Caribbean. She said it was so friendly it gave her an eerie feeling that it had her under some kind of top-secret surveillance."

Once Gaea and Don were aboard the raft, Dave and Christopher began paddling back to the *Cassiopeia*. Gaea removed her headgear and flippers, purposely not paying attention to the playful dolphin following them. She didn't dare give voice to her feelings. The curious mammal had spooked her. She couldn't explain why. It was just an impulse, or an unbidden thought that forced its way into her imagination and crept along her spine, making her shiver, just a little, inside. What her grandpa called having the sensation of someone stepping on your grave.

Superstitious thinking, she knew; but she couldn't shake it.

After wrapping a blanket around herself to ward off the chill, she bent and retrieved the Minolta and took several shots of the dolphin. Later, she would scrutinize those photos in order to reassure herself that she wasn't teetering near the edge of insanity. The odds of this dolphin being the same specimen she'd encountered in her childhood were a million to one.

"You forgot your topper," Don said as he pulled a black knit hat down over Gaea's tresses. "You lose heat faster from your head, remember?"

"All right, Daddy," Gaea said lightly, still clicking away with the Minolta. She paused to grin at Don. "Thanks."

He winked at her and leaned back to gaze at her thoughtfully. He wondered what was going on in her mind. They'd known each other three years, ever since he came to the institution from Woods Hole Oceanographic Institution in Massachusetts. He admired her perspicacity, especially her ability to decipher people. The students at Reed loved her and she had the faculty eating out of her hands. He, sometimes, found himself jealous of her accomplishments. However, the sentiment was fleeting because he knew she was a stand-up type and, unlike others he'd known in his career, would never stab a colleague in the back in order to further her own interests.

Consequently, he wound up wanting to protect her. Like, just now, when he'd placed her hat on her head, much like a brother would for his sister.

"Have you ever seen a bottlenose with a spot like that on his melon?" Gaea asked him.

Don sat up, peering at the dolphin. "No, never. Maybe it's an old scar."

"It's a peculiar size and shape for a scar, don't you think?"

"He could be a test subject in one of those sinister experiments the Navy is doing on dolphins," he joked. In the age of conspiracy theories, the charge that the Navy had been using dolphins in warfare was one of the favorites being bandied among mariners.

Some thought the idea pure fiction. Others, remembering the old adage there's always some truth in myths, tended to believe otherwise. Gaea hadn't given it much thought either way.

She laughed. "Yeah, right."

"I'm not kidding," Don said, his blue eyes twinkling in his suntanned face. "At this moment, he's probably filming us via a microscopic camera hidden in one of his teeth. You'd better put your camera away. The government is probably not too keen on having one of their experiments photographed."

"Jumping Jehoshaphat, Shear, I think you've been at sea too long," Gaea said, laughing so hard she couldn't focus the lens on the Minolta. She watched as the dolphin turned and swam away.

"See?" Don said triumphantly. "He's going back to report to his superiors about the nosy lady marine biologist who kept taking his photograph, and, tonight, while we're all asleep, Navy SEALS will board the *Cassiopeia* and steal the film, and maybe even spirit you away to question you." He found a comfortable spot on the floor of the raft and lay back, closing his eyes. "It's been nice knowing you."


As they drew nearer to the *Trickster*, which was still anchored aft of the *Cassiopeia*, Gaea's eyes scanned the decks of the smaller vessel. There was no one watching them via binoculars today. She wondered where Micah was, then quickly chided herself for being weak. There was no use harboring warm feelings for Micah Cavanaugh. They had nothing in common, save their love for the sea. So what if she'd dreamed about his kisses last night? She, of all people, knew that physical attraction was not the foremost factor in a relationship when longevity was desired. However, she had to admit that how a person looked was usually the first thing one noticed about the opposite sex. Therefore, she couldn't discount it entirely.

The fact was, he'd displayed a lack of sensitivity when he'd made jokes about her virginity. All right, it wasn't the first time a man had been so flabbergasted by her revelation that he resorted to joking in order to hide his nervousness. But for some reason, she'd expected more from Micah.

Still, she was big enough to accept his apology, if he chose to ask her to forgive him. And if he didn't, she was stubborn enough to never speak to him again.

As she put down the camera and lowered her cold body (next to Don for warmth), onto the floor of the raft, she decided she was going to allow nature to take its course. Whatever happened between her and Micah Cavanaugh wouldn't be orchestrated by her. He'd been right about one thing last night: it had been a long time since she'd let loose. That was the scientific mind-set. One always had to be in control. Well, she hadn't been in control last night; her body, her senses, perhaps even the moon had been, but not her.

She closed her eyes with a sigh.


Micah paced the floor of his cabin. His six-foot-two-inch-body was wound tight, which was unusual for him. He was an athlete and whenever he felt tense, a brutal workout usually did the trick. Five miles on the treadmill this morning hadn't done a thing to settle his troubled mind. Why should he care what

Gaea Maxwell thought of him? Two days ago, he hadn't even known the woman existed, for God's sake. Two days.

The muscles worked in his strong jaw as he recalled his reaction to her revelation last night. He fervently wished he could rewind the past twenty-four hours and have that day back.

And the expression in her beautiful almond-shaped eyes when she had looked up at him: pain, deep and relentless in its power. He knew, subjectively, that he hadn't been the cause of that level of hurt feelings. No, it had been there, festering in her heart for a long time. He'd just been the catalyst that made it surface, however fleetingly.

Xavier Cross was the culprit behind the disappointment, disillusionment and distrust he'd seen mirrored in Gaea's eyes. He still felt responsible though.

He didn't know why he'd felt his heart do a flip-flop when he'd first laid eyes on her, nor the reason why engaging her in conversation gave him such a rush. Even when they argued, he felt extremely vital, alive! It was as if her essence, what she was inside, complemented him, breathed life into him, gave him a booster shot, so to speak.

That inexplicable feeling was thrilling and frightening all at once. Thrilling because he wanted to get to know her better, to see where the tidal wave of emotions would take them. But it was scary, too, because he didn't want to care for someone, anyone, as deeply, perhaps even more, than he'd cared for Renata. Renata of the fickle heart. Renata whom he wanted to despise, but couldn't.

Now, here was this intriguing scientist with creamy toasted-chestnut skin and large, velvety-brown eyes, a mouth that begged to be kissed hard, whose very presence spoke to his soul. He didn't need this. But, he wanted it.

The phone on his nightstand buzzed, denoting a within-ship communiqué. He strode across the small room and picked up the receiver.

"Micah."

"Aerotechnic is up to its old tricks, my boy. We've got to get back to New York. I've made arrangements to fly home from Sakhalin. I thought you might want to say good-bye to Dr. Maxwell," Thad said regrettably.

"How soon do we weigh anchor?"

"Thirty minutes," Thad replied, sounding slightly put out. "But if you need more time . . ."

"No," Micah replied, knowing too well how swiftly Aerotechnic worked to foster divisiveness among the ranks in companies they wished to acquire. Poseidon Industries had successfully fought off one takevover bid from Aerotechnic. Now, apparently, their wounds had healed and they'd decided to attempt another skirmish. Okay, if they wanted a fight, he was up to it. Besides, waging battle against Aerotechnic might be just the diversion to give him the space and time to figure out what he was really feeling for Dr. Gaea Maxwell.

"No," he repeated, finally, "tell Captain Devere he can get underway on schedule."

A few minutes later, Micah stood in the control room with the handset grasped tightly in his right hand wondering what he was going to say to Gaea when Jason finally located her.

She sounded breathless when she picked up.

"Micah?"

"Gaea, something very pressing has come up and we've got to leave sooner than we'd planned to . . ."

"Today?"

His heart began beating faster at the note of disappointment in her voice.

"In thirty minutes."

"Oh."

"Gaea, forgive me for being an insensitive clod. You're the most fascinating woman I've met in a long time," Micah confessed, his baritone sincere. "Tell me you'll accept my calls when I phone you, because I will phone you."

There was more of a pause from the other end than Micah was comfortable with.

"I will," Gaea answered at last. Her voice wavered just a bit, which made Micah realize the depth of her convictions. Like him, she was both excited by the prospect of something wonderful happening between them and terrified of being hurt again.

"When will you be back in Key West?"

"We'll dock in Sakhalin in three days' time, another group of scientists will take over the *Cassiopeia* and we'll fly home. Today is Wednesday. We should be back home by Monday."

"Would Monday night be too soon?"

"No, Monday night is good," Gaea answered.

"It's a date then." His voice was husky, verging on sensual. "Good-bye, Gaea. Until next week . . ."

And their connection was severed.

Micah replaced the handset, a wide grin on his face. Even the sound of her voice made him shiver.

On the *Cassiopeia*, Gaea made her way from the control room to her cabin. She hoped she wouldn't encounter anyone in the hallway because she didn't think she'd be able to wipe this silly grin off her face and it was unseemly for a scientist to walk around looking like a total idiot.

# Six

The storm did hit, just as the weather service had predicted, however it didn't last long and by late afternoon, the waters of the North Pacific had returned to their calm state. The whales, though, appeared ready to move along, having lingered to take their fill of the krill and to nurture their young.

That night at dinner, Christopher announced that they, too, would be pulling anchor in a few hours.

"We've collected enough data to keep us busy correlating it for some time," he said, sitting back on the bench he shared with June and Dave in the galley.

Gaea, Don and Jason sat opposite them.

"With the photographs Gaea took, all the film recorded via the remote cameras and the whale song recorded by the hydrophones, we have achieved what we came out here to do. Of course, we planned to stay two more days, but it's my duty to watch the budget and I truly don't believe it would be to our advantage to stay on here the two remaining days," Christopher continued. He glanced at the others at the table. "Any objections?"

There were none.

"Then I suggest we get ready for disembarkation."

Aboard the *Cassiopeia*, it was traditional to spend the final night on ship playing poker. Whoever won the pot bought a round of drinks in the airport lounge before they boarded the plane for the United States.

Tonight, Dave couldn't lose. In the first game, he won easily with three of a kind.

Sitting on his right, Gaea looked forlornly at her hand. Two queens, a ten, a two and a six. There was no way she was going to make a good showing with those cards.

She threw out the two and pulled from the deck, hoping for another queen. Slowly turning the card over, she realized she'd pulled a ten of clubs in place of the ten of spades she'd given up.

Poker was a game of chance, however she attributed her bad playing to being preoccupied. Micah's image pervaded her thoughts. She hoped she hadn't seen the last of him. Sure, he'd promised to call, but it wouldn't be the first time a man promised to phone and reneged on his promise. According to her best friend, Solange, it was the nature of the beast. She, on the other hand, tried not to be as cynical as Miss Solange DuPree. He would phone.

Also, she had not had the opportunity to develop the photos she'd taken of the dolphin and that weighed heavily upon her thoughts. It couldn't possibly be the same dolphin of almost twenty years ago, but her mind wouldn't rest until she found out for certain. That might prove an impossible task, however. She had no photograph of that long-ago dolphin; only her memory, which was good, but nothing close to being photographic.

"Are you sleeping?" Dave asked Gaea, ending her ruminating. He was always obnoxious when he was winning.

"I fold," Gaea said, spreading her cards on the tabletop. The others groaned in sympathy.

"Anybody else?" Dave asked, gloating now.

The other three players, Christopher, Armand and Don all folded in turn. They knew Dave behaved this rambunctiously only when he held a sure thing.

His brown eyes were shining as he spread his hand on the tabletop. Three of a kind and a pair: a full house.

"Yeah!" he whooped. He greedily pulled the pile of bills that had accumulated during the course of the game toward him, raking it into a brown paper bag. "Anyone up to another game?"

"No," Christopher said, rising, "I know when to call it quits."

"I'm going to bed," Don said, sliding off the bench and standing. He looked down at Dave. "I hope you and your filthy lucre will be very happy together."

"Oh, we will be," Dave assured him, laughing.

"You're really unbelievably annoying when you win," Gaea said jokingly as she followed her colleagues from the table.

"Jealousy is so ugly," Dave returned, his brown eyes fairly dancing in his head.

"I'm ordering the most expensive cocktail on the menu at the airport," Gaea warned him with a grin. "Good night Mr. Moneybags."

She grabbed her coat and headed to the starboard deck. She wanted to see if that full moon was waning or if it remained as brilliant as it had been night before last, when she'd viewed it with Micah. No matter where he was, Micah could, very possibly, be gazing up at it right now too.

The celestial body was waning somewhat, but it was just as beautiful to Gaea. The sky appeared washed clean by the afternoon storms. She could even make out a smattering of stars in the black canopy above her. The cool breezes felt good against the warmth of her face. But there was no denying the chill in the air. She wrapped her arms around herself as she stood there against the railing.

It would be good to get home. They were in the middle of April and she didn't have a class to teach until the summer session. However, she wanted to return to her research of the Atlantic spotted dolphin. Their migratory habits coincided nicely with her remaining time off from the institution. The Gulf of Mexico population moved inshore in late spring and, sometimes, during summer. The Atlantic spotted dolphin looked very much like its cousin, the bottlenose dolphin, except for spotting all over its body. They were also friendly and inquisitive like their cousins. She recalled how the Atlantic spotted dolphin were unafraid when she approached them for a close-up examination last summer.

She was looking forward to seeing her parents, grandparents and Solange. Her mother, Lara, usually planned a welcome-home dinner the night she was scheduled to return. She'd give them a call when she arrived in Sakhalin to let them know she was going to be forty-eight hours earlier than planned.

Gaea heard a splash in the water and peered out into the darkness. She heard it again and quickly glanced in the direction the sound had originated from. Thanks to the luminescent full moon, she was able to make out the form of a dolphin riding the bow waves of the *Cassiopeia*.

Excited by the notion that the bottlenose they'd seen earlier was following them, she ran along the deck, trying to get closer. Without the aid of binoculars, there was no way she could verify the sighting.

Her heart was playing a lively staccato in her chest nonetheless. She felt a childlike wonder at the unfolding of the events. Was this the same dolphin? What could it possibly mean to her if it were proven to be?

"It's nonsense!" she yelled into the wind.

The dolphin continued to breach alongside the *Cassiopeia*, jumping into the air with abandon.

Gaea kept her eyes focused on him, wishing she had her binoculars or maybe even a pair of night-vision binoculars. Then, as the dolphin leapt into the air, it seemed to metamorphose into the shape of a human male. The breath caught in Gaea's throat. She gripped the railing tightly, thinking she was most assuredly losing her mind. Plus, she needed the feel of the cold steel of the railing to remind her she was here, in the physical world, and that she was not truly asleep in her bed and a visitor in the dreamworld.

The phenomenon lasted but a second or two. In her state of mind, she couldn't be counted on to rationally measure time. She just knew she saw a nude male in the place of the dolphin, and then, in an instant, it was a dolphin once more. Preposterous, she knew, but that's what she'd seen.

She turned away from the railing, gasping for breath because during the interim, she'd forgotten to breathe, and now she was overcompensating for it, almost hyperventilating.

When she turned back around, the dolphin had disappeared. Except for the audible thumping of her heart in her ears, silence reigned.

*It didn't happen,* she thought as she backed away from the railing. Suddenly, she collided with someone.

"Whoa!" a male voice said in her ear. Strong hands grasped her about the shoulders, steadying her.

She looked up into the face of Armand. His warm body appeared to be a safe haven for her now, and she leaned into him, her face against his chest. "Armand . . ."

"What's wrong?" he asked, his breath on the back of her neck. "You're trembling." He held her securely in his embrace, gently massaging her back.

"It's nothing," Gaea managed. She smiled weakly. "I think I've been working too hard, that's all."

She went to move out of his embrace. He loosened his grip and took a step back, looking down into her upturned face.

"Dr. Maxwell . . . Gaea. I think you know how I feel about you. I was simply trying to comfort you. I hope you don't think I'd take advantage of you."

"No Armand," Gaea said at once. "You've been very kind." She slowly backed away from him.

"Dr. Brennan told me about your fiancé. If I'd known, I would never have . . . well, perhaps I would have, you're so attractive. But I apologize if I've been too forward."

He stood there with his right hand over his heart as if he were about to pledge an oath with great solemnity.

Gaea decided now was not the time to set him straight about her relationship with Xavier. Armand's thinking she was betrothed worked to her benefit.

"You have nothing to apologize for Armand," she told him sincerely. "You've been the perfect gentleman."

"Well, not too perfect I hope," Armand said, moving closer.

"It's late. Good night, Armand," Gaea said. She spun on her heels and quickly walked away. Give a man an inch . . .

She didn't lessen her speed until she reached her cabin door. She took a deep breath and quietly unlocked the door and stepped into the darkened room. Grateful June wasn't a light sleeper, she went into the bathroom and closed the door behind her.

Switching on the light, she peered into the mirror. She still looked the same. Her eyes weren't bugging out and her hair wasn't standing on end. Her jaw hadn't gone slack with shock.

Sighing, she said in a whisper, "You need a vacation."


Yuzhno-Sakhalinsk, the largest city in Sakhalin, a small island off the eastern coast of Siberia, looked like utopia to June who was ecstatic to be on land again.

She and Gaea browsed the duty-free shop at the airport, looking through the handmade pottery and crocheted muffs and gloves.

Gaea was amazed by the number of people crowding the small airport. Besides Caucasians, there were also natives of Japanese lineage due to the island's proximity to Japan. For years, Russia and Japan claimed ownership of the 600 mile-long island. Then, in 1905, following the Russo-Japanese War, they divided the island between them with Russia taking the north and Japan taking the south.

However, the defeat of Japan in World War II meant that Russia gained total ownership of the tiny island.

The woman working behind the counter in the duty-free shop was Caucasian: a brunette with brown eyes.

"You like?" she said of the pair of ivory-colored mugs Gaea held aloft.

"Yes," Gaea said, smiling, "I like. How much?"

Ten-ten?" the woman said, unable to recall the English word for twenty dollars. She held up two fingers to denote she meant two tens.

Gaea handed her the money and waited as the woman wrapped the mugs in tissue paper and deposited them into a cardboard box.

"Thank you," said the woman, revealing a broken front tooth with her friendly grin.

"Thank *you*," Gaea returned.

As she moved away from the counter to allow another customer to make his purchase, June grabbed her by the arm and pulled her off to the side.

"Did you see him?" June asked excitedly.

"See whom?" Gaea inquired, looking down at her companion with an inquisitive expression.

"There was a man, staring at you through the store window," June explained. She frowned. "It was strange, really. He watched you intently the whole while you were at the counter, but, I suppose, before you could turn around and spot him, he left."

Gaea laughed as she and June walked out of the shop. "What makes you think he wasn't just window-shopping? He could have been looking in to see if he saw anything worth venturing into the shop for."

"Nah," June insisted. "He was watching you with a smile on his lips and a hungry look in his eyes."

"Can you describe him?"

"I'm not liable to forget him," June said confidentially. "Except for Micah Cavanaugh, he's the only black man I've seen in weeks . . ."

"Ah . . ." Gaea concluded, "that's it. He was black and I'm black therefore you assumed he was watching me. He could have been checking *you* out, doctor."

"Come on, Gaea," June disavowed, "you know me better than that. I'm not the type who makes those kinds of assumptions. No, he was most definitely watching you. He stood at the window and perused the shop and its inhabitants and then his eyes stayed glued to your form. The peculiar thing is, just before he moved on, his eyes took on a rather sad expression."

"You haven't described him yet," Gaea reminded June.

"He was six feet tall. His complexion was a little darker than yours. He had a nice face, sort of . . . innocent-looking."

"Innocent-looking?"

"That's the way I see it," June said. "He was young, maybe your age, clean-shaven and his hair was in a natural state, twisted, springy, sort of Whoopi Goldbergish. You know what I mean?"

"Dreadlocks?" Gaea asked, "down to his shoulders?"

"No, they were short and neat-looking. They framed his face nicely. He looked wholesome, I guess. Maybe that's why I thought he appeared innocent."

Gaea knew a number of African-American men who wore their natural hair in dreads, but couldn't imagine any of them being in Sakhalin, Russia, in the middle of spring. But then, here she was, so why couldn't a brother with dreads be here, too?

"Maybe you'll spot him again," she said to June. "Then we'll accost him and make him give up his name and identification."

As they entered the lounge, Dave stood up at a table across the room and waved them over. "This way, ladies."

"Look at him," June said as they walked toward the men. "He's still high from his win last night. That's the trouble with scientists: you have to allow them excitement in small increments because if it comes all at once, they behave like kids on a sugar binge."

Dave pulled out a chair for June, then for Gaea.

"Your shopping excursion left you two drinks behind, ladies," he informed them. "So drink up."

A young Japanese waitress stood ready to take their orders.

"An old-fashioned for me," June told her with a smile.

"Bottled water," Gaea said.

"What, no firewater?" Dave asked incredulously.

"You know I don't drink alcohol," Gaea reminded him lightly.

"After the last couple of days, I think I'm going to become a teetotaler," Christopher agreed wholeheartedly.

When the ladies' drinks arrived, Dave raised his glass in a toast. "To the best team I've ever worked with."

They touched glasses all around, the sound like that of bells being rung out of tune.

"To my final voyage," June told them, looking into each dear face of her five companions.

"What?" Christopher said, one bushy eyebrow raised in astonishment, "no more sailing for you, Dr. Ellison?"

"I didn't say that," June confessed, taking a sip of her old-fashioned. "I may take a pleasure cruise now and again, but no more monthlong voyages aboard cramped ships. This, my friends, was my epiphany. I'm now joining the ranks of those landlubber scientists who gladly work with data someone else has collected."

"We'll miss you," Gaea offered.

"Let's not get maudlin," Don said as he downed his beer. "Dave, order me another nonalcoholic brew, I'm going to get my money back out of you one way or another."


On the other side of the island, a housewife was reporting the theft of her husband's best trousers, shirt and coat that she had hung on the clothesline to dry earlier that morning.

The constable, a short, wiry fellow with dark hair and a thick moustache calmly wrote down everything the woman said.

"When did you first notice the items were missing?" he asked, his brown eyes taking in the worried look on the woman's face. Her husband was a fisherman and acquiring possessions didn't come easily for them, so losing something to thievery outraged her.

"Twenty minutes ago," she answered. "I went to my neighbor's home to telephone you right after that."

She tilted her head in the direction of the cottage to the left of them. It was identical to her own stone structure.

As the constable's eyes rested on the other cottage, a woman came running out the back door of the house.

"My husband's boots!" she cried as she jogged toward them. "I polished them and sat them outside the door on newspaper to dry. Now, they're gone."


"Hi, Mom," Gaea spoke into the receiver. She stood at one of the phone booths lined along the wall of the airline terminal.

"Hello sweetie," Lara Maxwell said in her slow, southern drawl. "How's my girl?"

"I'm fine, Ma. Listen, I'm phoning from the airport in Sakhalin. We're preparing to board the plane any minute now. I should be home tomorrow afternoon."

"I'll pick you up at the airport . . ."

"No, I'll take a cab. You have more important things to do, like cooking a pot of your collards for me. I'm starving for some real food."

"Sugar, your name's in the pot," Lara said with a deep, throaty laugh. Then in a more serious tone, she said, "Gaea, Xavier has been over here a number of times pleading his case. I wouldn't be surprised if he showed up at the airport. He has his spies, you know. Be prepared, sweetheart. He hasn't given up yet."

"All right, Ma," Gaea said with an exasperated sigh. "Thanks for the warning. Give Pop a kiss for me. See you tomorrow."

Gaea hung up the phone and began walking back toward the lounge when some unidentifiable impulse made her look in the direction of the electric doors that were the entrance to the terminal.

Standing two feet adjacent to the doors was a tall black man with short, well-kept dreadlocks, wearing a long black oilcloth coat like the ones the island's fishermen wore during inclement weather. On his feet were black leather boots polished to a high shine.

Gaea stopped in her tracks and allowed people to walk around her. The man didn't move; he simply watched her. Gaea was no more than sixteen feet away from him, so she got a good look at him. He was around thirty-five, it appeared to her. His brown eyes were widely spaced and held the light of the morning sun in their depths. She could say they glowed, but it wouldn't have been accurate to say that, exactly, because the room around them was sufficiently illuminated, and for something to glow, there needed to be a lack of light which would then heighten the contrast between dark and light. It was more of a subjective perception of benevolence she read in the eyes of the stranger that made her think of light and energy and goodness.

He had a square chin with a cleft in its center and high cheekbones. Of African ancestry, for certain, but until she heard him speak, she couldn't tell what part of the world he hailed from.

He was clean shaven, and his brown skin was smooth and unmarred. It was the red-brown tone of an Ethiopian. Her friend, Isme, who was from Addis Ababa, had skin the same shade of brown.

He smiled at her and raised his right hand in greeting. Gaea began walking toward him again. Maybe she'd met him somewhere before. It could have been anywhere: South America, West Africa, the Caribbean, Southern California, Massachusetts. Perhaps they'd met at the University of Miami where she'd done her undergraduate work. In that case, it was probably eight years ago that they last saw each other, and that's why he didn't look at all familiar to her.

She also raised a hand in greeting as she closed the distance between them. A young mother with two small children, the mother's hands full of luggage, crossed her path at the moment she was preparing to speak to him.

The smaller child, a tow-headed boy of three, stopped suddenly and Gaea nearly tripped over him.

"I'm sorry," she said, bending to make sure she hadn't bumped into him and inadvertently hurt him in any way.

"It's all right," the mother said. She was an American. A red-head with hard blue eyes that she turned on her son.

"Don't stand there like you're stupid, apologize to the lady," she spoke harshly to the little boy who was boring a hole in the floor with his eyes.

Gaea felt like shaking the mother for speaking to her child in such an unfeeling manner. Instead, she forced a smile and said, "It was my fault, really. I wasn't watching where I was going." To the boy, she said, "I'm just clumsy, I guess. Forgive me?"

"You're nice," he said, looking up at her with eyes the color of his mother's but with a genuine warmth emanating from them.

The mother grabbed the little boy by the arm and yanked him along. Gaea stepped aside and let them pass, then, as she looked in the direction of the dreadlocked man, she realized he was gone.

"Attention passengers: Flight 344, destination Tokyo is boarding now. Repeat: Flight 344, destination Tokyo is boarding now." That was her flight. She turned to walk back across the terminal, pausing to look behind her one last time.

June had been right. There was a dreadlocked man in the airport on that beautiful spring morning in Yuzhno-Sakhalinsk, Sakhalin. He did have her under scrutiny. The question was: why?

Less than an hour later, the 737's nose was pointing downward, heading for a landing in Tokyo.

At that moment, on the island of Sakhalin, a puzzled housewife was watching as her neighbor collected a pair of boots from the stoop at her back door. In the housewife's arms were the articles of clothing belonging to her husband that had been reported missing that morning.

The clothes were not soiled or damaged in any way. However, after examining the collar of her husband's shirt, the woman noticed a two-inch piece of seaweed hanging from the top button. She plucked it off and turned it between her thumb and forefinger. It was damp to the touch.

# Seven

On Friday morning, Micah sat in a meeting with Thomas Gray, chief counsel for Aerotechnics. They were in the east boardroom, which faced the Hudson River. Through the expansive double-paned windows, one could see the various barges, sloops and other vessels entering New York City harbor.

"Why don't we nip this fight in the bud?" Thomas Gray proposed. He was in his mid-forties, of average height, with steel-gray eyes, a large, straight nose that gave him a haughty appearance, and a round face. His wavy blond hair was receding, making his forehead rather prominent. He wore it tapered at the neck.

"Revenues are projected at twenty billion, making the new, combined company the Goliath of the aeronautics industry. Poseidon has outlived its usefulness in today's market. Thaddeus Powers has been a maverick in his field, but it's time he moved aside and allowed those who have vision to make their mark. Now, we're not dismissing Thaddeus' contributions . . ."

"No, that would be a mistake," Micah cut in, his brown eyes meeting Gray's across the mahogany table, "because Thaddeus isn't ready to roll over and play dead for Aerotechnics yet."

He passed a file folder across the table to Gray who picked it up and began reading the prospectus it contained.

"As you can see," Micah began, an amused glint in his eyes, "Poseidon and Benthic International have formed a partnership. As of this moment, Poseidon is the leading builder of seagoing vessels and ocean-exploring submersibles . . . oh, and submarines."

"But . . ." Thomas Gray began. Judging from the flushed red tone of the tips of his ears and his cheeks, Micah knew the disclosure had struck a nerve in the formerly confident attorney.

"But that's a whole different field!" Thomas Gray blustered. "Poseidon can't just up and change its entire direction. Thaddeus Powers would have to be insane to even entertain such a notion."

Micah humphed deep in his throat, and the smile he'd been holding back broke through.

"Poseidon can do anything it damn well pleases, because, as you know, Thaddeus Powers *is* Poseidon. And at this point in time, Thaddeus wishes to go sailing."

The bright red color had invaded Thomas Gray's entire face now. He rose from his chair and pointed a stubby finger at Micah's nose.

"This is a ploy to get us off your tails. I know it, and you know it. I'll investigate these allegations. I'll find out if you're bluffing, or not," he threatened.

"Be my guest," Micah calmly returned. He rose, too, towering over Gray. "In the meanwhile, I'd like it if you'd vacate the premises. We don't take kindly to corporate raiders around here."

Sensing he was beaten, Thomas Gray did what any wounded animal would do in a last bid effort to survive: he turned vicious.

"I read your file," he said to Micah now, a smirk on his lips. "You're the old man's godson." He chuckled. "Godson. What's that, a new euphemism for flunky? Or is there more between you two 'sailors'?"

Before Thomas Gray knew what was happening, Micah had leapt across the table and grabbed him by the throat. The attorney chuffed like a dog whose collar was too tight around its neck.

"I don't think you know what you're saying," Micah said through clenched teeth. "Just nod if you understand me. There will be no more acrimony between us, because as of now, you and Aerotechnics are a thing of the past."

The attorney nodded in short, quick jerks, which made Micah think the man might be having some kind of attack, so he let go of him.

Thomas Gray stumbled backward, his eyes full of contempt. His bottom lip was trembling, making his words sound slurred.

"I'll bring you up on charges for this!"

Sighing, Micah said, "Go right ahead. I took the liberty of recording the proceedings for future reference. I have your vile comments on the record. See you in court."

"You think you've won?" Gray wasn't ready to admit Aerotechnics didn't have a legal leg to stand on. He wasn't very steady on his own legs as he walked to the door and turned around to face Micah for effect. "I'm making it my personal vendetta to make you pay for accosting me, Cavanaugh. I'll see you behind bars."

"And I'll see you disbarred," Micah promised. The muscles worked in his strong jaw. He regretted losing his temper, however, Thomas Gray had it coming.

In the last five years, Aerotechnics had been doing its best to influence, infiltrate and generally cause dissatisfaction among Poseidon's loyal employees.

Thaddeus, a man who possessed more wealth than he'd ever be able to utilize in a lifetime, saw Aerotechnics as a threat to the future security of his employees, who lived on a salary and depended on their pension plan and group insurance.

Aerotechnics was like vultures flying in circles above carrion. If Poseidon had revealed one sign of weakness they would've gone in for the kill. Thomas Gray's lies about a merger were just a smoke screen and Micah had been aware of their true agenda: a takeover.

Therefore, to protect the company his father had founded and to ensure the futures of his employees, Thaddeus had gone to Benthic International with a proposal that would benefit them all. Benthic, looking to expand, had jumped at the chance to go into partnership with Poseidon. The details had been hammered out in a record twenty-four hours. And now, they could fend off the rabid dog that was Aerotechnics.

Micah left the room by another door, not trusting himself to refrain from throttling Thomas Gray, who was still hurling invectives at him.

"Pudge! Oh my God, you're a sight for sore eyes," Gaea exclaimed as she dropped her carry-on bag and ran into her best friend's outstretched arms.

Solange DuPree, whose childhood moniker had been Pudge, did not fit the description today. She was an elegant, brown-skinned woman with a heart-shaped face blessed with doe eyes of a golden-brown hue, a small, well-shaped nose and a mouth cover models had to get collagen injections to emulate.

She was two inches shorter than Gaea, however, one could never discern the difference because she was rarely seen in public without a pair of three-inch platforms.

She was wearing a lime-green linen jumpsuit that had a zip-front. In her ears were two-inch hoops to match and on her feet were the requisite mules in the same shade.

Her short pixie-cut framed her face perfectly and the red lipstick she wore made her full mouth appear bee-stung. She smelled of Ralph Lauren perfume.

Gaea felt like a boy next to her.

"How did you know what time I'd be arriving?"

"I have my sources," Solange said, turning to wink at a handsome black man behind the reservations desk. The man swallowed hard and attempted to loosen his button-down shirt at the collar with an index finger. Apparently unsuccessful, he fanned with a brochure instead and grinned foolishly in Solange's direction.

Solange blew him a kiss and smiled seductively.

"What did you have to promise him for the info?" Gaea asked, laughing.

"I didn't have to promise him anything," Solange replied, pulling her friend along. She didn't want to stay in one spot too long. That would give her latest victim the impression she was lingering with the hope that he'd get up the nerve to ask her out, which was the last thing on her mind. He was cute; but a man was a man was a man. Right now, she was on a fast career track and she wasn't slowing down for anything remotely resembling real love. Not her. Not the daughter of Haitian refugees. Not the girl who'd gone hungry more times than she cared to remember.

After they'd collected Gaea's luggage and camera equipment, they hurried out to Solange's waiting champagne-colored late model Toyota Camry.

"Ah, home," Gaea sighed, pausing to breathe in the early evening tropical island air of Key West.

"Get in," Solange ordered sharply. "Mama Lara says you-know-who could be skulking around. Let's make a fast getaway."

Pulling on her sunglasses, Gaea did as she was told and soon they were tooling down S. Roosevelt Boulevard, and into greater Key West.

It was seventy-five degrees and the sky was devoid of clouds. Gaea sat back on the plush seat and soaked in the warmth, her skin tingling.

"So how was Russia?" Solange asked. "Mission accomplished?"

"We photographed the first blue whales I'd ever seen," Gaea told her with a grin. "I got close enough to touch them."

"Which you didn't, right?" Solange said, a worried expression marring her lovely face. "If you did, don't tell Mama Lara, she'll have a fit, and you know it."

"I didn't," Gaea confirmed.

Solange breathed a sigh of relief as she pointed the car north, toward Atlantic Blvd. "Thank you, Lord. Girl, when are you going to accept a teaching position and stop gallivanting around the globe in search of that rush you experienced at age twelve when you first spotted a real, live dolphin?"

"Are you saying I'm a thrill junkie?" Gaea inquired, her brown eyes harboring an amused expression. "Because if you are, I've got a few choice words for you, girlfriend. Like: I'm not the one who ran off to Paris with that commodities broker who embezzled money from his firm . . ."

"I didn't know he was a thief when I boarded the Concorde with him," Solange protested. "Besides, it was a great opportunity for me to study my native tongue."

She giggled. "I was having a blast until the moment the police burst into the hotel room and carted Troy away."

"I must admit though, after that, you looked at every man with a clearer eye. No male was able to pull anything over on you; unlike yours truly," Gaea offered, to be fair.

"He had us all fooled," Solange said of Xavier. "Even I liked him." She reached over and grasped Gaea's hand, squeezing it affectionately. "You bear no blame for that fiasco, my dear."

"He said he was weak because I wasn't intimate with him," Gaea reminded Solange.

Solange sniffed derisively. "He knew you weren't going to give up the stuff when he asked you to marry him. What did he think, that after he got the ring on your finger, you were suddenly going to abandon your principles? You should be glad you didn't give him any. Right now, you'd be wishing you'd not been intimate with him. Believe me, I know. I've experienced enough of that kind of regret for the both of us, Gaea."

"I know I did the right thing," Gaea admitted more to herself than to Solange. "But, sometimes, I still wonder: what if? What if I had made love to him?" She sighed. "I'm thirty. Maybe it's time I let my guard down and went for it."

"You've waited this long, you can very well wait long enough for someone you love," Solange returned sagely. "Sex is no good without abiding affection. I know this. If you want release, buy one of those little gadgets. . . ."

"Girl, quit!" Gaea said, laughing so hard, tears came to her eyes.

"They don't roll over and go to sleep afterward and if it fails to please you, you can take it back to the store for a refund," Solange finished with relish.


Prior to 1822, when the United States bought Florida from Spain, Key West was the haunt of pirates who attacked ships sailing between Europe and the Caribbean. After the pirates were vanquished by the United States Navy, Key West became a haven for wreckers who took advantage of the dangerous reefs that plagued the route many ships took on their way to the Americas.

The damaged ships became the property of the first wrecker on the scene. They worked quickly, salvaging usable goods and selling them to the highest bidder, sometimes selling them back to the ships' owners.

Key West became the largest city in Florida and the richest in the United States. It thrived on the salvage business.

Then in 1912, The Overseas Railroad, built by Henry Flagler, became the initial overland connection to Miami where tourism had been big business for years. The railroad brought Key West a steady tourist trade. The Conchs, native Key Westerners, however, were mainly fishermen. Shipping also prospered, along with smuggling, which refused to go away.

Neither the depression of 1929, nor the Labor Day Hurricane of 1935 could keep Key West down for long. In 1938, The Overseas Highway, the only road into Key West, opened, and ever since then, tourists have been coming to the tropical island to play in the sunshine and party until the break of dawn.

Of course, many people associated Key West with Ernest Hemingway, who spent twelve years there in the twenties and thirties and wrote some of his most-loved novels while a resident.

To those who live there, though, Key West is just home. Residents put up with the drunken tourists and the island's reputation as a party mecca because they love it. And even though they are a part of the United States, they feel a spiritual connection to the Caribbean because so many of their people originally came from the islands. They will always be Conchs. Gaea and Solange were both third-generation Conchs.

There were advantages to living "at the end of the road." Average temperatures were between seventy and eighty degrees. You woke to the fragrant smells of ginger, hibiscus and sweet frangipani trees. And, in the middle of the summer, you could stroll into your backyard, pluck a mango from its branch, peel the skin back and bite into its succulent flesh. Paradise on Earth.

Solange pulled into the driveway of Gaea's parents' home on Simonton Street. It was a large bungalow with a wraparound porch bordered by Easter lilies.

Her parents had bought the house less than five years ago when they'd retired. They remained friends with the Langstons, however, Cameron no longer served as the Langstons' estate manager and Lara answered to no one except herself.

No sooner had the girls opened their car doors than Cameron and Lara came jogging out of the bungalow, screen door banging shut behind them.

Gaea ran to her parents and hugged them simultaneously. Cameron Maxwell, a good six inches taller than his daughter, nearly lifted her off the ground after Lara stepped aside.

"How are you, baby girl?"

"I'm fine, Daddy," Gaea said, beaming. She removed her sunglasses and, now, looked up into a pair of brown eyes the same exact shade as her own.

At sixty-two, Cameron had the skin of a man twenty years his junior. Caramel-colored, he had naturally wavy hair that he wore short and tapered at the neck. He had high cheekbones, courtesy of his West Indian ancestors; a long, proud nose; square chin and a wide, generous mouth, given to smiling.

He caressed his only child's cheek with one of his big hands.

"You get prettier every time I see you. After 'while, you'll have your mother beat."

"That'll be the day!" Gaea said. Her mother had hold of her right hand, her father, her left, as they strolled up the walk leading to the porch.

Solange hung back, smiling. She loved these three people as much as she loved her own small family.

Lara Maxwell was shorter than her daughter by three inches and fine-boned. She was darker-complected than her husband and four years younger. Gaea had inherited Lara's almond-shaped eyes and the same hair color. Cameron's hair was auburn, but Lara's, a blue-black as sooty as the inside of a chimney. She wore her crowning glory in a braid down her back that nearly reached her waist. She'd never cut her hair and was devastated when her daughter cut hers for the first time last year. Lara still had the braid, kept for posterity, in a Ziploc bag in her bureau drawer.

There was a gray streak running down the middle of Lara's hair today. She laughed whenever her female friends told her to dye the stubborn locks. "For what?" she'd say. "I'm proud of my gray. I've earned every one of them."

The air in the house smelled of collard greens, baked ham, macaroni and cheese and sweet potatoes. Gaea couldn't discern whether her mother had made candied yams or sweet potato pies. It didn't matter. Her mother made them both delectable treats.

"Ma, you've outdone yourself," Gaea complimented her mother, bending to plant a kiss on her mother's velvety cheek.

Lara smelled faintly of a fruity cologne and cinnamon. "How can you tell?" she asked, smiling her pleasure. "You haven't taken a bite yet."

"Because it smells heavenly," Gaea answered, fairly floating in the direction of the kitchen.

Laughing, Cameron let go of her hand. "You go on and check out the pots, sweetie. I have to go turn off the garden faucet."

Solange came into the house as Cameron was going back out and he paused to hug her as he would a second daughter.

"Thanks for collecting our girl, sugar."

"She's my girl too," Solange said and smiled her gratitude. This easy affection that she witnessed in the Maxwell home was a rarity in her mother's. Both her parents had led a hard-scrabble life and things like hugging and kissing were parceled out only on very special occasions. The last time her parents had hugged her was on the day she graduated from The University of Miami with a doctorate in anthropology, nearly four years ago.

She frowned as she followed Gaea and Lara into the kitchen. She hadn't realized it had been that long ago. Of course their inability to show affection did not mean her parents didn't love her and she was well aware of that. They simply weren't demonstrative.

The Maxwell kitchen was large and airy with all the up-to-date appliances any professional chef would covet. The center island was where Lara had placed the sweet potato pies to cool and a juicy ham, replete with pineapple slices reposed beside them.

Gaea went straight to the sink and washed her hands, a habit she'd picked up as a child because of her mother's constant reminders.

"What time's dinner?" she asked, peering up at the kitchen clock hanging above the sink.

"You know we don't stand on ceremony around here," Lara laughed. "Dinner's whenever you're hungry."

"Then it's dinnertime," Solange said, also scrubbing her hands at the sink. "I'll get the plates."

The three women worked companionably, setting the table, while subconsciously awaiting Cameron's arrival.

Ten minutes later, Cameron strode into the kitchen to see the three of them sitting at the table, all eyes on him, as if to say: "What kept you?"

After giving thanks, they dug in.

"The ocean was so beautiful beneath the surface," Gaea told them as they ate. "We saw a school of grunts, sea spiders, all sorts of anemones. It was fabulous. During our last dive, we even spotted a bottlenose dolphin. Or, should I say, he spotted us. He came right up to us and impressed us with his acrobatic skills."

"And what of the human animal?" Solange inquired, a smile lurking in her golden-brown eyes. She ate a forkful of collards and waited.

Gaea sipped her iced tea, wondering if she should tell them all about Micah now, or wait until he kept his promise to phone. Setting her glass back on the tabletop, she decided to wait.

Thaddeus Powers, however, was a safe topic.

"I met Thaddeus Powers. Maybe you've heard of him, he owns Poseidon Industries. They manufacture airplanes. He told me that when his father founded the company, they specialized in seaplanes, hence the reason they named the company after the sea god."

"Where did you meet him?" Cameron asked. "In the city?"

"No, believe it or not, it was in the middle of the ocean," Gaea told them. "Thaddeus Powers sails a yacht, a rather huge yacht, around the world photographing sea creatures in their natural habitats. He said he wanted to become a marine biologist when he was younger, but he got side-tracked."

"He sounds interesting," Lara put in. "Is he married? How old is he?"

Gaea knew then her parents didn't have the faintest idea who Thaddeus Powers was. They were not the type of people who read *Time* magazine. They read *Ebony* and *Jet* and on Sunday morning, shared the *Miami Herald* between them over break-fast. It wasn't surprising that they weren't aware of the business mogul.

To be honest, she only knew of him prior to their meeting because he was well known as a contributor to oceanographic institutions.

"He's in his late fifties . . ." Gaea began.

"Oh, then he's much too old for you," Lara said. She couldn't help it, every interesting male she heard of, she automatically wondered if he'd be a suitable match for her unattached daughter.

Gaea smiled. She couldn't fault her mother for wanting to see her married. Lara believed a broken heart was best mended by the emotional poultice of love. She and Cameron were as in love today as they had been when they were first wed, and she didn't see why her daughter couldn't have that same kind of happiness.

It was her maternal duty to ensure that her only child found a loving, enduring relationship before she, Lara, departed this world.

"Now, Lara," Cameron said, turning a patient eye on his wife, "don't start husband-hunting again. Give Gaea space to find out what she wants to do. I know the broken engagement put our becoming grandparents a little behind schedule, but we have to be supportive of our girl. She'll know the right man when she meets him."

That was a long speech for her father. It told her he'd given some thought to her breakup with Xavier and that he was sympathetic to her feelings. His heart went out to her.

"I know that, Cam," Lara said softly. She gazed at her daughter with such love in her dark eyes that Gaea found herself wishing she hadn't told her parents about Xavier's conduct and her subsequent decision to end the relationship. They were hurting because of her.

"Let's not lose sight of the fact that Gaea is a lot better off finding out about Xavier Cross's proclivities now, than later," Solange put in as the only nonrelative in the room. "She could have married him and two years down the road, a divorce would have been in the works, and a child could have been involved. . . ." Solange sighed. "I don't have to tell you what divorce does to a child's developing psyche."

No, they knew too well the pain Solange herself had gone through when her parents had divorced. She had been thirteen years old. If not for the welcoming love and warmth she found in the Maxwell home, she didn't think she would've survived that time of confusion and pain.

The funny thing was, if her parents had remained in Haiti, as devout Catholics, they would not have dared entertain the possibility of divorce, let alone the actuality of it. But, in the United States, they had exercised their newfound rights and privileges, opting to sever the marriage and go their separate ways. From thirteen onward, the only time she ever saw her parents in one place, together, was at her high school and college graduations and a funeral or wedding.

"You're right, of course," Lara said. She got up from her chair and walked around to the opposite side of the table. Standing between Gaea's and Solange's chairs, she placed an arm around the both of them, pulling them to her. "You're both perfectly fine without mates."

Lara excused herself after that and went to put the sweet potato pie on dessert plates.

Gaea and Solange turned to give each other knowing looks. Mama Lara meant what she said about their being perfectly fine without significant others, however, they also read her underlying meaning loud and clear: they weren't getting any younger, it was time to get on the ball.

"Forgive her," Cameron said in Lara's absence. "She worries about you two. I told her: get a hobby. But she says that until she sees you happy, she isn't going to have the peace of mind to concentrate on crocheting. I keep telling her that today, a young woman doesn't have to have a man in her life in order to feel complete. But, she's old-fashioned. She still thinks that a woman needs a man to love and protect her. These days, women can love and protect themselves. A good relationship? Well that's like the icing on the cake. Personally, I feel satisfied that my daughter is capable of making her own cake, and leave it at that."

Gaea and Solange were laughing happily when Lara returned to the table.

"What did he say?" she wanted to know. "Did he tell you what Gwen called here and asked me to do the other day?"

She served them each a piece of pie with a scoop of vanilla ice cream on top while Gaea poured fresh coffee into their cups.

Sitting down, Lara continued her story.

"That woman phoned me on Monday and asked me to take a trip around the world with her. Just the two of us. Can you imagine me and Gwen Langston traipsing around the globe visiting museums and drinking wine al fresco? Since Cyril died, she has too much time on her hands." She made it sound as if the idea was preposterous.

"What did you say?" Gaea asked, finding the idea less than ludicrous. It would be a great opportunity for her mother to get to know other cultures, see a bit of the world. New York City was the farthest north Lara had ever been and that trip had taken a truckload of pleading, cajoling and wangling from Cameron in order to convince Lara to go.

"I said, yes," Lara said, a smile on her face. She knew she had shocked Gaea and Solange.

Cameron reached for her hand and Lara gave it to him.

"I told her not to worry. Everything she knew and loved would be exactly as she left it when she returned."


Lara and Cameron tried to convince Gaea to spend the night at their bungalow. But Gaea wanted to sleep in her own bed, so Solange drove her across town to her house on Olivia Lane, off Duval Street.

Once in front of her small house, Gaea felt as though she was truly back home because, although her parents made it abundantly clear that their home was her home, she preferred having a place of her very own. Even if it was tiny, compared to theirs.

"Are you sure you won't spend the night here?" Gaea asked Solange as she climbed out of the Camry, her large suitcase in her right hand, and the camera bag and purse slung over her left shoulder.

"No, I promised my mother I'd stay the night over there," Solange said, sounding as though she'd rather stay with Gaea. "We don't see each other enough. Besides, she has a new boyfriend she wants to show off."

"Be nice," Gaea admonished gently.

Solange humphed. "Nice? If he's anything like the last one, he will be lucky if I'm civil, let alone nice. But, all right, sis, I'll be good." She laughed. "At least until he gets drunk and tries to toss us all out of my mother's house."

Solange wasn't being facetious. That incident had really happened with one of her mother's ex-boyfriends. No wonder she was presently down on men. Her parents' divorce. Her mother's poor track record with the opposite sex. It was enough to turn anyone off.

Now she trotted around the front end of the car and gave Gaea a quick peck on the cheek.

"Welcome back. Maybe next weekend, you'll tell me *everything* that happened on your trip."

"And what makes you think I haven't spilled all?" Gaea inquired innocently.

"I know you, that's all," Solange said simply.

She squinted up at the night sky. "That moon looks spooky, doesn't it?" She looked back at Gaea. "Gotta run. I love you, sis."

"I love you too," Gaea returned.

She ran up onto the porch while Solange shone the headlights in her direction, illuminating the dark steps. Gaea quickly put the key in the lock and turned. She then reached her hand inside the door and switched on the porch light.

Solange tooted the horn and was gone.

Gaea kicked the door the rest of the way open and dragged her suitcase inside. She then deposited the camera bag and her purse on the cherry-wood hall table adjacent to the front door.

The hairs on the back of her neck seemed to stand at attention. The house didn't feel right.

"So, you're back," a familiar male voice said.

# Eight

"Apparently, changing the locks on all the doors and windows wasn't enough to keep you out," Gaea said angrily, as she walked further into the room.

She swept past Xavier, who was standing in the foyer, and went straight to her desk near the French doors, paused to turn on the antique brass hurricane lamp and picked up the telephone receiver.

"What are you doing?" Xavier calmly asked.

"I'm doing what anyone would do upon returning home and finding an intruder: I'm phoning the police."

Xavier quickly closed the space between them, his long legs doing it in three steps. He placed his hand atop hers.

"I had to speak with you."

His voice wasn't pleading, nor apologetic. He'd simply made a statement.

Gaea slowly removed her hand from beneath his, took a step backward and watched him through narrowed eyelids. The shadows obscured his features, but she knew, too well, how he looked.

"I've said everything I had to say to you. I've listened to your excuses, heard all the pros and cons, thought long and hard on what I should do about us and made my decision. It's over."

As he drew closer, the light from the hurricane lamp on the desk illuminated his face and form.

Gaea inhaled sharply when she saw the inch-long scar above his right eyebrow. She refused to ask him about it, though. He might misconstrue her concern for interest in his welfare. She would leave no openings for him to take advantage of.

Xavier detected her change in breathing, however. His whole being was in tune to her and he knew she wondered how he'd been wounded. Gaea was soft-hearted. She couldn't stand to see any living thing suffer, be it man or beast. He stored her reaction to his scar for future reference.

His strong, utterly masculine face was unmarred otherwise. Dark, wide-set eyes with luxuriant lashes held a hurt expression in them. He had a rather long nose above a full mouth, which could be soft or a hard line, depending upon the situation.

His black, natural hair began at a widow's peak and grew to the nape of his neck like a thick, dense carpet. The widow's peak worked to give his face an authoritative aspect, especially when he slipped on his horn-rimmed reading glasses.

Tonight, though, he wasn't wearing his glasses, and, to Gaea, he just looked like a pest. An extremely handsome pest, but a pest nonetheless.

He was six feet tall and in excellent shape from daily jogs, which he took at dawn. He wore his favorite tweed jacket, a mixture of browns and blues, and a denim shirt with Levi's. Gaea didn't have to glance down in order to know his feet were encased in well-worn brown leather Rockports.

The faint scent of Aramis pervaded the room.

In spite of herself, her body reacted to his presence. Xavier had always had a strong physical pull on her senses. All those months they'd been together had been sheer hell for her. He had been the first man she'd seriously considered giving herself to without marriage. Now, as Solange had noted earlier, she was indeed glad she hadn't.

Her heartbeat accelerated and she felt her stomach muscles constrict, then a warmth suffused her. She was tired, therefore, her resistance wasn't what it should be.

"Please go," she said.

He did not. He went to her and pulled her into his arms instead.

Their cheeks touched and she inhaled his cool, mint-scented breath.

It was like accepting his essence inside of her, and she felt her legs grow weak.

So this was where the word *lovesick* came from. She thought there should be some kind of shot she could be inoculated with to ward off these unsettling chemical reactions.

She'd left him for good. He was a cad, a lout, a womanizer. She detested him. Somebody inform her body.

"Oh God, Gaea . . ." he breathed. His voice was a sigh, a whisper, a conduit through which his desire was translated.

"You know we belong together. I can feel it in you. The way your body quivers at my touch. Forgive me, Gaea. I'll spend a lifetime making it up to you."

She was tired, weary of it all. Why not relax and go with the flow? He promised to never stray again. Until his dying day, he would be true to her alone.

His right hand was at the base of her spine, massaging her there, whipping the spark into a full-blown inferno.

Their bodies pressed closer and she felt his distended member on her thigh. Ironically, the contact gave her a feeling of her own power. She'd elicited that reaction from him.

But then, the devil perched on her shoulder reminded her that others had excited him in the same way, and the realization was like a wake-up call to her senses.

She took a deep breath, marshaling her strength, and pushed out of his embrace.

Xavier was taken aback, and, frankly, his reaction amused Gaea.

"This little act isn't working," she told him, walking around him, maintaining a distance of at least three feet. He would not catch her off guard again.

"So, I'm a woman with normal sexual desires. But I also have a brain that tells me you're bad news, Xavier Cross."

She stopped and looked at him, arms akimbo. "I still love you."

He went to move toward her, and Gaea stepped back once more, her arms out in a defensive position.

"Stay where you are. If you come near me again, I'll go into the bedroom, lock the door, phone the police and have you arrested."

Xavier froze in his tracks and sighed in resignation.

"Let's be realistic," Gaea continued, her dark eyes meeting his across the room. "You were not unfaithful to me once. You had a bevy of lissome students who would do anything for you. Now, I had heard the rumors about you long before we began dating, but I'm not the type of person who listens to gossip; maybe I should have. But that's beside the point. When you say we belong together based on my response to the maleness in you, you're reaching."

"I thought you were a person who believed in the triumph of the human spirit," Xavier said quietly. "Is it entirely impossible for me to change, and grow from this experience? Do you know how many times people in a committed relationship have to forgive and go forward? Do you imagine your own parents haven't made mistakes and had to forgive each other over the years?"

Gaea knew her parents had had problems over the years, some of which she wasn't always privy to. But, whatever form those problems had come in, they were her parents' business. And by no stretch of the imagination did she believe, for one second, that those problems may have included infidelity. Her parents were thoroughly devoted to each other.

However, even if one of them had had an extramarital affair, it wouldn't change how she felt about either one of them.

"We weren't married," she finally said after having stood there simply amazed at his temerity at bringing her parents into the conversation. "You knew how much I valued fidelity, Xavier. We talked about it."

Xavier shoved his hands into his pockets, ruminating on her

words, then he peered deeply into her eyes and said, "All right, I've tried pleading and logic. They've both failed. Therefore, I'm forced to use my position to get you to see reason: Unless you agree to marry me, in August, as we planned, I will suspend you until further notice."

"On what grounds?!" Gaea shouted, coming around the desk to stand nose-to-nose with Xavier.

"It doesn't matter, I'll make up something," he told her smugly.

Gaea reacted instinctively, aggressively shoving him backward.

Xavier, though, outweighed her by sixty pounds and barely budged.

He laughed. "Let's not get physical, doctor."

Incensed, Gaea continued to push him backward, little by little until he was knocked off balance and nearly toppled. Catching himself in time, Xavier continued to laugh.

"I could bring you up on assault charges," he suggested.

"Do what you will," Gaea said angrily, "because I'll quit before I'll allow you to manipulate me."

"You can't quit, you have an ironclad contract with Reed," Xavier reminded her confidently.

"A contract, which is up in September," Gaea countered. "I can put up with anything for four months, even you."

"I'll pull the funds on your research project," Xavier threatened.

She could tell, by the gleam in his eyes, that he was enjoying what control he imagined he had over her. That only made her angrier than ever.

She wanted to shout that she'd already been offered another position. But she didn't want to give him any information that might prove advantageous to him.

Her research on the Atlantic spotted dolphin was in its final stages. She was close to proving that their migratory habits were not based upon following their food sources, as some scientists hypothesized, but because of the dolphins' genetic encoding.

However, even the cessation of her project would not induce her to marry this man.

She willed herself to pull in the reins of her emotions. Breathing deeply, she said, "Go right ahead. Wear yourself out. But, be forewarned: you'll only succeed in making me hate you even more than I do now."

Xavier pulled her into his arms and pressed his cheek to hers, his grip firm in order to resist her will.

"You don't hate me, Gaea. You just told me you love me."

He bent his head then and kissed her firmly on the mouth, ending only when Gaea bit his lip.

His hand went to the tender spot on his mouth when he released her, but he was still smiling. "You're turning into a real wildcat. I like that."

"Let's see how you like spending the night in jail," Gaea said, briskly walking over to the desk and picking up the receiver.

"I'm leaving," Xavier conceded and backed slowly toward the front door. "I've done what I came here to do. Think about what I've said, darling. If you'd seen reason, I could have had you cooing with pleasure by now, instead of snarling at me like a fishwife."

He turned and walked out of the house then.

Gaea followed him onto the porch.

"Wait a minute."

She held out her hand.

"You probably gave a locksmith a load of bull to get in here. I'm sure he supplied you with a new set of keys. I'd like to have them."

Laughing, Xavier went into his jacket pocket and retrieved a couple of keys on a ring. He gave them to her.

"Not much gets past you. That's one of the reasons I want you."

"Get used to not getting everything you want," Gaea advised him.

She then slammed the door in his face.

She stood with her back pressed against the door, listening

for the sound of his footfalls as he descended the front steps. He'd probably taken a cab, so there would be no telltale car door slamming or an ignition being fired.

She hoped he had trouble hailing a taxi. It would serve him right, breaking into her house and giving her grief upon her arrival back home. He'd stolen her sense of security.

Of all the places she'd called home, since leaving her parents' house, this little bungalow, which she was buying with her own hard-earned money, was where she'd felt most secure. Now he'd ruined that for her.

Satisfied that Xavier had left, Gaea picked up her suitcase, camera bag and purse and went into the bedroom.

She paused in the doorway and switched on the light. There on her pillow was a single, perfect long-stemmed red rose. She sat the suitcase and camera bag atop the bed and picked up the rose. Beneath the dewy petals of the flower was a white slip of paper with one word written on it in Xavier's bold scrawl: *Dream.*

She watched as if in a surreal daze as a drop of blood fell on the white paper and spread until it was the size of a dime; she'd pricked her thumb on a thorn. She absentmindedly placed the thumb between her lips and sucked on it until it had stopped bleeding.

In the morning, she felt rejuvenated. As she sat up in bed and felt around for her slippers, she vowed that today would be a good day even if she had to kill Xavier in order to make it so.

Rising, she went to the sliding glass doors, opened them and stepped out onto her backyard deck. Breathing in the honey-suckle-perfumed air, she smiled and sighed.

The sky was a blue, cloudless topper on the day. Another lovely day on "the island" as her folks referred to their home-town.

Going back inside, she made short work of the bed, plumping

the pillows just right. A fastidious housekeeper, she took solace in having everything in its place, which was probably one of the reasons finding Xavier in her sanctum last night unnerved her. He was not welcome here, nor did he belong here, only those whom she invited.

After finishing the bed, she went into the bathroom and caught a glimpse of herself in the mirror. Her short hair was tousled, but she combed it back in place with her fingers. Daintily rubbing the matter out of the corners of her eyes with her forefinger, she wondered if Xavier would still want her if he saw her performing that morning ritual. Maybe he'd insist on doing it for her. "Come here, baby. Let me kiss the crud out of your eyes."

She laughed aloud and reached for her toothbrush and the Colgate.

Ten minutes later, she'd rehydrated by drinking sixteen ounces of spring water, dressed in her sweats and running shoes and was heading out the door.

Six-thirty A.M. Three miles around the island and then breakfast at Pepe's Cafe on Caroline Street.

"Hey, Gaea, you're back!" Mrs. Williams, her elderly neighbor called to her as she trotted down the sidewalk. Eveline Williams, a black woman in her early seventies, was walking her Yorkshire terrier, Beau.

Beau growled and tried to nip Gaea's ankle as she passed them, as he always did. Mrs. Williams pulled back on his leash. "He doesn't mean it. He loves you," she said by way of an apology.

"I know it, Mrs. Williams," Gaea assured her brightly. *He just mistook my leg for a pork chop, that's all.*

She'd never say something like that directly to Mrs. Williams, of course. After her husband died, four years ago, Beau became the kind lady's constant companion. He showed a rather vicious side to everyone else; he loved his mistress. Which, Gaea thought, was worth the price of his kibble.

"You have a good day," Gaea told Mrs. Williams in parting as she jogged in place.

"You, too, sugar," Mrs. Williams returned her wishes. Beau bared his teeth in a menacing farewell. Gaea sneered at him when Mrs. Williams averted her attention for a moment.

She smiled as she picked up her pace, heading down Olivia Lane where she would turn onto Duval Street. Xavier often ridiculed her choice of jogging routes, stating that Duval was usually packed with tourists. But Gaea was a people-watcher and she enjoyed the early morning hustle and bustle. Duval wasn't nearly as congested in the morning as it was later in the day, or, especially, on the weekend.

In the height of the season, pedestrians, cyclists and those brave souls who chose to drive cars or ride scooters clogged the main artery, which was Duval Street. However, even with the crowds, crime was low in the historic district. Actually, on a whole, crime wasn't running rampant in Key West. Police routinely warned tourists away from Little Bahama, that area of the city west of Whitehead Street and south of Petronia, but Gaea felt the area had been unfairly singled out. Sure there was a certain criminal element in Little Bahama because it was one of the poorer sections of Key West. There were also good, decent people residing there who wanted their neighborhoods to be as safe as the swankier Margaret Street, where well-to-do boat owners docked their vessels at the Land's End Marina.

Today, there wasn't much foot traffic along Duval. Just a few hardy souls who hadn't imbibed too much last night and felt like a morning constitutional.

"Good morning!" several perfect strangers called to Gaea.

She returned their greetings just as merrily. She'd been told by a few of her northern friends that the act of greeting people on the street was a uniquely southern phenomenon. Maybe it had something to do with the warm weather, which, perhaps, had a positive effect on one's disposition.

Gaea just knew she'd grown up practicing the habit of calling hcllo to anyone she made eye contact with in passing, and she was a little too old to stop now.

She passed the two-mile mark as she approached the Wrecker's Museum. Built in 1829, it was the island's oldest building. Inside were a good collection of furnishings and other artifacts from the early 1800's: tools used by the wreckers, themselves; household utensils, objects those who lived at that time used in everyday living.

Because of her interest in the sea and Solange's interest in archeology, they had spent many hours at the museum in their youth.

She stepped off the red-brick sidewalk onto the paved road and crossed over to Caroline Street. Here, restaurants, cafes and bistros lined the street.

The aroma of freshly baked bread reminded her that she hadn't taken the time to have her glass of orange juice. She was hungrier than usual this morning.

She paused long enough to take a swig of spring water from the bottle attached to her fanny pack.

Being on Caroline Street triggered memories of her and Xavier meeting at Pepe's Cafe for coffee after their respective workouts. She'd purposely left the house an hour later in order to avoid him altogether. They were both creatures of habit. He wasn't likely to abandon his morning exercise simply to avoid her. However, she was more adaptable. She would alter her schedule in order to eliminate an unfortunate encounter with him.

Refreshed, she continued down Caroline Street, feeling energized and happy to be back home. Nothing was going to spoil her day.


Reed Oceanographic Institution was founded in 1943 when Julius Abernathy, a meteorologist and oceanographer, convinced Conrad Reed, a wealthy Philadelphia newspaper publisher, to invest in a little school that would devote its time to studying the only natural reef in the continental United States: the Florida Keys' reef.

Expanding from the Dry Tortugas, nearly to Miami, the reef is a unique ecosystem, which provides sustenance and a home to a diverse collection of life.

From its austere beginnings, Reed turned into an institution capable of rivaling any in the world. Today, it has thirty buildings on one hundred and fifty acres; nine hundred staff members and in conjunction with the University of Miami, fifteen hundred graduate students.

Like most institutions, Reed encouraged staff exchange with other institutions in order to ensure a steady flow of fresh ideas. In science, discovery was a sought-after commodity and Reed always wanted to keep abreast of any new ways of thinking.

Located on the southernmost tip of Key West, facing the Atlantic Ocean, it was approximately a fifteen-minute daily commute for Gaea.

She drove her white, late-model Ford Mustang convertible through the gate and waited as Cooper, the guard, verified her ID.

"Hey, Dr. Maxwell. Welcome back," he said, his voice amplified by the microphone in his guardhouse, which was the size of two old-fashioned phone booths back-to-back.

He was an African-American in his late thirties. Invariably chipper, Leroy Cooper had been with the institution for more than ten years.

"How's Diane and the kids?" Gaea asked, handing him her picture ID. It was a formality they went through for security reasons. And Coop, ever the conscientious worker, never shirked his duty.

"They're just great," he answered. Satisfied that she was who she purported to be, and not a spy with clever plastic surgery, Coop raised the gate and Gaea sped through.

"Have a good one," he called after her.

After parking in faculty parking, Gaea walked-jogged over to the biology building where her offices were located. It was a four-story brick building that had been among the first built. Now, newer edifices dotted the campus, all constructed to look as though they were all of the same era. The board of directors liked cohesiveness and structure.

Running up the steps of the biology building, Gaea was greeted by several of her students coming out of the building.

"Dr. Maxwell! Are you teaching Lab II next semester?" This from Luke Fielding, a graduate student in molecular biology.

They stood on the steps while other students walked around them. Gaea shielded her eyes from the sun as she peered down into Luke's suntanned face. He had curly light-brown hair and green eyes. She thought he looked like a surfer, probably because he wore those long shorts and wildly colored T-shirts surfers were known for.

"Yeah, I'll have Lab II," she told him. "I thought you were taking that this semester with Adams."

"Adams quit," Luke said, slinging his knapsack onto his right shoulder. "I heard he and Dr. Cross had some kind of fight. BUMP had been courting him, anyway."

Gaea hoped her face didn't mirror her surprise at learning Mike Adams had left Reed for an offer from Boston University Marine Program. That Xavier could provoke such action from a staff member was not hard to believe. She'd wanted to tell him to shove it last night herself.

"I'm sorry to hear that," she said now. "Mike is a good man."

Maybe he'd quit because the offer from BUMP had been too good to pass up, not because of anything Xavier had done.

"Well, all right," she said to Luke "I'm looking forward to having you. Don't forget to register."

Luke assured her he wouldn't and trotted down the remaining steps while she went inside.

The black-and-white tile floors appeared freshly washed and waxed. The maintenance staff was really on the ball. Approaching her office, she noticed a maintenance man, attired in the usual beige uniform, washing the glass in the upper portion of the office door. As she drew nearer, she saw that he wasn't cleaning the glass, he was painstakingly scraping the letters off the glass with a paint scraper; occasionally, he wiped the paint chips off with a cloth.

"What are you doing?" she asked, her voice rising.

She didn't know the man. He was Hispanic, around fifty, of average weight and height. He had soulful brown eyes, a thick head of dark brown hair, gray at the sides. He smiled nervously.

"Let me guess," he said, almost apologetically, "you're Dr. Maxwell, aren't you?"

Gaea nodded affirmatively.

Eyes narrowing, and breath beginning to come in short rasps, she sighed.

"Orders from Dr. Cross, I presume?"

"Yes," the man confirmed. "I'm sorry."

"You don't have anything to apologize for," Gaea told him as she turned on her heels. "But I know someone else who's going to be extremely sorry in just a few minutes."

"I sure wouldn't wanna be that someone," the maintenance man muttered under his breath when she was out of earshot.

She ran up a flight of stairs and, when she arrived at Xavier's office door, she paused to catch her breath. Mrs. Jenkins, his elderly secretary, had a heart condition, and Gaea didn't want to startle the woman.

So she smiled warmly as she entered his outer office.

Seeing her, Mrs. Jenkins smiled back. Her aquamarine eyes, behind tortoise-shell glasses, looked Gaea up and down.

"Well if it isn't the soon-to-be blushing bride." She got up from behind her desk to embrace Gaea.

Mrs. Jenkins was a buxom sixty-eight-year-old. She would retire at the end of this semester. Her hair was entirely white and she wore it in a bun, which, coworkers speculated, she didn't unfurl even when she went to bed at night.

Her perfume of choice was White Shoulders, with a touch of Ben Gay. (Gaea guessed her rheumatism was acting up.)

"He'll be happy to see you!" Mrs. Jenkins told Gaea as she released her. "Go right in, honey."

"Thank you," Gaea said. "And I love that blouse on you."

"My son took me shopping at Burdine's this weekend. Isn't it lovely? It's silk, you know," Mrs. Jenkins replied, fingering the lapel of the sky-blue blouse.

"Well it's very becoming," Gaea complimented her, backing toward Xavier's office door.

She opened the door and slipped inside. Xavier was at his desk, going over some papers.

He was wearing his reading glasses and it was difficult for her to see his eyes through them, but she was sure they weren't registering surprise. He'd expected her.

"Good morning," he said, removing his glasses and placing them on top of the sheaf of papers on his desk. He gestured to the burgundy, leather-upholstered chair directly across from him. "Please, sit down."

Gaea dropped her heavy shoulder bag onto the chair, but she remained standing.

"I like that color on you," Xavier told her, his eyes running the length of her jeans-clad body. She was wearing a sleeveless turtleneck pullover in brown crushed velvet with a pair of loose-fit Levi's. The dress code at Reed was casual. Some even joked that you could discern a staffer's rank by the sort of clothes he wore. If he dressed in suits, he was new and held little clout, but if he wore cutoff jeans and a holey T-shirt, he was probably a department head. At Reed, it was knowledge that made the man (or woman) not the clothes.

Gaea impatiently tapped the hardwood floor with her boots. She still hadn't spoken.

Xavier rose and went to lean against his desk, not three feet away from her. He cleared his throat.

"You're angry because I've suspended you," he surmised. One eyebrow rose as he watched her face. "I told you I would. But, don't worry. My reason was that you'd been working too hard, so I'm putting you on a sort of 'forced' vacation. At least that's what the board will believe. Your research can be put on hold for a month."

"A month!"

He was pleased he'd finally gotten a rise out of her. Smiling, he pushed away from the desk, standing with his arms crossed over his muscular chest.

"Of course, the time could be shortened considerably if you'd consent to an elopement. We can fly to Vegas this weekend and get married. It's just a matter of planning . . ."

Getting right in his face, Gaea said, "I'm not going to marry you, Xavier."

Pretending he hadn't heard that, Xavier grasped her by the waist and pulled her against him. "If you knew how much I want you, you wouldn't risk getting this close to me, darling. If you knew about all the tortured nights I burned for you in my bed, you would not dare come into my office looking so damned good." He breathed in her essence, a combination of a fruity skin lotion coupled with her own unique fragrance.

Gaea arched away from him, and he buried his face in her chest.

Raising his head, he looked down into her eyes. "Let me make you a woman, Gaea. Then we can go forward with our lives. When we've made love, you'll know how much I want to make you happy. We don't have to be at odds." He frowned. "I hate this. The way you're looking at me now, as if I'm a satyr, lusting after a young virgin to satisfy my carnal desires. I'm not evil, Gaea. I'm just a man. A man who wants you desperately."

Sighing, he continued to hold her. And Gaea no longer resisted. She knew she lacked the physical strength to break free of his hold.

"You broke my heart," she said in a low voice.

He looked confused and she knew she had his full attention.

"I loved you so much, I was prepared to be everything to you: a wife, a lover, your partner, your best friend. Everything. In you I thought I'd found my one and only soul mate. We were in the same field, so you would be understanding of my schedule, my dedication to my work. We even shared a love of running. We liked the same old movies and could dance all night to reggae."

He groaned and let go of her.

"How many times must I say I'm sorry?"

"Until I believe you!" Gaea said with conviction, being mindful of Mrs. Jenkins's presence on the other side of the door. "Until I know there's a heart beating inside your chest instead of some mechanized gadget that allows you to ride roughshod over other people's feelings. You expect me to just forgive you for cheating on me, and go on with our plans. Well, I can't do that, Xavier. I can't marry a man I don't trust."

Xavier ran a hand over his tight cap of hair. He met her gaze.

"What can I do to make you believe in me again?" he asked quietly.

Gaea was nearly nonplussed by his sincerity.

"Blackmail won't get you anywhere," she told him for a starter. "And if you truly love me and still want to marry me, you're going to have to back off and give me room to breathe. I'm confused and hurting at this point. I don't need you trying to force my hand; bullying me with threats to my career. That's the one way you can turn me into an enemy, Xavier: by taking my work from me."

Xavier's eyes never left her face. He raised his right hand to caress her cheek, thought better of it and allowed his arm to fall.

"All right. I'll reinstate you immediately, and have Mr. Mendez put your name back on your office door. That was rather childish on my part, I'm afraid. Please forgive me. . . ."

Thinking their conversation was at an end, Gaea made for the door. Xavier caught up with her and placed a hand beneath her elbow. "But, Gaea . . ."

She turned to face him. "Yes?"

"I am sorry. I've been a fool who allowed his gonads to lead him around by the . . . nose. But I woke up, darling. I came to my senses and realized you're the best thing that ever happened to me. I can't bear to lose you forever. I go a little crazy at the thought of it. That's why I've been behaving so irrationally, I suppose."

"I can understand that," Gaea told him frankly, "because I go a little crazy every time I imagine you with another woman."

Xavier couldn't contain his excitement at her admission of jealousy. In his mind, where there were jealous feelings, there was also passion.

He pulled her into his arms once again.

"Baby, I know we can work this out. Just give us time. I swear I'll make it up to you somehow. Say you'll allow me to court you once more. I know I can make you trust me again."

He gently rubbed her back. "Okay? Can we start fresh?"

"All right," Gaea said, her voice barely a whisper.

Xavier hugged her even tighter. "Thank you," he said, his voice rife with relief.

They stood there in each other's arms. He was so pleased with the outcome, that his brown eyes were lit from within with happiness and his full lips wore a wide grin.

Gaea, however, was grateful he couldn't see her face at the moment because she wasn't smiling and her sable-colored eyes were narrowed. Somewhere in the deep recesses of her brain, a plan was being hatched.

# Nine

Later that afternoon, Gaea went to Florida Keys Hospital to question Dr. Lynn Casenove, her personal physician, about her recent bout of dementia. Gaea had known Lynn, another hometown girl, since they were in the ninth grade at St. Mary's Catholic School.

Gaea waited a good half hour before Lynn strolled into her office at Florida Keys. As one of only two neurologists on staff, Lynn was kept busy consulting and caring for her private patients.

Gaea got to her feet when Lynn entered the room.

Lynn Casenove was five-ten and on the heavy side. She despaired of people, like Gaea, who seemed to be able to eat anything they wished and not gain an ounce; whereas, if she even looked at a piece of pie, she gained a pound.

She had beautiful red hair, which was wavy and fell down her back in a single braid. And she had the darkest brown eyes Gaea had ever seen on a Caucasian. They were very nearly black and thickly fringed: an unusual combination in a natural redhead. However, Gaea knew that Lynn had inherited her fair complexion and red hair from her English mother and her dark eyes and dark lashes from her Cuban father.

Lynn took one look at Gaea and started laughing. "If all my patients were as sick as you look, I'd be out of a job."

"There's nothing physically wrong with me," Gaea said, smiling. Lynn could always make her feel better. "At least I hope not."

The two women briefly embraced and Lynn went to sit on the corner of her desk, while Gaea sat back down on the faded forest green hospital-issue chair in front of the desk.

"Lynn," Gaea began, "have any of your patients ever had hallucinations?"

"I've treated patients who suffered from one psychosis or another, who reported seeing unusual things. A schizophrenic, for example, might have hallucinations," Lynn explained. She leaned forward, still unconvinced Gaea could be in her office for anything serious. "What? Has one of your dolphins shown signs of dementia?"

Gaea, however, had zoned out. Her thoughts had become stuck on one word: *schizophrenia*. She'd heard of people who'd developed the mental disease later in life. Around her age, for example. The thought terrified her.

Seeing the worried expression on her friend's face, Lynn frowned.

"It was a joke, Gaea!"

Gaea sat there, a fist pressed to her mouth, and silent tears streaming down her face. She hadn't known how frightened she was for her sanity until Lynn had given voice to her own fears. A mental disease. Something could be wrong with her brain.

She looked up at Lynn, her eyes glassy from the tears.

"Lynn, you've got to give me every test imaginable. I've got to know if there's anything wrong with me."

Lynn had risen and gone to her, squatting in front of her. She took her hand in hers. "I've never seen you so upset. What's happened?"

Gaea agonized over how much she could reveal to Lynn without appearing as though she'd taken a flying leap off the deep end. However, in order to treat her properly, Lynn might have to be privy to everything.

So she began at the moment she'd seen the dolphin with the silver-dollar-size mark on his melon, and concluded with the account of her sighting of a nude male riding the bow waves of the *Cassiopeia*.

When she'd finished, Lynn looked at her with real concern for her mirrored in those obsidian-like eyes.

"Don't worry, Maxie, we'll get to the bottom of this."

Gaea was heartened by the sound of Lynn's old childhood nickname for her.

Twenty minutes later, Gaea was lying prone on the table of the latest imaging apparatus at Florida Keys. Attired in a thin hospital gown, chill bumps had broken out all over her body. She knew the phenomenon was caused as much by her nervousness as the sixty-degree temperature in the room.

"Hold perfectly still," the X-ray technician behind the glass enclosure admonished.

Gaea heard a series of clicks and then the woman told her, "All right, you're done. You can put your clothes back on. Dr. Casenove will join you in a few minutes."

Gaea got up from the table and quickly slipped on her panties and bra. She then pulled on her socks and finally, the Levi's and crushed-velvet blouse.

She was fully dressed when Lynn entered the room, beaming.

"Good news, Maxie," Lynn told her. "There is absolutely nothing abnormal about your brain."

"Nothing growing in there?" Gaea asked.

"Believe me, Maxie, you're fine," Lynn reassured her gently.

"Then why did I see what I saw?" Gaea asked, not really expecting a reply, but hoping Lynn might have some explanation.

Lynn laughed shortly. "You're a Conch, and you're asking me about the strange and unusual? Girl, we grew up on the strange and unusual. Ghost stories about murdering pirates; tales of voodoo rituals where zombies danced the dance of the dead. I think I may have even seen a ghost myself once."

"You're kidding me. You? Miss Rationale 1998?"

Lynn hopped up onto the examination table beside Gaea and crossed her legs. She looked down at her watch. "I'm off in fifteen minutes. Hopefully no emergency will come in with his brains falling out of his skull between now and then."

She always joked to ease tension. She'd done that even when they were kids, Gaea recalled.

"It was after mother passed away," Lynn told her in a low voice. "I was a resident at Miami General. Existing on three hours of sleep a night and coffee that could burn a hole in steel. Mom had died a week before and I'd just returned from her funeral. I went straight to the hospital. I didn't want to go home. All I did at home was cry until my eyes hurt. I couldn't sleep, I couldn't eat. My stomach fluids were so acidic, every time I ate something, it would come right back up."

"You were a wreck," Gaea said in sympathy.

"I was a zombie," Lynn agreed. "Anyway, around two o'clock in the morning, I'm coming out of the staff lounge with another cup of poison, when my mother appears right in front of me, as large as life. 'Lynn,' she says, 'go home and get some rest. I'm all right. Stop worrying about me, and take care of yourself.' Well, I dropped the coffee, spilling it all over my shoes and fainted dead away. A nurse found me a couple of minutes later and they admitted me. I slept for twelve hours straight. And I never saw my mother's ghost again."

She shuddered at the memory.

Gaea trembled at the thought. "Well then," she said, "you're sane. So I suppose it stands to reason that I am too."

Laughing, Lynn got to her feet. "As sane as any woman can be who dives with sharks."

Gaea rose too. "I only did that once," she said, defending herself.

"Now that would have been an appropriate time for you to come to me doubting your sanity," Lynn told her frankly. "What you're suffering from now is probably just mental fatigue; like I was suffering from when I saw my mother. Of course," she added as an afterthought, "I have heard of women who contracted a rare form of dementia when they became pregnant. You're not pregnant, are you?"

"Not unless God has wrought another Immaculate Conception," Gaea replied, laughing.

"Stranger things have happened," Lynn told her, and said it without cracking a smile. "Let me know if you spot any more dolphin-men. As scarce as good men are, I might be interested in dating him. No, wait, he probably appeared to you because he's interested in you, so that leaves me out. I wonder if he has a brother at home? Where do you suppose he comes from, Atlantis?"

"All right already, Lynn," Gaea said, smiling ruefully. "I get the message. I'm going to go home and sleep for twelve hours."

They began walking toward the double-door exit.

"I'm not kidding," Lynn said. "If he has a brother, let me know. I always wanted my children to be really accomplished swimmers."

Sufficiently convinced that she was healthy both physically and mentally, Gaea decided to take a different tack on her problem. If the dolphin wasn't a figment of her imagination, that meant he truly existed.

Well, she had to admit the bottlenose existed because everyone in the raft on their last dive had seen him. She and Don had commented on the spot the dolphin had on its melon: Don saying he thought it was a scar; and she, disagreeing because of the size and shape of the spot.

As far as she was concerned, that left one alternative. Something wondrous was happening to her. Something unnatural; one could even call it supernatural. Of course the idea of a world, other than the one she resided in, existing boggled her mind.

Admittedly, she had been brought up in the Catholic church and was taught that God was a spirit and that He'd created angels and, yes, even demons and evil spirits existed. But had she truly taken any of the dogma seriously?

She believed in God, but had never given much thought to

what the existence of God meant. Now she had to accept the fact that if God could be real, then so could other beings who were not like humans. They could come in any form. They could be spiritual or physical, or a combination of both. And if they were some amalgam of flesh and vapor, then perhaps they had the ability to transmogrify, that is, transform into other shapes. Like from a dolphin to a human, for instance.

Her search for answers led her to the public library where she went up into the stacks and blew the dust off ancient tomes that looked as if no one had cracked them open in decades.

Alone in the stacks, she sat in the aisle and pored over the thick books, her legs folded beneath her.

She learned that sailors had told tales of the dolphin's intelligence from time immemorial.

Archaeologists had discovered prehistoric engravings in South Africa of men riding dolphins.

The Aegean civilization left behind innumerable vases and wall paintings of dolphins interacting with man.

In Ancient Greece, at Delphi (so named for the dolphin) it was thought that the God Apollo first appeared there in the form of a dolphin. The most famous oracle, or the place where the gods were purported to speak to the people, was located at Delphi. The dolphin was said to be sacred to Apollo.

Gaea read of myriad instances in which the dolphin acted as a savior to fishermen and sailors. They seemed to have a special liking for children.

She went back to the shelves, searching for something more modern and found a book written by a famous explorer whom she'd greatly admired when she was an adolescent; and, in fact, viewing his many adventures on television had been one of the reasons she'd become a marine biologist.

In his book, she read of a strange occurrence he had in the mid-1950's.

He had been in the Indian Ocean with a full crew aboard his research vessel when they noticed a certain school of dolphins passing the ship daily. He assumed they were swimming a route along an adjacent reef in search of food.

One day, he and one of his men took a launch and followed the dolphins.

He reported that on the other side of the reef, they noticed a dolphin come to the surface for air and then let himself straight back down. When the explorer and his crew member looked down at the spot they'd seen the dolphin sink to, they were amazed to see several dolphins sitting (perched on their tails) in a circle as if carrying on a conversation, perhaps even a meeting of sorts.

The water was extremely clear so there was no mistaking what the explorer had seen. He could not explain the strange behavior, however, and he rued the day he'd ever gotten into the launch without his camera, because he had no physical evidence of the occurrence.

In all her years of study, Gaea had never seen or heard of dolphins sitting in a circle, facing one another as if discussing business. She hoped the account was accurate though, because wouldn't it be fascinating if dolphins actually practiced organization in their everyday lives?

She'd read of sightings of huge schools of dolphins, sometimes as large as ten thousand of them, all heading for a certain destination.

No scientist really knew how dolphins behaved in the wild. They could not keep them under surveillance twenty-four hours a day while in the deep ocean. The cost would be astronomical. So the researcher had to be satisfied with short stints of observing the mammals in their natural habitats, hoping for some revelation into the operating of the animal's mind.

Then there were those who felt a close study of dolphins under controlled conditions, such as at oceanographic institutions or in marine parks, was sufficient. But Gaea didn't think so. Cetaceans behaved differently in captivity than they did in their own world.

Therefore, the dolphin remained, on the whole, a mystery to man.

Closing the much-admired adventurer's account, Gaea got to her feet. Glancing down at her watch, she was surprised to learn she'd spent four hours sitting and reading among the dusty stacks.

It was 7:20 P.M. Her stomach growled and she realized she hadn't eaten anything since eight o'clock that morning when she had consumed a raisin bagel at Pepe's Cafe.

As she jauntily descended the library steps, she felt energized instead of weary. She was all right. Something was happening to her that she didn't have a handle on yet, but she would learn as much about shape-changers as she could, and one day, she was sure, it would all make sense to her.

She would approach this much in the way she did any experiment: she would identify the problem and break it down into small, more manageable sections and then she would solve it piece by piece.

Looking to the west, she was chagrined to find out she'd missed the famous Key West sunset. Ah well, there would be another one exactly like it tomorrow evening.

There was a nice breeze and on it was the briny smell of the sea. She breathed it in. There was nothing like a mystery to make life intriguing.

When she arrived home, she removed her boots in the foyer and carried them with her back to the bedroom closet.

Sitting on the bed, she reached over and pressed the play button on the answering machine.

There were three messages on the tape. The first was from Don Shear: "A rumor's going around about Mike Adams and your fiancé. It seems they had a fistfight over funding for Mike's gestation project. Mike's quit. Do you know anything about it?

Gaea smiled to herself. So that's how Xavier had gotten that scar above his right eye. A little memento, courtesy of Mike Adams.

The second one was from her mother: "Your grandparents are coming for dinner Sunday. I'm sure they're looking forward to seeing you. You aren't going out in the boat again on the Sabbath, are you?"

Xavier's voice was animated on the final message: "I want us to pretend as though we've just met; so I was wondering if you'll go out with me tomorrow night. It'll be our first Saturday night date. I'll pick you up and you can be nervous all over again, the way you were a year ago, when we went to Christophe's in Miami. Remember? Wear that little white sheath you wore. But this time, it'll be different, because I'm already in love with you and I'll know how your lips taste before I kiss you good night."

A chill had come over Gaea. She lay back on the pillows and reached for the multicolored afghan her Grandma Omega had given her on her sixteenth birthday, and pulled it over her body.

How was she going to convince Xavier to leave her alone? She had given him hope today only because she needed time to devise a plan of action. Whatever it was going to be, it had to be a doozy.

At that moment, Xavier was floating in the Gulf of Mexico. As he drifted on the buoyant saltwater, he looked up at the stars.

He'd purchased this particular piece of property for its access to a private beach. No nosy neighbors to wonder why he took daily late-night dips in the ocean; or spying on him when he strolled, nude, out of the water.

Gaea's face appeared in his mind's eye and he grinned. Not being in control of his nature had nearly ruined his one purpose for being here. It had taken him longer to find someone of Gaea's unique attributes than he'd intended and time was winding down. Unless she quit stalling and consented to wed him within five new moons, he would have no choice: he would have to do something desperate.

The light from the waning moon reflected off the water's surface. It had been a night much like this one when he'd first come ashore in search of something more than his limited existence could offer. His family always told him he was never satisfied; they were right, he'd never be complete until he'd achieved his ultimate goal, and Gaea was the key to his success. With her, he could become anything. And their children . . . their children would be gods.

Xavier stood up, his long, black, muscular body glistening. Empowered from his swim, he took great strides, stepping on wet sand and seaweed, which reminded him of the primordial muck his ancestors climbed out of eons ago. In his opinion, he was evolving further, taking his race one more rung up the ladder to genetic superiority.

Stepping onto the beach now, he looked to the heavens and let out a joyous shriek. Throwing his head back, he continued to keen; the sound carried on the breeze.

In her bungalow, Gaea sat up in bed, listening. Her heart began beating rapidly. What could be making that mournful sound? It certainly wasn't Beau next door. Whale call. Yes, that's what it sounded like. But she was miles away from the aquarium. She shouldn't be capable of hearing the Orcas they kept in their tanks.

The cries ended abruptly and she settled back down on the bed, clutching a pillow to her chest. A sadness came over her.

"I knew I would find you here," Omega Maxwell said as she approached Gaea on a stretch of beach near Garrison Bight, the following morning.

If her grandmother had been five minutes later, she wouldn't have caught her, because Gaea was preparing to take a large skiff out to dolphin-watch.

The boat was a twenty-footer and was easily handled by one person, so she was going alone, as she'd done on numerous occasions.

Now, Gaea finished piling her equipment in the boat and went to embrace her grandmother.

Omega squeezed her so tightly, Gaea was momentarily rendered breathless; she was strong for a hundred-pound, five-foot-two-inch woman of seventy-eight years. It seemed to Gaea that a good breeze could make her airborne.

"You been on my mind, child," Omega said in her thick Spanish-accented voice. Born in the Dominican Republic, Omega had skin the shade of rich Dutch chocolate and her eyes, in stark contrast, were golden-brown with green flecks.

"And you've been on mine," Gaea told her. She smiled. "Why is it whenever I have a problem, you seem to home in on it?"

"It's in the blood," Omega told her. Taking Gaea's hand, she led her over to the boat where they stepped inside and sat down. "I been having dreams about you. You and the ocean. Makes me frightened, those dreams. I lost your grandfather to her. I'll never forgive her for that."

For as long as Gaea could remember, Omega had referred to the ocean as a female entity. And more often than not, Omega seemed to consider the ocean a personal adversary. Her husband, Cameron, Gaea's father's father, drowned when Cam was a baby. He'd been a fisherman in the Dominican Republic.

Omega remarried when Cam was four years old, and her husband, Aaron, gave the little boy his name: Maxwell. So Aaron, whom Gaea called Grandpa, was not related to them by blood, only by love and the passage of time.

Omega continued to grasp Gaea's cool hands in her warm ones.

"I don't want to frighten you with an old woman's superstitions," she said, looking into Gaea's dear face. "I only want you to promise me you'll be cautious and careful when you're in her. She's heartless, that one," her eyes glanced in the direction of the Gulf of Mexico, "and she doesn't care who she swallows up."

Sighing, Omega returned her gaze to Gaea. "Maybe my melancholia is caused by the season. It was in the spring when Cameron was taken. April nineteenth." Her eyes took on a happy aspect. "You're so much like him. He loved her too. He wasn't happy unless he was in her. Some nights, he would spend hours swimming. He was like a fish. Then, not two years after we were wed, he was gone forever. At least he left me your father. And now, there's you."

She affectionately squeezed Gaea's hand. "I don't want to lose you to her too. So be careful."

"I'm always careful, Gran," Gaea told her gently.

"All right then," Omega said softly. "Now, you tell your abuela what's troubling you. And don't hold anything back. Is it that devil, Xavier?"

Gaea laughed shortly. Of all her friends, relations and acquaintances, her grandmother was the only one who had not succumbed to Xavier's many charms. From the start, she'd said, "Don't marry that one, child. He isn't what he seems."

Gaea had never asked her grandmother to explain what she'd meant by that. She had a feeling she should seek elucidation.

For now, though, she'd tell Omega about her dolphin-man sighting and see what she had to say about it.

Gaea wasn't prepared for her grandmother's reaction to her tale.

Omega stood up, stepped from the boat and began walking in the direction she'd come.

Her long, multicolored caftan billowed out in the southerly breezes. With her balsa wood hand-carved cane thrust out before her, she looked like a bedouin crossing the desert.

"I've got to go, child. Your abuela has urgent things to do."

"Gran!" Gaea called, running after her.

Omega paused in her headlong rush and turned around. Her face was ashen.

Gaea grasped her by the shoulders. "You have heard something about them, haven't you? Maybe a folktale from the West Indies? If you have, you've got to tell me, Abuela."

She stopped and breathed deeply. She was upset, and she feared she might be causing her grandmother undue stress.

In a calmer voice, she said, "I don't think it's over, Abuela.

I believe he'll return, and if it's at all possible, I need to be prepared."

Omega's golden-brown eyes had held fear in them, but now the expression had changed to something akin to anger.

"It isn't over, child. It's just beginning. I will tell you all I know about them, but first, your abuela needs to gather her strength. Come to me tonight. Aaron will be at his lodge meeting. Six o'clock. Don't be late. I'll be recovered from the shock by then."

Gaea hugged her grandmother. "I'll be there, Abuela. Thank you. I thought I was losing my mind."

"No, child," Omega said soothingly. "It has nothing to do with your sanity. It's all because of a happenstance of birth. You will understand everything tonight, I promise."

Gaea kissed her grandmother's satiny cheek. Omega smelled of a combination of sweet, exotic spices. She mixed her own perfume from various herbs and flowers she grew in her garden.

"Show no fear," Omega whispered.


"Go home, Micah."

Micah looked up from the legal papers he was reading to see Thad standing in his office doorway.

Smiling wearily, Micah said, "I just have this last set of documents to proofread and then Joann can fax them to Benthic."

"All right," Thad said. He appeared particularly jovial tonight. But, then, Micah remembered Connor, Isobel and Angelica were due in from Long Island later this evening.

Connor brought the family into Manhattan one Sunday per month to spend the day in the city. They had brunch at Tavern on the Green, then the women went shopping, hitting all the stores on Madison Avenue.

"Give my best to Connor, Isobel and Angie," Micah said.

"What are you doing tonight?" Thad asked. "Big date?"

"I think you know the answer to that one," Micah said.

"You've done a great job on the merger," Thad sincerely congratulated Micah. "Why don't you treat yourself to a short trip? Key West is pretty this time of year."

"You're about as subtle as a steamroller," Micah said, laughing. "I don't want to frighten the doctor off by following her home."

"When I was courting Katharine," Thad said, "I followed her all the way to England."

"In your day, that was called displaying interest," Micah said. "Today, it's called stalking."

"She can do one of two things: send you away or welcome you," Thad insisted. "You're a big boy, you can take the rejection."

"She's worth the risk," Micah agreed. "But, the fact is, she isn't due back in Key West until Monday."

"You could be waiting for her with a bottle of sparkling grape juice, since the good doctor is a nondrinker, and nimble fingers with which you can administer a much-needed back rub."

Micah pushed his reading glasses back up on his nose. "I'll do it. I haven't been able to get her off my mind anyway."

"That's my boy!" Thad said enthusiastically. He turned to leave, "Give her my best. If I were thirty years younger . . ."

"You'd have one bitter rival," Micah finished for him.

The two men laughed and Micah could hear Thad chuckling all the way down the hall. He went back to his reading.

By the time he left the office, thanks to the miracle of the Internet, Micah had reserved a seat on an American Airlines flight to Miami the following morning. He'd also booked a suite at the Marquesa Hotel. The luxury inn was pricey, but according to the employee manning the keyboard at the Marquesa, the hotel boasted a four-star rating and every suite had a spectacularly lovely view of the city's sunset. Of course, Micah didn't care about the sunset. He was going to Key West with the express purpose of winning Dr. Maxwell's heart. She'd already stolen his.

It was after nine by the time he arrived at his building on the Upper West side.

Salvador, the doorman, a squat Colombian in his late forties with an ever-present grin, greeted him, his mood, as usual, enthusiastic.

"Hey, Mr. Cavanaugh, slay any dragons today?"

"A few," Micah said. "What's up, Sal?"

"Nothing much," Sal said, coming to stand close to Micah. "You, on the other hand, could be in for an interesting evening. Miss Jarrold is waiting for you in the lobby."

"Thank you, Sal," Micah said. "Have a good evening."

"You too, sir," Salvador replied, returning to his post.

Frowning, Micah continued across the lobby, making a beeline for the bank of elevators. He had nothing to say to Renata and hoped her attention was elsewhere while he traversed the length of the lobby and boarded an elevator for upstairs.

In their happier days, she had a key; and Salvador had been instructed to allow her access to his apartment in his absence. Now, she was forced to wait around the lobby when he wasn't at home. He should have instructed Salvador not to let her in the building at all, but that would've been petty.

He supposed it was inevitable that they would come face-to-face sometime. He couldn't foresee any reason why that should be the case. He could happily exist for the next fifty years without having to make polite conversation with Renata.

She'd made him feel like a fool for loving her.

"Mike?" That dulcet voice was painfully familiar.

He took a deep breath and slowly turned.

Renata stood behind him, attired in a black designer skirt suit. She was impeccable, as always. Not a tendril of coal-black hair strayed from her coiffure, which was piled high on her beautiful head.

She smiled, revealing straight, white teeth. Her fragrance wafted over him like a lover's caress.

But he was pleased to find out that his heart wasn't racing at the sight of her. And he was experiencing an unexpected freeze where his libido was concerned. Just being near her used to turn him on in an instant. Now? Nothing.

The realization made him surprisingly giddy.

He laughed suddenly. "Renata."

Renata stood five feet eight and was what some men called stacked. She had inspired all kinds of emotions in men: love, passion, desire, lust. But hilarity? No, not her.

She ignored his behavior for the moment, however. She had an agenda and would not be thwarted by anything short of a citywide conflagration.

Her body was within three inches of his as she looked up into his eyes. "Mike, it's over between me and Patrick. He didn't want a wife, he wanted another groupie."

She pouted prettily. "I spent all my time answering his fan mail. You would be shocked by the lewd articles he received through the mail from some women."

Micah wasn't in the mood to hear about her problems with the professional basketball player she'd dumped him for. Six months ago, she'd flaunted her relationship with the popular athlete. Now she was back grousing about him.

"I'm sure that if you work at it," Micah began, trying to sound sympathetic, "you'll be able to get past your personal quirks and get on with your lives."

He loosened his tie and placed his briefcase against his right leg as he stood there, hoping she'd get the hint and not try to back him against a wall. He didn't want to be cruel, but there was absolutely no possibility of a reconciliation with this fickle woman.

Renata reached out and placed the palm of her hand against his chest. "Be nice, Mike. I need someone to talk to, and you were the first person who came to mind. We used to be best friends. I could discuss anything with you . . ."

"That was before you left me for another man," Micah said. He wasn't angry though. Just resolute.

"That's what I want to talk with you about," Renata said, undeterred. Her eyes glistened with unshed tears. "Oh, Mike, he was mean to me. He said I was only with him because he's worth thirty million. He told me I spent his money like it grew on trees." She sniffed. "His mother hated me. She called me a gold digger."

She leaned against him and Micah placed his arms around her. He sighed. "I'm sorry you had to go through that, Renata. As someone who used to be your close 'friend,' I'm going to give you the gift of honesty; and I hope you accept it in the spirit in which it's given: you need to get in touch with your spirituality and stop putting so much emphasis on material things. Until you do that, and truly take care of yourself, you're going to be running from one man to another."

Renata wiggled out of his arms and looked at him as if he'd plunged a knife through her heart.

"I can't believe you're turning me away," she said incredulously. "I know you loved me, Mike."

"I did," Micah freely admitted. "But there's someone else in my heart now, Renata. And, somehow, I don't think she cares that I'll probably never earn thirty million a year."

He reached down and picked up his briefcase then, and turned to walk away. "Good-bye, Renata. Have a good life."

"You cold bastard!" Renata cried.

Hearing the end of the conversation, Salvador walked over and gently took Renata by the arm. "This way, Miss. Can I call you cab?"

# Ten

"What is the matter with you tonight, Meg?" Aaron Maxwell asked Omega that evening during dinner.

At their age, they ate sparingly; so their meal consisted of a hearty homemade vegetable beef soup and a loaf of Italian bread.

They were sitting at the table in the kitchen of their two-bedroom home near Cam's and Lara's on Simonton Street.

"You went to see Gaea this morning," Aaron said, gazing at Omega through his bifocals. "Ever since then you've been as jumpy as a pig on Bastille Day." In Santo Domingo, every year on Bastille Day, the men would dig a pit and roast a pig.

Omega smiled at her husband. After fifty years of marriage, he was attuned to her many moods; she'd been unable to conceal the fear and sense of foreboding she felt concerning their grand-child.

Her mother used to say that fate could not be thwarted. If fate was somehow averted, then it would try to reassert itself in future generations; and keep trying until what should have been in the beginning had, finally, come to pass.

That's what she believed was happening now. Tonight, though, she would tell Gaea everything, and perhaps something could be done to satisfy fate and ensure her granddaughter's safety. She continually prayed for mercy.

"The older you get," she jokingly said to Aaron, "the more

you fret about me. Don't you know by now that I'm made of steel, and not sugar and spice?"

"I know what that means," Aaron said knowingly. "You have a secret that you're not ready to discuss with me. But, as always, you will eventually tell me what it is."

He rose and bent to kiss his wife's cheek. "Thank you for the soup, it was delicious. I love you, Mrs. Maxwell."

"And I love you, Mr. Maxwell," Omega promised him, a twinkle in her golden-green eyes just for his benefit.

She watched as her tall, gangly husband, every hair on his curly maned head snow white, went to the sink and washed his dishes, rinsed them, then set them in the dish rack on the counter to drain.

He looked back at her before going into the bedroom to retrieve a lightweight jacket.

"Have your boyfriend out of here by the time I get back."

"I always do," Omega said, giving him her most coquettish smile.

She lingered over her coffee, glancing every now and then at the clock on the wall. It was five-thirty. If Aaron didn't dally, he wouldn't run into Gaea on the way out and there would be no need for a lengthy explanation as to why she was visiting on his lodge night. He looked forward to the pleasure of his granddaughter's company, too, and his feelings would be wounded if he were to be left out.

Aaron left promptly at five-thirty-five, and Omega set about cleaning the kitchen by washing the few remaining dishes and putting the soup in the refrigerator and the bread in the bread box.

Finished with that small chore, she went into her bedroom to get a manila envelope she kept locked in a metal box beneath their bed.

She was stooping, reaching under the bed when she heard a noise. Someone was coming in the back door. In case of an emergency, Gaea and Cam had keys to their home, so Omega wasn't unduly concerned.

It was probably Gaea, arriving a bit early for their appointment.

She stretched a bit and felt the cold metal box. After pulling it out, she sat on the carpeted floor and felt inside her blouse for the key, kept around her neck on a gold chain.

She unlocked the box, returned the chain to its place around her neck and began lifting old, time-yellowed black-and-white photographs from the box.

At that moment, she realized that whomever had come into the house hadn't called out to her upon entering. It was then that she felt a sense of wrongness about the noise she'd previously heard.

She dropped the photographs back into the box and slowly got to her feet. As an afterthought, she nudged the box, still opened, back underneath the four-poster bed.

"Who's there?" she called, her voice strong despite her nervousness.

A tall figure appeared in the doorway. Omega realized that at that distance, she would be unable to make out the person's face without her glasses. Curse the vanity of an old woman.

She knew instinctively, though, that it wasn't Gaea or Cam standing at the entrance to her bedroom, so she began backing away from the intruder.

"Listen, I don't know what you want here," she said, moving cautiously around the bed, hoping to get to the window where she could scream for help. "But, the jewelry box is on the dresser there, and the television set's in the living room. So take what you want and get out. I'm an old woman with bad eyesight, so I couldn't identify you even if the police showed me an eight-by-ten glossy of you."

She could hear his inhalations and exhalations, but that was the only sound emanating from him, which made her even more frightened. Why didn't he speak?

The silence grew thick between them, until Omega found herself trembling, imagining every form of violence man had ever perpetrated upon man. He hadn't made a move toward the dresser to get the jewelry she'd gladly offered him. He'd simply stood there breathing, his head cocked to the side as if he were trying to decide what he would do to her first.

"My granddaughter is due here any minute now," Omega cried, thanking God she'd remembered Gaea was sure to be there soon. *Please God, don't let her be delayed.*

That piece of information threw the intruder into action. He stepped into the room. Omega inched closer to the wall. She was right next to the window, but it was closed and locked. She didn't see much of a chance of being able to unlock it, raise it and scream loud enough for her neighbors to hear her before the man was on her and perhaps, strangling the life out of her. So she stayed put.

Finally he spoke: "Hablar es muerte. Comprendes? Muerte."

"Si, si, comprendo," Omega said urgently. "Comprendo."

He turned his back to her then and walked toward the exit, in no rush to vacate the premises.

Omega's heart was beating so fast, she was afraid she was going to pass out.

When he got to the doorway, he placed his right hand on the upper portion of the molding and turned his head to look back at her.

Even without her glasses, Omega could make out the grotesque, utterly inhuman image not eight feet away from her. She tried to scream, but the sound was choked off as she collapsed to the floor. Unable to process the reality of the extreme unreality of the situation, synapses in her brain had failed.

The last thing she remembered seeing was that horrific face, coming to peer down at her. Then, mercifully, everything went black.

After the old woman closed her eyes and succumbed, as if in death, the intruder's attention was drawn to an object protruding from beneath the bed.

He walked over and lifted the corner of the bedspread and reached down. His hand touched a single photograph. Pulling it out, he saw that it was of a very young Omega and a male, whose image was blurred. Much like his own image would be if he were ever photographed. This discovery made him get on his knees and probe further. Finding the cache of memorabilia, he carefully placed the photos that had spilled out of the box back inside, closed it and absconded with the entire box.

Omega's body jerked with convulsions.

Gaea rang the bell twice, and when her grandmother didn't answer the door, she used her key. Her senses already heightened from the peculiar predicament she found herself in, she was concerned by the funereal silence permeating the house.

"Gran!" she called.

She walked in the direction of the kitchen. If her grandmother had had to go out unexpectedly, she would've left her a hastily scribbled message stuck under one of the colorful refrigerator magnets on her Frigidaire.

There was no message.

Icy fingers of fear began climbing her spine. She knew something was wrong, she felt it in her gut.

Hurrying from the kitchen, she quickly checked the first bedroom, a small guest room that her grandmother used as a sewing room when it wasn't occupied by friends or family.

She checked the closet and the bathroom, just in case; not knowing what she would find, she didn't want to leave any place not properly scoured.

"Gran! Please answer me," she continued to call.

When she entered the master bedroom, she placed a hand on the molding above the door and came away with a green gelatinous liquid on her palm. The moment she began to wonder what the substance could be, she heard a faint moan and quickly followed the sound to her grandmother who lay slumped on the floor.

Kneeling, Gaea placed a hand beneath her grandmother's head.

Omega appeared as if she were sleeping. Her chest rose and

fell; and Gaea could see her eyes going back and forth as if in REM sleep. Every few seconds, she would moan, the volume barely detectable.

Gaea was usually the type of person who was calm in a crisis. Once, she'd been the only cool head in a room full of premed students when their instructor had clutched his chest and fallen headlong off the stage and suffered a heart attack. She'd been administering CPR when the ambulance had arrived.

But that was years ago, and the professor, Dr. Westfall, bless him, had survived and given her an *A* in his class (she'd earned it. He was grateful she'd saved his life. But, not *that* grateful).

The point was, he hadn't been someone she was emotionally attached to. Not someone she'd known all her life. Someone who'd loved her unconditionally for thirty-one years. Someone whom she adored.

She looked down now at the pitiful sight of her grandmother, and panicked. Her mind went blank for a moment. And then, an inner voice told her to get up and dial 911.

When the paramedics arrived seven minutes later, she had managed to take Omega's pulse: weak, but still there. And to telephone her parents who promised to swing by the lodge, pick up Aaron and meet her at the hospital.

The ride to the hospital, with the sirens at full blast, felt like an eternity to Gaea. She'd never seen her grandmother look so frail and helpless. Omega's warm, brown skin had lost its luster, and her mouth was slack. She still hadn't opened her eyes.

*Oh God, please don't let it be a stroke,* Gaea prayed.

When they arrived at the hospital, all Gaea could do was stand aside, feeling totally useless, as the emergency room personnel quickly wheeled her grandmother inside the building.

She followed them, almost running to keep up.

The paramedic who'd taken Omega's vital signs en route to the hospital quickly relayed the information to the doctor on the case.

"Blood pressure's 120 over 70. Heart rate's 53 per minute.

Real slow. No response, except slight sounds she makes at the back of her throat."

The doctor, a short, stocky man with pale blue eyes behind thick spectacles and long, brown hair which he wore pulled back in a ponytail, listened intently. He glanced back at Gaea.

"Family?"

"Yeah," Gaea answered. "Granddaughter. I found her. She was lying on the floor. Not moving. Eyes closed. No sound, except a low moaning."

"How old is she?" the doctor asked.

"Seventy-eight," Gaea replied. She quickly glanced at the name stitched on the top left pocket of his mid-length white coat. Dr. Jude Potemski.

"Any history of diabetes, heart ailments, stroke?" he inquired.

"None," Gaea said.

By this time, they were in an examination room. The paramedic left; a nurse drew a privacy curtain around the room and the only people left in the room were Gaea, the doctor, an African-American nurse in her early forties, and the patient.

Dr. Potemski began issuing orders for tests, which the nurse wrote down on the chart. In the meanwhile, he checked Omega's pulse and pronounced it strong. Then he listened to her heart with his stethoscope and said, "I don't think it's her heart, but we'll run an EKG anyway."

Gaea nodded, thankfully.

"What I'm afraid of," Dr. Potemski said, his forehead wrinkling in a frown, "is a brain aneurysm. Lucy, get Dr. Casenove down here. I think she's on call tonight."

"Right," Lucy, the African-American nurse, said curtly. She left the room.

"I'd like to rule that out right away," Dr. Potemski continued, his voice calm and reassuring. "The brain's a funny thing. Sometimes there can be a sort of short circuit and the patient is out for a while. Then he awakens as if nothing happened. The brain, in fact, repairs itself. Isn't that marvelous? I could be mistaken, but that appears to be what has occurred here. Her vital signs are pretty good. She isn't having any trouble breathing . . . Has she had a sudden shock that you know of?"

Gaea thought that a peculiar question to ask, but didn't say so.

"No. We were supposed to meet at six to discuss something. My grandfather had already gone to his lodge meeting when I arrived, on time. They never argue. I can't imagine what could have frightened her to such an extent."

Just as the doctor was about to ask another question, the technician, a young Hispanic man, walked through the curtains with an EKG machine in tow. He immediately began administering the test to Omega.

Dr. Potemski crooked a finger in Gaea's direction.

"Let's step outside, shall we?"

Gaea followed him into the corridor.

"We're going to do our level best to find out why your grandmother isn't responding. Was there nothing unusual about the room you found her in? No signs of a struggle? Nothing ransacked?"

"No," Gaea replied.

His question served to prick her memory about the green gook she had gotten on her hand and absentmindedly wiped on her jeans-clad leg when she'd rushed to her grandmother's aid.

She quickly decided not to tell Dr. Potemski about that. It couldn't have any significance to her grandmother's case anyway.

"Nothing," she maintained.

"Curious," Dr. Potemski said, shaking his shaggy head. His Nikes squeaked on the tile floor as they walked.

"You mentioned your grandfather. Has he been informed about his wife's condition?"

"Yes, he and my parents are probably in the waiting room by now."

"Good. Then you can tell them as soon as I know anything, I'll come out and let you know."

"All right. Thank you, Doctor," Gaea said softly. She felt as if she'd failed her grandmother in some fundamental way.

Could she have put Omega's life in jeopardy by her confession of that morning? What did her grandmother have to tell her that was so important that their meeting had to be cloaked in secrecy?

What if the strange occurrences of late had somehow been behind her dear abuela's illness? She'd never forgive herself should her grandmother fail to recover from this crisis with all her faculties.

As she had suspected, her parents and grandfather were anxiously fidgeting in the waiting room.

Lara was sitting next to Aaron on the beige couch, his hand firmly clasped in hers. But Cam was pacing back and forth, seemingly trying to wear a hole in the brown, tightly woven carpeting.

They all turned their eyes on her when she entered the room. Cam went to her and grasped her by the shoulders.

"Where is she?" he asked, his brown eyes boring into hers.

"She's in an examination room. They're giving her an EKG right now in order to make certain her heart's not the cause of the unconsciousness."

She took her father's hand and led him over to the couch where she made him sit down.

Still standing, she said, "Dr. Potemski is her physician. He doesn't think it's her heart and I told him all about her medical history." She looked into her grandfather's worried face. "There isn't anything I could've left out is there? Has she been complaining of any aches or pains lately? Anything you might be able to tell them could be of help in diagnosing what's wrong."

"You know your abuela," Aaron said, his voice hoarse. "She does not complain about anything. What about Dr. Baldonado? Has he been called in yet?"

Omega's personal physician. Gaea had forgotten all about him. His office would have her complete medical history on file.

"You're right," she told her grandfather excitedly. She bent to briefly give them a group hug. "I'll go tell Dr. Potemski to get in touch with Dr. Baldonado immediately. I'll be right back."

As she hurried off, she silently berated herself. Why hadn't she thought of contacting Dr. Baldonado? Too much was happening to give her sufficient time to think.

Turning the corner, she thought she saw Lynn Casenove walking a few feet ahead of her.

She quickened her pace, catching up with the tall redhead.

"Lynn?"

Lynn paused to smile at her. "Maxie, what are you doing back here? Another sighting?"

"It's my abuela," Gaea told her as they continued walking. "Isn't that why you're here? Dr. Potemski said he was calling you in to consult on the case."

Lynn's dark brows furrowed with concern. "You mean your grandmother is the comatose patient in examination room one?"

"Yes, Lynn, and I'm scared to death . . ."

"Banish that thought," Lynn said as they arrived at the curtained-off room. "No negative vibes permitted."

She pulled back the curtain and found the EKG technician unplugging his machine.

Recognizing Lynn, he said, "All's well with the ticker." Then, seeing Gaea, and thinking his remark might have sounded too flippant, added, "For her age, her heart's perfectly sound."

"Thank you," Gaea said.

"You're welcome," he said and quickly left the room.

"He didn't mean anything by that," Lynn said for Gaea's benefit. "Sometimes, when you work around sick people all day, you have to adopt an irreverent attitude toward life in order to cope."

"I know," Gaea said. Lynn was the most irreverent, humorous person she knew.

Going to Omega and taking her right hand in hers, Lynn bent down close to Omega's face.

"Well hello, Mrs. Maxwell. It's Lynn Casenove. Remember me? I used to eat your lemon pound cake as if it were going out of style. I still have the hips to show for it." Lynn glanced at Gaea, who was hanging back, out of the way. "Gaea's here. Gaea, why don't you tell your grandmother where she is and what's going on, just in case she's a little confused."

Gaea came forward and bent down close to Omega's face as Lynn had done. "It's me, Abuela. We're at Florida Keys Hospital. You passed out. I found you when I got to the house at six this evening. Grandpa, Mom and Dad are all in the waiting room, hoping to hear you're just fine. Plus, we have all sorts of questions that need answers; and you're the only one who can answer them. So wake up, Gran. Wake up. . . ." Her voice quavered and she stopped speaking, thinking that she didn't want Omega to hear the fear in it.

Lynn squeezed her shoulder reassuringly, .

"All right, Mrs. Maxwell," she said in her most boisterous tones, "we have real sick people here who could use this bed, so you get on up from there. Your family is counting on you. And I haven't had good pound cake in ages. Open your eyes and look into your granddaughter's beautiful face. Come on now."

Lynn walked over to the entrance and motioned for Gaea to join her. "I know this might seem unorthodox to you, but I maintain the opinion that comatose patients can hear and understand those around them. I've been told this on a number of occasions by people who awoke and told me what I'd said to them while they were unconscious. Therefore, I don't want you to say anything you don't want her to hear. And, like I said earlier, no negative vibes."

"What do you think happened?" Gaea asked her friend in a low voice.

A technician came in and handed Lynn a set of X rays. They were of Omega's brain. Apparently, while Gaea was out comforting her parents and grandfather, the X rays had been taken.

Lynn walked over to the lighted screen on the wall and placed the X ray against it.

"Mmm," she said, after a moment or two. "Her CAT scan looks normal." She studied the X rays for a couple more minutes. "The brain has a defense mechanism built in it, which guards against irreparable damage by shutting down some of the body's functions while it repairs whatever needs fixing. Do you get me?" She looked at Gaea.

"You're saying all you can do at this point is to give her tests, which will systematically rule out common ailments that could cause her symptoms. But you don't know what's wrong."

"Exactly," Lynn said, nodding. "She'll be in intensive care and we will keep her under close observation. Monitoring her vital signs to be sure she's still breathing well; which at this point, she is. She just appears to be in a deep sleep. All we can do is hope that the brain will do its job quickly and this episode will be of brief duration."

"That's not much to pin my hopes on," Gaea told her frankly.

"But that's all I have, Maxie," Lynn said regrettably.

Lynn returned to her patient. "As for you, Mrs. Maxwell, I want you to just relax. You're in good hands. And when you decide to open your eyes, your family will be here for you."

Lynn motioned for Gaea to follow her outside.

Once they were several feet away from examination room one, she said, "In the old days, when people would collapse and remain unconscious for any length of time, the family would just put them to bed and someone would remain at the bedside twenty-four hours a day, talking, singing, reading to the patient until one of two things happened: either the patient died or woke up and told the singer to shut up."

"We can do that," Gaea eagerly volunteered, seeing where Lynn was going.

"It's going to be difficult," Lynn said from experience. "Mom was in a coma for two weeks before she died. It can be a terrible strain on the family."

"I realize that," Gaea assured her. "But, there is nothing this family wouldn't do for Gran. She's the backbone, the strength that keeps us going. It's impossible to imagine life without her."

"I know what you mean," Lynn said sympathetically.

A male nurse walked up to Lynn, a chart in his hands. "Excuse me, Dr. Casenove. We need your signature in order to proceed with the tests for Mrs. Maxwell."

Lynn scrawled her unrecognizable name on the bottom of the form and waited until the nurse had gone before saying, "Like I've said, Maxie, I have a good feeling about this. I believe Mrs. Maxwell will come out of it on her own. That's *my* take on it. Of course, being trained in the medical arts, I can't rely on emotions. So, I'll consult the test results and if I'm not satisfied, I'll keep digging."

"I know you will, Lynn. That's just the way you are," Gaea said gratefully.

Lynn hugged her briefly. "In the meanwhile, I'll be praying."

"We'll all be doing that," Gaea said, smiling.

Lynn released Gaea and took a step backward. "There's something I've been meaning to ask you: Dr. Potemski mentioned to me that he'd suggested that your grandmother may have been frightened by someone. Do you think that's possible?"

"Anything's possible, Lynn. But there was no indication that anyone had been in the house. She was just lying on the floor, unconscious, when I got there."

"All right then," Lynn said. "I'm going to leave instructions for the nurses to allow you and your family in at any time. You bring your grandmother's favorite books and music, anything you can think of. Maybe we can pester her so much, she'll wake up and tell us to let her rest."

Micah had a few misgivings about winging his way to Key West. Number one on his list was: what if Gaea didn't want to see him? He was besotted with her, but that didn't mean she felt the same way about him. She could have just been being polite when she'd told him she'd look forward to hearing from him again. Although, it did appear to him that she was, if nothing else, attracted to him. She hadn't exactly spurned his kisses. Okay, so maybe she was physically drawn to him. That was a start.

He told himself, as he reclined in his seat on the plane, that he wasn't going through all the trouble of flying more than two thousand miles because he was hoping for a miracle. He would just be setting himself up for disappointment. No, he was committing this foolhardy act because he wanted to know if, upon seeing Gaea Maxwell again, he would experience the earth-moving emotions he'd felt when they'd met in the middle of the North Pacific. Would it be the same? That heady rush that only intensified the closer he got to her? Or had he imagined it all?

"Would you like anything from the bar?" one of the flight attendants, a young Asian woman, asked as she sidled up to his seat.

"No, thanks," Micah replied, smiling at her.

"Perhaps later," she said in a pert voice, her dark, liquid eyes lowering momentarily to his full mouth. "If you do get thirsty, my name's Lei." She smiled then, her ruby, heart-shaped lips turned up at the corners. "Enjoy your flight."

When she'd gone, Micah returned his attention to the article in *Sports Illustrated* he was attempting to read. Yet another jock grousing about his multimillion-dollar deal. He didn't think his agent had gotten him what he was worth. After encountering Renata in the lobby last night, Micah wasn't in the mood to sympathize with an athlete.

He placed the magazine in the slot on the back of the seat in front of him. Maybe the next person who had his seat would enjoy it more than he had.

His thoughts traveled to Russian waters. Gaea had said she would be home Monday night. It was Sunday. She'd given him her home and office numbers. Maybe she'd left a message on her answering machine with a number where she could be reached. He usually updated his recording two or three times a week. With voice mail, some people did updates on a daily basis. It wouldn't hurt to try. Her plans could have changed, and she wasn't going to be back by Monday night after all. He'd do well to find out.

The plane landed at Miami International at 11:35 A.M. He rented a convertible, planning to take U.S. Highway 1, the only road in, or out, of Key West.

It was seventy-eight degrees, and the sun was warm on his face as he pointed the white Mazda Miata westward. He was an excellent driver and derived pleasure from being behind the wheel. Besides that, he had a talent for directions. He liked being prepared for any contingency and had studied a South Florida road map while on the plane. But he wasn't prepared for Miami's particular brand of drivers.

By the time he reached Monroe County, where Key West was the county seat, he had been cut off by speed demons who flipped him the finger when he frowned at them in consternation; tailgated by a driver behind the wheel of an eighteen-wheeler who apparently thought seventy miles an hour was a snail's pace.

The trip became less stressful when he reached U.S. Highway 1 because many of his fellow motorists were in a more relaxed frame of mind, anticipating a vacation in the Keys. When he drove into Key West, it seemed to him that the air was charged with energy. At once, he felt the tension glide off him, and his mood became mellow. He didn't know if it was the generally laid-back aura of the city itself, or if the thought of seeing Gaea again worked to calm him. At any rate, as he drove down Roosevelt Boulevard, he experienced a kind of euphoria, a portent of good things to come.

In no hurry to get to the hotel, he drove down Duval, doing the tourist thing. It was 1:00 P.M., and pedestrians crowded the narrow sidewalks decked out in spring togs in various rainbow shades. The town, although ramshackled in some areas, was altogether pleasing to the eye.

He enjoyed the older residential streets where narrow sidewalks sat beneath spreading boughs of huge oak trees, the branches heavy with moss. He hadn't seen moss like that since he visited his mother's parents in Raleigh, North Carolina, as a child.

In Old Town, he came upon the Marquesa Hotel. The sign above the entrance said simply, Marquesa. Palms swayed in front of the unimposing structure.

He parked and let the top up on the car, grabbed his carry-on bag and was soon strolling into the lobby where he was immediately greeted by the full-time concierge, a middle-aged gentleman with a warm smile and an enviable tan.

"Welcome to the Marquesa, I am James McBride, the concierge. Right this way, and we'll get you registered."

Micah followed him across the red-carpeted, elegantly furnished lobby. He knew a little about antique furnishing and saw that they had acquired some truly exquisite pieces dating back to the eighteenth century. A Hepplewhite settee sat in the lobby, its upholstery a deep red brocade with intricate patterns.

"Good afternoon," said the desk clerk, a young brunette with light gray eyes. She smiled, revealing large white teeth in her round, pretty face.

"Hello," Micah said. "The name's Cavanaugh."

The desk clerk—her name plate read Julie—quickly entered his name in their computer and looked up at him with a pleased smile.

"Yes, here you are. We've put you in room 136. It has French doors that open onto the porch. If you step outside at sundown, you can see the sunset from your veranda."

"Thank you, I'll be sure to do that," Micah said, being polite. He was thinking of driving out to Reed Oceanographic Institution and, if possible, touring the facilities. By sundown, he would probably be on his way back to the Marquesa, not staring awestruck at the famous Key West sunset.

A natural-born investigator, he wanted to see where Gaea lived and worked. It would give him a better perspective on the woman herself. He didn't call this snooping. He thought of it as a good investment in the future. He hoped she would also try to learn everything she could about him. He was more than willing to tell her anything she wanted to know about him. She, on the other hand, struck him as a rather introverted, maybe even secretive person. Learning her would definitely be challenging. Fortunately, he was rather fond of challenges.

Julie gave him his room key. A real key, not one of those electronic card keys that were becoming so popular in hotels.

"Enjoy your stay," she said, her eyes lively. "And if there's anything I can do to make your stay more enjoyable, just let me know."

"Thank you, I will," Micah replied.

The room, just as the lobby, had antique furnishings. It also had a marble bath, with gold-plated fixtures and Caswell-Massey toiletries. After depositing his carry-on bag on the bed, whose pillows had Godiva chocolates atop them, he turned and opened the antique armoire. Hanging inside was a white cotton bathrobe.

"They do know how to make a guy feel welcome," he said with a short laugh.

In Omega's room in intensive care, Gaea sat next to the bed reading a passage from one of her grandmother's favorite Langston Hughes poems, "When Sue Wears Red:" "When Susanna Jones wears red / A queen from some time-dead Egyptian night / Walks once again."

She glanced up at Omega from time to time, hoping to see her eyes flutter open. But for the last two hours, as she'd sat there reading first the Bible and then the book of poems, Omega had lain so still, Gaea would rise at regular intervals to place her hand beneath her grandmother's nose to feel the warm exhalation lightly touch her fingers. It didn't matter that Omega was hooked up to sophisticated monitors that alerted hospital personnel of any minute change in her condition. Gaea needed the physical connection to her grandmother that being able to feel the breath of life within her provided.

At sundown, her father came into the room to relieve her.

He'd gone home earlier to take a nap. All of them: Gaea, Lara, Aaron, and Cameron were going to sit with Omega for stretches of four hours each. Aaron had protested, saying he wanted to stay longer, but Lara and Cam had insisted on his need for rest. They had to keep their energy levels up in order to be there for Omega.

On the drive home, Gaea had let the top down so that the wind could blow through her hair. She felt as though her life were spinning out of control. Tears sat in her large, sable-colored eyes. She wished she had never told her grandmother about the dolphin. What if Omega had been so frightened for her that something in her brain had come un-wired. Even Lynn didn't have a name for what was wrong with Omega. Would she ever hear her grandmother's voice again? See that twinkle in her brown-green eyes?

She thought her eyes were deceiving her as she pulled into her driveway on Olivia Lane. Because there, standing on her porch, was Micah Cavanaugh. She parked the car behind a white, late-model Mazda Miata and killed the engine.

She couldn't move. So many strange things had been happening lately, she'd learned to be cautious, even suspicious. However, when he began descending the steps, coming off the porch toward her, a gentle smile on his handsome face, an emotional dam seemed to burst within her and a deluge of tears began to fall

# Eleven

Micah had managed to get into Reed by saying he represented Thaddeus Powers, CEO of Poseidon Industries, who was thinking of making a sizable donation to the institute. All true. However, Thad had not told Micah that whether he chose to support Reed was dependent upon Micah's opinion of the facilities. Micah had his own reasons for wanting to get into the institute.

Pleased to see a brother representing a major corporation, Coop was especially nice about putting him through the third degree. The receptionist, a tiny woman in her fifties with auburn hair, sparkling brown eyes and a chirpy voice, made him feel at home.

She smiled, her mouth crinkling at the corners. "It's Sunday, so I may not be able to get a scientist. A lot of them have families and take the day off. But there are plenty of hungry research assistants who are probably in the lab today. Any of them can give you a rundown of what Reed is all about."

She had a pencil behind her left ear, and, glancing down, Micah saw that she'd been doing the crossword puzzle from Sunday's *Miami Herald*.

"If it's going to be a problem, I can return tomorrow," he offered gallantly.

"Oh no!" the receptionist answered immediately. She rapidly typed on the computer keyboard and frowned. "Wait a minute. Drs. Cross, Binder, Ellison and Maxwell all live here in Key

West. I'm sure one of them must be available. I'll give each of them a quick ring and explain the situation to them."

Micah could tell she was good at her job and wasn't about to allow the prospect of additional funding to slip through the institute's figurative fingers without a concerted effort on her part.

"I'd been informed that Drs. Binder, Ellison and Maxwell were on an expedition to Russia," he said.

The receptionist reached for her log book and thumbed through its pages.

"No, it says here that Dr. Binder's group returned ahead of schedule."

She then pressed several numbers on the touch-tone phone, took the pencil from behind her ear and gently tapped it on the desktop while she waited for someone to answer at Dr. Binder's residence.

A few moments later, her eyebrows shot up in surprise, so Micah assumed she'd gotten an answer.

"This is Doris Cox, receptionist at the institute. I'm trying to locate Dr. Binder." She frowned. "He won't be back till tomorrow? All right. Thank you."

She looked up at Micah with an expression of regret. "The maid said he and Mrs. Binder went to Key Biscayne for the weekend."

"Too bad," Micah said. "Perhaps you'll have better luck with Drs. Ellison and Maxwell."

"Believe me," Doris said. "I won't quit until I get one of them. Any preference?" Her brown eyes held a mischievous glint.

"Do you suppose Dr. Maxwell may be in town?" Micah asked, trying to keep the excitement out of his voice.

"We'll see in a moment," Doris told him chattily. "I'm the weekend receptionist, by the way; trying to keep busy since my husband passed."

"Oh, sorry to hear that," Micah said sympathetically.

Doris looked down. "Yes. He was a good man." She smiled

suddenly and raised her eyes to his. "But we were talking about Dr. Maxwell, a lovely lady. I saw her, briefly, yesterday. She hasn't been in yet today, but it's still early. She's dedicated, that one. Have you met?"

Micah decided to come clean. Doris seemed an intuitive person, as he found many women her age to be.

"We have," he told her. "And, to be completely honest, I was hoping to see her again while I'm here."

Doris leaned forward in her swivel chair. Her keen eyes surveyed his handsome, clean-shaven face and his conservative attire of dark blue Dockers, sky-blue polo shirt with the tiny polo player stitched on the left breast pocket and the black, highly shined soft leather loafers. Then she looked back up into his chestnut brown face and warm brown eyes.

"Why don't I try her number next," she suggested, turning smartly in her chair and reaching for the telephone receiver.

Micah leaned on the corner of Doris's desk while she sat with the receiver to her ear, her brown eyes fairly dancing at the interesting turn of events. He was no longer just a corporate benefactor, he was someone with a personal liking for Dr. Gaea Maxwell, whom Doris thought was one of the nicest people she'd ever known. It made her feel good that she could be doing Dr. Maxwell a favor. She'd heard rumors that Dr. Cross wasn't a very decent person. Rumors were best ignored; however, sometimes there was a modicum of truth in them, and this particular bit of gossip involved a female student. To Doris, it was forbidden for a professor to become personally entangled with a student. It was a severe infraction of ethics.

And this gentleman, Micah Cavanaugh, appeared to be just the right sort for Dr. Maxwell. He'd shown her his identification with nary a hesitation, joking about his photo on his driver's license. He was an attorney with Poseidon Industries. She'd heard the name before because she subscribed to *Time* magazine and had read the article about Thaddeus Powers, who also seemed like a nice fellow.

If Thaddeus Powers trusted him, then she could too.

She hung the phone up after a couple of minutes and sighed.

"I'm so sorry, but I can't get an answer at Dr. Maxwell's residence."

Micah sighed too. "Well, you tried."

They heard someone coming down the hallway and looked up to see Dr. Xavier Cross walking toward the exit.

"That's Dr. Cross," Doris said to Micah. "He and Dr. Maxwell are . . . friends. Maybe he knows how you can reach her."

Micah began walking toward Xavier, trying to catch the scientist before he left the building.

"Dr. Cross!"

Xavier paused and turned. The sun was high in the midday sky, and the light was extremely bright coming in through the glass doors that led to the lobby.

Xavier stood with his back to the doors as Micah approached him.

Micah didn't know what he expected the man Gaea had been engaged to to look like. The proverbial paper-pusher, probably. With a receding hairline, myopic eyes and a lisp?

Xavier Cross was a young forty. Trim yet muscular, with an athlete's gait. No glasses covered his brown, deep-set eyes. And though he had a widow's peak, his hairline was not receding.

He was two inches shorter than Micah, but, standing next to him, the difference was barely noticeable.

"Dr. Cross, I'm Micah Cavanaugh, chief attorney for Poseideon Industries."

"Poscidon," Xavier said, his well-modulated voice low but distinct. "Ah yes, you manufacture seaplanes for the government."

"And private businesses," Micah put in.

"What can I do for you, Mr. Cavanaugh?"

"I was told you're a personal friend of Dr. Gaea Maxwell. I'm in town for a short while and I was hoping to see her before I left."

Xavier's demeanor didn't alter one iota at the mention of

Gaea's name. His expression remained pleasant, although largely disinterested.

"As a matter of fact, I'm more than a personal friend of Dr. Maxwell's, I'm her fiancé. We're to be married in August."

This was said nonchalantly, as though getting married was a banal event with as much excitement attached to it as mowing one's lawn on Saturday morning.

"Then congratulations are in order," Micah said, offering his hand, which Xavier took, firmly shaking it. No use antagonizing him.

Xavier managed a weak smile. "Thanks. May I ask: How do you know Dr. Maxwell?" Not Gaea or my fiancée, but Dr. Maxwell.

Releasing the doctor's hand, and wondering at the coldness of it, Micah said, "We met in Russia a few days ago. Thaddeus Powers had invited me along on a photographic expedition in search of the blue whale; as you probably know by now, we were successful. At any rate, Mr. Powers invited the scientific team from the *Cassiopeia* to his yacht, the *Trickster*, for dinner. I met your fiancée that night and was intrigued by her. I'd never met a sister who was a marine biologist."

"There are a few of us," Xavier said. One eyebrow raised. "Although not nearly enough in my opinion." He smiled. "I can understand why you were impressed with Dr. Maxwell. She's not only brilliant, she's also charming and, might I add, easy on the eyes."

Micah knew a bait when he heard one. If he admitted to being attracted to Gaea, he wouldn't get any information out of Xavier Cross.

"Yes," he said, "she is all of that. She's an excellent role model. That's why I'm here. Well, actually I wanted to tour the facilities too. However, I also wanted to ask Dr. Maxwell to Career Day at A Step Up. That's a college-preparatory program I sponsor. Would you know where I can find her today?"

Xavier tilted his well-shaped head to the left slightly, as though he were considering Micah's query. Then he looked directly into Micah's eyes and said, "No, I'm sorry. I can't help you, Mr. Cavanaugh."

With that, he turned. "Forgive me, but I have an urgent appointment. I'm sure the receptionist will find someone to give you the five-cent tour."

Micah strolled back across the room, an amused smile on his full lips. The doctor was canny, he had to give him that much. Xavier Cross could probably smell competition a mile away. He wasn't about to give a young buck like him easy access to his lady.

Doris was smiling dreamily at him when he returned to her desk.

"I've been trying to figure out who you look like the whole while you've been here," she said triumphantly. "Denzel Washington. I rented *Fallen* last night. Boy, was it scary. Made me want to sleep with the lights on."

She laughed. "Dr. Cross wasn't forthcoming, huh?"

"I can understand his reticence," Micah said. "She is his fiancée, after all."

"Well then," Doris said, handing him a Post-it note, "I have something for you."

Micah accepted the slip of paper and grinned at Doris. "Why, Mrs. Cox, I believe you have a touch of the matchmaker in you."

"No, Mr. Cavanaugh, I'm just a firm believer in justice and fair play." She winked at him. "May the best man win."

So, by the time Gaea arrived at her small bungalow on Olivia Lane, Micah had been reclining on her porch in the white wicker rocker with the flowery cushions nearly two hours.

He'd risen from the rocker at the sound of the Mustang's motor and started walking down the four front steps.

The sun had met the horizon by then and it was difficult making out the face of the person driving the Mustang, so he walked closer. It could conceivably have been a friend of Gaea's coming to visit.

He smiled broadly when he saw that it was Gaea. But then

he stopped, frozen, as soon as he spotted the tears coursing down her cheeks.

"Gaea?" he said, confused. Concern for her propelled him forward. His hand was on the door's handle and he was opening the car door and Gaea was spilling out into his arms.

He pressed his cheek to her sodden one and breathed in. "My God, does the sight of me make you that sad?"

She was hugging him though, tightly, and that made him realize his unexpected appearance was not the cause of her crying jag.

Gaea laughed through her tears. "Micah. What are you doing here?"

"I'm breathing new life into an old custom, Gaea Maxwell. I'm courting you," he told her, and looked down into her face to see what her reaction to the news would be.

Gaea wiped her face with the back of her hand and grinned. "If you knew what kind of week I've had, you'd run for the hills, Micah Cavanaugh."

Releasing her and placing a hand about her waist, Micah began directing her toward the house. "Why don't you tell me about it and we'll see if I take off."

"All right," Gaea said reluctantly. It was against her better judgment, she knew, but, when she'd seen Micah standing there, looking so . . . right, on her porch, in her town, she had breathed her first good breath in days.

After they'd walked up the steps and she'd unlocked the door, she glanced back at him. "I can't believe you're here."

"You want me to pinch you?" Micah teased.

"No, but you can kiss me," Gaea said.

Micah placed one of his big hands at the base of her spine and drew her into this arms once again. Bending his head, he said, "What the lady wants, the lady gets."

Gaea went up on tiptoes in order to meet his mouth in a slow, deep kiss. Micah's hand slipped further down, resting on her shapely hips as they pressed closer. Gaea's core, which had seemed to freeze over with stress and worry the last twenty-four hours, began to slowly melt.

They moved out of the doorway, into the foyer, still locked in a kiss neither of them wanted to terminate. Gaea gently kicked the door closed behind them.

Micah raised his head and said, "Nice place."

"Thanks," Gaea replied, kissing his chin.

"You have great taste," Micah complimented her as he nibbled at her right earlobe. "And you taste good too."

Giggling now, Gaea peered up into his eyes. "Micah, why are you *really* here?"

"I wanted to hold you again," Micah said softly. His deep brown eyes held a happy expression in them. "I wanted to find out if what I was feeling for you was for real, or if I'd only wanted it to be real."

"And is it?" Gaea asked, searching his handsome face for any sign of doubt or indecision. She detected neither.

"It is," he simply said, and kissed her again.

This time, he lifted her off the floor and she wrapped her legs around him as he held her in his powerful embrace.

She was weak with pent-up desire when he loosened his hold, allowing her body to slowly slide down his before her feet met the floor again.

"Micah, Micah. Why couldn't we have met last month, or last year for that matter? Why now?"

Micah didn't like the sound of that. It had the ring of rejection in it. "I know you're a scientist, darlin', but there are some things you can't control," he said.

Blowing air between full, bruised lips, Gaea agreed. "The past few days taught me that."

Taking her chin between his thumb and forefinger, Micah tilted her head up. "You can trust me, Gaea. Tell me what's going on here. Why were you so upset?"

Sighing and lifting her chin out of his grasp, Gaea walked into the living room and sat on the blue-and-white-striped cotton duck upholstered loveseat facing the sofa.

Micah followed her. Sensing her mood, he sat opposite her on the sofa. She seemed suddenly protective of her personal space.

Gaea looked into his eyes. "Micah. You're sweet to come here, truly you are. But I'm not free to begin any kind of a relationship at this time. There are too many loose ends, too many problems that need solving. We're talking loads of baggage . . ."

"Gaea, I wouldn't be here if I weren't prepared for some kind of adversity. I took a chance. Maybe it was a crazy chance, but I'm here and I *want* to be here."

"Because you think you know me well enough to bare your soul to me," Gaea said. She shifted in her seat, sitting with her legs beneath her. Her long, summery dress was sleeveless and buttoned up the front. She'd left three buttons undone at the top, which revealed nothing of her ample cleavage. She appeared as innocent as a teenaged girl at her confirmation.

"I could be selfish," she continued, her eyes still on his face, "and ask you to stay, because I want you to. You make me want to believe in happy endings."

Micah rose then and went to sit next to her. He took both her hands into his and brought them up to his mouth, kissing the palm of each of them in turn.

As always, his nearness aroused Gaea to such an extent her body temperature shot up. She breathed in and slowly exhaled. His mouth was on her wrist and she ran a hand through his soft, natural hair. She loved the feel of it, playing between her fingers.

It was painful, though, wanting to hold him, touch him, but knowing she had no right to draw him into the mystery. Look what had happened to her grandmother. She would not involve anyone else in this until she knew exactly what, or whom, she was dealing with.

That's why she bent her head, gently kissed his cheek and said, "You have to go, Micah."

He looked up at her with his disappointment mirrored in his beautiful brown eyes.

She placed a finger on his lips before he could speak.

"I know I said I'd tell you what's going on, but I've decided I can't involve you in this. Please don't ask me to explain anything else. Just go."

Sitting up straight, Micah regarded her with clear eyes. "Are you being harassed by Xavier? Is that it? Has he been stalking you again? I met the man, and . . ."

"What do you mean, you met the man?" Gaea interrupted him, swinging her legs down and rising from the loveseat.

"I went out to Reed this afternoon and as I was at the receptionist's desk, he came through the lobby. The receptionist pointed him out and I introduced myself."

"As whom?" Gaea wanted to know.

"As someone who admires you a great deal," Micah said. "But I think he saw through that, because when I asked if he knew how I could contact you while I was in town, he clammed up," Micah answered, rising too. "What's the matter? You aren't engaged to him any longer. Why should my interest in you concern him?"

"He threatened to suspend me indefinitely unless I went through with the wedding," Gaea said. She walked over to the fireplace and turned back around to face him.

"That's sexual harassment," Micah said angrily. Chest expanding with indignation, he approached her. "What did you tell him?"

"I needed time to think, so I pretended to go along with him," Gaea said.

Micah opened his mouth to say something, but she cut him off with, "I know what you're going to say, Micah. I should have threatened to bring charges against him. But that's beside the point now. Yesterday, my grandmother collapsed. She's in a coma and I truly cannot expend my precious energies worrying about Xavier, or whether or not I still have a job."

"Oh my God," Micah said, contrite. She saw his sympathy

in his expressive eyes; and in the way his thick eyebrows drew together in concern. He reached out and grasped her by the shoulders. "I'm so sorry."

Gaea walked into his embrace and they stood there wrapped in each other's arms, not speaking or moving for several minutes.

When Micah looked down into her upturned face, he said, "I'm glad I came. I'm going to do all I can to make this easier for you. Forget that I'm crazy about you." He brushed a few stray hairs away from her forehead. "For the next few days consider me your good friend whom you can depend on for . . . whatever. No matter what it is, I'm your man."

Gaea smiled up at him. "Are you certain you can pull it off? No expectations whatsoever until the crisis has passed?"

"I'd do just about anything to be close to you, Gaea. There, I've said it. I'm a chump for you," he joked.

But it made her grin and for that, he was grateful.

When Xavier left Reed, he drove out to Pirate's Cove, a stretch of private beach so named because the locals believed pirates had buried treasure beneath the palm trees there years earlier.

The spot was special to Xavier because that was where he'd proposed to Gaea, on a moon-dappled night, nearly a year ago.

As he walked, barefoot, with his pants legs rolled up so as not to get them wet, he wondered why nothing between him and Gaea had gone well since she found out about Sharon Baker, the graduate student whom he'd taken as a lover.

He could not understand the human female's insistence upon fidelity. Practically every male of every species on the planet was promiscuous by nature. There was no logical reason why the human male should be exempt from nature.

However, if it took being faithful to her to win her back, he was willing to do it. Now, the only problem was, they'd argued, yet again, when he'd gone down to meet her boat yesterday afternoon in order to remind her of their date that night.

He had stopped by the florist and gotten her a single red rose. He always brought her a rose when they were planning to spend the evening together.

She had beached the skiff and was gathering up her camera equipment. She was wearing a pair of olive khakis, rolled up to mid-leg, and a white T-shirt that read: *Scientists experiment until they get it right,* on front. Her hair moved with the southerly breezes and when she looked up and saw him, an astonished expression crossed her lovely face.

"Xavier," she said, apparently surprised by his presence, "what brings you out here?"

"You never returned my call," he said, his voice patient. He didn't want to appear as though he were chastising her for her thoughtlessness.

"Sorry," she said with a small smile. "I was going to phone you as soon as I got home. I can't make it tonight. My grandmother needs to speak with me about something important. Family business, you understand, don't you?"

"Oh," he said, visibly disappointed. "And I already made the reservations."

Gaea adjusted her camera bag on her shoulder and began walking toward the car. Xavier walked alongside her, sand working its way between his toes, which irritated him even more than he already was.

"I don't like being ignored, Gaea."

Gaea paused to look up into his narrowed eyes. "You didn't even ask me if I wanted to go to Christophe's before you made the reservations, Xavier."

"Is that it?" He shook his right foot to expel the sand from his shoe. Blowing air between his lips, he said, "You aren't making much of an effort to get us back on track. What are you going to do, punish me for my transgressions for the rest of our lives?"

That remark seemed to get to Gaea. She humphed deep in

her throat and stood with her hands on her hips. She didn't speak for a number of seconds as she cocked her head to one side, then the other.

She glanced down at her watch. "It's five o'clock already, if I go home and take a quick shower, I'll just about make my six o' clock appointment with Gran."

He knew then that he'd been dismissed and it infuriated him.

"I can't for the life of me, figure out why I want such a contrary, argumentative woman," he spat out.

Gaea continued walking, ignoring him.

"I come out here, bearing a rose, which is your favorite flower, and you have nothing but flak for me."

"There are more pressing concerns in my life than you, at the moment, Xavier," Gaea yelled into the wind.

Xavier's strides were longer than Gaea's so he had no trouble keeping up with her.

"Such as?" he asked, sounding incredulous. In his inestimable opinion, nothing was more important than their getting together.

Gaea stopped walking and Xavier went to stand in front of her, awaiting her reply to his question.

"I told you, it's family business," she said, an amused glint in her dark eyes. "And we're not married, so that excludes you."

Her reminding him of their present status rankled.

"You can really be unkind when you want to be," he said, his nostrils flaring.

"I don't want to be unkind to you, Xavier," Gaea told him, her voice remarkably calm. "Even though I have the perfect excuse if I should choose to." She met his eyes. "I told you yesterday that if we get back together—and that's a big if—you are not going to be the one to call the shots. I can't see you tonight. Now, you're just going to have to accept that, because I'm not going to change my plans to please you. I'm done pleasing you."

A carload of teenagers arrived and the teens scrambled out of the old station wagon and began unloading their surfboards.

"That was the problem, wasn't it, doctor?" Xavier said with revenge for her remarks in mind. "You never did do very much to please me."

Her eyes glancing in the teens' direction and then cutting back to Xavier, Gaea said, "You're right. I suppose keeping my self-respect and holding on to my beliefs was more important than jumping into bed with you. And it still is. I have a great suggestion for you, Xavier. Why don't you consider this my resignation? I quit. I don't need this hassle in my life. And I can live the rest of my days without your continual badgering."

"I'm only doing what's best for you," Xavier said in that condescending way he had of making her feel like a chastised child.

"What's best for me right now is to get away from you," Gaea told him. "I'm going home."

She headed to her car, and this time, she didn't even look back at him.

"Nothing is going to get solved if you can't stay and finish a conversation," he called after her.

With her elbow straight, Gaea raised her right palm in his general direction. Xavier knew it was a gesture of complete frustration. She didn't have anything else to say to him.

Now, on Sunday afternoon as he strolled the beach at Pirate's Cove, he wondered about another interesting development, namely, Micah Cavanaugh.

He'd already known of Thaddeus Powers's presence in the North Pacific, and his generous invitation to the scientists to dine aboard his yacht. He'd gleaned that bit of information from June Ellison at the airport Saturday evening.

He'd been there, hoping to meet Gaea and drive her to her parents' home.

The only member of the team left at the airport was June, who explained the airline had misplaced a piece of her luggage. They'd found it in a matter of minutes, but jet-lagged and anxious to get home, June was in a temper.

"I can't believe this," she'd ranted. "Everyone else is long gone and I'm stuck here."

"It probably won't be a very long wait," Xavier consoled her. He gestured to two empty seats. "Tell me about the trip. Anything interesting happen?"

That was when she'd told him about Thaddeus Powers and how gracious the multimillionaire had been. However, she'd failed to mention Micah Cavanaugh, which piqued Xavier's curiosity.

Outside of their work, June and Gaea were good friends. If June had observed a budding romance developing between Gaea and Cavanaugh, she would think she was being loyal to Gaea by keeping that fact under wraps.

*Another fly in the ointment,* Xavier thought. Intriguing. He didn't, for one moment though, believe Micah Cavanaugh to be a worthy rival. The man was good-looking in an obvious, jejune manner. Plenty of males went to the gym nowadays and pumped up in order to attract women. But what did they possess by way of charm, magnetism and, yes, intelligence? Any woman worth her salt wanted a man with whom she could hold a decent conversation.

Cavanaugh seemed intelligent enough, but he was an attorney and Xavier put lawyers right up there with con men and used car salesmen. They had a way with words and could convince just about anybody of anything. A useful skill, no doubt. But it wouldn't turn Gaea's head.

He had to admit, though, that her reaction to his infidelity had been unexpected. She was a scientist and should have known his sexuality was the result of a chemical reaction and physical need, and not based on her definition of love, which also puzzled him.

She had some foolish notion that because her parents and grandparents had enjoyed happy, affair-free marriages, that she would follow in their exalted footsteps.

She knew the statistics: In the nineties, one in every two

marriages ended in divorce. So why hold him up to such strict standards?

The woman simply wasn't behaving like the scientist he knew and coveted. He could admit it to himself. He desired her. He could not wait to have her, but love was not a factor. Xavier Cross did not believe in fairy tales.

After Gaea decided to allow Micah to stay, she relaxed somewhat. She still wasn't going to tell him about the dolphin though, just in case.

He wanted to take her out to dinner that night, but she begged off saying she was tired and just wanted to sleep. So he left her, reluctantly.

The next morning, however, he was at her door, bright and early to accompany her on her morning jog. She wasn't due at the hospital until ten o'clock. She'd gotten two phone calls last night: one from her father saying Omega's condition was unchanged and the other from her grandfather saying much the same.

So as she and Micah jogged down Duval Street, she prayed that today would be the day her grandmother would open her brown-green eyes and speak to them, ending their vigil and their anxiety.

As they ran, she made a note of the admiring glances Micah received from several females—and males. He did have an impressive physique, from his sculpted pectorals, to his washboard stomach, to his long muscular legs. A woman could rhapsodize all day long about the beauty of his gluteus alone. Now she knew why Solange could quote poetry, albeit ribald ditties, about a man's butt.

She felt inspired to compose a few lines herself this morning.

He wasn't close to being out of breath by the time they'd done three miles and Gaea pointed toward Pepe's Café.

"Rest station," she said, feigning breathlessness.

Micah held the door for her.

"Hey, Gaea, who's that gorgeous hunk of male pulchritude with you this mornin'?" Marta, the smart-mouthed waitress-cum-writer, asked as Gaea and Micah sat down at a table in the back.

Marta was swiftly crossing the room toward them, a glass carafe of coffee held aloft in her right hand.

"That's Marta," Gaea explained to Micah in a low voice. "She's working as a waitress until she becomes the next Ernest Hemingway."

In her late twenties, Marta had dark brown hair that she wore chin-length in a wavy, tousled 'do. Her eyes were green today Yesterday they were blue. She had a collection of disposable contact lenses, which she wore to suit her various moods.

She was trim from riding her bicycle all over the city and wore her skirts tight and short.

Micah could tell by the way she was checking him out that Marta considered herself a connoisseur of men.

"Tell me he's your cousin from out of town," Marta joked.

"No," Gaea said, smiling. "No relation."

"Ah well," Marta sighed. She smiled at Micah and said, "What can I get you, sugar?"

"Ladies first," Micah said, looking at Gaea.

"Mmm," Marta said, "so it's like that, huh? Well all right. Miss Gaea Maxwell, you are one lucky raisin-bagel-eating, black-coffee-drinking woman."

She smiled roguishly at Micah after displaying her prodigious memory for customers' orders.

"A plain bagel, cream cheese, strawberry jam and a large café au lait," he said.

"Now that's a man who doesn't worry about calories," Marta said and sashayed down the aisle toward the kitchen.

"She's a character," Gaea said diplomatically.

"She's a nut," Micah countered.

Gaea laughed. "We have our share of squirrel food down here."

Micah reached across the tiny table to grasp her hand in his much larger one.

"I'm quite fond of you Conchs." His eyes lovingly swept over her face.

"I wish . . ." Gaea began, looking longingly into his eyes.

"You wish what?"

"I wish so many things, it's hard to pin down just one of them."

"Such as?"

"I wish we'd met before my relationship with Xavier," she began. "I wish that a certain recent incident hadn't occurred."

She hoped he assumed she was referring to her grandmother's illness. Which, she could have been.

What she was actually speaking of weighed heavily upon her mind. The thought of what might happen next kept her anxiety level at its peak.

# PART TWO

All the world's a stage
And all the men and women merely players—

> —from *As You Like It*
> William Shakespeare

When concocting a love potion
No emotion beats old-fashioned passion—

> —*The Book of Counted Joys*

# Twelve

"Dr. Maxwell, a Dr. Cross is in the waiting room. He insists on speaking to you," a young black nurse by the name of Barbara Padgett said to Gaea as she stuck her head in Omega's room. The expression on Barbara's face told Gaea that Xavier had been his usual demanding self.

She closed the book she'd been reading and smiled at Barbara. "Thank you, Barbara, I'll handle him."

Barbara returned her smile and left.

"Gran," Gaea said in a low voice, "I'm going out to speak to Xavier, I'll be right back."

Omega moaned, and this time, she moved her left leg as if trying to tug it from beneath the covers.

Excited by this development, Gaea pressed the call button for the nurse.

In a matter of seconds, Barbara was back in the room, coming to grasp Omega's wrist and take her pulse. Omega's leg was still now.

"Her heart rate's up," Barbara reported. Her dark brown eyes met Gaea's. "What happened?"

"I told her I was leaving for a few minutes and she made that sound she's been making and then she kicked her left leg."

Her eyes widening in astonishment, Barbara went to the foot of the bed and pulled the covers aside so that she could examine Omega's leg. Everything was as it should be. There was nothing irritating her foot. Barbara felt the temperature of Omega's feet to be certain they weren't inordinately cold.

"Nothing amiss here," Barbara said. She tucked the covers back under the mattress, making sure no draft could get in there. "Whatever happened, that's a good sign, her moving her leg like that. I mean, it wasn't in a jerky fashion, as if she were seizing or anything, right?"

"No," Gaea answered, her eyes on her Gran's face. Omega was frowning. "Oh, my God. Look, she's no longer slack-jawed."

Barbara smiled. "That's good too. Maybe she understood what you said. You go on and speak with Dr. Cross and I'll stay with her until you return, just in case she does something else."

"All right," Gaea replied. She was reluctant to leave Omega now. But she couldn't allow Xavier to harass the hospital personnel by throwing his weight around. She'd tell him to go away and hurry back to her grandmother's side.

Xavier stood in the waiting room next to the window, looking out. A few others were in the room also, so when he saw Gaea, he went to meet her halfway, and they strolled down the hall.

"How is your grandmother?" he asked. He had a day's growth of beard, which was unusual for him; and he was wearing well-worn Levi's, a denim shirt and a pair of white Reeboks.

Sensing only concern in his demeanor, Gaea answered with a polite, "She's about the same, thanks."

"I just heard," he said, shaking his head sadly.

They moved to the side as two orderlies and a nurse pushed a patient on a gurney down the hall.

While they were standing there with their backs pressed against the wall, he reached out and took Gaea's hand in his, squeezing it gently. "I wish you'd told me, Gaea. I could have been there for you."

Gaea experienced conflicting emotions. Who was he, really? Was he the man who'd berated her for not having dinner with him at Christophe's Saturday night, or was he this tender, compassionate man whose feelings were hurt because she'd excluded him from a family crisis?

"We'd argued only minutes before Gran collapsed," Gaea told him in a low voice. "I didn't think to phone you, Xavier. And now, well, there's nothing any of us can do except wait."

"She's a strong, feisty woman," Xavier said with a wry smile. "She'll pull through."

"We're all praying she will," Gaea said, feeling, now, that she should be getting back to Omega.

They continued down the hall, Xavier still holding her hand.

"Oh, by the way, a gentleman by the name of Micah Cavanaugh came by the institute Sunday afternoon. He said he knew you from your last expedition."

"That's right," Gaea said, seeing no reason to lie.

Xavier paused, turning to face Gaea. "Look, darling, I just came here to say I'm sorry for being such a selfish jerk Saturday; and to ask after your grandmother. I can feel the tension in you, but I'm not here to start another argument. And I only asked about Mr. Cavanaugh because whenever I sense another man is romantically interested in you, I feel a little . . . threatened."

Gaea almost laughed. Xavier Cross, threatened?

"And another thing: Your resignation is soundly rejected. We need you at Reed. I need you at Reed. You're right. I do try to control every situation, but I'm making an attempt to change my spots." He laughed shortly. "All right, I've kept you away from your grandmother long enough."

He released her hand and backed away from her. "Do you forgive me?"

Gaea opened her mouth to speak, but clamped it shut again because her throat had constricted and she was sure that the sound coming from her would be little more than a wheeze. About three yards behind Xavier, walking toward them, was the man she'd seen in the Yuzhno-Sakhalinsk airport.

Seeing the flummoxed expression on Gaea's face, Xavier looked over his shoulder.

The man walked within five feet of them and stopped.

This time he was attired in beige linen trousers with a thin brown belt around his trim waist, a billowy summer shirt with wooden buttons in white cotton and a pair of tan leather oxfords. All immaculate. His chin-length dreads were clean and shiny and the smile he wore was reminiscent of the one he'd worn when he and Gaea had first locked eyes across the terminal in Russia.

"Hello, brother," he said. This to Xavier.

Gaea's feverish mind tried to comprehend the meaning behind that greeting. It hadn't sounded general, or even casual. No, there was real tenderness in his cadence. As if he and Xavier were indeed blood brothers meeting again after a long, painful separation.

The muscles in Xavier's jaw worked. Gaea knew him well enough to recognize signs of stress. His mouth moved as if he were trying to decide whether or not to smile. He settled on keeping his lips pressed firmly together, as though any words he spoke at that moment would be inappropriate and it was best not to say anything.

He was definitely affected by the stranger's presence, and this fact made Gaea rethink her former hypothesis that the man had been following her. Perhaps she wasn't the person this mysterious stranger wished to speak with, but Xavier. She had simply led him to Xavier.

At any rate, she wanted answers.

She took a tentative step toward the stranger, and Xavier jerked her back with such force that she was nearly thrown off balance.

Looking back at Xavier, she said, "What's wrong with you? Who is this man? I saw him in Russia."

Her gaze fell upon the stranger who had not moved.

"Tell her, Serame," the man said in a deep, resonant voice. His large, golden-brown eyes beseeched Xavier.

Xavier breathed in and blew air out of his nostrils as if he were about to lose patience.

His fingers bit into the flesh of Gaea's arm.

"You're hurting me," she told him, trying to wrench her arm free of his viselike hold.

"Don't go near this man," Xavier said through clenched teeth. "He's insane. Don't believe a word he says."

"He hasn't said anything yet." Gaea couldn't believe her good fortune. Xavier had admitted to knowing the man.

The stranger cocked his head to the side and smiled radiantly at Gaea. "My name is Taras."

"Taras what?" Gaea asked.

Seeing that she wasn't going to obey him, Xavier pulled her along with him. Turning to look at the man who'd said his name was Taras, he cried, "Stay away from me and Dr. Maxwell, or you'll live to regret it."

Taras made no attempt to follow them as Xavier pulled-dragged Gaea down the hallway.

"Let go of me, Xavier," she threatened. "That man could possibly answer some questions I need answers to."

"What is more important to you, your grandmother's health or speaking to a madman?" Xavier inquired reasonably. He was looking straight ahead, his destination, apparently, Omega's room.

For the moment, the hallway was deserted except for them, otherwise, Gaea knew, Xavier would have had to release her, or someone would've called security to have him expelled from the premises.

"Who is he?" She wished she'd asked Taras, he would've probably told her. But she held out little hope of getting an honest reply out of Xavier.

"He isn't anyone you need to concern yourself with. I told you, he's unbalanced. He thinks I'm his brother. Apparently, he had a brother who was killed by police in Miami and I resemble the dead sibling. Every now and then, he pesters me. He's harmless, really. I just don't want you to be alone with him. There's no telling what a person with his inability to distinguish between reality and unreality is capable of doing."

They were at the entrance to the intensive care unit. "Gaea, for once in your life, you've got to listen to me and heed my warning. The man is totally around the bend."

"But he was in Russia, Xavier. I know I saw him at the terminal in Sakhalin. Why would he follow me there?"

"He has access to money," Xavier said. He'd calmed down a bit and since Gaea had stopped trying to get free of his grip, he seemed to be convinced she was going to cooperate with him. "He probably learned you and I are engaged to be married. He believes I'm his brother, whom, I suppose, he loved very much. Perhaps he thinks if he convinces you he is whom he says he is, you will intervene on his behalf and he and I will be reunited." He sighed. "I told you it was ludicrous."

He let go of her, finally.

Gaea gingerly rubbed her arm in the spot where he'd held her.

"I'm sorry," Xavier said. "But, you wouldn't listen to me."

Ignoring his apology because, frankly, he'd apologized to her too often in the past with a lack of sincerity, Gaea said, "If he's stalking you, you should go to the police."

"I have," Xavier told her. "It hasn't done any good. He stays away, sometimes for months at a time, and then he shows up, out of the blue, like today and resumes the madness. I'll inform the police. Just promise me, if you should see him, don't go near him."

Gaea didn't reply at once, and her silence incensed Xavier.

"Gaea," he said in a low voice, not wanting to draw attention to himself because they were only a few feet from the nurses' station. "Promise me."

"All right," Gaea said. "For the time being, I won't seek out this Taras person."

Xavier breathed easier. "I'll accept that." He raised his gaze to the double doors behind them. "You'd better go, you've kept your grandmother waiting long enough."

He bent and kissed her cheek. "Please don't cross me on this, darling. I swear, it is as I've told you. Nothing more. I'll get the police to escort Taras out of town. Don't worry about it. Go to your grandmother. Give her my best."

Gaea disappeared behind the double doors and Xavier turned to leave.

She hadn't believed a word of his explanation. Xavier was lying to her, but she couldn't figure out why. She went back over the recent chain of events in her mind. First, the bottle-nose dolphin appears in the North Pacific. It looks exactly like the one she'd seen in her childhood right here in Key West. Then, she takes a stroll on the deck of the *Cassiopeia* and sees an incredible sight: a dolphin metamorphoses into a human male. Only hours after that, the dreadlocked Taras appears in the airport when she is en route to the States. Then her grandmother acts peculiar when she reveals the fact that she has seen something very likely out of the supernatural.

Her grandmother tells her there is something very vital she needs to tell her, but before she can divulge this earth-shattering piece of information, she falls into a coma.

Now, Taras appears in Key West and he has some former connection with the man Gaea was to marry.

She was more confused than ever.

But, as she pushed open the door to her grandmother's hospital room, she vowed to get to the bottom of the mystery. Maybe she did need to confide in someone. Two brains working to unravel this mess was better than one slightly frazzled one.

When she walked into the room, Lynn was there studying a new set of X rays. As Gaea was watching Lynn, something occurred to her: she still hadn't developed the photographs she'd taken of the bottlenose while on the last dive in Russia.

When she got home this afternoon, that would be the first thing she'd do.

Lynn glanced in Gaea's direction. "So there you are. Barbara told me what your grandmother has been doing as of late. She's showing signs of trying to come out of it. Tell me exactly what you were talking about when she moved."

Gaea walked around to the left side of Omega's bed and

peered down into her grandmother's face. Omega had a faint smile on her lips.

"She knows you're here," Lynn said.

"Xavier showed up and asked for me," Gaea said softly, running her forefinger gently along Omega's brow. "I knew he would probably make a scene if I didn't go out to see him, so I told Gran I was going out to speak with him. She moaned and kicked her left leg as though she were trying to throw the covers off her."

Lynn laughed. "Well, you told me she didn't like Xavier. Apparently, she still doesn't. All right, I suppose that was what got that splendid reaction out of her. Maybe you ought to talk about Xavier more often."

"Not if it upsets her . . ." Gaea began.

"That's the point, Maxie," Lynn informed her. "Xavier may be the key to getting your grandmother back. So talk about him. Warn her that the wedding's back on unless she wakes up and stops it."

Her mother came in at two o'clock to relieve her. Lara's pretty face was drawn with worry. She'd pinned her everpresent braid up on her head and was wearing a royal blue, short-sleeve pantsuit with an empire neckline.

She bent and kissed her mother-in-law's cheek then hugged her daughter hello.

"How are you, Sweetie?"

"I'm fine, Mom," Gaea said, smiling.

"Any more movement since this morning?" Lara asked. Her dark-brown eyes looked hopeful.

"No, none," Gaea said, sighing regrettably.

"You go on home," Lara said. "Omega and I have things to talk about." She glanced at Omega, "Like the time she gave me her recipe for Jerk Chicken and left out a key ingredient, on purpose. Now that she's my captive audience, I can tell her everything I've been wanting to."

Gaea laughed. "Just keep the language civil, this is a hospital."

She left the two women alone, closing the door soundlessly behind her.

As she walked down the front steps of Florida Keys Hospital, she half expected to be accosted by Taras. She wished he would turn up again, this time without Xavier around to run interference.

Taras didn't look or sound insane to her. She wondered, though, why he hadn't spoken to her while they were in Russia. Perhaps he had only wanted a good look at her. If it was as she suspected, she was of interest to him solely because of her connection with Xavier Cross. She had to find out the real reason behind Taras's appearance in their lives.

She stopped by the supermarket on the way to Olivia Lane. Micah was coming to dinner at seven and she wanted to make Chicken Lo Mein for him. It was her mother's recipe; and Lara hadn't left out any key ingredients.

Arriving home at three o'clock, she unlocked the front door and placed the two bags of groceries on the hall table.

On the drive home from the supermarket, she'd been wondering how she could investigate Taras without knowing his last name. She could phone Solange and ask her to have her friend, Bill, who was a detective with the Miami Police Department, look into Taras's record. If what Xavier had told her about getting a restraining order to prevent Taras from harassing him was true, then Taras was in the system. Then, too, if Xavier was lying, as she suspected, Taras wouldn't have a record and she'd be back at square one.

In any event, she'd be doing something, and not twiddling her thumbs.

After putting the groceries away, she went into the bedroom to see if she had any messages.

Kicking her shoes off, she lay back on the pile of pillows and put her feet up. Ten-hour days at the institute didn't make her as weary as four hours spent beside the bed of an ill loved one. It was the stressfulness of the situation, she was sure. That, plus the fact that she blamed herself for her grandmother's condition.

There were no messages, so she just lay there on the bed a few minutes, counting the ceiling tiles.

Ten minutes into her attempt at relaxation, the phone rang.

She picked up the receiver, bringing it to her ear. "Hello."

"You sound tired, Gaea," Micah said.

"I'm mentally worn-out," she admitted. Sitting up in bed, she swung her legs down and rose. "What have you been doing to keep busy?"

"Oh, I went back out to the institute and was given the grand tour by Dr. Ellison, who said I rescued her from a dreary hour in the lab. We spent the whole hour talking about Thad."

Gaea laughed. "Then you know she has a tiny crush on him."

"And it's reciprocated," Micah said, also laughing. "She told me about the annual fund-raising event and wondered if Thad was coming."

"The Conch Republic Ball," Gaea said. "I'd forgotten all about that. It's the biggest event of the year."

"You've been understandably preoccupied," Micah said, his voice husky.

Gaea felt a warmth invade her, beginning in the lower regions and spreading to her entire body.

"Actually," she said, trying to concentrate on mundane things so that she wouldn't be standing in the middle of her bedroom, getting turned on by the sound of Micah's voice, "the Conch Republic is a week-long celebration. The whole city goes a little crazy. It's like carnival in Rio de Janeiro. However, the institute chooses this time of the year to coax philanthropists to the island and hit them up for huge donations."

"Sounds like fun," Micah said.

"A good time is had by all," Gaea said. "Last year, the institute made budget with that particular fund-raiser. Xavier usually tags me to make the presentation on cetaceans.

"Come to think of it," she continued, "this year they'll probably use the footage we shot of the blue whales."

"I'd love to see that," Micah said.

"Which reminds me," Gaea said suddenly, "I've got to do some darkroom work."

"I'll let you get to it then," Micah graciously replied.

"Dinner's at seven," Gaea reminded him. "Bring a hearty appetite."

"Why don't you let me cook for you tonight, while you relax," Micah suggested. "I'm in the mood to pamper you."

"You can treat me when I come to *your* town," Gaea said. She imagined his handsome face with a look of surprise on it.

"So, there *is* a possibility of this going farther than just today," Micah proposed, speaking of their growing relationship.

"I can see it going as far as . . . next Tuesday," Gaea joked.

"Or Wednesday, if we're lucky," Micah responded, playing along.

Gaea was grinning, the tension had dissipated and she was absentmindedly wiggling her toes in the plush carpeting.

"You make me feel good, Micah Cavanaugh."

"I hope so," he said. "Because I've made it my mission in life to make you smile."

"I'm going to have to do my homework to come up with a reply to that one," Gaea said. But his words had warmed her heart, so she said, "Thank you."

"See you soon," Micah said.

After they'd hung up, Gaea slipped her shoes back on and went to the darkroom adjacent the kitchen. It had been a laundry room when she'd purchased the house, but she'd had shelves put in to hold all her camera equipment and the various supplies and chemicals needed to develop photographs. Photography was an indispensable part of her work. Years ago, it used to be that the marine biologist sketched specimens in order to better study the intricacies of an organism. There were still a few die-hard practitioners; she even dabbled at it from time to time. But, on the whole, photography and, more and more, computer graphics, were being utilized.

Now, she went to the small, apartment-size refrigerator she

kept in the darkroom where she stored undeveloped film, and retrieved the black plastic canisters that held the film from the Russian expedition.

She'd labeled the roll she'd shot of the dolphin with a large, black question mark atop the canister's bright yellow lid.

For the next few minutes, she concentrated on getting the photos as clear as possible. She recalled that she'd had no trouble focusing with the Minolta on the day she'd shot the pictures, therefore if she developed them correctly, she should have some excellent close-ups of the dolphin.

It wasn't surprising to her, when she'd hung the photos to dry, that the best shots were the ones she'd taken on the surface. The sun hadn't been at its brightest on the last day they'd spent in the ocean, so the clarity of the underwater shots weren't as good.

Still, every photo of the dolphin, itself, was blurred. She switched on the overhead lamp above the work station to be certain she was seeing what she thought she was seeing. Yes, everything surrounding the dolphin in the shots was sharp. In one of the surface shots, she'd gotten part of Don's head, and *his* image was as clear and delineated as it should be. But the dolphin, which had been performing for his human audience, dancing on his tail with abandon, was blurred.

Taking the magnifying glass from the shelf next to the lamp, she peered closer at the photograph. The shape of the dolphin was unmistakable. There could be no doubt that there was a dolphin of some size in the photograph. The blurred image was the same color of the dolphin, only foggy around the edges.

She could not make out the silver-dollar size mark on its melon, but she could tell where the head began. Sighing, she placed the magnifying glass back on the shelf and left the room. They were all ruined. Now, she had no physical evidence of the bottlenose they'd encountered in the North Pacific.

She removed latex gloves and deposited them in the wastebasket next to the back door. It seemed every theory she'd come up with had been shot to Hades. Without a photograph, it was going to be impossible to convince anyone, even herself, that the dolphin she'd seen in the North Pacific had been the same one she'd seen in a lagoon in the Gulf of Mexico nearly twenty years earlier.

But then, she reasoned, as she went to the kitchen sink to scrub her hands and arms all the way up to her elbows, maybe that wasn't so important anymore.

She felt the crux of the mystery lay in discovering what Xavier's connection was with Taras. That name sounded so familiar to her. It resonated in her mind. She knew she'd heard it, or seen it, somewhere recently.

She mulled it over while she chopped the carrots, broccoli, onions, celery, mushrooms and red peppers for the lo mein.

By the time she'd finished, she'd remembered where she'd seen the name. It was in one of those ancient tomes she'd read at the library a couple of days ago. In mythology, Taras was the son of the sea god, Neptune.

*All right, girl,* she thought. *Now don't go there.*

Her mind was racing forward though. She'd spotted the dolphin-man in the waters of Russia and not twenty-four hours later had seen Taras in the airport terminal in Sakhalin. Coincidental? A person well-grounded in reality would answer with a resounding, yes! However, she'd been thrust into a mystery rife with supernatural undertones. She'd learned there was more than one reality.


When Xavier left the hospital, he went in search of Taras. He knew though, as he climbed into his midnight blue Range Rover, that Taras could not be found unless he wished it. And, his senses, though not as keen as they used to be when he lived among his own, told him Taras was no longer in the vicinity.

What disturbed him was the fact he hadn't sensed Taras before he got within speaking distance. Now that Gaea knew about Taras, was it possible she would also stumble upon the true reason he needed to wed her?

Pointing the Range Rover west, he decided the only way to prevent Taras from telling Gaea everything would be to get rid of Taras permanently. Physical violence was out of the question, though. If he should spill Taras's blood, the entire Council would be on his case. And if he were to be left to live out his natural life in relative peace, he could not go against the Council. Maybe he could reason with Taras. After all, Taras had been in his position once, many years ago.

Taras was, if he chose to be honest, the reason he could carry out his plan with a hundred percentile ratio of success.

He smiled as he cruised down the boulevard. Yes, one could say that, if everything went as planned, Taras was the father of a new race, a better race.

He mentally tossed Taras from his mind for the time being, because if Gaea didn't become his wife, the whole matter would be moot anyway.

While he was with her, he was certain he'd detected Cavanaugh's odor on her. He'd wanted to throttle her for allowing the interloper to touch her. But such behavior was contraindicated. She would definitely have nothing to do with him if he resorted to brute force. Women.

What he had to do was fight for his woman. If she wanted a smooth operator, as he suspected Cavanaugh was, then he'd adapt. He'd swept her off her feet once, he could do it again.

He pulled the car into the parking lot of a florist shop.

Getting out, he strode into the shop exuding confidence and charm.

"May I help you, sir?" the clerk, a petite woman in her twenties with a dark, boyish cut asked eagerly. It'd been a slow day and she was able to count the number of customers they'd had on one hand.

"You're a woman," Xavier said, his expression askance. "What sort of flower do you send a woman when you want her to know you adore her and will never give her up?"

He could swear the woman was about to swoon. She'd probably never heard anything so romantic in her short life.

Her big doe eyes held a glimmer of avarice in them, however.

"Roses are beautiful and red roses denote passion and ever-lasting love," she said almost breathlessly. "But if you really want to impress a woman, do it with orchids. We just got in several varieties from South America this morning. They're exquisite."

"I'll take a dozen long-stemmed red roses and each variety of orchid you have," Xavier told her.

"But sir, we have fifteen different varieties," the woman half-heartedly protested. If she made this sale, she'd look like a real go-getter to her boss.

"You do take Visa Gold?" Xavier asked, producing the card and holding it under the woman's nose.

She glanced down at it and snatched it from his hand before he had the chance to reconsider.

Turning his back to her, Xavier breathed in the heady aromas pervading the shop. His olfactory gifts were heightened today. Perhaps it was because he'd come into contact with one of his own. So few of them ventured out. Sometimes he'd go for months at a time without encountering a brother or sister.

Behind him, the clerk was rapidly adding up charges on the Visa Gold. When she got the total, she frowned. It was equivalent to the cost of providing flowers for a small wedding party.

When she gave Xavier the bad news, he merely smiled and signed the receipt.

"Money, I can get any day," he said. "But she's one of a kind."

The clerk sighed longingly. "Who's the lucky lady these are going to? I'll have our man deliver them right away."

"Not a drop of dew is to evaporate from those petals," Xavier admonished lightly.

"I'll deliver them myself," the clerk offered, excited by the notion of true love. Besides, she wanted a look at the woman who inspired this kind of devotion.

Xavier produced a card with Gaea's name and address on it.

The clerk read it and said, "Dr. Gaea Maxwell. Even her name sounds special."

Xavier left the shop feeling a bit more in control of the situation. Now, all he had to do was get back into Gaea's good graces. And he knew just how to do it.

# Thirteen

Micah showed up at Gaea's door bearing gifts. He was hidden behind a mountain of roses, and Gaea got a sinking feeling in the pit of her stomach when it occurred to her it might be Xavier.

"It's me," Micah said. His handsome face pecked out from behind the roses. "Since, technically, this is our first date, I brought a couple of things I thought would please you."

Gaea laughed and stepped back so that he could enter. As far as she was concerned, all he needed to bring was himself. *He* pleased her immensely.

Micah placed the roses in her arms. They were tangerine-colored with tightly closed petals. The sweet, heady fragrance wafted upward and Gaea breathed in their essence. "They're heavenly."

He then handed her a five-pound box of Godiva chocolates. "You aren't one of those women who won't allow her lips to touch sweets, are you?"

"I personally don't know any of those women," Gaea told him. "Please come in." She led him to the living room, where she sat on the sofa and placed the flowers on the coffee table. With the box of chocolates on her lap, she unwrapped it and chose a piece without nuts.

Micah followed her, delighted with her reaction to his gifts. He sat beside her on the couch and watched as she bit into the chocolate and closed her eyes as she savored it.

"That's good stuff," she said after swallowing. Their eyes met.

"Not half as good as this," Micah begged to differ. He leaned forward and took the box from her, depositing it, with the flowers, onto the coffee table, then pulled her into his arms for a slow kiss.

Gaea wrapped her arms around his neck and met his kiss with enthusiasm. All her senses were involved as she inhaled his unique fragrance, a combination of a woodsy aftershave and his own fresh, masculine scent. She could feel his back muscles playing against her fingertips as she held him. His mouth tasted clean as his tongue pressed against her lips. She opened her mouth to allow him in, and the sensation made her think of a more intimate act, which she found herself longing to share with him as well.

Had Xavier ever kissed her like this? She was sure he had, but she couldn't recall ever succumbing to Xavier in this manner.

Micah's right hand was at the base of her spine and his left one was in her hair. She felt her body go limp as the kiss deepened, and her arousal was nearly complete when he abruptly raised his head and gazed down into her eyes.

"Forgive me, but you looked so beautiful, I couldn't resist," he said, his voice husky.

"Don't apologize. I enjoyed it just as much as you did," she told him. Still weak, she didn't move at once, but lay there getting her breath.

Micah rose, pulling her up with him. "All right. I'll behave myself for the rest of the evening."

"You'd better," Gaea admonished jokingly. "Otherwise, I'm not going to have the strength to finish preparing dinner."

She reached for the flowers then. "I should go put these in water."

Micah observed her, a satisfied smile on his face. She had no guile, this woman. Didn't she know that you were never to reveal how you really felt about another person in the beginning of a relationship? Renata called it holding your cards close to your chest until you knew what your opponent's hand looked like.

Of course, Gaea knew that he'd come all the way to Key West just to spend time with her. So, maybe she already knew she had a winning hand.

He let his nose lead him to the kitchen and when he entered, he found her on a step ladder, reaching up to get something from the top shelf of the cabinets above the sink.

"Smells good in here," he complimented her. Then, "Let me help."

Gaea had her hand on the vase she'd been trying to locate by then and stepped off the ladder, clutching the crystal vase to her chest. "I've got it, thank you."

She was wearing a simple cotton linen sheath in a deep shade of purple. It was sleeveless and the hem fell two inches above her knees. It was the first time Micah had seen her legs, and he admired the shape, length and curvature of them. Golden brown, like the rest of her, they were tanned slightly darker than her face or arms. And, peering closer, he saw, her left knee had an inch-long scar on it.

"How'd you get that scar?" he asked.

Gaea had placed the vase in the sink and was running cold water into it. She smiled to herself. He'd noticed her legs.

Micah went to lean on the counter next to her so that they were face-to-face as she finished her task.

"A softball game when I was seven," she said, smiling at him. "It was the bottom of the ninth and I was sliding into home. The umpire called me safe, our team won and I got this scar as a reminder of the day. It took five stitches to close. My mother wanted me to quit playing, at least for the summer; but Pop told her that would only teach me to give up. I had a blast playing ball that year."

"What else did you like doing when you were a kid?" Micah wanted to know.

Gaea placed the roses into the vase one by one. "Anything that was outdoors," she said, her voice low. She looked up at him. "I played football, soccer, volleyball on the beach. I was on the swim team in high school. But, I think my all-time favorite thing to do was snorkeling."

"Who introduced you to that?"

"My pop. He used to go diving in the Keys nearly every weekend with friends. Mom and I would go and wait for them in the boat. Even when I was small, I always envied them. I wanted to go down too and see what they were seeing. So when I was ten, he started me out with snorkeling. Then, when I was fifteen, I went under with my pop and his diving pals." She laughed. "They still talk about it when they get together to play cards and shoot the bull. I was the only girl they'd taken down. Before that, they thought females were too fragile for the sport. They were a bunch of male chauvinists. But I loved them."

"Where did you go to college?"

"The University of Miami and California State, for my doctorate," Gaea answered lightly. "Where'd you go?"

"New York University and Yale for my law degree," Micah replied nonchalantly.

"You went to Yale?" Gaea said, impressed.

"On scholarship," Micah told her. "I worked part-time. My folks couldn't afford to send me and I wasn't about to accept any money from Thad."

"Why not? He's your godfather," Gaea said.

"Yeah but my old man is a proud individual who managed to instill the same fierce independence in his son. I just would not have felt good about myself if I'd relied on Thad's money."

"I understand," Gaea said, smiling. "And I agree with your reasoning. The Langstons offered to pay for my schooling, but my parents and I discussed it and decided against it. Pop always says it's best not to owe anyone too much, no matter how good a friend they may be."

"He sounds like my father," Micah said.

"Tell me what you were like as a kid," Gaea said, picking up the vase and carrying it into the dining room, where she placed it in the center of the oak table.

Micah followed. "I was into ball too," he said. "In high school, I was a running back on the football team."

Gaea looked up at him. "There's that modesty again. You were a running back. Is that all?"

"All right," Micah conceded reluctantly. "We went to State four years in a row and won three out of four times."

"Then you were good."

"I was okay."

"You were probably great," Gaea said. "One of these days, you'll feel more comfortable with me and be able to tell me anything."

Micah smiled, the lone dimple in his left cheek more pronounced. "I'm already comfortable with you," he said. His eyes sought hers. "I just don't believe in blowing my own horn. Nor, I might add, do you."

"Oh?" Gaea said, walking closer to him.

"No," Micah answered. "I've been making use of the time I spend apart from you while I've been here. You're quite the celebrity, Dr. Maxwell. Last year, you were featured in *Science American* as a scientist to keep an eye on. You've had articles published in quite a few journals and according to one of your colleagues, you're being courted by several universities and institutes. Yet, you remain here. Why is that?"

"That's simple enough," Gaea said, her eyes on his clavicle revealed by the collar of his white silk shirt. He'd dressed semicasual for the occasion, choosing the long-sleeved shirt, a pair of black pleated slacks and Georgio Armani loafers in black leather.

"You were saying?" Micah reminded her after a few dead seconds during which Gaea had just gazed into his eyes.

"It's home," she added. "Everyone and everything I love is here. I spent some time away from here when I was in college and shortly after I got my doctorate, I went to North Africa in order to help document the behavior of some dolphins in relation to a coastal, nomadic tribe called the Imragen."

"Behavior?" Micah inquired, his interest aroused.

"Yes. Apparently, every year around December, dolphins would arrive, like clockwork, in the coastal waters of Mauritania, where the Imragen lived, and help the fishermen capture mullets in their nets, by forcing the fish to shore."

"Every year?" Micah asked incredulously.

"For decades, maybe centuries. It's difficult to document a phenomenon like that when the people one is studying have no written language. But, the oldest members of the tribe all related how their grandfathers also spoke of dolphins exhibiting the same sort of behavior when they were boys; so it must have been going on for a long time."

"Incredible," Micah said.

Seeking the opportunity to get out of his presence a little while so that her heartbeat could return to its normal rhythm, Gaea said, "I'll check on dinner. Why don't you go in the living room and relax? What would you like to drink? A beer, a glass of white wine?"

"Nothing right now," Micah said. "I could roll up my sleeves and help you . . ."

Gaea walked past him. "No, you're my guest."

"Then, if you don't mind, I'll go sit on your front porch. We don't have porches in New York City. I rather enjoyed yours while I was here yesterday."

"Go right ahead," Gaea told him happily. "I'll join you in a few minutes."

She left him then, turning in the direction of the kitchen while he walked back through the living room to the porch.

In the kitchen, Gaea opened the refrigerator door and stuck her head inside. "Girl, you'd better cool off or you'll have broken your vow of chastity before the night's over."

She closed the door and leaned against it, fanning her face with her right hand. Analyzing her reaction to Micah, she came to the conclusion that she was looking for comfort. The last week had been amazingly stressful, what with her believing, at first, that she could be suffering from dementia. And then her grandmother fell into a coma, making her feel guilt-ridden and helpless to ameliorate the situation.

She wanted to let go, and Micah was, conveniently, here. Looking so fine. Feeling so fine. Smelling so fine. The man *was* fine. No doubt about it.

And here she was, a woman who'd been saving herself for just the right man. Well, what if the right man never came along? What if she died without ever making love to anyone? What if . . .

"What if you get dinner on the table?" she said aloud and laughed shortly. "And let tonight take care of itself."


Xavier seethed with rage when he learned, from an anonymous nurse at Florida Keys Hospital, what Gaea had done with his flowers.

She'd taken them down to the hospital and asked the nurses to distribute them among patients who hadn't received any during their recuperation.

She made a point of telling the nurses that they were from Dr. Xavier Cross.

The nurse who'd phoned had sounded so grateful, he was loath to be rude to her.

"You don't know how much your gesture cheered up some of those patients," she said, sounding as though she was near tears herself. "It's people like you," she continued, "who remind me of the reason I do this job. Thank you, Dr. Cross."

"You're welcome," he'd said, anxious to end the conversation so that he could phone Gaea and confront her about her duplicitous shenanigans.

After getting off the phone with the nurse, however, he wasn't able to get Gaea at home. He didn't leave a message because he wanted to speak with her directly.

While he sat at his desk at work, it gave him time to think. If he should phone Gaea and tear into her with one of his usual angry tirades, that would be adding fuel to the fire. She expected him to behave in that fashion.

The best thing to do would be to ignore her volley. He was certain she'd done it to incite him to anger. Giving away his gesture of love and commitment communicated how much she detested him. She wanted nothing to do with him and therefore wouldn't accept his gifts.

All right, he would see if she would be capable of turning down his next gesture.

Gaea had set the round table on the covered patio out back. The early night was cool, around seventy degrees, therefore they would not be pestered by mosquitoes; plus the pungent smell of ginger made the night air a pleasure to breathe.

The light on the patio was dimmed and she'd set candles on the table.

When everything was ready, she went to the front porch and extended her right hand to Micah. "Dinner's served."

He rose from the rocker and allowed himself to be led along, but once in the foyer, he stopped and pulled her into his arms.

"I could get used to this," he said in her ear. She heard him inhale. "A man could get lost in you, Gaea. Just drown in your scent, and the feel of you. He'd die with a foolish grin on his lips." He peered down at her.

"I've been accused of many things," Gaea said, smiling up at him. "But never murder by proximity. Come on, big guy. Let's get some food into you. That should quell the intoxicating effects of being too close to me."

They continued across the room.

"You mock me," Micah said. "But I'm serious. You make me high. And I don't need stimulants to feel this way."

He paused yet again and turned her around to face him.

"You have a way of avoiding being candid with me, Gaea. So I'm asking you now: how do you feel about me?"

"Feel about you?" Gaea said softly. Their eyes met and held.

"I have to stand in front of the refrigerator with the door open in order to cool off after I've been in your arms. Does that tell you how I feel about you?"

Micah laughed shortly. "A little bit. But what I want to know is: what do you sense about me?" He went on to explain. "The first moment we met, I sensed in you a woman who knew what she wanted from life and exactly how to get it. Then, after talking to you, I knew I'd been right. I also knew I had to know more about you."

Gaea smiled. "The first moment I met you, I thought to my-self, 'he's so good-looking, he'd never be interested in me; so I'd better keep my distance if I don't want to get my feelings hurt.' "

"What?" Micah exclaimed, disbelieving. "You're pulling my leg. You reeked of confidence when we met. You haughtily sized me up through those binoculars, then put me in my place."

"That was because I figured you were sticking your nose where it didn't belong. But, after I'd met you, up close, and I'd gotten the full effect of your overpowering masculinity . . . and after you'd made that joke about my snubbing you, I felt a tiny bit intimidated."

"But you apparently got more comfortable as the evening waned, because you were comfortable enough with me to tell me about you and Xavier," Micah reminded her.

"I did feel as though I could trust you," she admitted. She looked down, then back up at him. "But, for the life of me, I don't know why. I blurted out a very personal, and embarrassing episode in my life. You should have stopped me."

Laughing, Micah said, "Stopped you? I could have talked to you all night long."

"Micah, the food's getting cold. All this stalling, you're going to make me believe you're afraid of my cooking," Gaea said, slightly exasperated. Once Micah started talking, it was hard to shut him up. No wonder he was an attorney.

On the patio, Micah complimented her on the table and pulled out her chair for her.

Gaea served them, then Micah said grace.

"Thank you, Father, for the company, the beautiful setting, and for what we are about to receive, may we be truly grateful."

"Amen," Gaea said softly.

In the glow of the candlelight, she thought he looked like a dream come to life. She was content for the moment, and she had Micah to thank for that.

Micah took a bite of the Caesar salad, chewed and swallowed. "You know what I like best about the South?"

"What's that?"

"You have yards and porches that you take advantage of. I cannot imagine a New Yorker sitting on his porch sipping a glass of iced tea. But here, it's commonplace. You probably don't realize how fortunate you are."

"New York has its advantages," Gaea said. "You have plays, the ballet, the opera. Wonderful restaurants. Anything you can imagine needing, you can find it in the city. Here?" She laughed suddenly. "Here? Well, if you don't have it, you figure you can do without it. That's our attitude."

"You mentioned earlier that you'd traveled extensively, but never considered anyplace else home. Could anything tempt you away from Key West?"

Gaea chewed thoughtfully. "If I got a really stupendous offer, I'd consider it."

"Does that offer have to come from a university or an oceanographic institute, or could it come from a man?"

Gaea sat up straight and regarded him with a surprised expression in her warm brown eyes. She had no reply to that. Maybe it was a rhetorical question, with no personal interest involved.

His deep brown eyes held an amused glint in them. "I see I've stumped you." He speared a slice of chicken and ate it. "Take your time."

Okay, her assumption of it being a harmless query was blown out of the water. She'd found that the best defense was a good offense; so she said, "Would you leave your job, family and friends for a woman?"

"If she were *my* woman, I most definitely would," he immediately replied. "This is delicious, by the way."

*Good,* Gaea thought. *You enjoy it, while I sit here with it stuck in my throat.*

She swallowed hard and took a sip of mineral water.

"Yes," she finally said, her voice sounding hoarse. "I would, if he were my man."

The doorbell rang. She'd never been more grateful for an interruption in her life. Rising, she smiled at Micah and said, "Excuse me."

Micah returned her smile and continued eating.

Gaea walked swiftly through the house to the front door, where she paused to look through the peephole.

She'd neglected to switch on the porch light earlier, and turned it on now.

Initially, all she saw was a mass of black hair, then the person on the other side of the door raised his head.

The air caught in her throat and she quickly unlocked the door and flung it open.

"Your fiancé told you not to trust me," was the first thing out of Taras's mouth.

"If I listened to everything Xavier . . ."

"Serame," Taras corrected her.

"Whatever," Gaea breathed excitedly. She stepped aside. "Come in."

Taras crossed the threshold. He was still attired in the billowy white shirt, beige slacks and tan oxfords.

Now that she had him up close and personal, she was able to inspect him at her leisure. He was trim, but, judging from the outline of his chest showing beneath the shirt, he was well-muscled.

His skin tone was a healthy reddish brown, smooth and unmarred. Clean shaven. His eyebrows looked as though they'd been sculpted, but she was sure they were simply naturally that beautiful.

But it was his hair, like something alive, that caught her interest the most. Shiny, springy, it moved with him as he looked around the room.

"Are we alone?" he asked.

"No, I have a guest," Gaea told him.

"Then I'll be brief." His eyes met hers and she felt as though she were gazing into the eyes of a holy man. Not a madman, as Xavier had referred to him.

"You should not couple with Serame. The consequences could be disastrous."

"How do you know we haven't already . . ."

"I would know," he said. And what's more, she believed him.

"As a matter of fact," Gaea told him, "the wedding has been canceled. I called it off."

"Serame has always been somewhat of a hedonist," Taras said, his voice kept low so as not to alert whomever Gaea's guest was to his presence. "In all the years I've known him, he has gone from female to female. It is not our way, you understand. But Serame has always been a rebel. Our ways were too restrictive for him."

"Listen," Gaea said, "why don't I meet you someplace where we can talk undisturbed. A public place."

"In case I am a lunatic?" Taras said with a gentle smile.

Hearing footsteps approaching from the kitchen, Gaea hurriedly ushered him back out the door. "Pepe's Cafe at eight tomorrow morning."

"But where is this Pepe's?" Taras asked.

"Ask anyone, they'll tell you," Gaea said frantically. "Go now, Taras. I don't think I could convincingly explain you to my guest."

Taras stepped onto the porch and bowed from the waist. "By your leave," he said.

Gaea smiled. "I'll see you tomorrow."

She closed the door and locked it.

"I was getting lonely," Micah said, as he entered the living room from the hallway.

"It was just a kid hawking candy bars for his elementary school," Gaea said, regretting having to lie to him. But she wasn't about to tell him the truth.

Glancing down at her empty hands, Micah observed, "You didn't buy any."

"I made a donation instead," Gaea said. That was the trouble with lying. Once you told one, you had to tell another to support the first, and they continued to pile up, like so much cordwood, until the whole stack came tumbling down.


At the hospital, Aaron was leaning over Omega's bed, trying to hear what she was saying.

He had been sitting next to the bed, reading Barbara Neely's *Blanche Among the Talented Tenth* to her, when he heard her mumble.

At first, he thought it was the television set, because he had left it on in order to see the ball scores on CNN. But the set's volume was so low, it was barely audible. So, he'd sat down again, thinking it must have come from the hallway. Hospital personnel were constantly passing on their way to one task or another.

The purpose of being in a hospital, he'd thought, was to rest and get round-the-clock medical care. He conceded to the medical care, but he couldn't see how anyone got any rest, what with nurses coming in every two hours to poke and probe and stick you with needles.

Then they'd give you a sleeping pill to facilitate rest, and an hour or so later, come back and wake you up for some other pill or treatment.

He'd been there for three hours when he'd heard the words being spoken low, quickly and with a raspy voice; he'd looked up toward the entrance. The door was kept open twenty-four hours a day, in case personnel barreled through it in answer to an emergency. He'd seen no one passing in the hall though.

He returned to the book and five minutes later, there it was again. This time, his eyes went to Omega and he saw her lips move. He got up from the chair so fast, the book fell to the floor and the chair rocked on its back legs, but righted itself.

"Meg?"

He was at her side, holding her cool right hand in his, and bending down so that she could see his face well without her spectacles should she open her eyes.

"Meg? What did you say, sweetheart? I'm here, Meg."

But Omega was as still as before. She breathed, unperturbed. Her expression was peaceful, and she was as unresponsive as ever.

"Meg, I know you said something. You're just stubborn. Always have been, always will be. Stubborn, that's you."

Tears of frustration sprang to Aaron's eyes. "Don't you dare leave me, Meg. That's not how we planned it, I'm supposed to go first. I told you I couldn't take it if you went first. What are you trying to do, scare me to death? That policy ain't worth that much, Meg. Come on, girl. Wake up. I promise I'll quit smoking that damnable pipe you hate so much."

Omega slept on.

"I'll give up the lodge. You never were comfortable with me having secrets. I'm going to tell you now, Meggie: We are just a bunch of old men sitting around telling lies. Honest. No secret ceremonies. No girls dancing on tables. Fact is, nine times out of ten, it's so boring at those meetings, I wish I'd stayed home with you and watched some television. We just know it upsets our wives to be left out. And let's face it, Meg, women control everything on this planet. You tell us when to get up, what to eat, what to wear, when to go to bed. Girl, we'd be lost without you. So, once in awhile, we like to pretend we're in charge. It's pitiful, I know, but it's all we've got."

Hearing footfalls behind him, Aaron turned his head to see a tall black man enter the room.

He'd never seen the fellow before and squinted in order to see what was written on his nameplate. Francis Wolford, RN. *All right,* Aaron thought. *I reckon if women can be doctors, men can be nurses.*

The young fellow approached the bed. "Hello, Mr. Maxwell, I'm here to take Mrs. Maxwell's vital signs."

Aaron stepped aside. As the nurse walked past him, Aaron experienced a rush of warm feelings. A sense of well-being that he hadn't felt since this whole crisis began. Suddenly, his body was suffused with a lightness, an all-around positive burst of confidence that Omega would pull through. He hadn't been at all certain of that fifteen minutes ago.

"If you'd like to go get a cup of coffee, I'll stay with Mrs. Maxwell until you return," Nurse Wolford said.

"All right, I will," Aaron said. He didn't want any coffee, but his bladder needed relieving and he didn't like using the bathroom in Omega's room. What if a nurse turned up while he was using the toilet?

Nurse Wolford smiled pleasantly. "Take your time, I'll be a few minutes."

Aaron left the room, content that he'd left Omega in good hands.

As soon as Aaron left, the nurse went to Omega and placed his hand on her forehead. He closed his eyes. "What are you afraid of, my dear? Tell me so that I can share your burden."

Omega moaned softly.

"You don't have to be afraid," the nurse spoke into her ear in a low voice. "Look at it, Omega. Face it, and then you can come back to your loved ones. They miss you. Just now, your husband had tears in his eyes. He's afraid. Too much fear, Omega. Someone has to break the cycle of fear. Let that someone be you, Omega. My brave little Omega. Angelita Negra."

Omega moaned again and sighed as though she was tired. Then, her eyes opened. "Cam?" she said. "Is that you?"

Nurse Wolford smiled, and reached for the water pitcher sitting on the tray. He poured a few ounces of water into a cup and raised it to Omega's parched lips.

She leaned forward and took a few sips and lay her head back down. "You're not Cam. For a moment, your voice . . . you sounded like my son."

"No, I'm not Cameron," Nurse Wolford said. "But I'm sure he'll be thrilled you're awake. How do you feel, Mrs. Maxwell?"

"I feel fine. I could use something to eat."

Nurse Wolford laughed. "You've been asleep for two days, I suppose you would be hungry. I'll inform your doctor. Maybe he'll let you have a cup of broth or something."

"Broth? That's not enough to make a gnat burp," Omega said. "Where is my husband? I could swear he was here a minute ago."

"He stepped out for a moment, he'll return soon."

Nurse Wolford held Omega's hand for a second or two and slowly placed it back on her stomach. "I've got to go now, Mrs. Maxwell. I'm sure you'll be going home soon."

"You're a nice young man," Omega said. "Are you married?"

"I was a long time ago," Nurse Wolford replied as he backed out of the room. "She was the most beautiful, the sweetest girl I ever knew."

"Oh," Omega said, her expression sad. "You lost her?"

"Yes, I did. And I'm afraid I've never recovered from the tragedy."

"Poor baby," Omega sympathized.

Seeing he was intent on leaving, she added, "Come back and see me again sometime, you hear?"

"If only I could," Nurse Wolford whispered. "I will," he said for Omega's benefit.

When Aaron returned from the bathroom, his hackles rose when he noticed the nurse hadn't kept his word and stayed with Omega until he got back. He would make a formal complaint. He didn't care if the nurse was a black man. There was something to be said for honesty and reliability. You couldn't count on anyone nowadays.

He was going to complain so loudly . . .

Omega was sitting up in bed sipping from the cup of water. She lowered the cup and smiled at him. "Where have you been?"

Aaron started crying all over again. "Where have *I* been? The question is, my dear: where have *you* been?"

"I needed the rest. I guess you should've taken me on that vacation when I asked you to," Omega joked.

Aaron was hugging her so tightly, she groaned loudly. "Aaron, Aaron. I'm a sick woman. I need to breathe."

"Oh you were breathing fine, Meggie," Aaron told her. "We simply missed that sassy tongue of yours."

"Well it's back now," Omega said. "I've got lots to talk about."

She gently caressed his dear face.

"But first, I need to build up my strength. Call the nurses and get me some food in here, sugar. Your wife is starving."

"I'll call them right away," Aaron said at once, reaching for the remote call button.

"Then call Cam, Lara and Gaea," Omega said.

"Ah, Meg, you're back," Aaron said happily, commenting on her take-charge attitude. "The world can rest easy now."

"And what was that you said about giving up that rancid pipe?" Omega said, her brown-green eyes twinkling mischievously.

"Now, Meg, I never said . . ."

"Sure you did, but I won't hold you to it," Omega said with a warm smile. "I love you, Mr. Maxwell."

"And I love *you*, Mrs. Maxwell," Aaron said, bringing her hand up to his lips and lovingly kissing each beloved finger.

# Fourteen

"What do you believe in?" Gaea asked Micah over coffee in the living room. She hadn't made any dessert, so she'd brewed a pot of Columbian coffee and they were partaking of the box of Godiva chocolates.

They were facing each other: she with her legs underneath her in one corner of the sofa and he, next to her with about twelve inches between them.

She'd put a Cassandra Wilson CD on the player and the stirring sounds made the mood in the room mellow and inviting.

"You mean religious beliefs?" Micah asked. His eyes swept over her face. He was inwardly pleased that she'd broached the subject. That meant that her interest in him went deeper than physical attraction. She wanted to know how he thought. What system of beliefs he relied upon when faced with tough life decisions.

"Religious and spiritual," she said. She drank some of her black coffee and placed the cup atop its saucer on the coffee table. Her eyes returned to his as she awaited his response.

"My parents brought me up in the African Methodist Episcopal church," he said, sitting back on the sofa. "They are both still active in the church. But, I have to tell you, I rarely go except on special occasions. It isn't that I stopped believing in God, because I believe in Him. I think it's more because I considered it a part of my childhood, and when I grew up, went away to college, I had other interests and didn't put enough emphasis on spiritual things."

"I know what you mean," Gaea said. "I was brought up Catholic, attended Catholic school from kindergarten to twelfth grade. But when I went to college, I neglected that part of my life. It was as if I figured I was on my own, no longer under my parents' rule, therefore, I could skip Mass if I wanted to. But, like you, I still went on special occasions.

"The rudiments, however," she continued, "are in my heart. I do believe what my folks taught me to be good rules to live by: for example, do unto others as you would have them do unto you; try to help those less fortunate than yourself; and so on. As a way of life, I practice my faith all the time, but I sometimes ask myself: how strong is my faith if I don't attend Mass regularly?"

"It could be," Micah said, turning on the sofa to see her better, "that you don't see the importance of regular attendance because you aren't a mother yet. Your parents set a good example for you. My parents did their best to give me an excellent foundation. Maybe when we're parents, we'll also see the need to teach our children what our parents inculcated in us."

Laughing, Gaea said, "You think so? It isn't that we're just a couple of heathens?"

"No, I don't think so," Micah said, smiling. "Once we've settled down, things will change."

"Now for the tough questions," Gaea said.

"Those weren't the tough questions?"

"No," Gaea said, shaking her head. She sat up and swung her legs down, crossing them. "These questions may change the way you feel about me. To be honest, they may make you leave here and never want to return."

"I don't think anything could make me want to leave you, Gaea," Micah told her, his large brown eyes sincere.

"Are you serious about that?" Gaea asked. "Because I do care for you, Micah. And if we are going to be together, you have to know what's been going on in my life."

She paused. The worst thing that could happen would be for him to hasten back to New York believing she was a kook of the first order. A total loon.

However, if she wanted him in her life (and she'd decided she did), then he had to be apprised of the situation he was involving himself in. It wasn't fair to him to allow him to walk, blindly, into whatever was happening to her.

"Gaea?"

She'd hesitated so long, Micah had assumed she'd lost her train of thought.

"Have you ever experienced anything out of the supernatural?"

Micah's eyebrows arched in surprise. However, he quickly wiped that look off his face, remembering the way he'd reacted to her news that she was a virgin. He didn't want a repeat of that episode.

"Such as?"

"Anything unnatural," Gaea said. "Like ghosts or UFOs or even attending a séance. Have you had any experience of that kind?"

"No, I can't say that I have," Micah replied thoughtfully.

"Then that makes it doubly hard for me to tell you what I have to tell you if we're going to become more involved with each other than we already are," Gaea said, afraid that she wasn't making sense.

Micah leaned forward. "Huh?"

It was best simply to say it and get it over with. "Micah, when I was in Russia, I saw something totally out of the ordinary that I cannot explain. It shouldn't exist. It's impossible to contemplate anything like it being real. But I saw it and I know I saw it. And it's made me question my sanity. I've had my brain scanned because I thought I might have a tumor, or something . . ."

"What?" Micah said, reaching for her.

Gaea placed both her hands in his. She was talking too fast. She took a breath and slowly exhaled. "I know you're going to think I'm nuts, but I'm going to tell you. Try to have an open mind, Micah. Remember that I'm a scientist and not some flake who bays at the moon and consults my horoscope each morning before taking a step outside. Try to remember that you said I'm a together, confident person whom you're very attracted to. You *will* remember that, won't you?"

"Now you're scaring me," Micah confessed.

He moved closer to her and attempted to pull her into his arms, but Gaea held back.

"I need to see your eyes when I tell you," she explained.

"All right," Micah said. "Let's have it."

Gaea frowned. She didn't want to lose him. He made her feel as if her dream of a committed, forever-after relationship was possible. He'd made her realize that Xavier was the one with the problem, not her. He'd given her the strength to come back home from Russia and sever her ties with Xavier once and for all. Xavier no longer had any power over her emotions. He could bluster and bellow all he wanted, but she would not marry him. *Could* not. Not when she felt this way about Micah.

"I was standing on the deck of the *Cassiopeia*. It was night, but, if you recall, there was a full moon. I heard something splashing in the water and looked in the direction of the sound. Riding the bow waves was a large bottlenose dolphin. Earlier that day, when Don Shear and I were diving, a bottlenose had approached us and spent a few minutes impressing us with his acrobatic skills."

"All right, so you saw a dolphin," Micah said, following her narrative closely.

"I watched him for a minute or so and then, he wasn't there. In his place was a nude human male, diving in the waters of the North Pacific. Do you know how cold those waters are? Below thirty degrees during springtime. And there was this nude human being swimming in them. I blinked and the dolphin appeared again. I tell you, I was freaked."

"A dolphin that turned into a man and then back again," Micah said, his voice low and skeptical.

"That's not all," Gaea said. "The next day I spotted a tall black man in the airport in Sakhalin. He was watching me. I can verify his presence, because June Ellison saw him too and commented on his appearance, and the fact that you didn't see many black people in Sakhalin. This man and I were probably the only two on the island. Well, just today, the same man showed up here in Key West. He approached me and Xavier while we were having an altercation in the hallway at Florida Keys Hospital. He introduced himself as Taras and referred to Xavier as 'brother.' He also said Xavier's real name is Serame."

Seeing the confusion in Micah's eyes, she said, "I know it all sounds unbelievable. Especially the part about the dolphin changing into a man, but all of it is true. And, what's more, when the doorbell rang earlier in the evening, it was Taras. We have an appointment to meet tomorrow morning. He wants to tell me something, and I have a million questions to ask him."

Micah released her hand and pinched the area just above his nose and between his eyes, as if he had a migraine.

"That's a lot to decipher," he said. He looked up at her. She hadn't moved. Her hands sat on her lap, her back was straight and she appeared as if she were girding her loins for his rejection of her after hearing such a preposterous tale.

For one fleeting moment, he thought, *Why are all the beautiful souls a little daft?*

Her expression hadn't wavered. She would not look away, as though she were ashamed of having lied to him. She didn't nervously reach up and grab a chunk of her hair and twirl it between her fingers. This woman was cool and collected. She was solid, rational, reliable. And she believed she'd seen a dolphin transform into a man. And then that man had followed her to Florida. He'd come to that conclusion because it was the next logical step. Logical?

The silence separating them grew so thick, Gaea felt she had to say something or burst.

"You don't have to believe me," she said, talking fast again. "If it hadn't happened to me, *I* wouldn't believe it either. Sometimes, I think I must have been dreaming. But then there's Taras. I know he's the same man I saw in the airport in Russia. Once you've looked into his eyes, you can never forget him. He has that effect on you. It's his connection to Xavier that puzzles me. Why did he have to get a good look at me while in Russia? Why didn't he just come to Key West, where he knew Xavier lived? And if he's his brother, why hasn't Xavier ever mentioned him to me? We were supposed to be getting married. He told me he'd been orphaned young and had been a ward of the state. After that, I never questioned him about his family because I figured dredging up the past was too painful for him."

"Breathe . . ." Micah instructed her.

Gaea let out a breath, closed her eyes and inhaled. When she opened her eyes again, Micah was smiling at her.

"I believe you," he said. "I'm going on faith here. I believe in you; therefore, I believe you."

"You believe me?" she asked incredulously.

"I believe you saw what you think you saw. 'There are more things in heaven and earth, Horatio, Than are dreamt of in your philosophy,' " he ended, quoting Shakespeare.

Gaea threw her arms around his neck, hugging him fiercely. She sighed. "Thank God. I don't know what I would've done if I'd chased you away with my unique problems."

They held each other a few more precious moments, and then she regarded him with sober eyes. "Micah, I *will* get to the bottom of this. You're only the second person I've told about it."

"Who was the first?"

"My grandmother," Gaea replied. "And that's another thing; the day I told her about the sighting, she seemed upset, maybe even a bit frightened. But she wouldn't explain why. She asked me to come to her house later that day. She had something important to tell me. But before she could tell me what it was . . ."

"She fell into a coma," Micah finished for her.

Gaea nodded in the affirmative. "When we got to the hos-

pital, the emergency room doctor asked me if she'd been frightened by someone, or something. At the time, I really wasn't
thinking clearly; but now, I wonder. Could someone have known
she was about to reveal an important piece of information to
me and gone there to warn her not to?"

"What kind of information?" Micah asked, wanting to know
what she was thinking.

"Gran has lived a long time. She's from a country where
people believe in the supernatural. Maybe she's heard something
about a race of men who could transform themselves. I mean,
is it impossible that they exist? If God created us, maybe he
created all sorts of other beings as well."

"A race of men who share the earth with us, but stay separate
from us for their own reasons," Micah proposed. Gaea smiled.
It was nice having someone she could talk to about this.

"Right," Gaea said, getting into the conversation. "Perhaps
a long time ago, they'd coexisted with us. The myths about the
gods must have come from somewhere. Imagine if you're a
human being and you see another supposed human being transform into a dolphin before your very eyes. Wouldn't you attrib-
ute godly powers to that being?"

"Then too," Micah said. "Maybe men became frightened of
these beings and began hunting them. They had to hide in order
to preserve the race and now there may be so few of them, that
they are not spotted as often as they used to be."

"The question is," Gaea said, "why did Taras call Xavier
brother? And tonight, when he was here, he told me not to make
love to Xavier. He said the consequences could be disastrous.
And another thing, he knew I hadn't been intimate with Xavier.
How he knew that, I have no idea. But he did. And when I told
him I'd called the wedding off, he seemed relieved."

"That makes two of us," Micah joked.

Gaea laughed. "No," she said, "that makes three of us."

Micah thought she deserved a reward for that comment, and
leaned over and drew her to him. Her full, red lips were soft
and pliable beneath his, and she tasted, faintly, of rich chocolate.

"Micah, I'm so glad not to be in this alone anymore," Gaea said, her voice husky with longing. "I've been so afraid of what's going to happen next."

"Show no fear," Micah said. And because her grandmother had uttered the same words to her the last time she'd seen her up and around, tears came to Gaea's big sable-colored eyes.

"It's okay," Micah murmured, wiping the tears away with his forefinger. "I know you've been under a lot of stress recently. Your nerves are frayed. But I'm here to help. We'll find out what's going on together, darlin'. Don't worry."

"My mind just went to Gran," Gaea told him. "What if she never awakens? All the years I've known her, I always thought of her as a tower of strength. There was nothing my Gran couldn't do. When it comes to chutzpah and sheer grit, she's my role model. She came from the Dominican Republic on a refugee raft. She was twenty-two years old with a small child, but she made it. And now, to come to this? . . . It isn't fair."

"Isn't there a chance she'll come out of it?" Micah asked. "I haven't asked you about her condition because I was afraid it would upset you further." He took her hand into his, squeezing it reassuringly.

"The doctors can't tell us anything, except to pray, which we knew already," Gaea said helplessly.

"You haven't given up, have you?" Micah asked, searching her eyes.

"No, I can't give up," Gaea answered.

The phone rang.

Gaea rose from the couch, reluctantly dropping Micah's big hand.

He watched her walk over to the desk with the antique hurricane lamp on it and pick up the receiver, bringing it to her ear.

His heart was doing double time, because it was at that instance that he knew. He hadn't come here to see if what he'd felt for Gaea Maxwell was real, he'd come here in order to define those feelings.

He was in love with her.

He knew it as well as he knew that tomorrow, the day would dawn anew and the Key West sunset, at which he'd previously scoffed, would be just as lovely as the day before.

He loved her. And there was nothing he wouldn't do for her.

So, when she began screaming, he was at her side in a heartbeat.

"What? What's wrong?"

Gaea was grinning through fresh tears. "Gran's awake," she said. "I'm on the way," she spoke into the receiver. After hanging up, she walked into Micah's open arms and he hugged her tightly. "I believe in miracles," she breathlessly said.

At that moment, so did Micah Cavanaugh.


Omega was weary of doctors. First, Dr. Cesar Baldonado arrived to confirm her condition. He'd taken her vital signs, smiling all the while. "Omega," he'd said, "You had us worried there. I'm relieved to see those unusual eyes of yours again."

Omega had thanked him and asked when she would be allowed to go home. "There's no telling what condition the house is in," she'd added, glancing in her husband's direction.

Aaron had shrugged her insinuation off with: "Cleaning the house is the last thing you should be thinking about."

"That can wait," Dr. Baldonado, a tall Mexican gentleman in his late forties, agreed. His dark, liquid eyes looked tired. "You're doing so well, I don't see why you can't go home in the morning."

"In the morning?" Omega protested. "Why not tonight?"

"We'll see about that after I speak with Drs. Casenove and Potemski. But, don't count on it," Dr. Baldonado told her firmly. "Of course, the staff is going to move you to another room. This one is needed for more serious patients."

He placed his stethoscope back about his neck after listening to her heart and lungs and smiled at Omega. "Drs. Casenove and Potemski will be in to examine you shortly. Don't be in a rush to get out of here, Omega. And once you're home, I want you to take it easy for at least a week. I'll see you in my office next week sometime. Phone Susan and make an appointment, all right?"

"All right," Omega reluctantly answered.

"She'll be there doctor," Aaron promised.

Dr. Baldonado smiled warmly at the both of them, then took his leave.

Drs. Casenove and Potemski arrived together, to Omega's great relief. She figured they could examine her in tandem, saving time; then her family, who was waiting outside, could come in. She had a lot to tell them, and the minutes seemed to be rushing by.

"Lynn!" she exclaimed. "It's been a long time. How is your father?"

Laughing, Lynn walked around to the left side of Omega's bed to briefly hug her. "Dad's fine. He remarried a couple of years ago, you know. He and Deana, that's the ex-dancer's name, live in Miami, where he put up the money for her to open an upscale dress shop. Can you imagine?"

"I don't detect a note of bitterness do I, child?" Omega said in her best grandmotherly tones. She only used that voice when she wanted young people to check their attitudes.

"Maybe a tiny bit," Lynn admitted. "You're right though. It's his life. I didn't ask his permission when I married Jeff, and divorced him."

"So you're single now," Omega noted, her keen eyes going to Dr. Potemski, who pulled nervously at his shirt's collar.

Jude Potemski had been secretly attracted to Lynn for some time now. But he didn't hold out any hope of the big redhead falling for him. He was short. A good two inches shorter than her. He was certifiably blind without his glasses and his hair was too long, even by Key West standards.

"And who is this young man?" Omega inquired.

"You can call me Jude," Jude said, stepping forward and shaking Omega's hand. "I'm so glad to meet you, Mrs. Maxwell."

"I take it you've seen me before, I simply wasn't up to being introduced to you," Omega said. She smiled warmly. *"Dr.* Potemski, I presume?"

Jude struck his forehead with the butt of his right hand. "Yes, it's Dr. Potemski." Being in Lynn's presence made him so self-conscious, he wasn't thinking straight.

His reaction wasn't lost on Lynn, who stood a bit more erect, her ample chest thrust forward. With her career, and her heavy schedule, it wasn't every day that her feminine wiles made a grown man break into a sweat. All right, it had never happened before. But it was happening now, and she was enjoying it.

Jude figured if his hands were busy, it'd give his brain time to get in gear. So he took Omega's vital signs, pronouncing them normal, and then stood aside as Lynn checked Omega's eyes with a penlight, and peered into her ears with an instrument that had a cone-shaped attachment that went inside the ear with a magnifying glass on the opposite side which the doctor used to search for abnormalities.

"How do you feel?" Lynn asked Omega after putting her instruments away. "Any dizziness, nausea, blurred vision, floaters?"

"No, no, no, and no," Omega replied, displaying her ability to think clearly by answering each of Lynn's queries separately.

"Well," Lynn said, stepping back. Jude moved out of the way to avoid being stepped on. "We'll do an MRI to be on the safe side, okay? But it looks to me that you're perfectly fine." She deferred to Jude. "What do you think, doctor?"

"She looks wonderful to me," Jude said, smiling at Omega.

"Then what are you two doing here?" Omega asked. "Go get a cup of coffee or something. Two young, healthy people like yourselves ought to be out having fun instead of wasting your time with a patient who should be home."

"That's a hint if I've ever heard one," Lynn said, laughing. She looked at Jude, who pushed his glasses back up on his nose. "What do you say, doctor. Shall we release her?"

"After the MRI tomorrow," Jude said, "I don't see why Mrs. Maxwell shouldn't be able to go home tomorrow morning."

After they left, Aaron said, "I thought you were laying it on a little thick, Meg. Those two people are about as opposite as they come. Why, he looks like Woody Allen standing next to that model, Cindy Crawford."

"They like each other," Omega said.

Outside in the hall, Lynn turned to Jude. "Coffee does sound good right about now. Are you busy?"

"No," Jude said, swallowing hard. "Nothing pressing for the next few minutes."

They walked toward the elevators via which they'd go downstairs to the cafeteria. Lynn studied him. He had a strong chin. His body was pretty firm-looking for an over-forty male. He obviously cared enough about his health to work out.

Jude smiled up at her. And he had dimples. He was kind of cute at that.

The elevator arrived and they waited as other hospital personnel exited the conveyance. Then they stepped in, the only occupants, both of them attired in blue hospital-issued surgical scrubs and white athletic shoes.

Both of them with braids hanging down their backs.

Lynn, suddenly nervous, wondered what they would talk about over coffee. Up until a few minutes ago, she would never have thought she'd be attracted to Jude Potemski. She admired his skill as an emergency room physician. And he was also a good surgeon. But she hadn't spent any time imagining what it would feel like to be kissed by him, until now.

It was all this recent talk about magical things occurring. She could feel something in the air tonight. When Omega had obviously attempted to make a match between her and Jude, she should have ignored it, but, for some unfathomable reason, she'd begun to see Jude in a different light.

Jude cleared his throat. "I know you were just being kind back there, doctor. If you'd rather not have coffee, I'd understand."

Lynn chuckled. "Stood up in the space of five minutes! That's a record."

"I didn't mean it that way," Jude began, his words halting. "I meant, if you'd rather not be seen with me . . ."

"Jude . . . I may call you, Jude?"

"Of course."

"Jude, I haven't been out on a date in months. My life is this hospital and my office. It would be nice to sit down and have a conversation with an attractive, intelligent male."

"Do you see one around here?" Jude joked.

Laughing, Lynn said, "Yes, I do."

Their eyes met and held. Jude felt like getting on his knees and thanking The Almighty for this instance, this moment in time. while Lynn thought, *He has the clearest, kindest eyes I've ever seen.*


Gaea ran up the steps leading to the entrance at Florida Keys Hospital, Micah at her side.

The night was mild, so she hadn't even hesitated long enough at the bungalow to grab a coat.

The fluorescent lighting in the hospital's halls was exceptionally bright, coming from outside, but their eyes quickly adjusted. They walked swiftly to the elevator, their shoes making clicking sounds on the green-tiled floor.

Her grandfather had said the staff was preparing to take Omega to the third floor since her condition had been downgraded to serious from critical. So Gaea half expected to be denied entrance to intensive care.

However, when they approached the nurses' station in the intensive care unit, Barbara Padgett simply waved them past.

"Go on in, Dr. Maxwell," she said, smiling.

"Thank you, Barbara," Gaea said, so happy, she felt like running the rest of the way.

Micah's hand remained firmly clasped in hers.

He hung back when they got to Omega's room door.

"You go in, I'll wait here."

"No," Gaea insisted, "come meet everyone."

Omega was sitting up in bed wiping her mouth with a paper napkin, after having been allowed a small bowl of beef broth and gelatin. She smiled broadly when she saw her granddaughter. "There's my baby!" she said, opening her arms to Gaea.

Aaron moved away from the bed as Gaea went to embrace her grandmother. "Oh, Gran, I'm so relieved to see you holding court again," she said, her throat tight from trying to suppress tears.

Aaron went to sit on a straight-back chair next to his son. Lara was sitting on the foot of Omega's bed. She turned and smiled at Micah as she rose.

"Hello, dear," she said, extending her hand.

She didn't know who he was, but she did know one thing: Gaea wouldn't have brought him into their midst unless he meant a great deal to her. Therefore, she was interested in getting to know him.

Gaea continued to hold her grandmother's diminutive body in her arms. Their faces were pressed together. "Don't ever scare us like that again, Abuela"

"Don' worry, child," Omega said, her voice low and comforting. "I'm going to be around to see my great-grandchildren." Then, she said, "Who's the handsome fellow?"

Gaea released her grandmother and reached back for Micah's hand.

Micah placed his hand in hers and came around to be introduced to Omega.

"Gran," Gaea said, "this is Micah Cavanaugh. We met in the middle of the North Pacific on my last expedition."

Omega clasped Micah's hand and held onto it for a few moments.

"Nice face," she said. Her brown-green eyes looked him up and down. "And nice form too. Aren't you glad you didn't throw him back?"

"Yes," Gaea answered, looking up at Micah, who seemed at ease and thoroughly delighted with Omega.

Turning, Gaea said, "And this is the rest of my small family: my mother, Lara . . ."

Lara came forward and actually gave Micah a hug.

"The pretty lady with the warm hello," Micah said amicably.

"A pleasure, dear," Lara said.

"My father, Cameron . . ."

Cameron, at the same height as Micah, looked the young man squarely in the eyes. He gave him his best father-meets-suitor-for-the-first-time grimace and Micah just grinned.

Cam smiled back and vigorously pumped Micah's hand. He liked a man who couldn't be intimidated.

"Good to meet you," Cam said.

"Same here, sir," Micah returned.

He had manners too.

"And this is my grandfather, Aaron," Gaea said.

Aaron nodded his head in greeting. "Hello, son."

"A pleasure, Mr. Maxwell," Micah respectfully said.

With the introductions done, Gaea returned to her grandmother's side, while Lara and Cam monopolized Micah.

"We still haven't had that talk," Omega said quietly. Her eyes adopted a faraway look. "It all happened so long ago, I hope I won't forget some salient point." She focused on her granddaughter. "But that will have to wait until later."

"I confided in Micah, Gran," Gaea said near her grandmother's ear.

Omega cut her eyes in Micah's direction. He was sitting beside Lara, smiling at something Lara had said. Then, she looked into Gaea's face. "It must be love. For no other reason would a man stay after that kind of revelation."

"I think so, Gran," Gaea admitted. She'd been afraid to voice the words, even in her mind. But she did love Micah. She loved everything she knew about him. It hadn't been love at first sight, although the briefness of their union could probably qualify.

How could she be sure?

Love wasn't something she could put into a test tube and reduce to its minutest parts. She had to rely on faith.

Therefore, she loved him with her heart, soul and mind. The physical aspects of their love would be explored, in detail, at a later date.

"Then it's okay to bring him with you when you come," Omega told Gaea now, bringing her back to the issue at hand. "I should be out of here tomorrow sometime. Come to the house tomorrow night at seven. I'll have told your grandfather everything by then. I should have confided in him years ago, but I figured this problem would never surface again."

"All right," Gaea said. "Tomorrow night. Seven."

She bent her head to kiss Omega's silken cheek. "Welcome back, Abuela."


Later, after Micah had driven Gaea home, they sat on the porch, in the white wicker swing with the flowery cushions. They were sitting close, his arm draped about her, and her head on his shoulder.

"I can almost see the end of the tunnel," Gaea said of their present situation. Her mood was elevated after having spoken to her grandmother.

Omega was all right. So perhaps everything else would be fine as well. Perhaps Taras was indeed just a man. And Xavier? Xavier had taken the hint and resigned himself to being her department head alone. If she had a wish on one of those brilliant stars, it would be to live the rest of her life in peace, with Micah at her side.

She placed her nose in his chest now, inhaling his scent, which she'd come to covet like the air itself. To go to sleep with him beside her. What would that be like? A slice of heaven, no doubt.

He gently rubbed her bare arm. "It's getting a little chilly out here. And I don't have a coat to offer you."

"I'm fine," she said. And she was, as long as she was close to his warm body.

"It's getting late," Micah said, the sensible one. "I should be getting back to the hotel."

"Why don't you stay the night?" Gaea suggested innocently. "I've plenty of room. . . ."

Smiling down at her, Micah said, "Gaea, when I spend the night with you, it's going to be in your bed."

He got to his feet, bringing her up with him. "Now, unless you feel Taras or Xavier will be a problem, I'm heading back to the Marquesa."

"No, I don't think I'm in any danger," Gaea replied truthfully. "But, I don't want you to go," she added, pouting.

Then she caught herself. Here she was, a thirty-year-old virgin being petulant with a gorgeous man who, man of the world that he was, was trying to be a gentleman and help her maintain her standards.

"Sorry," she said. She tiptoed and kissed his cheek. "Thanks for being so sweet about it. I'm so keyed-up, what with Gran waking up and everything, that I wanted to make the moment last. You're right though. I'm the one with the no-intimacy clause."

"I'm available whenever you choose to break it," Micah joked.

"Not tonight," Gaea said regrettably.

"Then I'll wait until you're ready, sugar," Micah said, coining a Southern expression. "I like that: sugar."

He bent and kissed her soft lips.

"It's appropriate for you."

He let go of her and walked down the steps. "Go get some rest, doc. You've had a long day."

# Fifteen

The next morning, Gaea was out and running by seven. The temperature was in the sixties, so she'd worn a light-blue fleece jacket over her white tank top and navy biker shorts. A navy headband held her raven locks in check.

There were colorful banners above shop doors heralding the Conch Republic Independence Celebration. Only a week away, the festivities brought revelers from all over the globe. To locals, the celebration symbolized their unique heritage. Although citizens of the United States and Floridians, by choice, they were Conchs first and foremost.

Duval Street was relatively quiet this early in the morning. A few joggers, like herself, several elderly couples getting the morning air into their lungs; shop managers unlocking and preparing for the seasonal onslaught of shoppers.

When she passed the Wreckers Museum, she was in her stride, her heart and lungs working at optimum capacity. Legs feeling good and strong.

As she turned on to Caroline Street, however, she momentarily felt as though she'd hit the imaginary jogger's wall. Standing outside of Pepe's Cafe was Xavier, attired in running clothes, looking the picture of health.

Gaea jogged in place. He hadn't spotted her yet. His interest was on the morning paper in his hands. She thought of ducking into one of the restaurants on the block and waiting him out. But then Taras would arrive for their meeting and come upon an angry Xavier. There was no telling what Xavier would do if he saw Taras at Gaea's favorite cafe. He'd undoubtedly put two and two together and come up with perfidy. He'd know she'd ignored his warnings and poor Taras would suffer because of her.

Glancing at her watch, she saw that it was seven-thirty-two. If Taras didn't arrive early, she might have time to get rid of Xavier before he put in an appearance.

Steeling herself, she jogged right past Xavier, pretending she hadn't noticed him. Laughing, Xavier sprinted after her. "You don't expect me to believe you didn't see me standing there," he good-naturedly accused her. "And when have you ever gone past Pepe's without stopping?"

"I thought I'd forego the raisin bagel this morning, I've picked up a few pounds," Gaea said by way of explanation. She was taken aback by his effusive attitude. She'd thought her actions would make Xavier combative. He hated a public scene, which would, in turn, induce him to beat a hasty retreat. At least, she hoped he would.

"You look fine to me," he said, his dark eyes admiring the curve of her hips in the skintight biker shorts. "I like those. You should wear them more often."

"Is this your new avocation?" Gaea asked dryly, "accosting women on the street?"

Xavier chuckled as he leaned in and, actually, playfully touched the tip of her nose with his forefinger. "My, my. If you'd let me make love to you, you wouldn't wake up with such a big chip on your lovely shoulder."

Gaea turned her pert nose up at him "You should be good. You've had enough practice. What's the number now? One million served?"

"And sharp-tongued too," Xavier observed, his mood unchanged.

"All right, all right, let's have it," Gaea told him, ceasing her jogging and facing him. She rocked from one leg to the other in order to keep her muscles loosened up while they talked.

"You would not be here unless you had an anvil to drop on my head. And you're in such a gleeful mood! What's it this time? Another threat? Like cutting my salary? It's already ridiculously low. Pulling the funding on my Atlantic dolphin project? You've already threatened to do that, haven't you?"

"I'm sending you to the Rosenstiel School to work on the tumor project," Xavier stated. He watched her face for some reaction.

Gaea just stared at him. Scientists from the Rosenstiel School of Atmospheric Sciences had discovered several specimen of South Florida dolphins with malignant tumors caused by Immune Deficiency Syndrome. Dolphins were known to create antibodies which, usually, left them immune to cancerous tumors. But these South Florida dolphins had died, or were dying, from a form of lymphoma. Some of the scientists theorized the malady was caused by pollution.

Gaea had been interested in the project from the beginning— and had been invited to join the team at Rosenstiel. However, Xavier had said he couldn't spare her.

"You start next week," he was saying now. "The project lasts until early August. You'll live in Miami, of course. You should have no problem finding a place to live. Solange would probably love to have you stay with her."

"What do I have to do for that bone?" she asked suspiciously.

Smiling and shaking his well-shaped head, Xavier placed the rolled-up paper under his arm and sighed. "You don't have to do anything—except a good job. You're representing Reed, so be your usual brilliant self and help find a solution to the mystery."

"I don't believe you," Gaea maintained. It was a quarter till, and Xavier was in no hurry to be on his way. She had no choice. She would have to start an argument. "First you dangle the carrot in front of me—and then you snatch it away when I bite. Well I'm not playing your game anymore."

"Suit yourself," Xavier said, checking his watch. "Take the carrot, or let the choice morsel go to some other hungry diner.

I offerred it to you because I know how much you care about the local dolphin population. But, if you'd rather I gave it to someone else . . ."

"I didn't say that," Gaea edgily returned. "It's difficult to determine whether or not your offers are genuine. We both know where your generosity usually leads: to fresh demands. You want me to toe the line. I want you to back off. We butt heads when we try to reach any sort of compromise."

Xavier peered down into her eyes. "No strings attached. Except perhaps my heartstrings. I love you, Gaea. I want to see you happy. And if there is an ulterior motive, it's that I know I've been a fool and I want to make it up to you. End of discussion." He bent over and gave her a buss on the cheek. "Gotta run."

Gaea permitted him a bemused smile as he sped off, his trim body getting into the rhythm of his forward-motion dance.

She had to give it to him: The man was a cool character. Nothing she'd done had served to exasperate him. It was a good thing he had an urgent appointment to get to.

She watched until he was out of sight and then slowly walked back to Pepe's.

The cafe was crowded with mostly locals who'd been coming here for years. The air was redolent with strong Colombian coffee, eggs, bacon, hickory-smoked ham and fresh-baked bread all juxtaposed to create a mouthwatering aroma.

She sat at the counter and Marta wasted no time coming over to her.

Marta's green eyes were fairly sparkling. "Hey, girl. Guess who's in the corner booth?"

"I give up," Gaea said, smiling at her. "Who?"

"That delicious Yankee with the big hands you brought in yesterday. Did I ever tell you what they say about men with big hands?"

"Yeah," Gaea interrupted. She was sitting next to an elderly woman whom she didn't think would appreciate Marta's ribald jokes so early in the morning. "I'm not meeting him here today. I'm waiting for another guy. Tall, dreadlocks. He been in?"

"Nah," Marta replied, turning on her heels, "be back soon with your RB and BC."

She was back in under five minutes. "Since you've lost interest in hunk number one, can I throw him a line?"

Buds didn't fish in another bud's pond without permission.

"Sorry, Marta, but he's special. However, number two may be unattached. You're welcome to inquire."

Gaea had been buttering her bagel and hadn't noticed Marta had gone silent.

Marta stood with her mouth agape. She carefully placed the carafe of coffee she'd been holding on the countertop.

Gaea followed her friend's line of sight. Taras had arrived. All that was missing was the fanfare. Yesterday, he'd been wearing light-colored clothing. Today, he was entirely in black. Black pleated trousers and a loose-fitting, long-sleeved cotton shirt with a mandarin collar, and black oxfords polished to a high gloss.

Black. In spring. On the island. And it was *right* on him.

The women in the room were craning their necks to get a better view of the perfect male specimen. The males cast envious glances his way. Gaea just smiled at him as he approached her.

"You were right," Taras said amiably as he joined her at the counter. "The first person I asked for directions knew exactly where Pepe's Cafe was." He picked up a colorful menu. "I'm famished. I see you've already ordered."

He turned his golden-brown eyes on Marta.

Marta still hadn't snapped out of her trance.

Taras, who was less than twelve inches away from her, favored her with a sidelong appraisal. "From your spiffy attire, I assume you're the waitress. How are you today, my dear?"

Marta smiled weakly. Could it be that Key West's infamous man-eater had finally met her match? Gaea wondered.

"I'm Marta," Marta said at last. "I mean, I'm fine, thanks. What can I bring you?"

"A stack of hotcakes, bacon, eggs, ham, hot coffee; keep it coming. I usually have at least three cups," Taras rattled off, smiling radiantly at Marta.

"Geez, where do you put it all?" Marta guffawed, regaining her bravura.

Taras laughed. "I like you."

"Sugar, there's more to like than meets the eye," Marta said. She winked at him, whereupon she walked away, her jeans hitting every curve of her lithe hips.

"Where do you put it all?" Gaea asked him seriously in Marta's absence.

Taras's golden eyes met hers. "I swim several miles a day. Works it off like that," he ended, snapping his fingers.

"Okay," Gaea said. She paused to take a sip of her coffee. "Shall we begin now or would you rather wait until after we eat? Because I have plenty of questions for you."

"I'm sure you do," Taras said, his eyes never leaving her face. His gaze was so mesmerizing, Gaea had the feeling he was looking through to her soul. Peering at a part of her she wasn't sure yet she wanted to share with him. He was a stranger to her and the intense jolt he gave her with just the power of his presence was unsettling. It put her nerves on edge.

"You don't have anything to be nervous about," Taras said as though he'd read her mind.

Gaea looked up defensively. "Some strange things have been happening."

"Define strange," Taras said, his voice compellingly gentle.

"I saw you in Sakhalin, Russia. Why were you there?"

"I wanted to see you up close. It was an accident, really. I was in the North Pacific on business for my father when I saw you again after many years. You're special, Gaea."

"How so?"

"Your grandfather, Cameron, was one of us."

"One of whom? You haven't explained anything. You're

speaking in riddles. My grandfather, Cameron, was from the Dominican Republic. Is that what you mean? You're from the same part of the world, as well?"

"More than that. Your grandmother hasn't told you anything? Your father? He must know. He must have questioned your grandmother when he was growing up. Our people share certain traits. They are diminished in you, because you are only a quarter Aquarian. But, in your father, the traits would be more pronounced. He would be extremely fond of swimming, for example. And he would age at a slower rate than air-breathers."

"Aquarians? The water-bearer? Air-breathers? Humans?"

"It has nothing to do with astrology. Aquarians are what we are. I'm making this as easy for you as I possibly can, Gaea. You are three-quarters human. Our scientists figure that makes you, in essence, human. Although you have the ability to stay underwater longer than the average human. What can you do, seven minutes, or perhaps up to ten?"

That shocked her. She could stay underwater eleven minutes. A talent she'd never boasted about because she figured it made her a freak of nature. The longest length of time ever recorded for free diving was two minutes, nine seconds by a Cuban, Francisco Ferraras, of Grand Bahama Island in 1993.

Taras continued to observe her. "Gaea, I suppose if I am to convince you of my sincerity, I have to be totally honest with you."

"You haven't been honest up to this point?"

"To an extent," he said. He squeezed her hand and paused, as though he were marshaling his resolve. "Many years ago, a young Aquarian was curious about the air-breathers. Did they think like us? Did they love like us? So, being shape-changers by design, he took on the countenance of an air-breather and went ashore for an experiment. The result? He found out that the air-breathers were no more, no less than an Aquarian. They lived, they loved, they died. Of course, they had no shape-changing ability. They lived pitifully short lives. But they weren't inferior to us."

"Is that how he thought before his experiment, that we air-breathers were inferior to you?"

"Pretty much," Taras said, nodding his handsome head. "Our elders taught a form of racial superiority, I believe, in order to keep the youths from being too curious about air-breathers. To prevent something happening like crossbreeding, which proved viable."

Gaea laughed shortly. "Otherwise, I wouldn't be here."

Taras nodded as if in deep thought.

"Don't think of your father's birth as an experiment, Gaea. Cameron loved your grandmother. He still does. He couldn't stay with her because . . ."

"Because when she was seventy-eight, as she is today, he would look much younger," Gaea said sarcastically. "And, of course, there is the shape-shifting to be considered. You can't have friends over for dinner when your husband is a dolphin. Do you serve the fish cooked, or do you serve sushi?"

Taras snorted in laughter. "I admire the human's ability to joke when faced with something truly horrifying."

His eyes narrowed somewhat when he turned his gaze on her. "But, the real reason Cameron didn't stay with your grandmother was because when he—what is the term?—came clean with her, she was so repulsed, she asked him to leave her and never come back. For the sake of their son, she said. Young Cameron must never know what his father was."

"And she never told him," Gaea said, a note of wonder in her voice.

"Apparently not," Taras agreed. He frowned. "Which left her granddaughter vulnerable to Serame's schemes."

"Xavier," Gaea said. "Xavier is an Aquarian."

"Who wants to follow in Cameron's footsteps," Taras replied. He stopped and turned his head to the left.

Marta arrived with his order.

"Serving you is going to throw my sacroiliac out of whack," she complained as she sat the stack of pancakes before him, followed by scrambled eggs, crisp bacon and a thick slice of ham with pineapple on top, swimming in red gravy.

"Don't forget how sweet I was about the heavy labor when you tip me," Marta said in parting.

"I'll be sure to take that into consideration," Taras assured her as he poured maple syrup on the stack of pancakes and taking knife and fork in hand, cut into them.

"So you've been pining away for my grandmother all these years," Gaea said.

Taras dropped his utensils.

His golden-brown eyes met her much darker ones. "How could you know I'm that long-ago boy?"

"My grandmother has always said I'm very intuitive," Gaea said. Tears sat in her eyes. "Besides, for some reason, you and my father have the same eye color. Is it your choice? When you assume a human form, do you always select this one?"

"I'm fond of this one," Taras confirmed with a small smile. "I went to see Omega last night. I was afraid she'd recognize me, but she didn't."

"She didn't have her glasses," Gaea provided.

"But she said there was something about my voice that reminded her of her son's."

"Not much gets past her."

"She's more beautiful than she was as a girl," Taras said, his voice catching. He cleared his throat. "But, that's not why I'm here. We must stop Scramc from using you to propagate his mutated race."

Propping her chin in her hand, Gaea looked at him. "Why does Serame need me for that? Aren't there any other half-breeds walking around?"

"No, thank God," Taras told her.

"How did your people do it?" Gaea wondered aloud, "go undetected by man for all these years? And why would Xavier risk so much in order to father a new race of beings? What will it benefit him? I don't understand what motivates him."

Taras paused to drink some of his coffee. "There are two

factions among Aquarians: Some believe that in order to preserve the purity of our genes, we must not crossbreed with the air-breathers. The group Serame belongs to believes that we can remain intact as a people, plus become stronger if we breed with air-breathers. We don't interfere in the air-breathers' government. But Serame's group feels we can become more powerful if we were to, little by little, infiltrate your government. He has proven, by living among you for so long, that it can be done. Now, more Aquarians are beginning to think in this manner. The only way to stop the madness is to bring Serame back to the fold a failure."

"Well he's not going to get my cooperation," Gaea said emphatically. "The wedding's definitely off. I don't want to be the mother of Serame's New World Order."

"You're as repulsed as your grandmother then?" Taras inquired, his eyes taking on a sad aspect.

"That's not it," Gaea said truthfully. "By your calculations, I'm one-quarter Aquarian. I wouldn't be repulsed by you even if I weren't. I happen to love dolphins . . . is that the main shape Aquarians favor?"

"Are you asking what we look like in our purest form?"

"Yes."

"I can show you," Taras suggested. "Though, not here. We can meet in the lagoon where I spied on you when you were a child."

He was smiling at her so tenderly that it dawned on Gaea that she was, indeed, sitting and talking to her grandfather. Inside this handsome, thirty-something man was the heart and soul of an ancient being whose blood coursed through her veins.

She placed a hand atop his. "I know we can never get back the time that has passed. But if we could, I'd wish I'd grown up knowing you."

"Me, too, dear one," Taras said, his voice low. "Me too."

"Gran wants to talk to me tonight," Gaea told him, wiping a tear from the corner of her eye with a finger. "I believe she's going to finally tell us about you and what really happened."

"Good," Taras said. "I'm proud of her. She's gotten over her fear."

"Fear," Gaea said, laughing. "Fear is a word I would never have associated with that woman. Intrepid, yes. Heroic? Yes."

"You're right, of course," Taras amended. "Omega acted to protect Cam, and then, you. She didn't realize she had no reason to fear me. I was a monster to her. Sixty years ago, people were much less sophisticated. Today you have films and books about alien invasions. Films that depict aliens in positive ways as well as negative. Mass media has been preparing the human psyche for the possibility that they aren't alone in the universe for some time now. But when I knew your grandmother, she knew of only one being who manifested himself in forms other than man, and that was Satan. She thought I was a demon, or something."

"Or something," Gaea echoed. "As a devout Catholic, she had learned that Satan could take on many forms. Your shape-changing ability probably confirmed her suspicions for her. Today, however, she has matured and I believe she's more prone to think you simply belong to a different species. One no more or no less than human."

She sipped her coffee. "Eat, Gramps, your food's getting cold."

Taras laughed and ate happily, looking at her from time to time and laughing all over again.

When he'd finished, he placed two twenties on the counter.

"That's way too much," Gaea told him, thinking he was unaware of the custom of tipping fifteen percent.

"It was worth every penny," Taras begged to differ. He smiled down at her as he rose. "Will you meet me tonight at the lagoon?"

"It might be late," Gaea said.

"That's okay. The water's warm there," Taras said. "I'll linger."

"Then, I'll be there."

She watched him as he crossed the room and the ladies, once

again, followed his progress. Marta caught up with him at the door and thanked him for the tip.

"My sacroiliac and I, both, thank you," she joked.

Taras had grinned, his delight shining in his eyes.

Gaea turned and walked to the back of the room, where Micah was waiting.

She sat down across from him and he clasped both her hands in his. "How did it go?"

She sighed. She didn't know what to tell him. How *much* to tell him. "Micah, you've been through so much already. Finding out what a mess my life is . . ."

"All things beyond your control," he gently reminded her. His dark eyes looked straight into hers. "Don't hold anything back, Gaea. It's my life. I should be the one to decide upon how far I want to go with this thing. And to make that decision, I have to be apprised of everything. You said as much yourself a few hours ago."

"I know I did," Gaea said, hating herself for bringing him into this. "But it's even more complicated than I ever imagined."

Micah didn't want to press her. He knew she was at war with her conscience. She was trying to weigh the pros and the cons. Would what she told him put his life at risk?

The question was: Did she love him? Because, if she did, she would distance herself from him. She'd use everything in her arsenal to make him go back to New York.

He waited.

Gaea cleared her throat.

She rose and zipped up her jacket, preparing to leave.

Micah rose, too, removed his wallet from his coat pocket and dropped a couple of bills onto the table top.

Gaea opened her mouth as though she were about to say something, then clamped it shut.

She turned and walked away, heading for the exit.

Micah frowned. She was going to be difficult.

Outside, Gaea walked swiftly, the morning breezes whipping

about her face, making her light jacket billow out. She zipped it up further and kept walking.

She didn't look around, however, she knew Micah was dogging her steps. She could hear his footfalls.

"Go home, Micah. I've got things to do, and I don't need a greenhorn mucking up my plans."

"Oh, then you have this all figured out now," he said. In a couple of strides, he was at her side. "You're afraid, Gaea. You're afraid and you don't want to admit it."

She refused to stop walking, so Micah caught her by the arm and ceased her forward motion.

Gaea blew air between full, moistened lips. "Give it up, Micah. I'm not caving in this time. You're not going to convince me that you belong here, because you don't. The fewer people involved in this, the better." She looked into his eyes and then, hastily, looked away. "It just wasn't meant to be. Go find yourself a normal, red-blooded American girl who can love you the way you deserve to be loved. Someone you can have children with and grow old with. Someone with no secrets."

"And where would I find that paragon?" Micah inquired, his dark eyes devouring her lovely face.

"I wouldn't know," Gaea replied, crestfallen he'd even asked. He was supposed to say he'd already found his woman. His woman. Was she really a woman if she were one-quarter Aquarian?

He would do well to get as far away from her as he possibly could. The problem was, she didn't want him to go. She longed to be in his arms, right now. She just wanted him to hold her and continue to hold her until she felt human again. Until the noise in her mind had diminished to a whisper.

She wanted him to go. And yet, she wanted him to stay.

Micah had loosened his grip on her. She hadn't noticed because she was watching his mouth. Wishing he'd kiss her one last time, to give her something to remember him by. Something to dream about and hang her hopes on.

She was still watching his full, mobile lips when they parted, and he said, "I love you, Gaea."

Her heart thumped in her chest. She raised her gaze to his eyes, and saw that those dark orbs held an amused glint. He could not possibly know what her reaction to his declaration would be, yet, he had faith in her.

"You gonna make me stand here with my heart on my sleeve?"

"You're nuts," Gaea announced suddenly. But she was smiling, and the next thing he knew, she was in his arms, kissing him.

She pulled away. "Didn't your parents teach you not to get involved with a woman who has more problems than you do?"

"Your problems are external," Micah said reasonably. He hugged her to him. "There's absolutely nothing wrong with you, Gaea Maxwell. As far as I'm concerned, you're perfect. Perfect for me. So that's why I'm asking you to marry me."

"Right here on Caroline Street?" Gaea joked, smiling up at him. She tiptoed and kissed his dimple. "I'll tell you what, Micah. If after I've told you about my conversation with Taras, you still want to marry me, I will, because I love you too . . ."

"Oh, baby," Micah breathed, kissing her lips. He worked his way down to the side of her neck, where he nuzzled her. "We'll get through this together. And then, we'll get married and have a house full of kids."

"Nothing would make me happier," Gaea assured him, taking his hand.

She tried to urge him forward, but Micah was intent on kissing her again. His strong arms enveloped her and his lips claimed hers and she felt she'd been granted her wish of a few minutes ago. He held her as though he'd never let her go. And she felt human again. Anything was possible as long as he was beside her.

What's more, she wasn't aware of the strangers moving around the two of them as they stood on the sidewalk wrapped in each other's arms.

* * *

"I'm pregnant."

Sharon Baker said these words after coming out of the shower wrapped in a fluffy white towel and still dripping wet.

Xavier was lying in bed flipping through the channels with the remote. They were in a motel on Petronia Street. She was his important appointment.

After seeing Gaea this morning, he was so turned on, he had to find release or burst; therefore, he'd phoned Sharon and she'd been accommodating, as usual. She was a minx, that girl. So energetic and eager to please. Never any strings attached. She was an unusual female; one who had sex for the pleasure derived thereof and not for any sort of promise that he'd be there in the morning.

"I'm pregnant," Sharon repeated.

She sat on the edge of the bed and began brushing her black, shoulder-length hair. Her brown skin was the color of chestnuts and her eyes, which were regarding him with contempt at the moment, were light brown.

"You're impossible," she said. "Are you going to sit there and ignore me, you cold bastard?"

She threw the brush at him, connecting with his right shoulder.

"Unless you do right by me, I'm going to that fiancée of yours and tell her you never quit seeing me. What do you say to that?"

Xavier threw the covers back and stood. Nude, he walked over to the chair where he'd flung his clothing an hour ago and calmly picked up his shorts and stepped into them.

He didn't bother looking at her. "If you are pregnant, the brat isn't mine."

"It most certainly is yours. I haven't been with anyone else in nearly a year."

Xavier sniffed the air, then turned his well-shaped head to glare at her. "You were with another man last night."

"You have no proof of that," Sharon said, her voice breaking. "You'd say anything to get out of marrying me . . ."

"Marrying you?" Xavier laughed.

"My father's a minister. I am not going to have a child out of wedlock. Either marry me, or I'll report you. How long do you suppose you'll be head of your department when they learn you've been making it with a student?"

"You're twenty-seven years old," Xavier said dismissively. "You're hardly an ingenue."

He finished dressing and went to stand directly in front of her. She rose and he pushed her back down onto the bed.

"I don't like threats, Sharon. I don't know what sort of game you're playing at, but you knew I was only in it for the sex from the beginning. I don't love you. I don't even like you very much. You're just a body to me. A vessel to be used and tossed aside. Frankly, I don't care if you are pregnant. It isn't my concern, because there is no way the child could be mine. When I decided to seduce you, I took a hair sample from you and mapped your DNA. You and I are incompatible."

Sharon spat at him, catching him on his left hand.

Xavier wiped the spittle on the front of her towel, and violently wrapped both hands around her slender neck.

"Don't ever approach my fiancée about this, Sharon; because if you do, I'll have to kill you," he said, smiling menacingly. "I believe you know me well enough to know I don't make empty threats, like you do."

He let go of her and stood, wiping imaginary dirt off his clothing. "I should have known getting involved with the likes of you would leave me feeling soiled." He cut his gaze back to her frightened face. "Although, I must say, you were spirited in bed."

He walked over to the bureau and went into his wallet. Removing two one hundred dollar bills, he placed them in the ashtray.

"For services rendered."

Sharon was clutching her sore throat as she sat up on the bed.

"I hate you," she croaked. "You're a monster."

"Sticks and stones," Xavier said with a smirk.

He left, leaving the door wide open.

Sharon got up and slammed it after him.

She stood with her back pressed against the door for some time, trying to think.

Xavier had been correct when he'd guessed the child wasn't his. The baby belonged to Bradley Chamonix, another graduate student. However, Brad was as penniless as she was. She needed financial support.

She couldn't believe Xavier's gall, saying he'd mapped her DNA in order to make certain they weren't compatible before taking her to bed. She was humiliated.

She'd like to throw a wrench in his illustrious plans. Dr. Maxwell was a simpleton if she actually went through with the wedding after catching her and Xavier in bed together.

Sharon smiled. She could still remember the look of utter shock on Dr. Maxwell's face.

It was a cool night in November and she and Xavier had been holed up in his house. Dr. Maxwell was supposed to be in Miami visiting a friend, so Xavier had brought Sharon to his home for the first time.

Sharon had been impressed with his digs.

He lived well beyond his means. She'd jokingly asked him what bank he'd robbed and he'd said, "I don't need to rob banks. I know where to find all the gold and jewels I'll ever need. The Gulf of Mexico is full of treasure."

They had been in a playful mood that night, so she hadn't taken him seriously.

They'd made love and were still in bed, enjoying the afterglow, when she heard a noise coming from downstairs.

Xavier shrugged her off with, "You're hearing things. No one could get past the security system."

A few minutes later, though, Dr. Maxwell appeared in the

doorway; for, since they were alone in the house, they'd left the door open.

Xavier had sprung out of bed, grabbing the sheet to cover himself, all the while running toward Dr. Maxwell who'd taken one look at the scene and spun on her heels, getting out of there.

Sharon had gotten a perverse satisfaction being in the center of the chaos which ensued. Dr. Maxwell, though she'd never done anything to Sharon, needed taking down a peg or two. And Xavier had gotten what he deserved. He was a cheater, and cheaters deserved to get caught.

She didn't, for one moment, disbelieve him when he said he'd kill her if she went to Dr. Maxwell with her present grievance.

No. He'd kill her. She was certain of that.

She walked over to the phone and picked up the receiver. Maybe Brad's parents were worth something.

# Sixteen

"I've told you everything, Cam," Lara said for the fifth time. She pulled their forest-green late-model Ford Taurus behind Gaea's Mustang in Aaron and Omega's driveway. "Omega just said to get over here by seven, and that's all she said."

"I don't understand why she has to be so cryptic," Cam said, sighing tiredly. He turned his golden gaze on his wife's pretty brown face. "You don't suppose she's worse off than . . ."

"No," Lara immediately replied. She leaned over and planted a kiss on Cam's brow. "You worry too much, sweetie. Your mother is going to outlive us all." She reached for the door's handle, "Maybe this last episode has frightened her enough to do something about a will. You've been telling them they need to get that taken care of for years."

"Maybe," Cam agreed, but he didn't sound convinced.

"We're here now," Lara said reasonably. "Your curiosity will be satisfied in a few minutes, I'm sure."

They got out of the car and strolled up the walk leading to Cam's parents' small bungalow.

As they stepped onto the porch, they were greeted with the sound of voices raised in laughter. Gaea, Aaron, Omega, and (Lara guessed) that nice young man, Micah Cavanaugh.

"It must not be anything of a too-personal nature," she commented to Cam before they went inside. "Otherwise, Gaea wouldn't have brought Micah."

"Probably not," Cam said, smiling for the first time since being summoned to his mother's house.

The aroma of fried fish pervaded the bungalow. They walked through the living room and the dining room and emerged in the kitchen where everyone else awaited them.

Omega came forward and embraced the both of them.

She was attired in one of her colorful caftans, and her long, thick, wavy white hair fell in a cascade to her shoulders, held back by a headband in the same material as the caftan. She looked radiant.

"I didn't know you were throwing a party," Cam said with a grin. He was happy to see his mother in such good spirits.

"I'm calling it an enlightenment party," Omega said, her brown-green eyes dancing.

She let go of Cam and reached up to pinch his cheek, just as she used to do when he was a boy.

"Mama," Cam said, annoyed.

"I just felt like doing that," Omega said, unapologetic. "Come children, the fish's hot. Let's eat, and then we'll talk."

Lara and Cam went over to the table where Cam shook Micah's hand and affectionately grasped his stepfather's shoulder.

Lara pulled Gaea aside. "Do you know what's going on here?"

"Some," Gaea admitted. "But I think you ought to hear it from the beginning from Gran later. Believe me, it's worth waiting for."

"All right," Lara conceded. "As long as it isn't that crazy notion of hers to move back to the Dominican Republic and reclaim the family's land. I'm too old to haul water up a mountain."

Laughing, Gaea briefly hugged her mother. "I promise, it isn't that."

"Good," Lara said, smiling. "Now," she continued in a low voice, "what's going on between you and that good-looking New York City boy?"

Gaea looked into her mother's eyes and simply smiled.

Lara hugged her tightly. "Oh, baby. I'm so happy for you."

She released her daughter and went to throw her arms around Micah's neck.

Micah, being much taller, had to stoop in order to receive her token of affection. "What's that for?" he asked pleasantly.

"Just for being you," Lara said.

She then went to sit next to her husband. But, throughout the meal, she'd glance in Micah's direction and smile warmly at him.

They feasted on fried grouper, baked potatoes, garden salad and key lime pie. While they ate, Gaea's family regaled Micah with stories about her.

Some of them were downright embarrassing, such as the tale Aaron wove about her senior prom.

"She was dating a fellow by the name of Spike McGraw," Aaron began. "So named because when he was seven, he was bitten on the behind by a dog with the same moniker. The kids in the neighborhood henceforth called him Spike. Anyway, Spike, being a big fellow, was courted by the football coach to become a defensive end. He went on to gain some acclaim during his high-school career. So our Gaea was rather impressed, and smitten I might add, with Spike."

"Grandpa . . ." Gaea protested. "Don't embellish."

"As if I ever would!" Aaron exclaimed heartily.

"At any rate," Aaron continued, "on the night of the senior prom our Gaea was dressed to the nines. Looking so beautiful, her parents, her grandmother and I took enough photographs of her to fill an album. We'll show them to you later this evening . . ."

"Over my dead body," Gaea said emphatically.

"The before photos, not the after ones," Omega piped in.

"Oh, all right," Gaea agreed.

"Off our little Gaea went to the party of a lifetime. Both of them splendidly turned out. Not a hair out of place, clothes immaculate. Five hours later, Gaea walks into the house covered from head-to-toe in mud. Pieces of leaves and branches sticking out of her long hair. The dress, which she'd saved her allowance for months to buy, was ruined."

"Some of the kids got the bright idea that it would be romantic to go out to Great White Heron National Wildlife Refuge in the middle of the night. There we were, parked out there, when Spike tried to get fresh. I slugged him and got out of the car. He gave chase and I ran into the swamp. I began sinking and some of the kids pulled me out and brought me home. I never spoke to Spike again."

"But I certainly did," Cam said. "He, his father and I had a real nice chat."

"That landed you and Frank McGraw in jail," Lara added.

"It was still a nice chat," Cam maintained. "My fist spoke to his jaw. He had the nerve to defend his son, claiming that all teen girls were asking for it. It was worth a night in jail."

"Did you press charges?" Micah asked, his big hand grasping Gaea's.

"No," she answered. "I wasn't physically hurt. Spike had been drinking that night, something I wasn't even aware of until he grabbed me in the dark and I smelled his breath. He'd never tried anything like that before, so we agreed to drop it."

"It was just a case of youthful stupidity," Cam explained. "After his father and I were released from jail the next day, the boy apologized to Gaea and me. He even apologized for his old man's behavior. I came to realize that with a father like his, the boy had a hard row to hoe."

"You're definitely understanding folks," Micah commented, alluding that, under the same circumstances, he would not have been.

"Who wants more coffee?" Omega asked, rising. The tone of the evening was becoming too serious for her. She wanted the mood to be light when she launched into her tale. This family had been through enough crises to last a lifetime. Now, there should be a lifting of the veil of sadness as it were. She wanted her revelations to be looked upon as something positive, not as another weight to deflate her family's collective spirit.

Everyone wanted refills, so Gaea got up to help her grandmother in the kitchen.

Once they were alone, she said, "Gran, if it were possible to see Grandpa Cameron again, would you want to?"

Omega put the coffee pot back on the warmer and turned to look her granddaughter in the eyes.

"I have seen your grandfather again, child. Not twenty-four hours ago. Seeing him made me certain of what I have to do. He told me I have nothing to fear, and I'm going to take him at his word."

She grasped Gaea firmly by the arm. "What I'm about to say is for your ears only, my love: Xavier is one of them. It was Xavier who scared the wits out of me. At first, I couldn't make him out clearly. I wasn't wearing my glasses. After I'd fallen to the floor, though, he leaned over me. I saw him then. I saw his human face and I saw his other face, as well."

"I know what he is now, Gran," Gaea said, surprised by the calmness of her tone. "He isn't human. He's a being who has the ability to shape-shift. Taras, who is Cameron to you, told me about them."

"Then you're in danger," Omega said, her eyes widening in fear.

"No, no, Gran," Gaea said softly, hugging her grandmother's petite body in her youthful arms. "I'm going to be fine. Everything is going to be all right now. We're armed. We know about them."

Looking into her grandmother's upturned face, she smiled.

"What I need for you to tell me is: is it possible that one of your parents had some shape-shifter blood in his, or her, veins?"

"There were stories," Omega began quietly. "Things my mother told me when I was a child, about men who walked from the sea and coupled with island women. But I assumed they were just fairy tales of a sort."

"However, now we know they do exist," Gaea said. "I have a theory. I believe that in order for Aquarians to successfully impregnate a human woman, the woman has to first have

Aquarian genes. That's why you had Dad. And that's also why Xavier wants me."

"It makes sense," Omega said softly.

"Taras also told me that Xavier, whom he calls Serame, believes that mating with me will bring forth some sort of superhuman race. Their attributes, such as longevity, shape-shifting, coupled with our ability to breathe air makes for quite a few advantages. Xavier apparently has political aspirations for his future offspring too."

"Another madman seeking to control the world?" Omega joked.

"Or his part of it," Gaea replied. She released her grandmother and went to retrieve the coffeepot. "I almost feel sorry for him. Perhaps his life with his people was too restrictive for his tastes, so he decided to try the other side. But he can't fight his nature. He's Aquarian. So he comes up with a plan. He'll prove to his people that crossbreeding with humans is a good idea; maybe he can have the best of both worlds. He can live among humans and visit his people when he gets homesick."

"No ostracism?" Omega put in, understanding.

"Mmm hmm," Gaea said. "The only drawback is: me. I want no part of his plans. There's a dearth of suitable women to choose from. So, what will he do now?"

"Something drastic," Omega predicted.


"I have a favor to ask," Micah spoke into the receiver.

Thad, on the other end of the line, sounded even farther away than New York City. "What is it, Micah?"

"A leave of absence."

"Is something the matter?" Thad asked, concerned. His deep baritone rose an octave.

"Yes. But, I'll have to leave it at that, Thad. I'll explain it all when I see you."

"What can I do to help?"

"Nothing at the moment. I may have to call on you later."

"Whatever I have is yours. And, Micah, be careful. From the sound of your voice, I can tell something very serious is happening there. You and Gaea keep safe, you hear me?" Thad urged him, his tone grave.

"We will," Micah vowed.

Micah rang off and went outside onto the deck and stood with both hands on the railing, staring up at the quarter moon.

If Micah didn't know better, he'd think he was the main character in an episode of *The Twilight Zone*. Up until a few days ago, his life had been so ordered, so by-the-book, so mundane. Now, all of a sudden, he was thrust in the middle of something strange, yet wonderful.

Strange, because now they had evidence of another race of beings residing on earth alongside mankind. Beings who were not limited to one form. Beings who were amphibious. From what Omega and Gaea told them all earlier tonight, these "people" had been crossbreeding with humans for quite some time. Gaea's father's father was one of them. Which made Cam half-Aquarian. Which made Gaea one-quarter Aquarian. The woman he loved. Not quite human. It was mind-boggling.

Where had they come from, these Aquarians? Were they created by the same God who created mankind? Were they part of the primordial mix, which gave humans the genetics to climb out of the bog and become Homo sapiens? Could they have preceded man?

His thoughts were racing. And there was a grain of fear, in the pit of his stomach, steadily growing. It wasn't for his own safety.

He was afraid that, when the time came, he wouldn't be there for Gaea. The disadvantage of dealing with the unknown was that you could never guess what would happen next. There were no past precedents to compare the present to. One had to fly by the seat of one's pants, so to speak.

Still, the situation left him with a feeling of being a young boy again, about to embark on a great adventure. He'd been made privy to a wondrous event and if they all made it out alive, it would make one magnificent tale to tell his grandchildren someday.


The Langston estate sat on the northeastern tip of Key West. From a distance, the white sandstone structure resembled an Islamic mosque, for there was a gold dome atop the highest turret of The Villa, as the Langstons had dubbed it when it was built thirty-five years ago.

Since Cyril's death, Gwen Langston could not bear to reside at The Villa year round and she was presently visiting her mother in Minnesota. However, The Villa was fully staffed, even in her absence. And when Gaea telephoned the caretaker, Mr. Cerrano, with the request that she be allowed access to the lagoon, he assured her that she would be welcomed with open arms. She had but to come to the house and ring the bell. Gwen had left instructions that all the Maxwells should be allowed access to The Villa whenever they wished. A privilege the Maxwells rarely took advantage of.

"Will you be bringing guests?" he asked, sounding not at all put out if she was. In fact, he sounded bored and the prospect of live bodies on the estate was something to look forward to.

"No, I'll be alone," Gaea said. There was no use explaining that there would, indeed, be another guest, however, he would arrive under his own steam and leave in the same manner. And he would be in the form of . . . well, that was yet to be seen.

Once they were in the lagoon, she and Taras would have complete privacy, so there was no fear of their being interrupted, or spied upon for that matter.

When she rang the doorbell at The Villa, Mr. Cerrano answered and ushered her in.

He was a Cuban gentleman in his late sixties. His bronze skin was unwrinkled by the sun, save the crinkles around his eyes when he smiled, which was often. His thick, wavy hair was salt-and-pepper.

At six feet tall, he bent at the waist when he kissed Gaea's hand, a custom he invariably observed when she visited. She was charmed by his courtly manners.

"A pleasure, Senorita Gaea," he said in his deep, Spanish accented voice.

"It's good to see you, Senor Cerrano," Gaea said, smiling.

He wore an off-white evening suit in linen. His tie knotted perfectly and gold cuff links shining at his wrists.

Gaea had worn her white maillot swimsuit. Over it was a multicolored wrap-skirt whose hem fell to her ankles.

"You still enjoy a dip at night, I see," Jorge Cerrano observed with an appreciative glance at her graceful arms.

"Yes," Gaea said, stepping into the foyer. "The house is so quiet."

"A house this size begs for the pitter-patter of small feet," Jorge said regrettably. "Perhaps you and Dr. Cross will help to supply us with that wonderful sound one of these days, aye?"

The housekeeper, Miss Haile, appeared at that moment, saving Gaea from having to make a reply.

Carmen Haile had been with the Langstons for nearly forty years. These days, she rarely did any physical labor herself; her duties were limited to supervising the household staff.

She was a tall black woman in her early seventies. She'd never married or had any children, so she became particularly attached to Gaea when she and her parents lived at The Villa.

Carmen warmly embraced Gaea now, pressing her to her ample bosom. Her scent was a mixture of Evening in Paris and talcum powder.

"Miss C, you never seem to age," Gaea exclaimed happily.

"Hello, child, it's good to see you too," Carmen said. She was trim and fit and was dressed in a smart navy blue skirt-suit and a crisp white cotton blouse with a Peter Pan collar.

"Come on back to the kitchen, Mrs. Ramirez just made a pan of cinnamon rolls. You have time for one, don't you?"

"Could I have a rain check?" Gaea asked, her expression regretful. "I really need to get down to the lagoon. How about in a couple of hours? Would that be too late?"

"Dear, we're not on any kind of schedule when the mistress is away," Carmen said. "That would be just fine wouldn't it, Mr. Cerrano?"

"Indeed, Miss Haile," Jorge returned amiably.

"All right then," Gaea said. She said a quick hello to Mrs. Ramirez as she went through the kitchen to the back patio and soon, she was jogging down the sandy slope leading to the lagoon several hundred yards behind The Villa.

Entering the beach, she stopped next to a palm tree and removed her wrap. Folding it, she placed it in her big canvas bag and leaned the bag against the base of the tree.

Slipping out of her sandals, she wiggled her toes in the sand.

"I'm here," she called into the wind.

The quarter moon didn't do much to illuminate the beach, however Mr. Cerrano had been kind enough to turn on the tennis court lights. It was sufficient to see how to walk down to the water without stepping on any sharp objects.

She stepped into the water. The silken feel of the wet sand beneath her feet gave her the momentary sensation of sinking. She waded in up to her thighs.

There was no sign of another living creature, although she knew that these warm, shallow waters nurtured myriad forms of life.

Snails, crabs, worms, all made the sand near the shore their home. On the bottom, coquinas, lavender-hued clams the size of thumbnails, lived. They fed on microscopic nutrients. Birds and fish fed on them.

"You love it, don't you?" a deep male voice said from behind her.

She turned and saw Taras walking toward her. He wore only a pair of baggy white slacks tied with a cord at the waist. The legs were rolled up to his calves.

"The sea," he explained. "You love everything about her."

"I do, and I always have," Gaea allowed, smiling at him.

Carried on the breezes was the piquant odor of ginger.

"Why do you love her?"

He stood a few feet away from her, awaiting her answer.

"There's no logic behind my feelings for the ocean. How can I describe a wave? Or the power of an entity which can shape continents? I'm in awe of her. And I deeply respect her."

"She's a part of you, you know. She's a part of all of us. From the tiniest creature, to the largest. We all had our meager beginnings in her."

He approached her now and reached for her hands, which she raised and placed in his.

"May I hold you for a moment?" he asked.

"Yes."

He drew her into his warm, strong arms. Her head lay against his bare chest and a calmness descended upon her like a feather floating from heaven. She inhaled and exhaled and listened to the rhythmic beating of his heart.

He released her after a while and smiled down at her. "I never thought I'd get the opportunity to do that."

They held hands as they walked down the length of the beach.

"Tell me about yourself," Gaea said. "What do you do? Do you have a wife? Other children?"

"My father, your great-grandfather, is the leader of our people. You could say he is king. Our government isn't exactly a democracy, although, it is not a dictatorship either. The leaders are all descended from our line. Your great-grandfather, Deocles, has ruled for many decades."

"How many?"

"Nine. He is advanced in age now and one of his children will soon succeed him so that he can live out the rest of his life without the constant pressure of the monarchy."

"Then your society isn't sexist?"

Taras laughed shortly. "My dear, your great-grandmother, Sabina, is one of our most renowned scientists. She will be thrilled that you also show an aptitude for science. No, our females are revered, and are equals in every sense of the word."

"And what do you do in the service of your father?"

"I am an ambassador. I keep the lines of communication open between all Aquarians worldwide."

"How many of you are there?"

"How many humans populate the earth?"

"That many?"

"We've been on this planet for eons."

"Then you're not . . ."

"Aquia, was our home planet."

"Was it destroyed?"

"No, on the contrary, it thrives to this day. Aquia was becoming overpopulated. Those who left Aquia were explorers, and colonists. When they arrived, man was still largely cave dwellers. They painted images of our ships on cave walls. Those early colonists tried to communicate with mankind, but mankind was too backward. They thought the Aquarians were gods and tried to worship them. It was then that the elders decided it was best to remain apart from the air-breathers."

"But the myths persisted," Gaea said. "Poseidon, the sea-god. Your name, Taras, is the name of the son of the sea-god."

"Taras is a name that has been handed down for generations in our family."

"About you, personally," Gaea began. "Who do you have waiting for you back at . . ."

"Aquia. The colonists named their new home after their former one. And there is no one. After your grandmother, I could not bear to care that way again. I devote my life to my work. Plus, I have a love of travel, which occupies my time when I'm not working."

"Haven't you been lonely?"

"Lonely? No, not really. I stay too busy to become lonely. Tell me something, Gaea. That young man who was in the diner this morning. Is he someone special to you?"

"It's not easy pulling the wool over your eyes, is it?" Gaea replied, laughing softly.

"I cannot blame you for not trusting me. You didn't know

me. But, here we are now, alone. So you must believe in me now."

"I do. And, in answer to your question: Yes, I love him. He's asked me to marry him, and I want to."

"Then do it," Taras said.

"It's not that easy."

"What's so hard about it? As I understand your customs in this part of the world, you get a license, a blood test and then have a ceremony."

"I've only known him a few days."

"How long must you know him before you can wed him?"

"There's no certain length of time . . ."

She stopped in her tracks and dropped Taras's hand. "That was a trick question, wasn't it?"

"You have to watch us," Taras said, smiling. "We're a tricky bunch. However, since you've admitted there is no general length of time one has to observe before the nuptials, what prevents you from marrying this . . ."

"Micah Cavanaugh."

"Micah Cavanaugh? He appears a decent sort. I assume you've told him of your present predicament?

"He knows everything."

"Even about our meeting here, tonight?"

"Even this."

"Then, what more is there to be said? He must love you. It takes a strong individual to know what he knows about you and stay by your side in spite of it."

"You don't have to convince me of that," Gaea told him.

"Then marry him right away, Gaea. You'd be safe from Serame if you should wed Micah Cavanaugh."

"Why is that? Does Serame require a virgin for his experiment? Is that it?"

"In order for an Aquarian to mate successfully with an air-breather, the air-breather has to have the correct DNA."

"Mmm hmm," Gaea said. "Gran and I were discussing that earlier. We came to the conclusion that Aquarians need a human mate who has some Aquarian blood in order to produce off-spring."

"You're close," Taras said, crossing his muscular arms at his chest. "The fact is, some humans, for lack of a better analogy, retain amphibious DNA, which is compatible with Aquarian DNA, while other humans do not. As you know, the human embryo goes through several stages in utero. Some humans, by an accident of evolution, don't lose their amphibious DNA. Of course their outward appearance is no different from any other human's. But blood will tell."

"Oh, I see," Gaea said, her voice awe-filled. "Then Gran didn't have to be part Aquarian in order to have Dad."

"Serame's desire for you has to do with the degree of Aquarian blood in you," Taras explained. "With your DNA and his, your children will have all the traits of an Aquarian and not require the daily rejuvenation process Serame has to go through in order to remain among you. On an evolutionary scale, they would be a new species."

"You mean I'm the only human on this planet with one-quarter Aquarian blood?"

"Unless you have a brother or sister."

"I don't."

"Then you're it."

"Well that's a chilling thought," Gaea said, her voice rising. "Where have you all been for the past few months? I could've married Xavier by now and been pregnant with his child already!"

"We were watching," Taras assured her. "We've always kept Serame under surveillance. And I, of course, took a special interest in the case. However, it took a great deal of wangling on my part to convince the elders to send me to speak with you. They felt I couldn't maintain a sense of detachment since I'm your grandfather."

"And they were right," Gaea said, not meaning to hurt him, but he needed to face reality. "What is the recommendation of the elders? How do they want to solve this problem?"

"They wish you to go along with Serame's plans a while longer. And then, at the appointed time, they want you to bring him to a set of designated coordinates. We'll handle it from there."

"When, and where?"

"I haven't been contacted with the particulars yet. But it will transpire soon, very soon."

"In the middle of the Conch Republic celebration? This town is going to swell with tourists."

"And some will be Aquarians."

Sighing, Gaea continued walking, kicking at the oncoming tide.

"I'll tell you what, Gramps. I'm trying my best not to blow a synapse like Gran did. This is too much."

Taras caught up with her and grasped her by the arm, turning her around to face him.

"You can handle it, Gaea. I wouldn't have come to you if I didn't believe you could."

"But you had a personal interest in this," Gaea reminded him. "You wanted to see your Omega once more. And then there's your son and your granddaughter. Maybe the elders were right. You may not have been the best choice for this mission."

"You're right. I did have a personal interest. You and your father are the only descendants I have. I've wondered about you. I've dreamed of the day when I could hold you in my arms. Nearly twenty years ago, my curiosity got the best of me and I came, in the form of the bottlenose, to see you."

She had her opportunity to ask him, now, a question that had been bothering her for years.

"What would've happened if I'd followed you that day?"

"I wouldn't have stolen you, if that's what you're wondering," Taras said with a chuckle. "I would've brought you back to shore if you had tired. I wouldn't have let anything happen to you. Just like I won't let anything happen to you today."

"Would you do it again?" Gaea asked. Her dark eyes sought his.

"Do what, my dear?"

"Could we swim together, like we almost did all those years ago?"

"It would be my pleasure," Taras said and let go of her.

Gaea watched as he walked into the water and waded up to his waist. She followed slowly, the water up to her chest, since she was much shorter than he was.

He stood five feet away from her. She started to get closer, but he warned her off with an outwardly raised palm in her direction. "Stay where you are."

His body began to glow. The outer edges were bright yellow, then the color changed to a dark golden hue, until it finally faded to a green. It was like he was suspended in a tank of green sea water. His body then changed to an amorphous lump so quickly, Gaea wasn't certain whether she'd seen the transformation or imagined it.

There was a loud splash, and before her was the dolphin. It swam away and circled back to her, seemingly getting its bearings.

Gaea dove into the water and met him. She smoothed her hand over his melon and grinned. "That's quite a feat, Gramps."

Taras nudged her in the back with his beak. It was time to swim. Laughing, Gaea followed his sleek body farther out to sea and they frolicked, like children, for quite some time.

When the knock came, Micah was sound asleep. He awoke with a start and reached for the lamp on the nightstand, turning it on.

He was dressed solely in a pair of Joe Boxers. The ones with the bulldogs on them. He grabbed the white terry bathrobe the Marquesa provided for guests and quickly put it on.

Just for future reference, he glanced at the digital readout of the alarm clock on the nightstand before approaching the door. It was 1:10 A.M.

"Yeah?"

"Micah, it's me."

He wasted no time getting the door open. Gaea stood outside, an enigmatic grin on her lips.

She stepped inside and went straight into his arms. Micah shut the door as they walked, locked in each other's arms, into the room.

Her warm skin smelled of papaya and it made him think of the first time he'd kissed her aboard the *Trickster*. Their faces were pressed together and the silken touch of her skin against his aroused him. He wondered what her body, its full length against his, would feel like.

His hand was in her soft, sooty locks. "What are you doing here so late?" he asked, his voice husky.

"I needed to see you. After I left Taras, I went back to The Villa and spent a few minutes catching up with Miss Haile and Mr. Cerrano. Then I drove home and went to bed, but I couldn't sleep."

Her nose had been buried in his chest, but now she turned her head and her lips were beneath his. She looked up into his dark, sexy eyes. "Micah, I know what it means to burn for someone now. I lay in bed, wishing that you were there with me, holding me, touching me, making love to me."

"Baby . . ." Micah breathed. "You don't know how much I'd like to make that wish come true."

"Then let's do it, Micah," Gaea said, as she wrapped her arms around his neck.

Micah bent his head and met her mouth. One of her hands moved upward to rest in his curly hair as the kiss deepened.

She was wearing a black trench coat and had slipped a pair of sandals onto bare feet. Micah wondered, fleetingly, what lay underneath the coat.

Tense with desire, his hand ran down the length of her body and rested on her shapely buttocks. Gaea moaned deep in her throat and inched closer to him. She fit so well in his arms, it was as if they'd been born expressly for each other.

"Oh God, Micah, I don't think I can wait much longer," she

said. His tongue followed the curve of her lower lip, and then he gently took it between his teeth.

"You taste so good."

Gaea arched her back, throwing her head back so that he could kiss her neck and work his way downward.

His big hands undid the sash of her coat and the garment fell open revealing Gaea's lush body enveloped in a lacy white teddy that left very little to the imagination.

"As if showing up at my door in the middle of the night wasn't enough," Micah said wonderingly.

Her large dark eyes raked over him suggestively. "What are you wearing underneath that?" she asked, fingering the lapel of the robe.

"Little or nothing," Micah said, his eyes meeting hers.

Gaea undid the belt and placed her hands inside, against his smooth, muscular chest. His pectorals jumped, astonishing her.

"Do that again," she said, giggling.

He did, making first the right side jump and then the left.

"You're one talented fellow, Micah Cavanaugh."

With that, she reached up, pushed the robe from his shoulders and gravity did the rest.

She doffed the trench coat, tossing it onto a chair that stood near the door.

"Let's get this straight," Micah said, backing up. "You've decided *not* to wait until we're married? You've made a conscious choice?"

Placing a finger on his lips, Gaea said, "Stop being an attorney, Micah. I want you now. Tonight. This isn't something I've rationally thought out. I just know I need you."

Micah caught her by the wrist of the hand she'd pressed to his mouth. Smiling, he said, "Baby, that's all good. But I love you too much to have you wake up in the morning with a guilty conscience. You've waited this long. You can wait a while longer."

Gaea gazed downward. "That's not what your body's saying."

Micah laughed. "But my brain rules my body. So my body will just have to take a cold shower."

"I'm not leaving," she said, adamant about it.

"No one said you had to leave," Micah told her. He took her by the hand and led her to the bed. "Get in."

Gaea climbed into bed and moved over, leaving the side he'd been sleeping on for him.

Micah went and picked up the robe and put it back on.

He then doused the lights and got into bed, pulling Gaea close to him. "Now, go to sleep, little girl."

Gaea snuggled down and closed her eyes. "I don't believe this."

# Seventeen

"Cam, you've got to get some rest. You haven't slept a wink all night," Lara said gently as she lay her arm across her husband's chest.

Sighing listlessly, Cam continued to gaze at the ceiling in their darkened bedroom. "I don't think I'll ever be able to sleep again."

Lara snuggled closer and lay her head on his shoulder. "Cam, you're the same man tonight as you were when you woke up this morning. Nothing has changed."

Laughing, Cam said, "How can you say that? You're living with a half-fish-man."

"Well the important half happens to be all male," Lara said in an attempt to lighten the mood.

"How can you joke about it?" Cam asked, sitting up in bed.

"You just joked about it," Lara reminded him. She sat up, too, and switched the lamp on.

"Well I can joke about it, it's my affliction. But you can't, because when you do it, it's just plain cruel."

Rising, Lara regarded him through narrowed eyelids. "If you want to get testy with someone, go yell at your mother, who kept this a secret for sixty years. And while you're at it, you can look in the mirror and curse the fool whose reflection you'll see."

"What are you getting at, Lara?"

"You, you big lunk head. Do you mean to tell me you never noticed you were different from the rest of us?"

"No, I never noticed," Cam said truthfully.

Shaking her head in frustration, Lara said, "You look at least ten years younger than you are. And, honey, it ain't just the melanin talking. You're rarely ill, and when you are, you recover at a faster rate than the rest of us. And what were you doing the night we met?"

"Strolling on the beach after a five-mile swim."

"Mmm hmm," was all Lara said. She caught his gaze and held it with the sheer obstinacy of her own.

"A five-mile swim. Something you still do at the age of sixty-two. Every day, rain or shine. Now why do you do that, Cam? You're not an athlete training for a decathlon."

"It makes me feel better," Cam replied off-handedly.

"Because you can't survive without the ocean," Lara said as if he were possibly the densest male who ever drew a breath.

Cam sat as though he were stunned, not uttering a word for several minutes, while Lara let him stew in his own juices.

After a while, though, she went to him and put her arms around him. "I love everything about you, Cam. And I'm going to love you until the day I die. Be depressed. Sort it out in your mind. Take all the time you need. But I think it would be a mistake if you missed the opportunity to speak with your father while he's here, because you can't get over the fact that you're not whom you thought you always were. You should get Gaea to set up a meeting between you and . . . what was his name?"

"Taras."

"Yes, Taras."

She looked into his beloved golden-brown eyes. "It's like being given a second chance, Cam. You thought he was dead. I'd give anything to be able to talk to my mother again."

Cam's arms tightened around his petite wife. "Lara, Lara. What would I ever do without you?"

"You wouldn't get kicked in the seat of your pants as often," Lara said with a throaty laugh.

"Sometimes I need a good, swift kick," Cam said, kissing her forehead. His big hand smoothed her hair back. She wore it loose to bed because he liked to feel it, spread out over his arm, as they slept. "Your beauty goes much deeper than this precious face of yours," he said, as he kissed her lips.

Lara playfully pushed him back onto the bed. "Put up or shut up, daddy."

Grinning, Cam rolled her over and was on top of her in an instant. "Is this all you ever think about?"

"Pretty much," Lara said as she pulled him down for a soulful kiss.

"Are you sure you want to marry me?"

They were lying in spoon fashion, with Gaea's head in the crook of his arm. She could feel his warm breath on the back of her neck and his right arm lay across her midsection.

"I'm sure."

"How can you be sure? With everything that's happened, don't you have any reservations?"

"Here you are, in bed with a man you've known less than two weeks. Do you have any?"

"No, because I believe I fell in love with you the first night we kissed. And it made me so sad when I came to that realization."

"Why is that?"

"I figured you'd be reluctant to get involved with a woman who was doubting her own sanity."

"The problem comes in when you don't question your sanity after going through what you've been through," Micah said, his voice reassuring. "And I fell in love with you before I knew about your troubles. That's why I came to Key West, to see if what I was feeling was real."

Gaea brought her hand up to grasp his. "You won't regret loving me, Micah. I promise."

Micah kissed the back of her neck.

"And I'm making the same promise to you. You know, there could be worse things in a relationship than one of the partners being one-quarter Aquarian."

"Such as?"

"I could pass gas in my sleep."

Laughing, Gaea turned around to face him. "I'd invest in a gas mask. But I'd never give you up."

"I could drool uncontrollably."

"I'd change the pillowcases every day."

"I don't do those things, you know. I just wanted you to understand that my love for you transcends anything and everything. I've never loved anyone the way I love you, Gaea. And I don't believe I'd ever be lucky enough to find anyone else half as wonderful as you, the original, are. So, yes, I'm sure I want to marry you. And I'm sure I want to spend the rest of my life with you, whether it's here in Key West, or anywhere else we might travel in this great big world. So, have you any more questions?"

"Kiss me again before I go to sleep?"

She placed her small hand on his cheek. He reached up and grasped it, bringing it to his lips and kissing each of her fingers.

Then they moved closer until the knot in his robe's sash was irritating Gaea's navel.

"That robe has got to go," she complained.

"Baby, if this robe goes, so does your chastity. So, the robe stays," Micah replied, after which, he kissed her.

She didn't have the strength to speak, let alone complain, after that. They slept soundly.

Gaea rose before Micah awakened the next morning and left him a hastily written note: "If I'm going to pretend to still be engaged to Xavier, as Taras wishes, then I couldn't be seen leaving your room this morning. Key West has eyes and ears everywhere. I love you, Gaea."

Micah read the note and folded the slip of paper, placing it in his wallet. It was the first missive, however short, he'd ever received from her and he wanted to keep it.

He had his breakfast on the patio and lingered over his coffee. At around ten that morning, there came a knock on his door.

Expecting the caller to be Gaea, he didn't look through the peep hole, he simply swung the door open. Xavier stood on the other side, looking immaculate in a beige summer suit in raw silk. He was tieless and had left the collar open on the white shirt.

Micah was dressed casually in navy blue Dockers and a white, short-sleeved polo shirt. His biceps strained the fabric on the sleeves.

"Dr. Cross. To what do I owe the pleasure of this visit?"

"Do you mind?" Xavier said coolly as he crossed the threshold.

Micah stepped back. "Please. Come in."

Micah closed the door and walked across the room to the patio, sure that Xavier would follow.

The day was bright and clear, the temperature still in the seventies. Micah had been enjoying it until this moment.

"Would you like to sit?" Micah asked, indicating the chairs around the glass-topped patio table.

"I won't be long," Xavier said, joining Micah at the railing. He looked up into Micah's brown eyes. His own nearly black ones held an unreadable expression in them.

"I don't suppose you're willing to admit you're here to seduce my fiancée? So I'll take a different tack with you, Cavanaugh. Threatening you wouldn't be wise. You're younger, bigger and probably stronger than I am. So I'm going to appeal to your sense of decency. Gaea is an innocent. I know she's over the age of consent, but that's neither here nor there. She's never been touched, and her condition may leave her vulnerable to a man like you."

"And what kind of man is that?" Micah calmly asked.

"Virile, good-looking. I'll speak frankly, Cavanaugh. You are not capable of holding her interest in the long run. She's a scientist. You're an attorney. She needs the kind of intellectual stimulation only I can provide. We were made for each other. You? You are a passing fancy. If you truly care for her, you'll leave and never return. She has the chance for a happy marriage with me. A marriage of minds as well as hearts. With you, she'd probably enjoy some passionate nights and live to regret it. What do you say? Will you be a gentleman and leave her alone?"

"You don't deserve her," Micah said, containing his anger better than he'd imagined he'd be able to, under the circumstances.

Xavier surprised him by saying, "I know I don't. But, I love her. I've loved her for years. How long have you known her?"

"The length of time is of no consequence," Micah said, his voice rising. He lowered it somewhat before continuing. "This conversation is moot, actually, Dr. Cross, because Gaea has already told me she's marrying you. I'm going back to New York today."

Xavier was nonplussed. A frown crossed his handsome face before a slow smile replaced it. "She's a woman of her word." He held out his hand. Micah reluctantly took it and they shook. "However, since we've come to a civilized agreement, there is no need for you to leave our fair city. Your employer, Thaddeus Powers, has been invited to our annual fund-raising gala. Why don't you come, as well? We're all adults here. Dr. Maxwell and I will be pleased to have you."

"I'll think about it," Micah said noncommittally.

"Do that," Xavier urged, pumping Micah's hand. "Well, I'll be going. Good day, Cavanaugh."

"It was," Micah said.

It took Xavier a moment to grasp the meaning behind Micah's comment. Laughing, he said, "Yes, I suppose you have a point."

Micah preceded him and opened the room door for him. "Congratulations on your upcoming marriage, doctor. I'm sure you'll be happy."

"No similar wishes for the bride?"

"Personally, I think she'd be happier with me; but she's made her choice."

Xavier made no reply to that, however, Micah noticed there was an added bounce to his step as he left, that wasn't evident when he had arrived. The doctor was definitely pleased with the outcome.


Gaea stood looking at her reflection in the mirror. It had been five hours since she'd left Micah at five-thirty that morning. Wednesday morning. He'd been here since Sunday. Four days. She felt as though she'd known him much longer. Being in love had a way of suspending time.

She wished she could go up on her rooftop and shout out to the world, "I love Micah Cavanaugh!"

Instead, she had to engage in a ruse which might prove fatal if not carried out correctly. How would she perform? Would Xavier sense her true feelings when he tried to pull her into his arms and her body, in automatic response, tensed?

She held up the jade blouse she was thinking of wearing. It made the brown-red tones in her skin look richer, deeper. It was one of those cropped tops which generously displayed the belly button. Xavier's blood began to boil whenever he saw her in anything remotely sexy. And that was the desired effect, wasn't it? To convince Xavier she'd come around to his way of thinking, she had to be nice to him. She had to behave like a besotted bride-to-be. At least in private. Hopefully, she'd only be playing to an audience of one.

The situation created a conundrum for her: was it so wrong for Xavier to want to further his race by siring offspring who could assimilate into human society more easily than their father? In some ways, it reminded her of her grandmother's life-threatening voyage to America. Omega, an impoverished refugee, seeking life, liberty and the pursuit of happiness in America. Wasn't that what Xavier wanted, as well? The chance to become more than he was?

His mistake was using her without her knowledge or consent. Plus, according to Taras, the Aquarians did not want the experiment to come to fruition. They regarded Xavier as a renegade whose actions needed curtailing.

Gaea wondered, though, what would happen if Xavier found out about the Aquarians' plot to foil his plans and take him back into the fold? Would he do something desperate?

And if he should learn that she willingly aided the Aquarians, would he take that as an act of betrayal? Exactly what did Aquarians do to traitors?

She went to the closet and hung the blouse back up. She selected, instead, a denim shirt and a pair of Levi's. Dressing sexy for Xavier might make him too suspicious. It was best to maintain the status quo.

Fifteen minutes later, she was walking into his outer office. Mrs. Jenkins looked up from her typing. "Hello, dear. Go right in, he's been seeing staff all morning and I'm sure he'd be pleased to see your pretty face."

"Thanks, Mrs. J. Love the haircut," Gaea said brightly.

"Do you, dear? Oh, I agonized over it for ages. But I thought it was time to get rid of the bun. Folks had started naming it." Her aquamarine eyes danced. "Dr. Cross said it makes me look like a teenager. He's quite the charmer, that one."

"I couldn't agree more," Gaea said, backing toward Xavier's office, her hand on the doorknob, ready to turn it should Mrs. Jenkins give her an opening.

Mrs. Jenkins resumed her typing and Gaea disappeared into Xavier's office.

She heard him in the bathroom when she entered the room. She sat on the corner of his desk and waited. He emerged a minute or so later, drying his hands on a paper towel. He tossed the crumpled paper towel into the trash receptacle next to the desk.

"Good morning," he said, his eyes looking her up and down. He walked over and kissed her cheek. "You're rather fetching this morning. Why aren't you out documenting the habits of the Atlantic dolphin?"

"I'm going out later this afternoon. There's something I needed to talk to you about."

"Oh? You've decided to take the Rosenstiel offer?"

"Well, yeah. I'd like to do that." She stood and faced him. "I've decided to marry you, Xavier. I realized that, aside from your past behavior, which you've promised never to repeat, everything else about our relationship was perfect. . . ."

"Yes," Xavier said excitedly. He went to her and drew her into his arms. His dark eyes were sparkling with delight when he gazed down into her upturned face. "Gaea," he breathed, "Gaea, that's what I've been trying to get you to see. I made a mistake. I'll always regret it. But we were destined to be together. I will cherish you, my darling. I *do* cherish you. I'll make you forget the foolish mistakes I've made. My life will be devoted to your happiness."

"I'll never forget, Xavier. Let's make that perfectly clear," Gaea was quick to tell him. She willed herself to relax in his arms. "But I had to face reality: I loved you once. And, even though I think what you did was reprehensible, I still have feelings for you. So I'm willing to forgive you and go through with our plans; that is, if you're serious about never cheating on me again."

"I am, darling. You're the only woman I want. You're the only woman I need."

He bent his head and kissed her lips, his own tender at first, then more demanding.

*He's going to sense how I really feel,* Gaea thought.

However, Xavier interpreted her reticence as shyness. He pressed her closer to his hardened body and raised his head to meet her eyes. "Don't worry darling. When we're married, I'll instruct you in all the pleasures you've been denying yourself."

He kissed her neck, ending with a flicker of his tongue, which sent chills throughout Gaea's body, because she thought he was going to bite her. Xavier smiled, and his brown eyes became lighter, almost hazel. **Gaea's** heartbeat thundered in her ears. She trembled.

She supposed his eyes changing colors like that was another part of his shape-changing abilities. The trick had caught her off guard, however, and she was slightly shaken. Her breath was coming in short rasps.

Xavier assumed her reaction was purely lustful. He grabbed her by the hips and pressed her to his tumescent member. "You're ripe, my dear. I believe you will be quite the tigress when the moment arrives."

Gaea was so repulsed, she didn't trust herself to speak.

Xavier kissed her on the lips one last time and released her.

"You'll have to go now, darling. I'm expecting Christopher Binder any minute, and if he sees you in this state, he'll know exactly what we've been up to."

He smiled warmly at her and walked her to the door. "Let's have dinner tonight to celebrate, shall we? Eight o'clock, at my place? I'll cook."

"All right," Gaea said. she raised her eyes to his and gave him a fair rendition of a smile.

Once outside though, she went straight to the ladies' room down the hall and rinsed her mouth out. After that, she splashed water on her face and dried off with a paper towel.

She was angry at Taras for putting her in this position. She wanted to go to him and tell him everything was off. She couldn't pretend to love Xavier. His touch made her nauseous.

"You're okay," she spoke to herself soothingly as she held onto the porcelain sink for support. "You can do this."

A toilet flushed, and a woman strode from one of the stalls. The smell of vomit wafted into the antiseptic air.

Sharon Baker nearly stumbled into the tall, metal trash receptacle standing next to the door, in her haste to leave.

Puzzled by the woman's behavior, Gaea stared after her. Why would the sight of her strike terror in the heart of a woman who'd brazenly slept with her fiancé?

She would never forget the look of triumph in Sharon Baker's eyes the night she'd caught her and Xavier in bed together. Now, where was her defiance? The woman had looked as if she was being pursued by a pack of ravenous wolves. Curious.

In his suite at the Hyatt, Taras reclined on the sofa, the phone to his ear.

Stuart Cohn, a local gold dealer, was on the other end of the line explaining that several buyers were interested in the gold coins Taras had brought him two days ago.

"We've decided to auction the pieces off, if that is satisfactory with you."

"When would the auction take place? My business in Key West is winding down," Taras told the dealer.

"We could hold it as early as tonight," Mr. Cohn eagerly offered. His voice sounded expectant. Taras supposed Mr. Cohn's commission would be considerable.

"All right," Taras said after a long pause. "Do it."

"We'll phone the interested parties right away. Will you be able to join us?"

"I'm afraid not," Taras said. "However, you can reach me here afterward."

"Sir . . ." Mr. Cohn began, reluctant to ring off, "my associates were curious as to where you obtained the coins."

"They've been in the family for years," was all Taras would say. "Good day, Mr. Cohn."

After hanging up, he rose and headed for the door. There was a good deal of daylight left. He had to see a man about a boat.

As he turned the corner, he froze. Serame was exiting the elevator a few yards away. He thought of ducking back into the suite and not answering the door when Serame came knocking. He had plenty to do today and he didn't wish a confrontation with Serame, who could be coming to see him for no other purpose.

He did not choose that course, however. He kept walking, meeting Serame midway.

"Hello, brother," he said. Their usual greeting was to press the palms of their right hands together. Taras held his out, but Serame did not. A clear indication of intent.

"I want you gone," Serame said, his eyes as dark as a stormy sea.

"You know I have to abide by the elders' recommendations," Taras said quietly.

A young couple, probably honeymooners, passed them in the hallway.

"We'll talk in my room," Taras suggested.

Serame nodded his agreement and followed Taras back to the suite.

Once inside, Taras locked the door and turned to Serame. "How long did it take you to find her?"

"Two years," Serame replied. He looked around him. "I'll never get used to all the chemicals the air-breathers use in the manufacturing of their furnishings. This place reeks."

"Yes," Taras agreed. He wanted to remain on the subject, however, which was Gaea. "When I told you about her, I never . . ."

"It never occurred to you that I had an agenda," Serame finished for him. "That's your problem, Taras: You have the mentality of a holy man. You're good to the very core."

He walked over to the picture window and peered out at the adjacent marina. Boaters were mooring their hundred-foot yacht at the dock. "Back to your question. It took me two years to find her. It took me much longer to establish my identity as Xavier Cross, though. I couldn't come to her as myself, could I? I had to become someone she could respect and revere. I worked hard to gain clout at the institute. When I did, I wooed her away from the University of California. It wasn't difficult; she has her grandfather's sensitive nature. She wanted to be near her family. So, I made her a generous offer. Soon after that, I began pursuing her for my true purpose."

"And all went well until you seduced a student and got caught in the act," Taras said.

"She told you?"

"No one had to tell me, Serame. Just as you know my nature, I know yours."

"Yes, well," Serame replied, looking Taras directly in the eyes, "what is it going to be? I don't believe I come under the rule of the elders any longer. I've been on my own for nearly fifteen years, during which time, the elders have kept me under close observation. But they can't stop me from marrying Gaea. Not if she consents to it. What could they do, kill me? It's against everything Aquarians believe in."

"It is against our beliefs; it isn't inconceivable to our baser natures," Taras corrected him.

Serame laughed. "Is that a threat?"

"It is not," Taras disavowed.

"What will you do, Taras?" Serame asked smugly. "You have more at stake here than a faceless committee of elders do. It was your slip-up that sent me halfway around the world in search of a dream. Is that why you're here? To clean up your mess?"

"You're still a boy, Serame," Taras spoke soothingly. "You don't realize the repercussions of your actions. All you know is your desire for power and control. You don't think, or care about, the people you'll harm in your quest."

"What have people ever done for us?" Serame asked with vehemence. "They hunted us, killed us, sent us into hiding because we were different; because we were superior to them . . ."

"You hate them so much, you want to be like them?" Taras said in wonderment. "That's demented thinking, Serame."

"Oh, is it? And how were you thinking when you seduced a teenaged girl, then left her high and dry when the elders discovered you were posing as a human? Exactly what were you thinking, Taras?"

"You don't have your facts straight," Taras informed him calmly. "I didn't return to Aquia because the elders decreed it. I returned because Omega told me to leave after she found out what I was. She was afraid of me. Just as Gaea will be afraid of you when you reveal yourself to her."

"Gaea's not that ignorant islander you lay with. She's a scientist. She will understand. And she loves me. Therein lies the reason why my experiment will succeed and yours failed."

"Experiment?" Taras said, angered for the first time. "My granddaughter is an *experiment* to you?"

He had crossed the room and had his hands around Serame's throat in a split second. Taller by two inches, and more powerful due to his advanced age, he lifted Serame by the collar. Serame's feet dangled above the floor. "I should kill you, you pup. I'd be doing both worlds a favor. You are not human and you're not Aquarian; you have become your own creation. An abomination."

Using one hand, he tossed Serame away from him, onto the sofa.

Serame stood a bit shakily.

"I have what I came for," he said, looking up at Taras. "I now know who my opponent is. It's you, not the elders."

Serame walked to the door. "I'd be surprised if they even know you're here. You came because of love. Love!" He laughed incredulously.

"Love is the most important thing in this world or the next," Taras readily admitted. "Yes, I'm here because I love my granddaughter, and I'd like to save her from the fate you have in mind for her. And I'll do it, Serame. Be forewarned. You will not have her."

"You are mistaken, old man," Serame said, a smile, as poisonous as a cobra's, contorting his handsome features. "She just told me today: The wedding's back on."

"You're lying," Taras accused him. However, he had his anger in check now. "Gaea is too smart to fall for your insincere promises. She'll see through you."

"No, old man. She's forgiven me. She ditched the air-breather she was infatuated with and has come back to me, ready, no, *hot* to get the ceremony over with so that we can consummate our union. Isn't that wonderful? She will make a splendid wife and mother."

"Get out of my sight," Taras said, his voice barely audible.

At that moment, he had but to think it, and Serame's lifeless body would be lying on the suite's floor, his blood gushing copiously from it in gelatinous pools.

Serame left.

Taras sat down on the nearest chair, drained.

Gaea thought she would never come to a juncture in her life when it would be difficult for her to concentrate on her work. However, as she spied the white-sided Atlantic dolphin through her binoculars later that afternoon, she realized, she'd reached it.

The skiff rocked with the moderate waves and the southerly winds felt good on her face. The sky was azure, dotted with white, cumulus clouds. She couldn't have ordered a more perfect day.

The dolphins were romping, having just fed on a school of grunts, and some of them were of a mind to come close to the skiff and check out the human on board.

She took photos of these curious ones.

She was snapping photos of a large male, when it occurred to her that in the ten years she'd been in the field, beginning with her graduate studies, she'd seen thousands of dolphins. Now she wondered how many of those dolphins had been Aquarians in disguise. Was what Taras had said about his having kept an eye on her over the years true? He had no reason to lie.

No use worrying the thought, she decided. If she picked apart every detail of her encounters with dolphins in the past decade, trying to see significance in trivial occurrences, she'd drive herself crazy.

It was best to go on with her work as if she were unaware

of the Aquarians' existence. Best for them. Definitely best for her peace of mind.

She put her camera down and picked up the binoculars. In the distance was a large racing boat. She'd noticed it a few minutes ago, but it was farther out to sea then. Now, it was closing in on her, which piqued her curiosity.

Hers had been the only boat within her eyesight until she'd spotted the speedboat. Why would it be approaching her now, and at such high speeds?

Thinking it was better to be cautious, she stood and started the motor. She wasn't getting much done today, anyway. The outboard motor sputtered, but caught, and she sat back down and began steering the skiff toward shore. That meant her back would be to the oncoming boat, so she took quick glances behind her as she steered.

The boat was about two hundred yards away now, and the driver hadn't reduced his speed. She could see the boat's occupants clearly. Four sun-tanned youths. Two males. Two females. All in swimsuits. One of the boys was drinking a beer from a long-necked bottle. Heavy metal music was blaring from a boom box.

The driver came within six feet of her before veering off to the left. Water sprayed inside the skiff, soaking Gaea and her camera equipment.

The boy was coming back around for another pass at her, egged on by his inebriated companions.

She wiped her face with the bottom of her T-shirt, fleetingly chided herself for not wearing a life jacket and gunned the motor. Drunken boaters. Where was the Coast Guard when you needed them?

Peering behind her, she was horrified to see the boy who'd been drinking the beer throw the empty bottle at the skiff. The bottle fell a few feet short of her boat.

"Are you nuts?" she shouted, certain they couldn't hear her above the racket the boats' motors were making.

The driver of the high-powered racing boat came within three feet of her this time; the backdraft almost tipped the skiff over. Gaea had to lie flat on the bottom of the boat in order to balance its weight. Bile rose in her throat, but she swallowed it, afraid that if she succumbed to illness at this point, she might risk losing her life. She had to be prepared for them when they came back.

Pulling herself up, she peered over the side to see the racing boat coming in for the kill. This time, the driver didn't appear as if he intended to swerve. He'd reduced his speed somewhat. However his course was straight-on.

When he got within twenty feet of her, Gaea sprang from the skiff, over the side.

She dove five feet, kicking her feet so as to put some distance between her and the skiff. Coming to the surface, she saw the racing boat crash into the skiff broadside.

The skiff capsized. The racing boat faltered. The driver tried the engine, but it wouldn't engage. In the abrupt silence, Gaea heard one of the girls wail, "You idiot. How are we supposed to get back to shore?"

As she floated in the Atlantic Ocean, miles away from land, Gaea wondered that herself. Then, she felt something on her leg and a sleek body brushed up against her. She blinked. The saltwater was stinging her eyes.

A seven-foot white-sided Atlantic dolphin swam beneath her right arm, raising it. Its musical series of squeaks seemed to serve to buoy her confidence. He let her wrap her arms around him and hold on to him as he swam.

Gaea turned her head to the left, her face lying on his body as he swam, in order to avoid inhaling and swallowing sea water. She floated as he swam, his streamlined body shooting through the water at thirty-five miles per hour. Gaea had an image of how they must appear to an onlooker: like a mother whale with her calf.

She fretted about his destination. Where was he taking her? But she had little choice in the matter. The skiff was capsized, and she couldn't risk swimming over to the speedboat, whose occupants had tried to kill her. Seeing they had failed, they might try to rectify the situation.

For most of the ride, she kept her eyes shut, but from time to time, she would look up and find that he'd taken a southwestern direction. That raised her spirits. If he kept in that direction, they'd end up on the shores of Key West.

She didn't know how long she'd been holding on to him, but her arms were growing weak and, suddenly, her grip loosened and she was floundering in the ocean.

She held her breath as she sank. She kicked with her legs, hoping to break the surface, but her arms were numb and without her arms she couldn't get any propulsion.

She knew she could hold her breath well enough to give her sufficient time to get back to the surface. But unless she had some way to get back to the surface, she would still drown eventually.

Looking around, frantically, for the dolphin, she was unable to see him. Somewhere in the back of her mind, she'd believed the dolphin wasn't actually a dolphin, but an Aquarian, sent by Taras to keep an eye on her. Now, in her panic, she wondered if it had been just a dolphin all along. And she was drowning. Steadily falling to the depths of the Atlantic.

# Eighteen

The kids in the speedboat were on spring break from Michigan State. Jared Clarke, twenty-one; his girlfriend, Courtney Silvermann, also twenty-one; Billy Strieber, twenty, and his date for the holiday, Jane Richer, nineteen.

After Billy rammed the skiff, and they found themselves adrift in the Atlantic, their alcohol-induced recklessness was transformed into genuine panic. They'd never been in trouble with the law before. Jared was premed, with a 4.0 average. Courtney was a political science major. Billy's father was a well-known novelist and Jane's mother, a member of the House of Representatives.

Jared heaved over the side of the boat. He felt as though his stomach had turned inside-out. Courtney went to him. "We've got to do something," she said in a low voice so as not to be heard by Billy and Jane. "Billy's a lunatic. He killed that woman."

Jane, a petite blonde, was huddled in a corner, crying. "Oh, my God. Oh, my God. Oh, my God. Oh, my God. Billy, you killed her."

"*I* killed her?" Billy said, disgusted. "You were all goading me on. If I go down, you all go down with me."

Jared straightened up and faced Billy. "Isn't there a radio aboard? We've got to call someone for help."

"Someone?" Billy said sarcastically. "You mean the Coast Guard, don't you, Jared?"

He walked over and aggressively shoved Jared in the chest with both hands. "I'm not going to jail for this. It was an accident, do you hear me? An accident!"

Jared gingerly rubbed his chest. "All right. It was an accident. But we still have to get someone out here to look for that woman, Billy."

"Why? She's gone. Do you see her anywhere? She's fish food, man."

"Yeah well, we're going to be fish food, too, if we don't get a tow back to Key West. How do you think we're supposed to get back, Billy? We've got to use the radio."

"No!" Billy shouted, spittle flying from the corner of his mouth.

He purposefully headed toward the radio, but Jared tackled him from behind. They fell to the floor with a resounding thud, and Courtney stumbled out of the way as they rolled from one side of the deck to the next in each boy's struggle to overpower the other.

Jared gained the advantage. Straddling Billy, he hit him on the side of the head with all his might, rendering him unconscious.

Getting off Billy, he looked up at Courtney. "Find something to tie this fool up with."

Jared got on the radio and soon, he was speaking with the Coast Guard dispatcher.

As best he could recall, he gave the Coast Guard their coordinates, explaining what had happened.

"We haven't been able to spot the woman. I saw her jump just before her boat was capsized. That's the last thing I saw of her. Yeah, I believe I can describe her. Now? Well, she was a black woman. Small-boned. Alone? Yeah, she was alone. The boat? Maybe a twenty-footer. Small. Outboard motor. A name on the boat? Wait a minute, I'll go look."

He put the handset down and went over to the side of the speedboat to crane his neck in the direction of the overturned skiff.

Going back to the radio and speaking into the handset, he said, "I can make out the word *institution* that's all."

"Could it be Reed?" the dispatcher asked. "There's a local oceanographic institution in the area."

"Maybe," Jared said, frustrated. "Probably. Look, man, get somebody out here, okay. . . ."

"Someone's already on the way," the dispatcher informed him crisply. "In the meanwhile, I have some pertinent questions for you. I'll need all the names of those aboard your boat. . . ."


Gaea didn't know how deep she'd fallen, however, when she looked upward, the surface appeared very far away. The light was growing dimmer. She couldn't discern whether her eyesight was failing or sunlight simply didn't illuminate this depth so readily.

A soporific malaise invaded her body. It would be so easy to close her eyes and sleep. No more struggling against the water pressure; her lungs were burning now. She wouldn't be able to hold her breath much longer.

She was beginning to see brilliant colors all around her. The chemicals in her brain were making her see mirages. Images that couldn't possibly exist in real life.

A beautiful woman with brown skin, a white sarong covering her sleek, lithe body swam toward her, a look of utter love in her golden eyes. Everything around her was so sharp, highly defined now.

*So this is how it feels to die,* she thought.

A man appeared behind the woman, swimming swiftly toward Gaea.

He wore only a white loincloth.

He was brown-skinned too. With long, dark, flowing dreads, which seemed like live snakes in the buoyancy of the ocean. His brown eyes looked into Gaea's and she stopped struggling. But, at the moment she ceased fighting the water pressure, and let go, her body began sinking farther into the depths.

The man swam underneath her and took her into his arms. He then covered her mouth with his. Gaea allowed the darkness to take her.


Micah paced the floor of his suite. Gaea was supposed to have phoned two hours ago. He hadn't been able to reach her at the institute or at her place. He was loath to concern her parents.

Under normal circumstances, he would not have been worried, but these were not normal circumstances. Xavier Cross was unpredictable. What if he'd seen through Gaea's profession of undying affection and gone into a violent rage?

Micah couldn't bear the waiting. He had to do something. Taras. Gaea had mentioned he was staying at the Hyatt on Front Street.


Taras stood on the dock behind the Hyatt awaiting the fifty-foot yacht slowly making its way into the marina. Night was falling and the bright orange sun hung low in the western sky.

He could make out four figures on the deck of the yacht. Three males and a female. Another man was in the wheelhouse, piloting the boat.

"Taras?"

Taras turned. He recognized the young man right away. Micah Cavanaugh.

Micah sprinted across the wooden planks. "Taras, do you know where Gaea is?" he asked without preamble.

Taras didn't have to see Micah's face clearly in order to know how anxious he was. Fear was a palpable emotion coming, like waves, off of him.

"I haven't seen her all day," he replied truthfully. "She told me, yesterday, that she was going out to dolphin-watch this afternoon."

"She would've been back by now," was Micah's response to

that suggestion. He stood within three feet of Taras. "Look, she told me about your plans. I believe they could put her in danger. What are you all waiting on anyway? If you're going to take Xavier back to wherever he came from, do it. Do it, and allow Gaea to get on with her life."

"That's precisely what I'm doing," Taras said quietly. He inclined his head in the direction of the yacht. "My associates have arrived."

"Good," Micah said. "But that still doesn't answer my question. Where is Gaea?"

Gaea opened her eyes. Her limbs felt miraculously heavy. That meant she was no longer in the ocean.

When her eyes came into focus, she saw a ceiling. It was above her, so it had to be a ceiling. It was also, however, a gigantic mural. The painting depicted a large bottlenose dolphin with an exquisite nude, brown-skinned woman on its back. The style reminded her of Michelangelo Buonarroti's painting of the religious figures on the Sistine Chapel.

She wished she had her camera.

Raising her arms to see if they were back in working order, she was pleased to see that they were. So were her legs.

She sat up in bed. The down comforter fell away and she saw that she was nude. Not a stitch of clothing.

The room was small with just the bed, a bureau built into the right wall, a minuscule closet and a nightstand next to the bed.

A cabin on a ship. She knew now that the feeling of being slightly off-balance was caused by the gentle rocking of the boat she was on, and not because she was dizzy.

She got out of bed and went to the closet, hoping there was something in there she could use to cover herself with.

The closet was full of women's clothing. She chose a pair of slacks that was a bit short on her, but otherwise fit fine, and a black T-shirt that was dark enough to conceal the absence of a bra.

On the floor of the closet were several pairs of designer shoes. All of them too small for her size eight feet.

She needed to use the bathroom, so she went to the door and turned the doorknob. It wasn't locked. That was a good sign. Whoever had pulled her from the drink didn't wish her any harm.

Stepping into the hallway, which was lit by a line of decorative lights, she paused to listen. She could faintly hear people conversing to her left. She went in that direction, thinking that the sooner they knew she was awake, the sooner she could get back to Key West. She was sure that someone must realize she was not on the skiff by now, and they were probably frantic with worry. She remembered telling Micah she would phone him after she returned from dolphin-watching this afternoon.

Without a watch, which she'd lost somewhere in the Atlantic Ocean, she had no way of telling what time it was; however, her body clock told her it was considerably later than the time she'd promised to phone.

Micah was probably under the misapprehension that Xavier was somehow involved in her absence, when it was a boatload of drunken kids who'd been the cause of her near-death experience.

At the end of the hall, there was a set of steps leading to the upper deck. She took them, and emerged in the wheelhouse of the boat. A man sat at the wheel, his back to her.

He turned around suddenly, as if he'd heard her. Gaea was certain he couldn't have heard her. There had been no creaking of the stairs and besides, she was barefoot.

He was a black man. Around twenty-five, with short, natural dark brown hair and brown eyes. He smiled at her.

"It's the mermaid," he said, his deep voice suppressing a chuckle. "Hey!" he shouted forward.

Gaea peered straight ahead through the glass enclosure. Three men and a woman were on deck, sitting on cushioned built-in seats. They looked in the direction of the wheelhouse.

Gaea's heart began hammering in her chest. Beyond the four-some were lights and a marina. Key West?

She ran from the wheelhouse, onto the deck.

The lone female of the foursome approached her. It was the woman she'd seen in the vision she'd had when she was drowning.

She was tiny. Perhaps five-two. Gaea glanced down at the slacks she was wearing. They undoubtedly belonged to this petite woman.

"How wonderful to see you up and about," the woman said in a Spanish-accented voice. Gaea thought there was another, familiar, patois beneath the Spanish. Yes, her abuela put the same spin on her pronunciation of English words.

"I am Catia," the woman said. "Taras is my brother."

"I'm . . ." Gaea began.

"You are Gaea," Catia said warmly as she reached for Gaea's hand.

She led Gaea over to the three men who'd risen from their seats and were eyeing her with interest.

"Gaea, these robust men are my sons: Saurus, Annias and Deocles. You've already met, Jarus, my eldest."

"I can see the resemblance," Gaea said. Indeed, they were all well over six feet tall, well-built and, except for Jarus, wore dreadlocks in varying lengths. Annias was the man who'd breathed life back into her while they were in the depths.

They all took turns warmly grasping her by the hand and holding it a while before letting go of her.

Gaea felt a bit as though she were under a microscope. Here she was meeting her Aquarian relatives. What must they think of her? Was she to be looked upon as an oddity? A freak to be ogled and pitied? Taras had mentioned that the elders had promoted a sense of racial superiority in Aquarians. Did they feel she was just one step above a tree monkey?

Catia continued to hold her right hand in hers. But, after her sons had been introduced to Gaea, she stepped in front of Gaea and said, "May I embrace you, child?"

Gaea was relieved to be asked. Catia opened her arms to her and Gaea walked into them.

From a scientific point of view, Gaea might chalk the feeling she experienced up to pheromones, or some other natural pleasure-inducing chemical found in the body. Whatever it was, Catia's embrace gave her a safe, warm glow all over.

"You and your father are our blood," Catia whispered in her ear. "Taras has longed to be with you. And whom Taras loves, we love."

For Gaea, those words cemented their bond. Family, she understood. She felt the same way about her parents and grandparents. And Micah. Micah, who was probably going out of his head with worry.

"Thank you," Gaea said of Catia's sentiments.

Their eyes met. "When this is over with," Catia said, "I hope you will visit us. Mother and father wish to meet you."

Gaea didn't reply because at that moment, Jarus cut the engine and his three brothers ran to secure the boat to the dock. Catia was looking toward the dock with a smile on her lips. Pointing, she said, "Look."

Gaea raised her eyes to see two men running toward them, their heavy footfalls pounding the wooden planks of the dock.


Xavier was at home when he got the call from Capt. Benjamin Abercrombie of the U.S. Coast Guard. Capt. Abercrombie had gotten Xavier's home number from the receptionist out at Reed.

"Dr. Cross," Capt. Abercrombie began in his southern-accented baritone, "I'm sorry to bother you at home, but we have a report of a missing boater and we'd like to check some facts with you. There was an accident this afternoon out near Sand Key. The officers on the scene have identified a skiff belonging to your institution. Can you tell me if any of your personnel were out in that vicinity this afternoon?"

Xavier's mind had already gone to Gaea. He knew she had taken the skiff out near Sand Key.

"What do you mean, 'if any'? You identified the skiff; surely you have Dr. Maxwell aboard your boat by now?"

Capt. Abercrombie paused on the other end. He didn't know how to proceed. Dr. Cross sounded very upset. "Well, no, sir, we do not. The occupants of the other boat that was involved in the accident say they saw a woman go into the water. Is Dr. Maxwell a black female? Small-boned?"

"Yes, yes!" Xavier said angrily. "What are you doing to find her, Captain?"

"Our divers have been down a number of times, Dr. Cross. They've found no sign of Dr. Maxwell. I'm very sorry."

"I'm coming out there," Xavier said.

"Only authorized personnel are allowed in the area, Dr. Cross. I'm afraid that's out of the question."

"Dr. Maxwell is my fiancée, Captain Abercrombie. I'm coming," Xavier informed him and hung up.

Xavier stood and began peeling off his clothes. Sand Key was only a few miles away. He could swim there swifter than a boat could get him there.

Night had fallen. He sprinted from his back porch and onto the beach. The quarter moon looked like a suspended sickle in the dark sky.

His feet had barely touched the water before he transformed into a great, blue porpoise, and pointed his beak eastward. Gaea could *not* be dead. To come this close to having his dreams fulfilled, then to be thwarted by fate? He wouldn't believe it. Not until he saw her with his own eyes.

The divers, with their artificial breathing apparatus, were hindered by their man-made gadgets. They could have missed her. And with Gaea's Aquarian DNA, there could be a chance of saving her if she hadn't been drowned too long.

He swam with determination. He swam as though the woman he loved was in peril.

Arriving on the scene, he swam beneath the U.S. Coast Guard trawler. He heard the vibrating footsteps of several men aboard. A couple of wet-suited divers were below. They hadn't spotted him yet, and, even if they did, they'd see a porpoise. An unusual species in these waters, but they probably wouldn't be aware of that distinction.

He dove to forty feet, then fifty. He scoured the bottom. No sign of Gaea. After a few minutes, he had to go up for air, and as he was rising, out of the corner of his eye, he spotted a shiny object. Cruising in a circle, he saw a watch, lying on the bottom.

He transformed back to his human form and picked up the watch. It was the silver, water-resistant Seiko Gaea wore. He dropped the watch and it floated back to the bottom.

Where was she? Transforming into the porpoise, he swam to the surface and took great gulps of air. The trawler was moving away. They'd given up the search.

They were towing the skiff back to Key West.

Xavier saw no reason to maintain his porpoise form when there were no humans around to be astonished by the appearance of a nude male in the middle of Sand Key. He changed back to his human identity. The shape had certain advantages that the porpoise form did not share, such as hands. Also, being Aquarian, he wasn't affected by water pressure; therefore, he could search the bottom without fear of Caisson disease, or the bends.

He swam to the bottom, which was thirty feet down in some spots and upwards of sixty in others. His eyes had adjusted to the dimness. He swam from one end of the cay to the other, hoping to spot Gaea. At times, praying.

However, after three hours of searching, he'd come up with nothing except the watch. He knew Gaea had had her camera equipment with her. She kept it in a watertight case. Perhaps the Coast Guard divers had recovered it.

He turned toward Key West, the bitter gall of defeat eating at him. If Gaea had drowned, then where was her body? Had it been taken by some sea creature? It was a possibility. Sharks weren't unknown in these waters; although he hadn't seen any the whole while he'd been out here. The dolphins? Dolphins were known to keep the dead bodies of their companions afloat for days out of their apparent confusion concerning the nature of death. Until, finally, the body began to decompose and then they would let go of it and allow it to sink to the depths.

However, he'd never heard of a dolphin performing the act on a human's behalf.

One could never predict the behavior of dolphins, though. They could have carried Gaea's body off somewhere.

Or . . . an even better possibility was that they'd aided her before she drowned. They'd observed her for months now as she conducted her study of them. They could have taken a liking to her, and when she'd gone into the water, they had helped her get to shore.

Changing back to the porpoise, whose body was aerodynamically designed for speed in the water, Xavier vowed to swim the shoreline until he saw some sign that Gaea had survived.

"I'm never letting you out of my sight again," Micah murmured as he hugged Gaea to his chest.

"You won't have to," Taras said, coming up behind them.

Earlier, he, Catia and her four sons had left Gaea and Micah alone while they went below.

"For all intents and purposes, you're dead, Gaea. Our people report that the Coast Guard has given up the search for you."

Micah and Gaea gave each other knowing looks.

Gaea looked her grandfather in the eyes. "How do you suppose Xavier will take the news?"

"That remains to be seen," Taras said wisely. His golden-brown eyes narrowed. "That's no longer your concern, however. You've been through quite enough. I want you to leave town with Micah. Go to New York. Get married. Go on a honeymoon. Just go. When your body doesn't wash up on the beach, Xavier will be forced to make a decision. Either stay here and be ostracized by his people forever, or return to Aquia with the rest of us. He must, however, be firmly convinced that you're dead.

So you must leave at once. Don't go back to your place to pack. Simply go."

"But what about my folks?"

"Don't worry, I'll go to them and tell them you're fine and that you'll contact them in a few days."

Micah's hand was warm at the base of her spine.

"Let's do it, Gaea," he encouraged her.

"What'll I do for ID?" Gaea asked. "I can't get a plane ticket without ID."

Taras produced a ladies' purse from behind his back. "Use Catia's. You're both about the same complexion, nearly the same height . . ."

"I'm four inches taller . . ."

"It'll work, Gaea," Micah said. "A busy reservations clerk isn't going to pay that close attention to height."

"If this is going to work, you have to move fast," Taras warned.

"Okay," Gaea said.

Catia came forward and took her by the hand. "Come little one, you need more appropriate clothing, and I have an idea as to how we can change your appearance so that if anyone who knows you should see you, they won't recognize you."

Fifteen minutes later, Micah sped out of the Hyatt's parking lot in the white Miata with a heavily made-up redhead, curly hair down to her shoulders, at his side.


The next morning, Thursday, Taras phoned Xavier's office and was told by Mrs. Jenkins that Dr. Cross wouldn't be in today, he was in mourning for his fiancée.

Her voice had broken in midsentence. "Are you a personal friend? Did you know Dr. Maxwell?" She sounded as though she needed to talk.

"I knew her," Taras told her. "I was sorry to hear about the accident on the local news last night."

"Accident!" Mrs. Jenkins said, outraged. "Those kids were

drinking. The paper said that if Gaea doesn't make an appearance soon, alive and well, they'll be charged with manslaughter. I want them prosecuted to the full extent of the law."

She sniffed. "Dr. Cross is at home if you'd like to try and reach him there," she said politely.

"Thank you, I will," Taras said and hung up.

He smiled to himself as he replaced the receiver. The ruse was a success, so far.

At ten after eleven, he arrived on Xavier's doorstep.

He rang the bell. No one appeared.

He rang again and waited. Still nothing.

Walking around the house, to the back patio door, he peered inside. Xavier was sitting at the kitchen table nursing a bottle of bourbon.

Taras tried the door, it was unlocked. He opened the door and strode inside. "You know we can't get intoxicated."

"It gives me a slight buzz," Xavier said without looking up. "What are you doing here? Shouldn't you be with the bereaved family, or don't they want a fish-man in their midst?"

"Maybe you are drunk," Taras said. "No, I'm here to tell you we're departing for Aquia tonight. There's no longer any reason to stay. Gaea is gone. My son doesn't want anything to do with me."

"So why tell me this?" Xavier said, looking up. His eyes were bloodshot. Not from the liquor, but from lack of sleep.

"Just following instructions," Taras said mildly. He walked over to the sliding glass doors and gazed out at the calm sea. He turned. "You're welcome to return home, Serame."

"How noble of you," Xavier said sarcastically.

Taras laughed. "Nobility has nothing to do with it. You're one of us. You will always be one of us. You can live here among the air-breathers, but you'll never be one of them. Gaea loved you. You can cherish that memory. Even though you didn't deserve her love, you had it. Has the experience taught you nothing?"

"Do you want to hear something ironic?" Xavier returned,

rising from his chair. "Last night, when I was searching the waters around Sand Key for her body, I felt something I'd never felt before. I am bereft, Taras."

He threw the glass he'd been drinking from onto the floor. The glass shattered, sending shards in every direction.

"You're disappointed because your experiment failed?" Taras asked with no censure in his tone.

Tears sat in Xavier's eyes. "No. I'm angry at myself because I truly did love Gaea, the woman. All I could see was my goal. I put my emotions in a box and locked it. I told myself she was just a means to an end. And now, I find I don't want to live without her. Oh, God, Taras. I had a miracle in the palm of my hand and I let it slip through my fingers."

He fell to his knees, sobbing.


Gaea and Micah arrived at his apartment on the Upper West side early Thursday morning, whereupon they fell into bed and slept until noon.

Gaea awoke before Micah and went in search of something to eat. She found his refrigerator better stocked than she'd expected. He had fresh milk and eggs. Cheddar cheese.

In a few minutes, she'd whipped up two omelets, made some toast and brewed a pot of coffee.

Micah came into the kitchen wiping the sleep from his eyes.

He smiled when he saw her, attired in one of his big T-shirts, holding a plate of food aloft in each hand.

"I guess I didn't dream it and you did sleep in my bed last night," he joked, taking one of the plates.

"Yeah, that was me snoring my head off," Gaea returned.

Micah gave her a peck on the cheek.

"What was that? We haven't been living together eight hours yet and I'm reduced to a pitiful kiss like that?"

"Get real, girl. This morning breath is kicking. Let me kill the dragon first."

Laughing, Gaea went to sit at the table. Micah sat across from her and poured coffee into both their cups.

"The first thing we have to do today," he suggested, his brown eyes on her face, "is to go shopping. You can max-out my credit cards."

"I only need a few things to last me until I can go back home," Gaea said, after which she took a sip of the coffee.

"You'll need a wedding dress," Micah said quietly. He watched her. "We also have to get a license and blood tests."

"You want to elope?" Her expression was shy all of a sudden.

"No, I want our parents to be there. I'd like Thad to come. The main thing is: I want you to be happy," Micah said, clasping her hand across the table.

"As long as you're with me, I'll be happy," Gaea assured him.

For the next few weeks the talk on campus at Reed Oceanographic Institution concerned the tragic death of Dr. Gaea Maxwell and the subsequent disappearance of Dr. Xavier Cross, her heartbroken fiancé. Sharon Baker was secretly relieved and hoped he was gone for good.

On her return to Key West, Gaea explained to the authorities that she'd been rescued by the crew of a Cuban trawler fishing, illegally, in Florida waters. It had taken her weeks to secure passage on a boat returning to the U.S. And, since she refused to press charges, the Michigan State students' sentences were reduced from manslaughter to time served and they were fined and sent home. Gaea figured three weeks in jail was punishment enough for one drunken episode which hadn't resulted in anyone's death or dismemberment.

On May thirtieth, the backyard of Cameron and Lara Maxwell's house on Simonton Street was resplendent with a seven foot arch, amply decorated with white roses. On either side of the arch were rows of whitewashed folding chairs.

Cam had made certain the lawn was like a velvety green carpet and the aroma of orange blossom pervaded the air.

The weather was warm, if slightly breezy. The sky, a cloudless crystalline blue.

Gaea was upstairs getting into the simple, white empire-waist gown. Her mother, her grandmother and Solange were helping her by riding commentary on everything she did.

When she started to put on the dress before her hose, her mother said, "If you put on your hose first, you won't risk wrinkling the dress."

She was going to wear her short hair combed away from her face in her normal style. But Solange suggested, "Why not wear a band of orange blossoms?" She looked tearful. But, as always, she was beautiful in her sky-blue bridesmaid dress with pouf sleeves, a sweetheart neckline and a hem that fell two inches above her knees.

Gaea dutifully placed the band, which she thought a bit garish, on her head.

Finally, when she stepped into the white pumps, her grandmother almost screamed, "You forgot the garter!"

"I don't have a garter, Gran," Gaea told her.

Aghast, Omega said. "Don't go downstairs yet. I'll find you one."

For Gaea, that was the last straw. Her nerves were frayed and they weren't making things easier.

"Hold it," she said, looking first at her mother, then Solange and her grandmother. "This is my day. And I say I don't need a garter." She reached up and removed the band of orange blossoms. "And I don't want anything on my head. I love you all, but I'm already a bundle of nerves and your constant adjustments of my decisions are making me crazy."

Laughing, Lara said, "Oh, sugar, we didn't mean anything by it. We're just so happy for you, we don't know how to act."

"You're right," Solange said, running her fingers through Gaea's hair to create the tousled do Gaea liked. "Who needs those dorky orange blossoms anyway?"

Tears, rolled down her cheeks. "I'm losing my best friend. What'll I do when you're in New York, teaching at Benson College and having babies with Micah? Listen to me. I'm so selfish."

"You're not selfish," Gaea told her. "I'm gonna miss you, too, girl. But we'll visit each other often, you'll see."

"Well I have something that will cheer you up," Omega said. She went into her purse and produced a long, white envelope. "It's from your grandfather. He made me promise to give it to you before you left for your honeymoon in Santo Domingo."

"Where is Grandpa?"

When Omega got closer, she said in a low voice, "It's from your *other* grandfather." Taras had delivered the letter, along with Omega's box of memorabilia that Xavier had stolen, before they'd set sail for Aquia.

Gaea accepted the envelope and looked at the three women surrounding her. "Could I have a moment alone?"

They readily agreed, each of them planting a kiss on her cheek as they filed out of the room.

Gaea sat at the vanity and opened the envelope.

A note from Taras read:

*My dear Gaea: I wish I could be with you on your wedding day. But we both know that it is more than miles that separate us. I love you. I think you know that. If you should want to see me again, there are a few humans who know of us and who can get a message to me. One of them is your soon-to-be-husband's godfather, Thaddeus Powers. Enclosed is a wedding gift to you and Micah. It is the proceeds from a little something that had been in the family for quite a while. May you always be happy. Gramps.*

Gaea unfolded the other slip of paper in the envelope. It was a cashier's check in the amount of five hundred, forty-three thousand dollars.

She felt faint as she sat on the spindly chair in front of the vanity.

Micah had reserved the same suite at the Marquesa that he'd occupied on his first visit to Key West.

After spending the requisite time at the reception, he and Gaea had slipped away, leaving their guests to party without them.

At the door of the suite, Micah swept Gaea up into his arms and carried her across the threshold.

She wrapped her arms around his neck and rained kisses on his cheek. He grinned infectiously, that sole dimple doing overtime duty. Joy infected their hearts, their minds, their souls.

Gaea hadn't stopped grinning since Micah had said, "I do."

Her marital status was a source of sheer happiness for her.

Micah looked so handsome in his tuxedo. The orchestra had played beautifully. Her mother, grandmother and Micah's mother, Lily, had cried throughout the ceremony. Her father had given her away, saying, "This isn't a loan now, you've got to keep her forever."

To which Micah had replied, "That's my intention, sir."

Thad and June had been there, looking very much in love. Drs. Casenove and Potemski had barely been able to keep their eyes off each other. Love was the order of the day.

Now, she and Micah were alone, at last.

He put her back down and she looked around the suite. A bottle of sparkling grape juice was chilling on ice next to the bed. She knew it was grape juice because Micah knew she didn't drink champagne, and he was considerate like that.

The bed was turned down, and red rose petals were sprinkled on the white sheet. She walked over to the bed. A sheer white lace gown lay across the foot of the bed.

She picked it up and held it against her. "It's lovely."

Micah took it from her and placed it back on the bed. "Not half as lovely off, as it will be on."

He bent his head and nuzzled her neck.

"I'm, suddenly, very nervous," Gaea admitted. She smiled into his dark brown eyes. "I was so brazen the night I came here and threw myself at you. Now I'm nervous. Why is that?"

"Maybe it was because you knew, instinctively, that as a gentleman, I would put the brakes on any antics that night," Micah said, his voice husky. He kissed her lips. He tasted, faintly, of the champagne he'd drunk at the reception.

Gaea sighed when the kiss ended. She felt intoxicated with desire. That wasn't the problem. She wanted Micah so much, she was in pain. But she was afraid that, due to her inexperience, she would disappoint him. What if after thirty years of waiting, she was an absolute dud in bed?

"You know what your problem is, doc?" Micah said as his hands were undoing the line of covered buttons on the back of her dress.

"Tell me," Gaea said. "I welcome any diagnosis."

"You think too much," he said. He turned her around so that he could more easily get at those buttons.

Gaea stood, giggling. "Don't rip it. I want our daughter to be able to wear it someday."

"Too many buttons," Micah grumbled good-naturedly.

Finished, at last, he pulled the dress up, over Gaea's head and she stood before him in a white teddy, sheer stockings, a garter belt holding them up and white pumps with three-inch heels.

"Now that's what I call a wedding gift," he said.

Gaea, in turn, removed his bow tie, cummerbund and shirt, taking her time. "Can't you go any faster?" Micah joked.

"I like the anticipation," Gaea told him.

"Well, I've been anticipating for some time now. I want to *participate,*" Micah said.

Gaea ran her hands over his bare chest. "Micah, you're so beautifully made, I wish I could sculpt, just to be able to sculpt you."

"I'm already putty in your hands, sugar. Mold me," he said, as he pulled her into his arms and against his hard body.

He kissed the side of her neck, working his way downward to her shoulders. Gaea reached up and pulled the right strap of her teddy down off her shoulder. Micah kissed the spot.

She threw her head back and he trailed kisses down the length of her neck, ending with his face in her cleavage.

Her breathing was labored, and a fire had begun to burn in her nether regions. Micah pulled her closer to him and she could feel his erection on her thigh. She burned hotter still and her nipples hardened.

Micah gently pulled the teddy down to her waist, and the air caught in his throat when he saw her voluptuous breasts, the nipples brown and pointing north. He took one in his mouth and touched it with the tip of his tongue.

Gaea arched her back in her ecstasy. "Micah, I want you now . . ."

"Not yet," Micah said.

He took the other nipple between his lips and slowly manipulated the bud with his tongue.

Gaea moaned.

Micah pulled on the bottom half of the teddy and the garment fell to the floor. Gaea stood in just a skimpy pair of white bikini panties, and the stockings with the garter belt still around her waist. She'd kicked the shoes off when Micah had taken her nipple into his mouth.

Trying not to seem too anxious, Micah pulled her panties downward and once they were past her hips, Gaea sat on the bed and he removed the panties, the garter belt and the stockings in one movement. Gaea scooted back on the bed, looking into his eyes all the while.

"Good God," was all Micah could say as he hurried out of his shoes, socks, slacks and jockey shorts.

Gaea's gaze went south. "Oh my," she sighed.

Micah knelt on the bed, crawling slowly toward her. "You can't get any further in the corner. The bed isn't that big."

Gaea laughed and launched herself at him, grabbing him

around the neck and pulling him down on top of her. "It feels so natural, being naked with you."

"Good, because I plan to have you naked quite often," Micah said, and kissed her mouth.

As the kiss deepened, Gaea's legs wrapped themselves around Micah and her hips relaxed as he slowly, gently entered her.

She arched her hips and Micah said, "Not yet."

"But I need to, badly."

"I don't want to hurt you."

He felt her body tremble.

Gaea wanted to cry with the sense of fulfillment and wonder having Micah inside of her gave her. There was a little pain, but only initially; now there was only pleasure, and she wanted her husband to know she loved him and would always love him.

"I'm all right, Micah," she said, her voice husky.

"I love you," he breathed. "I love you."

Then, he was fully inside of her and Gaea cried out. Micah kissed her brow. "I'm sorry, I'm sorry."

"You just feel so good," Gaea said, sighing happily.

"A screamer," Micah joked. "I'm married to a screamer."

Dear Reader,

I hope you enjoyed reading *Out of the Blue* as much as I enjoyed writing it.

The ocean and its inhabitants have always fascinated me. I especially love dolphins.

I suppose it was only a matter of time before I wrote a story incorporating the ocean, dolphins and romance.

Until our next adventure together.

Sincerely,

Janice Sims
P.O. Box 811
Mascotte, FL 34753-0811

## Coming in January . . .

BEYOND DESIRE, by Gwynne Forster     (0-7860-0607-2, $4.99/$6.50)
Amanda Ross is pregnant and single. Certainly not a role model for junior
high school students, the board of education may deny her promotion
to principal if they learn the truth. What she needs is a husband and
music engineer Marcus Hickson agrees to it. His daughter needs surgery
and Amanda will pay the huge medical bill. But love creeps in and soon
theirs is an affair of the heart.

LOVE SO TRUE, by Loure Bussey     (0-7860-0608-0, $4.99/$6.50)
Janelle Sims defied her attraction to wealthy businessman Aaron Dever-
reau because he reminded Janelle of her womanizing father. Yet he is
the perfect person to back her new fashion boutique and she seeks him
out. Now they are partners, friends . . . and lovers. But a cunning
woman's lies separate them and Janelle must go to him to confirm their
love.

ALL THAT GLITTERS, by Viveca Carlysle  (0-7860-0609-9, $4.99/$6.50)
After her sister's death, Leigh Barrington inherited a huge share of Cassiopeia Salons, a chain of exclusive beauty parlors. The business was
Leigh's idea in the first place and now she wants to run it her way. To
retain control, Leigh marries board member Caesar Montgomery who is
instantly smitten with her. When she may be the next target of her sister's
killer, Leigh learns to trust in Caesar's love.

AT LONG LAST LOVE, by Bettye Griffin   (0-7860-0610-2, $4.99/$6.50)
Owner of restaurant chain Soul Food To Go, Kendall Lucas has finally
found love with her new neighbor, Spencer Barnes. Until she discovers
he owns the new restaurant that is threatening her business. They compromise, but Spencer learns Kendall has launched a secret advertising
campaign. Embittered by her own lies, Kendall loses hope in their love.
But she underestimates Spencer's devotion and his vow to make her his
partner for life.

*Available wherever paperbacks are sold, or order direct from the Publisher. Send
cover price plus 50¢ per copy for mailing and handling to Kensington Publishing
Corp., Consumer Orders, or call (toll free) 888-345-BOOK, to place your order
using Mastercard or Visa. Residents of New York and Tennessee must include sales
tax. DO NOT SEND CASH.*

# WARMHEARTED AFRICAN-AMERICAN ROMANCES
## BY *FRANCIS RAY*

FOREVER YOURS             (0-7860-0483-5, $4.99/$6.50)
Victoria Chandler must find a husband or her grandparents will call in loans that support her chain of lingerie boutiques. She fixes a mock marriage to ranch owner Kane Taggert. The marriage will only last one year, and her business will be secure. The only problem is that Kane has other plans for Victoria. He'll cast a spell that will make her his forever.

HEART OF THE FALCON          (0-7860-0483-5, $4.99/$6.50)
A passionate night with millionaire Daniel Falcon, leaves Madelyn Taggert enamored . . . and heartbroken. She never accepted that the long-time family friend would fulfill her dreams, only to see him walk away without regrets. After his parent's bitter marriage, the last thing Daniel expected was to be consumed by the need to have her for a lifetime.

INCOGNITO                 (0-7860-0364-2, $4.99/$6.50)
Owner of an advertising firm, Erin Cortland witnessed an awful crime and lived to tell about it. Frightened, she runs into the arms of Jake Hunter, the man sent to protect her. He doesn't want the job. He left the police force after a similar assignment ended in tragedy. But when he learns not only one man is after her and that he is falling in love, he will risk anything to protect her.

ONLY HERS                (07860-0255-7, $4.99/$6.50)
St. Louis R.N. Shannon Johnson recently inherited a parcel of Texas land. She sought it as refuge until landowner Matt Taggart challenged her to prove she's got what it takes to work a sprawling ranch. She, on the other hand, soon challenges him to dare to love again.

SILKEN BETRAYAL            (0-7860-0426-6, $4.99/$6.50)
The only man executive secretary Lauren Bennett needed was her five-year-old son Joshua. Her only intent was to keep Joshua away from powerful in-laws. Then Jordan Hamilton entered her life. He sought her because of a personal vendetta against her father-in-law. When Jordan develops strong feelings for Lauren and Joshua, he must choose revenge or love.

UNDENIABLE                (07860-0125-9, $4.99/$6.50)
Wealthy Texas heiress Rachel Malone defied her powerful father and eloped with Logan Williams. But a trump-up assault charge set the whole town and Rachel against him and he fled Stanton with a heart full of pain. Eight years later, he's back and he wants revenge . . . and Rachel.

*Available wherever paperbacks are sold, or order direct from the Publisher. Send cover price plus 50¢ per copy for mailing and handling to Kensington Publishing Corp., Consumer Orders, or call (toll free) 888-345-BOOK, to place your order using Mastercard or Visa. Residents of New York and Tennessee must include sales tax. DO NOT SEND CASH.*

# LOOK FOR THESE ARABESQUE ROMANCES

AFTER ALL, by Lynn Emery                 (0-7860-0325-1, $4.99/$6.50)
News reporter Michelle Toussaint only focused on her dream of becoming an anchorwoman. Then contractor Anthony Hilliard returned. For five years, Michelle had reminsced about the passions they shared. But happiness turned to heartbreak when Anthony's cruel betrayal led to her father's financial ruin. He returned for one reason only: to win Michelle back.

THE ART OF LOVE, by Crystal Wilson-Harris  (0-7860-0418-5, $4.99/$6.50)
Dakota Bennington's heritage is apparent from her African clothing to her sculptures. To her, attorney Pierce Ellis is just another uptight professional stuck in the American mainstream. Pierce worked hard and is proud of his success. An art purchase by his firm has made Dakota a major part of his life. And love bridges their different worlds.

CHANGE OF HEART                          (0-7860-0103-8, $4.99/$6.50)
by Adrienne Ellis Reeves
Not one to take risks or stray far from her South Carolina hometown, Emily Brooks, a recently widowed mother, felt it was time for a change. On a business venture she meets author David Walker who is conducting research for his new book. But when he finds undying passion, he wants Emily for keeps. Wary of her newfound passion, all Emily has to do is follow her heart.

ECSTACY, by Gwynne Forster                (0-7860-0416-9, $4.99/$6.50)
Schoolteacher Jeannetta Rollins had a tumor that was about to cost her her eyesight. Her persistence led her to follow Mason Fenwick, the only surgeon talented enough to perform the surgery, on a trip around the world. After getting to know her, Mason wants her whole . . . body and soul. Now he must put behind a tragedy in his career and trust himself and his heart.

KEEPING SECRETS, by Carmen Green          (0-7860-0494-0, $4.99/$6.50)
Jade Houston worked alone. But a dear deceased friend left clues to a two-year-old mystery and Jade had to accept working alongside Marine Captain Nick Crawford. As they enter a relationship that runs deeper than business, each must learn how to trust each other in all aspects.

MOST OF ALL, by Louré Bussey            (0-7860-0456-8, $4.99/$6.50)
After another heartbreak, New York secretary Elandra Lloyd is off to the Bahamas to visit her sister. Her sister is nowhere to be found. Instead she runs into Nassau's richest, self-made millionaire Bradley Davenport. She is lucky to have made the acquaintance with this sexy islander as she searches for her sister and her trust in the opposite sex.

*Available wherever paperbacks are sold, or order direct from the Publisher. Send cover price plus 50¢ per copy for mailing and handling to Kensington Publishing Corp., Consumer Orders, or call (toll free) 888-345-BOOK, to place your order using Mastercard or Visa. Residents of New York and Tennessee must include sales tax. DO NOT SEND CASH.*